Might of the Phoenix:

The Restoration of the Dominican Republic

Rafael Morillo

ISBN:
978-0-578-59243-5

"Dios, Patria, y Libertad."
"God, Homeland, and Liberty."

"Y la verdad os hará libres."
"And the truth shall make you free."
—*Gospel of John, 8;32*

"Antilles for the Antillerans."

I dedicate this novel to my friends and family as well as the Latino community and anyone who yearns to learn about Caribbean history. I particularly dedicate this novel to the people of the Dominican Republic and the Dominican Diaspora. May we learn from all aspects of our Dominican history and improve our beloved Dominican Republic. May we help each other throughout the Dominican diaspora worldwide. To my beautiful Quisqueya, I love you!

CONTENTS

President José Núñez de Cáceres

Republic of Spanish Haiti (1821)

The Founding Fathers of the Dominican Republic (1844)

Juan Pablo Duarte

Francisco del Rosario Sanchez

Matias Ramon Mella

Queen Isabella II of Spain

General Pedro Santana

President Ramón Buenaventura Báez

"Los blancos, morenos, cobrizos, cruzados, marchando serenos, unidos y osados, la patria salvemos de viles tiranos, y al mundo mostremos que somos hermanos."

"The whites, browns, copper-colored, the mixed, marching serene, united and daring, to save the homeland from vile tyrants, and to the world we will show that we are all brothers."

"La Nación está obligada a conservar y proteger por medio de leyes sabias y justas la libertad personal, civil e individual así como la propiedad y demás derechos legítimos de todos los individuos que la componen."

"The Nation is obliged to preserve and protect through wise and just laws the personal liberty, civil, and individual rights as well as the property and other legitimate rights of all the individuals that compose it."

"La Nación Dominicana es la reunión de todos los dominicanos. La Nación dominicana es libre e independiente y no es ni puede ser jamás parte integrante de ninguna otra Potencia, ni el patrimonio de familia ni persona alguna propia ni mucho menos extraña."

"The Dominican Nation is the union of all Dominicans. The Dominican Nation is free and independent and is not and can never be an integral part of any other Power, nor the family patrimony or any person of its own, much less strange."

—Juan Pablo Duarte

"The Antilles now face a moment that they had never faced in history; they now have to decide whether 'to be, or not to be'. ...Let us unite. Let us build a people, a people of true Freemasons, and we then shall raise a temple over foundations so solid that the forces of the Saxon and Spanish races will not shake it, a temple that we will consecrate to Independence, and in whose frontispiece we will engrave this inscription, as imperishable as the Motherland itself: 'The Antilles for the Antilleans.'"

—Ramón Emeterio Betances y Alacán

"I wish that they will say: In that island (Puerto Rico) a man was born who loved truth, desired justice, and worked for the good of men."

—Eugenio María de Hostos

"Every human being has within him an ideal man, just as every piece of marble contains in a rough state a statue as beautiful as the one that Praxiteles the Greek made of the god Apollo."

"Men are like the stars; some generate their own light while others reflect the brilliance they receive."

—Jose Marti

"I would unite with anybody to do right and with nobody to do wrong."

"Those who profess to favor freedom and yet deprecate agitation are men who want crops without plowing up the ground; they want rain without thunder and lightning"

—Frederick Douglass

"Labor is prior to, and independent of, capital. Capital is only the fruit of labor and could never have existed if labor had not first existed. Labor is the superior of capital and deserves much the higher consideration."

—Abraham Lincoln

"Nothing is more rational and fair than that the owner of the house should be the one to live in it with his family and be the one who furnishes and decorates it as he likes and that he not be forced against his will and inclination to follow norms imposed by his neighbor."

—Generalissimo Máximo Gómez y Báez

"A people without the knowledge of their past history, origin and culture is like a tree without roots."

—Marcus Garvey

"I am convinced there is only one way to eliminate these grave evils, namely through the establishment of a socialist economy, accompanied by an educational system which would be oriented toward social goals. In such an economy, the means of production are owned by society itself and are utilized in a planned fashion. A planned economy, which adjusts production to the needs of the community, would distribute the work to be done among all those able to work and would guarantee a livelihood to every man, woman, and child. The education of the individual, in addition to promoting his own innate abilities, would attempt to develop in him a sense of responsibility for his fellow-men in place of the glorification of power and success in our present society."

—Albert Einstein (*Why Socialism?*, 1949)

"If I cannot see for myself the liberation of this nation, I will see it through my ideas."

"There is no weapon more powerful than the truth in the hands of the good."

"For us there is nothing as admirable, beautiful and great as man, nothing can be more admirable, beautiful and great than the Dominican people."

—Juan Bosch

"Education is the passport to the future, for tomorrow belongs to those who prepare for it today."

"I'm for truth, no matter who tells it. I'm for justice, no matter who it's for or against."

—Malcolm X

"Call it democracy, or call it democratic socialism, but there must be a better distribution of wealth within this country for all God's children."

—Martin Luther King Jr.

"Me don't dip on nobody's side. Me don't dip on the black man's side, not the white man's side. Me dip on God's side, the one who create me and cause to come from black and white."

—Bob Marley

"If they sending Indians to India
And Africans back to Africa
Well somebody please just tell me
Where they sending poor me?
I am neither one nor the other
Six of one, half a dozen of the other
So if they sending all these people back home for true
They got to split me in two"

—Clatis Ali

"Preservation of one's own culture does not require contempt or disrespect for other cultures."

—Cesar Chavez

"The Dominican Republic is my holy land, my Mecca."

—Raquel Cepeda

PROLOGUE
THE REPUBLIC OF SPANISH HAITI
(DECEMBER 1, 1821)

José Núñez de Cáceres y Albor, the political leader of the independence movement, declared independence from Spain in 1821 and became the President of the *República del Haití Español* (or the Republic of Spanish Haiti). This was declared after the overthrow of the weakened Spanish authority on the eastern part of the island of Ayiti now renamed Hispaniola. The Governor of Eastern Florida and the previous Governor of Santo Domingo (Sebastian Kindelán y O'Regan) was replaced by Pascual Real, who was overthrown by the Dominican leader José Núñez de Cáceres y Albor. The Spaniards ruled the island of Ayiti (or Kiskeya) since the arrival of Cristóbal Colón in 1492. For most of its colonial history since, the Spaniards held control of Santo Domingo and began to expand their empire throughout the Caribbean and Western Hemisphere. The Spanish Empire expanded from its capital of Santo Domingo towards the rest of the Americas as they conquered the various native civilizations. Initially led by King Carlos I (or King Charles the V) and his son King Philip II, the Spanish Empire successfully defeated numerous native societies—including the powerful Aztec Empire, the weakened Mayas, and the Incas of South America. After the native Taino population rapidly decreased due to Spanish disease and violence. The Hapsburg Spanish Empire brought West African slaves from different tribes (Igbo, Ajas, Fulbe, Kalabari, Yoruba, Akan and Mandinka) starting in 1501. The Muslim Wolof slaves, who were later brought to Hispaniola, would rebel near the city of Santo Domingo in 1521, marking the first African slave revolt in the Americas.

The African slave rebellion began on the sugar plantation of the son of Cristóbal Colón, Diego Colón. The first African slave maroons spread around the island and many slave upheavals arose, such as a revolt led by Sebastián Lemba in 1532. The native Taino leader (Cacique Enriquillo) would start a rebellion that lasted from 1519 to 1533 and would involve natives and Africans against their Spanish oppressors. As the Spanish Empire expanded, other rebellions would also form—including in the island of Cuba by the native leader Hatüey, who escaped Hispaniola and later Guamá who led a rebellion in the 1530s. Hatüey was subsequently executed by the

1

Spanish authorities in 1512, and became one of the first leaders to rebel against the Spaniards. He was later celebrated as "Cuba's first National Hero". Meanwhile in Puerto Rico, the native leader (Cacique Agueybana II) would lead an impressive uprising against the Spaniards, initiating the Battle of Yagüecas (or the Taíno Rebellion of 1511). The African rebel leader, Gaspar Yanga, would successfully resist the Spaniards near Veracruz Mexico and earn self-rule over the maroon settlement named San Lorenzo de los Negros as well as San Lorenzo de Cerralvo. The maroons helped slaves escape bondage and live freely among Africans and their descendants who were once slaves and those who were always free from chattel slavery.

African and native slaves would escape and live in maroons in the island of *Xaymaca* (or Jamaica), which was initially controlled by the Spaniards. As the first sighting of land, Cristóbal Colón named what is now St. Ann's Bay as "Santa Gloria". Nearby the first Spanish settlement and capital of Jamaica was Sevilla, which was later replaced by the capital of St. Jago de la Vega (or Spanish Town) in 1534. The Spanish Empire would rule Portugal and unify the Iberian Peninsula. The Hapsburg-led Spanish Empire would govern both the Spanish and Portuguese global colonies, earning the title *"el imperio en el que nunca se pone el sol"* or "the empire on which the sun never sets". Initially, the Spanish Empire controlled the Americas from the capital of Santo Domingo and governed Asia from their capital of Manilla in the Philippines. Various other European powers would gain colonies in the Americas, Africa, and Asia—including the Dutch, English, and French. After the dissolution of the Iberian Union (which lasted from 1580 to 1640), the Spanish Empire began showing signs of weakness as British and French pirates gained power and influence. Soon after, the Spanish Empire would be rivaled then surpassed globally by the British and French Empires.

The Spanish Empire would lose their various territories to their rival European powers. In the island of Hispaniola, the French would officially create their own colony in 1697 named Saint-Domingue. After the Nine Years War (or War of the League of Augsburg) between France and the Grand Alliance of England, Spain, the Holy Roman Empire, and the United Provinces, the French were forced to renounce various territories while gaining Acadia and Saint-Domingue, which would become Haiti. The French were excessively brutal, frequently importing West African slaves to the western side of Hispaniola. The French wars and the Treaty of Basil led to the acquisition of Santo Domingo by the French in 1795, leading to complete French control of the island of Hispaniola under King Louis XVI, who was then executed after the French Revolution.

In 1801, with the aid of the English, the Haitian leader Toussaint Louverture took over Santo Domingo in the east, gaining control of the entire island before he was captured and imprisoned by the French Army sent by Napoleon Bonaparte. The strength and determination of the Haitian Army and diseases—including yellow fever—helped defeat the outnumbered French Army as the Haitian leader (General Henri Christophe) drove the French from most of Eastern Hispaniola. General Christophe, however, would sow discontent among the people of Santo Domingo after the sacking of the towns of Santiago de los Caballeros and Moca.

Rebellions against Spanish rule were now occurring in other colonies in the Caribbean. In Curacao, Tula Rigaud led a large slave revolt against the Dutch in August 1795. At the Knip plantation of slave master Caspar Lodewijk van Uytrecht at Bandabou Curaçao, Tula led an uprising of over forty people. Caspar Lodewijk van Uytrecht informed the slaves to appeal to the Luitenant Governor in Amsterdam, however other leaders joined Tula—including Bastian Karpata and the French slave Louis Mercier, who led revolts at the plantation of Saint Kruis. Karpata imprisoned the commandant, van der Grijp, and ten mixed race soldiers as prisoners. The rebel leader Pedro Wakao killed the Dutch slaver, Sabel would join the rebellion of Tula as the Dutch attempted his rescue. Negotiations failed; Tula only agreed to full emancipation of the slaves—he argued that since the Netherlands was recently conquered by the French and observed the revolutionary movement in Saint-Domingue, slaves in Curaçao should now earn their freedom as well. Governor Johannes de Veer ordered Commander Wierts of the ship *Medea* to defend Fort Amsterdam. Commander Wierts sent both black and white soldiers to attack the rebels and on September nineteenth, Tula and Karpata were betrayed by a slave, ending the rebellion. Tula and the rebel leaders were executed, however the spirit of rebellion would continue in the Caribbean and the island of Hispaniola.

Led by General Jean-Jacques Dessalines, the Haitian Revolution of 1804 established Saint-Domingue as the first black independent nation in Western Hispaniola, which was renamed Haiti after the native Taino name of Ayiti. The Haitians defeated the English, French, and Spaniards; Dessalines was proclaimed Emperor Jacques I, and ruled until his assassination by Haitian conspirators in 1806. With the aid of the Spaniards, the Dominicans were also able to defeat the Napoleon French forces in Spanish territory. On November seventh, 1808, at Palo Hincado savanna (near El Seibo in the colony of Santo Domingo), a force of 1,800 Spanish Dominican troops (led by General Juan Sánchez Ramírez) defeated over 500 men belonging to the French Army of Napoleon (led by Governor General Marie-Louis Ferrand). Governor Ferrand, who was subsequently overwhelmed by depression, committed suicide with a pistol shot to the head. Juan Sánchez Ramírez reintroduced slavery however, slavery served a small role in society.

The Haitian revolution inspired the other Caribbean islands and various territories to revolt against the Spanish Empire, creating independent Latin American nations. This also paved the way for rebellions against the Spanish in Santo Domingo, leading to the establishment of the Republic of Spanish Haiti in 1821. President José Núñez de Cáceres was declared the leader of the new republic, and he attempted to join Spanish Haiti with Gran Colombia (led by Simon Bolivar). The people of Spanish Haiti rejoiced, and the flag was modeled after the flag of Gran Colombia. Many Spanish Haitians (Dominicans) celebrated the end of Spanish rule in Santo Domingo at the hands of General José Núñez de Cáceres, who was widely accepted as president of the new Spanish Haitian Republic.

President José Núñez de Cáceres was a popular writer and fabulist who used his writing to invigorate rebellion against the Spaniards. He was part of the criollo social class, which were of predominantly Spaniard ancestry; the *criollos* were historically below the Iberian-born Spaniards, who were called *peninsulares*. However, the *criollos* had gained considerable authority—particularly in Santo Domingo—as Spanish authority weakened. Since the arrival of the Spaniards in 1492, a racially blended society emerged in the eastern side of Hispaniola from the various African tribes, the Taino and other natives, along with Spaniards. In 1820, President Jean-Pierre Boyer sent Colonel Dezir Dalmassi to nearby towns—including Las Matas, San Juan de la Maguana, and Azua—to convince locals to join a Haitian Republic that would provide them with jobs and great benefits. However, under rumored threats of possible invasions from the French and Spanish in the east and a desire to unite the entire island under his rule, President Boyer began plans to annex the Spanish-speaking eastern side of the island.

On November 9, 1821, General José Núñez de Cáceres defeated the Spaniards; on December first of that same year, a constitutive act was ordered to petition the union of Spanish Haiti with Gran Colombia. In 1822, the Haitians who had abolished slavery in 1804 were petitioning for unification of the island of Hispaniola under Haitian protection. President José Núñez de Cáceres initially opposed the unification, but many black Spanish Haitians (or Dominicans) and those who desired to see slavery abolished outnumbered him. President José Núñez de Cáceres petitioned Simon Bolivar repeatedly for Spanish Haiti to join Gran Colombia, but subsequently agreed with the demand of President Boyer after the Haitian Army marched towards Santo Domingo with a veteran Haitian military force numbering over 12,000 soldiers.

President Jean-Pierre Boyer entered Santo Domingo on February 9, 1822. President Núñez de Cáceres offered him the keys of the Palace, but Boyer rejected the offer, stating, "I have not come into this city as a conqueror, but by the will of its inhabitants." The Haitian government soon began restricting the use of the Spanish language and other cultural practices, including cockfights in the former Spanish Haiti. A young man was present during the initial independence from Spain and during the unification of the island of Hispaniola under the Haitian government. This young man was Marco Aurelio Medina.

Marco Aurelio Medina was born near the central regions of Spanish Haiti where it was said to occasionally snow, which was unheard of in most of the Caribbean—this region was most likely the only place it occurred. Afterward, the family moved to Bani. Many were there to celebrate the proclamation of Spanish Haiti and the subsequent unification of the island under the Haitians. An eighteen-year-old Dominican man named Marco Aurelio Medina was just as excited for what was to come.

CHAPTER 1

THE LEGACY OF DUTTY BOUKMAN & THE UNIFIED HAITIAN ISLAND
(1835)

Anibal Hector Medina Taveras was born nine years after the proclamation of the Republic of Spanish Haiti in 1830. President Jean-Pierre Boyer governed the island as the second president of Haiti, after succeeding President Alexandre Pétion who ruled from 1807 to 1818. Secretary Joseph Balthazar Inginac implemented various policies to strengthen and centralize the Haitian government under President Jean-Pierre Boyer. Previously, Emperor Jacques I implemented strict laws to keep labor in the Haitian sugar industry and plantations without the brutal institution of slavery. Despite this practice being abolished in Haiti, Jean-Jacques Dessalines ruling as Emperor enforced a strict agrarian policy which angered black Haitians. Members of Jean-Jacques Dessa-lines' administration (including Alexandre Pétion and Henri Christophe) began to plot against Emperor Jacques I, leading to his assassination in Pont Larnage just north of the Haitian capital of Port-au-Prince. On the seventeenth of October 1806, as the emperor was on his way to fight the rebels, a bullet to the head ended his life. The Haitian assassins pounced on Emperor Jacques I and after he unceremoniously collapsed in the public square, the conspirators mutilated his corpse as they shouted, "The tyrant is dead!"

Marco Aurelio Medina particularly loved African, Greek, and Roman history. He shared his love of the subject with his young son, Anibal Hector Medina Taveras. Marco Aurelio Medina was named after the Roman leader (Emperor Marcus Aurelius) and he studied and read some of the works of the Roman emperor. Marci Aurelio's love of history also led to the naming of his first-born son Anibal after the famous leader General Hannibal of Carthage. One of the first books Marco Aurelio was interested in as a teenager was the Meditations, which was a series of twelve books written by Emperor Marcus Aurelius. Marco Aurelio also taught his son about the history of the island referred to in the native Taino language as Ayiti or Quisqueya, meaning 'land of mountains' and 'mother of all lands'. Marco Aurelio often spoke of the first slaves of Africa brought by the Spanish in 1501 as well as the first African and native rebellions against the Spaniards.

Marco also spoke about an African woman who set up a small hospital in Santo Domingo in 1501 in her *bohio* (or home) and was affectionately called la Negra del hospital (or the black woman of the hospital). She was believed to be a free black woman who created the first hospital for all people. Throughout the generations, the natives became a mixture of various West African tribes, Spaniards, and the few remaining native Tainos who were now the Spanish Haitians or Dominicans. Marco Aurelio possessed a dark complexion and he believed he was a descendant of some of the first African rebels who formed the first maroons in the Americas led by the valiant Sebastian Lemba and Diego Ocampo. The spirit of rebellion against Spanish colonialism later continued under different leaders including Ana Maria, who led one of the last known rebellions in the area of San Cristobal known as Nigua on the thirtieth of October in 1796. It was a history that Marco Aurelio Medina was proud of.

Marco Aurelio Medina's wife was named officially Maria Altagracia Taveras de Medina and was of a light complexion which was due to her Spanish ancestry. She was born in the northern region of the Cibao known for its rich, fertile soil. Maria Altagracia was five years younger than her husband, who married her in a Catholic wedding during a hot day in June of 1828. Maria Altagracia was proud of the man she married and admired his respectability and thirst for knowledge. Like his father, Marco Aurelio was a deeply pensive man. Jairo Antonio Medina was similar to his son Marco; both were traditional and thoughtful men unlike their younger unmarried brother, Julio Manuel Medina.

The Medina men were emancipated black Dominicans who lived freely in the central part of the nation previously declared as Spanish Haiti. Although they were freed men, their ancestors were slaves—just as thousands of black Dominicans continued to be before slavery was abolished. There was an interesting difference, however, being that the population of slaves as well as the general population in eastern Spanish Haiti was much smaller than that of western French Haiti by the early 1800s.

Marco Aurelio explained to his young son the terrors that the Spaniards unleashed under the leadership of Cristóbal Colón: violence to the native Taino populations as well as the African slaves in the island renamed Hispaniola, Cuba, and San Juan Bautista (commonly called Borinquén in Spanish after the native Taino word for the island Boriken, meaning 'land of the valiant and noble lord'). Many traders would commonly refer to the island of San Juan Bautista as Porto Rico or Puerto Rico after its capital city. Marco Aurelio was proud of his ancestors and their fight against the Spanish conquistadors; although he did not agree with some of his policies, he was an admirer of José Núñez de Cáceres. Marco Aurelio also praised Jean-Jacque Dessalines and identified with his rough upbringing as a black slave under the French for over thirty years, however he opposed some of his decisions as a ruler.

Haiti (previously called Saint-Domingue) was the wealthiest colony in the Caribbean. It generated great wealth for the French monarchy and subsequently Emperor Napoleon's French Empire. The French exploited their African slaves, severely limiting their life expectancy to several years and as low as several months for those who were sick and weak. Many

Haitian slaves such as the maroon leader François Mackandal led devastating rebellions against their French colonizers. François Mackandal used his knowledge of plants to help poison French slave masters and soldiers until his capture and execution by burning in 1758. The Jamaican leader Dutty Boukman was sold and transported to Saint-Domingue and would later lead a ceremony which generated a rebellion against the French. An educated man, Dutty Boukman carried a Koran and quoted from the Bible and used them to unite the slaves against their French masters. Dutty Boukman and Cécile Fatiman led a religious ceremony at Bois Caïman in August 1791, sparking the Hai-tian Revolution. Various Haitian leaders skilled in the French military had joined the rebellion—including François-Dominique Toussaint Louverture.

François-Dominique Toussaint Louverture was a highly skilled veteran who fought for the Spanish against the French, then for France against Spain and Great Britain, and then for Saint-Domingue against Napoleonic France. He sought to liberate Saint-Domingue and create a free nation. By 1801, the French colony of Saint-Domingue was nearly autonomous with its constitution declaring Toussaint Louverture Governor-General for Life—against the wishes of Napoleon Bonaparte. Toussaint Louverture was nicknamed the black Napoleon and the black Spartacus by many of his supporters. He and his wife, Suzanne Simone Baptiste Louverture, were the leaders of what was to become the free nation of Haiti until Toussaint's betrayal and capture. Toussaint would subsequently die in captivity in France.

Toussaint's lieutenant and successor, Jean-Jacques Dessalines, was a veteran commander who quickly took leadership of Haiti. A former slave, Dessalines was born in the plantation of Cormier near Grande Riviere du Nord. Originally named Jean-Jacques Duclos by his French master, he worked in the plantation alongside his brothers Louis and Joseph Duclos. Jean-Jacque Duclos rose to the rank of foreman and subsequently, he was sold to a black Haitian named Dessalines. After the age of thirty, he was renamed Jean-Jacques Dessalines—it was a name he would keep as a free man. Jean-Jacques Dessalines joined the slave uprisings of 1791 led by Jean François Papillon and Georges Biassou, enlisting in the Spanish Military in Santo Domingo.

After the French declared an end to slavery in 1794, Dessalines followed his leader Toussaint into the French Military and rose to the rank of Brigadier General by 1799. Dessalines participated in the battle against the English and French and the capture of the cities of Jacmel, Pet-it-Goâve, Miragoâne, and Anse-à-Veau. In 1801, Dessalines impressively broke the northern rebellion of Toussaint Louverture's nephew General Moyse. The Haitians soon learned that Napoleon's laws for the common Frenchman did not extend to the black people of Haiti and Toussaint's subsequent capture and death led to the election of Dessalines as leader of Haiti. The French Enlightenment ideals were not meant for the black people of Haiti and they were motivated to forcefully emancipate themselves from slavery and live in freedom. The life experiences of Dessalines led him to view the white French slave owners negatively, as well as the Haitian mulatto slaveholders and the slavery-supporting Haitian population.

From June to December of 1803, the British fleet blockaded Saint-Domingue. British Royal Navy squadrons encircled the French-held ports of Cap Français and Môle-Saint-Nicolas on the Northern coast. In order to eliminate communication between French outposts and to capture or destroy French war ships, the Royal Navy dispatched a squadron under the leadership of Sir John Duckworth from Jamaica to patrol the region. The French commander Rochambeau procrastinated until the last moment and was eventually was forced to surrender to the British commander. French General Louis de Noailles refused to surrender and sailed to Havana, Cuba in a fleet of small vessels on the third of December 1803, but was intercepted and mortally wounded by a Royal Navy frigate. Under the leadership of Dessalines, the slave rebellion subsequently defeated the French troops and the Republic of Haiti was declared in the following year of 1804. Like Toussaint, Dessalines proclaimed himself leader for life and was named emperor of Haiti.

The Haitian revolution was a disaster for the French Military and the Polish regiments commanded by General Charles Victoire Emmanuel Leclerc (who was married to Napoleon Bonaparte's sister, Pauline Bonaparte). The experienced Haitian leadership previously led by Toussaint and then Dessalines fought bravely against the French Army, which was weakened by yellow fever. The disease, along with advancing Haitian forces, crippled the English Army in Haiti and would degrade French forces. General Leclerc, who previously imprisoned Toussaint, would suffer defections from the black and mulatto Haitian soldiers who joined the Haitian rebellion—including experienced black and mulatto officers such as Henri Christophe, Alexandre Pétion, and Dessalines. General Leclerc's desperation increased as he ordered the execution of over 1,000 black colonial troops in Le Cap by tying sacks of flower to their bodies and pushing them overboard as an answer to the executions of hundreds of Polish soldiers under the orders of Henri Christophe. General Leclerc would advocate for a war of mass genocide against the Haitian people as he wrote to Napoleon, "We must destroy all the blacks of the mountains—men and women—and spare only children under twelve years of age. We must destroy half of those in the plains and must not leave a single colored person in the colony who has worn an epaulet."

General Leclerc would soon succumb to yellow fever in November 1802. He was succeeded by General Rochambeau, who would lose the

Battle of Vertières to the Haitian officer François Capois. General Rochambeau called a temporary cease-fire to celebrate the bravery and efforts of Officer François Capois, who charged uphill over four times against overwhelming French firepower. The Haitians subsequently won their independence in 1804.

Regional rivalries in Haiti between Nord, Sud, and Ouest as well as class and racial tensions between white, black, and mixed Haitians (called free people of color) persisted after the Haitian victory over the French in 1804. Dessaline's 1805 constitution held racial laws which stated that all Haitians were black and could not marry white foreigners. Many of these laws were later abolished during rule of the third leader of Haiti, President Charles Rivière-Hérard. Dessalines subsequently ordered the execution of most of the white population of Haiti that were suspected of conspiracy, which would also include women and children. The mixed-race Haitians were also encouraged to take part in the massacre of the Haitian white population to make the activity a combined effort of all Haitian people of color against their French colonizers. Thousands of white men, women, and children were executed in brutal fashion. Some whites who supported the Haitian black population, did not escape death. The white Haitian minority were prevented from escaping Haiti and through his ministers, Emperor Jacques I advocated for the use of silent weapons (including machetes and knives) to carry out the executions, as gunfire might alert the remaining white population. Many of the whites were paraded in Port-au-Prince in front of foreign merchant vessels and drowned while some moderate Haitian generals and officials attempted to dissuade Dessalines and his planned mass killings—including his wife who hid several white women and children from execution.

Some Haitians protected the whites and creoles as Dessalines exacted revenge against the French and their suspected allies, who had brutalized the Haitian slaves. Desperate whites fled towards the Spanish east and other Caribbean islands like Cuba and Puerto Rico. During the white massacre in Haiti, many of the French colonists who also had some African ancestry attempted to pass as Creoles (who were Haitian natives). Emperor Jacques I and his advisors devised a test to weed out French imposters who attempted to pass as Mixed Haitians by forcing the French colonists to sing *Nanett alé nan fontain, cheche dlo, cricha li cassé* or "Nanette went to the fountain, looking for water, but her jug broke." Many of the French colonists spoke continental French and could not properly pronounce the Haitian Creole words or the African cadences found within the melody and were promptly put to death. Emperor Jacques I traveled from city to city within Haiti to confirm that his orders were carried out. Dessalines reminded Haitians who questioned the mass executions of the wickedness of the French and European colonizers throughout the Caribbean and the Americas.

Whites were viewed with contempt for their brutality and colonization in Haiti as well as their continuing colonization of the Americas. Many whites were excluded from Haiti with the exception of some Polish soldiers and Americans who aided the efforts of the Haitian Revolution. Dessalines proclaimed all Haitians "black", but black Haitians were viewed as authentic Haitians (or authentiques). Haitian society categorized various mixtures from darkest to whitest as authentiques, *sacatra, griffe, marabout, mulatre, quarteron, metis, mamelouque, quarteronne,* and *sanmele.* However, the Haitian mulattos still maintained a privileged place in society while maintaining ownership on most businesses. Elite Haitians were mostly Catholic and spoke French and looked down on the dark-skinned Haitians who often spoke Creole and practiced Voodoo. The Haitian mulatto minority still maintained a high place in Haitian society and rich blacks (or gwo neg) were considered mulatto while poor mulattos were considered blacks (or neg), perpetuating a negative stereotype of black people. Over ninety percent of Haiti's population was composed of black Haitians and in times of societal instability, the black Haitian population would manifest their deep anger and suspicions of the mulattos in the destruction of their businesses.

The Empire of Haiti quickly dissolved, and would split into two nations after the assassination of Emperor Jacques I. The Haitian Constitution of 1806 ended the authoritative regime of Dessalines, creating three separate branches of government and empowering the citizens. However, the Legislative Branch representing the Senate remained the most powerful. In 1807, the northern region would be called the State of Haiti led by the black President Henri Christophe, and the southern region would be called the Republic of Haiti led by the mulatto and free person of color President Alexandre Sabès Pétion. The State of Haiti would subsequently become the Kingdom of Haiti and on the twenty-sixth of March 1811. President Henri Christophe would proclaim himself Henri I, King of Haiti; he ruled alongside his wife, Queen Marie Louise Coidavid, after eliminating many of his enemies—including the brave François Capois (who was nick-named the "black Achilles"). King Henri I of Haiti named his legitimate youngest son as heir and gave him the title Jacques-Victor Henri, Prince Royal of Haiti. When the United States once again entered the war against Britain in 1812, King Henri I made an agreement with the British to not disrupt the surrounding British colonies in the Caribbean and in turn the British would provide intelligence to Haiti regarding French movements in the Caribbean and possible French attacks.

The Northern Kingdom of Haiti was Ruled by King Henri I and a black Haitian royal family while the Southern Haitian Republic was led by mixed-race Haitians and President Alexandre Pétion, who was a *gens de couleur libres* (or free man of color). The Northern Haitian Kingdom grew wealthier than the Southern Haitian State, causing further friction between the two. King

Henri I began extensive construction projects—six castles and eight palaces to include the Sans-Souci Palace and the Citadelle Laferrière fortress built to protect the kingdom from potential French incursions. King Henri I also created a Haitian noble class in the hopes of maintaining Northern Haitian nobility and the stability of the Haitian Kingdom after his passing. Ironically, King Henri I modeled his kingdom after the French and Europeans they had expelled. King Henri I created a marvelous palace influenced by the palace named Sanssouci that belonged to King Frederick the Great in Potsdam; nearby hamlets were given names to include Marmelade and Limonade. Thousands died in the building of the Citadelle, and rumors spread that to prove his soldier's loyalty, Henri I ordered them to march off the edge of the structure.

Support for King Henri decreased as plots against his life and negative propaganda increased; he suffered a stroke and subsequently committed suicide by shooting himself in the chest on the eighth of October 1820. Prince Jacques-Victor Henri, Prince Royal of Haiti, was assassinated ten days later by Haitian revolutionaries at the Sans-Souci Palace. In the Southern Haitian Republic, President Alexandre Pétion—who championed democracy and the redistribution of wealth from the rich gentry to the poor working class—declared himself President for Life on the second of June 1816. Called the good-hearted father for his redistribution of land towards the peasantry and improvements in education and social programs for the poor, President Alexandre Pétion became an autocratic ruler. However, the southern region of Haiti continued to lose state revenue, and President Alexandre Pétion succumbed to yellow fever and was succeeded by General Boyer, who took control in 1818. President Jean-Pierre Boyer quickly moved to reunite Northern and Southern Haiti as well as the Eastern Spanish territory in an effort to rule the entire island of Hispaniola.

The eastern Spanish-speaking population of Hispaniola was mostly racially mixed through many generations of intermarriage, which differed from the large majority black Haitian population. Other regions of Latin America were also largely mixed and various Latin American leaders supported interracial marriage—including the lawyer and authoritarian leader of Paraguay, Dr. José Gaspar Rodríguez de Francia, who made a law forbidding whites to marry other whites. Intermarriage by law created a more egalitarian society while at the same time curbed the power of white elites in Paraguay. Known as the Supreme and Perpetual Dictator of Paraguay, José Gaspar Rodríguez de Francia was commonly known as El Supremo (or The Supreme). José Gaspar Rodríguez de Francia advocated for the full independence of Paraguay from the United Provinces of the Río de la Plata and the Empire of Brazil. El Supremo held liberal views regarding sex and marriage and declared prostitution an honorable profession after catching his daughter Ubalda García de Cañete prostituting herself outside his palace. Paraguay performed well economically although El Supremo had many critics, including Charles Darwin. He ruled Paraguay from 1814 until his death in 1840.

President Boyer sought a quick end to the regionalism within Haiti and brought his rule to the entire island, uniting both Haitians and the Dominicans. President Boyer sent envoys towards the eastern Spanish territory in order to gain support for the unification of the island as José Núñez de Cáceres was seeking independence from Spain and an alliance with the Gran Colombia. After the announcement of the Republic of Spanish Haiti in 1822, José Nuñez de Caceres reluctantly lowered the Colombian flag of the Republic of Spanish Haiti and raised the Haitian flag after the entrance of Haitian soldiers into Santo Domingo. President Boyer now ruled a unified island and continued his policies to liberate people of color from Spanish rule throughout the Americas. His predecessor, President Pétion, gave military and financial assistance to the revolutionary leader Simón Bolívar, which helped him liberate the Viceroyalty of New Granada and bring about the Gran Colombia. Haiti and the experienced Haitian Army was sought to maintain a stable government and the unification of the island of Hispaniola.

The former president of Spanish Haiti, José Núñez de Cáceres, endeavored to reclaim the previous independent and separate state of Spanish Haiti for the Dominican people. His clandestine efforts were reported to President Boyer, who quickly exiled José Núñez de Cáceres when he sought refuge in the Gran Colombia as he continued his efforts to gain support for the establishment of Spanish Haiti. José Núñez de Cáceres and his family relocated to Maracaibo, Venezuela and subsequently to the city of Caracas, where he established a printing press. José Núñez de Cáceres fell out of favor with Simon Bolivar and joined General José Antonio Páez, who desired to create an independent Venezuelan state. He was appointed secretary and advisor to General José Antonio Páez until the year 1827 when the movement stagnated, forcing José Núñez de Cáceres to move to Mexico in the city of San Luis Potosi and then in Ciudad Victoria (capital of Tamaulipas). José Núñez de Cáceres practiced law in Mexico and would later serve as a prosecutor to the Mexican Supreme Court and a senator in Tamaulipas.

José Núñez de Cáceres would no longer directly influence politics within the territory formerly known as Spanish Haiti. However, he remained outspoken regarding the Dominican people that were under the rule of the Haitian government led by President Boyer. Anibal learned of José Núñez de Cáceres from his father, but he only knew of the government of President Boyer. The Haitian government remained relatively stable despite Haiti's tumultuous path towards independence and post-independence governments which suffered from Haitian regionalism, racial instability, and classism. The Dominican population lived relatively peacefully despite past grievances regarding the violent Haitian Military incursions into the eastern Spanish-speaking territory. The Haitian Military previously committed violent acts towards the Dominican populations, however peace momentarily returned to the island as President Boyer decreased direct Haitian control and attempted to increase Dominican participation in the military. Anibal and his family continued to live in peace, but the relationship between the Haitian government and the Spanish-speaking Dominican population began to strain.

☐

CHAPTER 2

THE PRO-COLOMBIANS

(1836)

In an attempt to increase the stability of Haiti and the safety of the island, President Boyer secretly made an agreement with the French government. After the defeat of Emperor Napoleon Bonaparte and the victory of the Seventh Coalition, Napoleon was exiled to the island of Saint Helena and King Louis XVIII was restored to the throne. Napoleon died in 1821 and the culmination of the European wars allowed the French to concentrate on their country's weakening grip on their colonies—including the former Saint-Domingue. In 1825, King Charles X demanded that Haiti reimburse France for the loss of money and trade resulting from Haiti's independence. He reportedly sent fourteen heavily armed French war ships to patrol the coast of the Haitian capital of Port-au-Prince, although various observers reported more. President Boyer agreed to sign the Royal Ordinance of Charles X and pay France 150 million francs within five years while also taking out a of thirty million francs, which dealt a devastating blow to the Haitian government.

President Boyer attempted to continue Haiti's involvement in foreign affairs following his diplomatic support for various rebellions in the Americas as well as events in Europe—including his previous support for the Greek Revolution against the Ottoman Empire. His troubles increased within the island of Hispaniola as the Haitian economy worsened. Anibal Hector Medina and his family lived in relative safety as his knowledge of world events slowly filtered through the words of his knowledgeable father. H told his family stories of the War of 1812 and the factions of native groups that allied themselves either with the United States, Britain, or the powerful Tecumseh Confederacy. The Confederacy of Tecumseh rallied around the teachings of the Shawnee Prophet named Tenskwatawa, who was the younger brother of the Confederacy's leader the Shawnee Chief Tecumseh. Although facing disease and the expanding United States, the natives on the mainland were still an active force while the Tainos of the Caribbean were largely removed as a society. The Taino people, however, were not entirely eliminated; they were integrated among the African and European populations and thus were represented by the Dominican people. Marco Aurelio Medina often spoke about the peaceful, honorable Taino who fought along with the enslaved Africans against the Spanish Empire.

Despite the relative stability of the Haitian government, tensions within Haitian society steadily increased as President Boyer became autocratic and attempted to continue his policy of establishing a nation where black people could be free from slavery. Black people previously arrived in 1824 from the United States—particularly from the cities of Baltimore, Philadelphia, and New York. The Society for the Colonization of Free People of Color of America (or the American Colonization Society (ACS)) was established in 1816 in an effort to plan the migration of free African Americans to the continent of Africa. The American Colonization Society was founded by Robert Finley, who briefly served as the President of the University of Georgia until his death in 1817. With their plan to resettle 100,000 free people of color within ten years, the ACS founded a colony of free and black people within Cape Mesurado and Cape Palmas in the Western Coast of Africa commonly called the Pepper Coast for the melegueta pepper found there. Many black people within the United States protested the ACS as they viewed their goals as racist—including the African Americans James Forten and David Walker, who believed they deserved to live freely in the land of their birth in the United States. The Haitian government worked alongside the ACS and Loring D. Dewey, who planned to resettle black Americans to Haiti along with free people of color who had fled during the Haitian revolution.

President Boyer and his assistants, Joseph Balthazar Inginac and Jonathas Granville, eventually agreed with the ACS to bring American black people to Haiti. However, thousands returned to the United States as the Haitian economy continued its decline. Thousands of African Americans remained and settled in Haiti, particularly in the northern regions of the eastern Spanish side of the island in the Samaná region. As the Haitian economy declined, President Boyer attempted to increase production by enforcing his Code Rural upon the population while the Haitian Military became increasingly corrupt. Enacted in 1826, the Code Rural forced the peasants to their farmlands as a quota system was forced upon the Haitian populace. The wealth gap enlarged as Haiti's wealth was redistributed from the working-class black Haitians towards the minority mulatto Haitian elite and Haitian government officials. President Boyer, along with his mixed-race brethren, remained in power as the lower-class Haitians grew frustrated by the stagnating economy and their forced labor to pay their former colonizers.

The Dominicans who were employed in the Haitian Army would also participate in the corruption involving the underpaid Haitian Military, who would prey upon the Dominican population as the Haitian government continued to destabilize under its crippling debt to France as well as its decreasing production. A growing number of black Dominicans who initially favored the unification of the island under Haitian rule began to support the idea of a separate eastern nation under a Dominican government. Many nationalistic Dominicans began to exploit the growing dissatisfaction of President Boyer and the Haitian government. As the economic situation worsened, the Haitian Army grew weaker and were unable to enforce Haitian laws—including the Code Rural. Growing friction increased within the Haitian population while some Dominicans began to secretly speak against the government.

Anibal Hector Medina and his family noticed open discontent among some Dominicans away from the ears of the Haitian Military patrolling the streets. The Haitian revolution was initially a success, however the Haitian government failed to gain economic stability in a world that was not ready to accept a black independent nation. The United States saw Haiti as a threat to its domestic politics and its ongoing institution of slavery predominantly in the Southern United States. Information regarding the fragile Haitian government and world affairs slowly spread throughout the Haitian and Dominican populations. Many of the Pro-Colombian Dominicans that previously supported their new nation of Spanish Haiti to unite with Simon Bolivar's Gran Colombia in 1821 were now joining Dominican nationalists who desired to liberate themselves from Haitian rule.

Marco Aurelio Medina grew increasingly frustrated with the Haitian government and was unsettled by the stories of abuse towards the Dominican people by the Haitian Military and their allies. His wife, Maria Altagracia, was raised in a deeply religious, conservative Catholic family and she saw the government closing the churches as Haitian overreach. Many Haitians and even some Dominicans understood why the Catholic church was closed as the Spaniards and French used the Catholic faith to legitimize European colonization and their brutality. Marco Aurelio Medina was not a religious man, but he believed in God and read the Bible; he was aware of the hypocritical position of the Catholic Church and the political participation of the Pope and his predecessors towards conquest and negative policies against the Africans and Tainos.

Marco Aurelio and many Dominicans were secretly offended by the Haitian government's suppression of the Catholic faith and Spanish language. Despite Marco Aurelio's feelings against the politics and past actions of the Catholic Church, he still believed Dominicans should be free to decide if they wanted to participate in the Catholic faith. Marco was overjoyed with the establishment of Spanish Haiti and he was somewhat indifferent when the unification of the island under the Haitians occurred, as he agreed with some of the Pro-Haitian arguments made by free black Dominicans and enslaved black Dominicans.

Marco's younger brother, Julio Manuel Medina, was swayed by the Pro-Colombian argument—as was Marco Medina's wife, who desired an alliance with Gran Colombia. The Pro-Colombians believed the Haitian government was fragile and the Dominican people would suffer under its mismanagement. Anibal would listen to some of these private discussions and would sometimes question his father on the topic whenever they spent their day at the farm. Julio Medina was not as accepting of the Haitian government as his older brother Marco. Julio was angered by the presence of Haitian soldiers in Santo Domingo soon after the Republic of Spanish Haiti was established in 1821. The Code Rural also felt similar to slave labor to many of the Haitian black working class, while the continued autocratic rule of President Boyer angered many Haitians and Dominicans.

Opposed to his father and brother, who worked as farmers and cattle ranchers, Marco Aurelio Media was an educator who was previously employed as a teacher in history as well as mathematics. Marco Aurelio Medina's success as a teacher led to an opportunity to teach at the Universidad Santo Tomás de Aquino (or the University of Saint Thomas Aquinas) during the short-lived Republic of Spanish Haiti. However, his prospects diminished after the Haitian government controlled the island. Marco Medina subsequently sought to expand his father's business alongside his brother as they pursued a partnership with a young Dominican named Romulo Andujar. A wealthy landholder, Romulo Andujar's ancestors were African Moors and Arabs who married with Spaniards and had become successful ranchers. Romulo married Milagros Muñoz, who was part of the Dominican elite who initially welcomed the Haitian government—although now their family felt increasing unease with the instability within the Haitian government.

As Marco Medina and his son Anibal approached the ranch, Andujar emerged riding a dark brown Dominican horse. It was a Spanish mix-breed horse of the Paso Fino (or Fine Step) lineage. Inherited from the Spanish Jennet breed first brought by Cristobal Colón in 1493, it was the oldest native breed in the Western Hemisphere.

Andujar slowed his steed, quietly stating, "Bringing your son to work, I see. It is a good thing for young Dominicans to understand the value of work."

Marco Medina laughed as he replied, "That is correct, Mr. Andujar. My son should not only be educated with books but also in the school of hard work and life. Children need to understand the value of education and its applications to real life."

Romulo Andujar climbed down from his horse. "I am happy you have joined your brother in the farming and cattle ranching business. I am sorry you have lost your opportunity to teach at the University, but perhaps you can teach at a local school and you can apply to teach at the University of Saint Thomas Aquinas in Santo Domingo if the Haitian government reopens it. Petitions by Dominicans have already occurred against various Haitian resolutions and it is my hope we can bring change to the Haitian government."

Marco Medina agreed, but secretly believed—like many Dominicans—that the enactments against the Dominican populace like restrictions of the

Spanish language, closing churches and schools, prohibition for Dominicans running for public office, curfews, and general economic instability would soon result in a violent rebellion.

A majority of white Dominicans lost their lands, however many mixed mulatto Dominicans such as Romulo Andujar could keep theirs if he continued to support the Haitian government under President Boyer. Many black Dominicans who did not wish to continue working their lands or did not own any joined the mixed Dominican Military unit Battalion 22 under Colonel Pablo Ali (called the morenos libres or the free mulattos). Julio Medina briefly joined the free mulatto Army in an effort to gain military skills and possibly seek inclusion in the Haitian political process. Though he served for several years, he grew dissatisfied with the corrupt practices of the Haitian Military and the failure of Colonel Pablo Ali to control what was happening within his own battalion. Some Dominicans left the battalion as they joined the Pro-Colombians who secretly began joining the ranks of the Dominican nationalists. Julio Medina chose to serve his agreed upon term of service and subsequently joined his family and settled back into civilian life.

Marco Aurelio Medina believed that his son Anibal should receive a good education in various disciplines, including gaining necessary skills in farming and cattle ranching so he could provide for himself and his family. Marco Medina also believed that his son should prepare himself to survive, even during times of social upheaval and economic downturns. Julio Medina spoke negatively regarding the Haitian government, and he supported the growing number of Pro-Colombian Dominicans who previously backed the Republic of Spanish Haiti and Gran Colombia. These Nationalistic Dominican groups were uniting older and younger Dominicans who wanted autonomy from Haiti. These activists were slowly gathering support from many in the Dominican elite who aided these young Dominicans. Marco Medina feared that his younger brother Julio was secretly meeting with Dominican Nationalists and advised him to not involve himself with groups against the Haitian government.

Julio Medina broke his silence one day and spoke directly to his older brother: "The Haitian government has grown corrupt and has punished the Dominican people, erasing parts of our Dominican culture. I cannot even enjoy cock-fighting like I used to."

Marco Medina replied, "You know our family always looked down on cock-fighting—there are more important things than drinking and betting at the cockfights. It is okay to engage in these activities occasionally, but gambling, just as any other vice, can overtake a man and lead him to ruin. You have to be careful who you associate with and who you share your political opinions with because although the Haitian government has become corrupt and weak, it is still dangerous to speak against President

Boyer. At the moment, we need peace and stability. Later we can form our own government with enough time."

Julio Medina responded quickly, "The Haitian Military has spilled innocent Dominican blood in the past and continues to do so now. Dessalines and his Haitian armies killed innocent Dominican women and children and the Haitian Army continues to subject the Dominican people to disrespect and violence. Dominicans have witnessed and suffered horrors from the Spaniards and we agree that this Haitian revolution was successful in giving the people of these islands hope to be free from the yoke of the Europeans—a freedom that possibly the people of Puerto Rico and Cuba will one day experience. However, we must continue to be free as Dominicans with our own state once again."

Although he sought a peaceful path to freedom as he cared for the safety of his family and the Dominican people, Marco Medina agreed with his younger brother. He had reason to be cautious regarding a possible rebellion: primarily, the recent pregnancy of his wife Maria Altagracia. Marco Medina would speak to his son Anibal and later his family about the arrival of a new baby. Altagracia was pregnant for a few months and her body was beginning to manifest the fruit of her love with her husband while Marco Medina worried about his brother Julio's growing involvement with the Dominican nationalists.

CHAPTER 3

JUAN PABLO DUARTE & THE DOMINICAN SOCRATES

(1838)

Clandestine meetings had been taking place among Dominican nationalists for several years. Various Dominicans would lead these nationalist movements, and a determined young Dominican named Juan Pablo Duarte would soon create and lead La Trinitaria (or The Trinitarians). Juan Pablo Duarte belonged to the criollo Dominican group (or the Creole Dominican class) who had fled after the arrival of François-Dominique Toussaint Louverture. To escape the turmoil in the island of Hispanola during the Hation Revolution, Juan Pablo Duarte's parents sought safety in neighboring Mayaguez, Puerto Rico in 1802. Juan Pablo Duarte's father was José Duarte Rodríguez, a Peninsular from Vejer de la Frontera, Kingdom of Seville, Spain; his mother was Manuela Díez Jiménez from El Seibo, Captaincy General of Santo Domingo, which subsequently became the Republic of Spanish Haiti after the Dominicans declared independence in 1821.

As the Napoleonic Wars raged in Europe, the English and Spanish fought against the French in the Caribbean. The Napoleonic French Army was led by Governor-General Marie-Louis Ferrand against the Spanish allied Army. Juan Sánchez Ramírez led Puerto Rican and Dominican soldiers, launching the first attack at the battle of Palo Hincado on November seventh, 1808. Born in 1762 in Cotuí, Santo Domingo, Juan Sánchez Ramírez was determined to defeat the French. General Ramírez placed on his right Manuel Carvajal and his left Pedro Vasquez. Miguel Febles served as adjutant, while the Milicias Españolas (or the Spanish Army) was under the command of Captain Tomas Ramirez Carvajal. The Spanish and Dominican troops devastated the French Napoleonic forces, leaving many French corpses on the battlefield. A few of the Spaniards who died were two cavalry unit leaders: Captain Antonio Sosa and Captain Vicente Mercedes. They were later buried in El Seibo. The retreating French soldiers fled to Santo Domingo and were chased by a squadron commanded by Spanish Colonel Pedro Santana. At the subsequent battle for Santo Domingo, Juan Sánchez Ramírez defeated French forces led by General Dubarquier and was appointed governor and recognized by King Ferdinand VII of Spain as sovereign at La Junta de Bondillo (or The Assembly of Bondillo). Juan Sánchez Ramírez reopened the Universidad Santo Tomás de Aquino or the University of St. Thomas Aquinas and reopened the Dominican ports, however the economy of the territory declined as the Spanish Empire was locked into various conflicts throughout South America.

This was the third major war symbolizing "the triumph of Dominican will". The first was the victory over the British in 1655, and the second conflict was the Battle of the Sabana Real in 1691. After the Spanish reconquered Santo Domingo, the Duarte family returned from Puerto Rico. Juan Pablo Duarte had nine siblings, and his sister Rosa Protomártir Duarte participated in the independence movement. The University of St. Thomas Aquinas was established in 1538 and became the first university of the Americas. Juan Pablo Duarte enrolled in this school and studied under Professor Dr. Juan Vicente Moscoso Carvajal, who taught at the Universidad Santo Tomás de Aquino (or the University of Saint Thomas Aquinas) in Santo Domingo before the university was closed by the Haitian government in 1823. The Dominican students were subsequently forced to enlist into the Haitian Military.

Juan Pablo Duarte acquired a higher education in Law, Philosophy, and Latin under the tutelage of Dr. Juan Vicente Moscoso Carvajal, and he traveled to the United States and Europe to further his education. Duarte would form La Trinitaria, and other prominent Dominicans—including Juan Isidro Pérez, Pedro Alejandro Pina, Jacinto de la Concha, Félix María Ruiz, José María Serra, Benito González, Felipe Alfau, and Juan Nepomuceno Ravelo—would become the earliest members. Many of the people in La Trinitaria were unknown to most Dominicans, however the members of this secretive group (including Julio Medina) were slowly uncovered by other Dominican nationalists. Juan Pablo Duarte led La Trinitaria and allied himself with older liber-al Dominican thinkers while also aiding the creation of other more public nationalist Dominican organizations.

Dr. Juan Vicente Moscoso Carvajal and his teachings captured the minds of many young Dominicans. He graduated from the University of Santo Tomas de Aquino in 1798, acquiring a doctorate of canon and civic law. He became a lawyer, politician, educator, and assessor of the royal artillery of Santo Domingo. Dr. Juan Vicente Moscoso Carvajal was one of the signatories of the Declaration of Independence for the Republic of Spanish Haiti on December first, 1821 along with other Dominicans—including José Nuñez de Caceres and Manuel Carvajal. Dr. Juan Vicente Moscoso Carvajal was an avid reader; he digested a multitude of books; he especially enjoyed the ancient history of the Egyptians, Greeks, and Romans. The Socratic method became a favorite teaching style for Dr. Juan Vicente Moscoso Carvajal.

The ideas of Socrates were written and preserved by his famous disciple Plato, including the Socratic Method—famously demonstrated in Plato's Theaetetus (written around 369 BCE). The Socratic Method invoked internal reflection and helped students question previous ideologies. In the Fifth Century BCE, Sophists encouraged and convinced people to agree with their points of view, but Socrates proposed an alternative. This method was accredited by some people to Socrates' predecessor, Protagoras. The method of elenchus is the cross-examination or scrutiny of ideas and a form of cooperative argumentative dialogue. It is based on asking and answering questions to stimulate critical thinking and to draw out ideas and underlying presumptions (also known as the Socratic Method). Plato would write over thirty dialogues in which Socrates was the main participant. Often, Socrates stated that he is a simple man, and he would discuss with others who proclaimed advanced knowledge on various subjects. Socrates would subsequently demonstrate that the other person's views were inconsistent. Socrates believed that a person could attain knowledge through recognition of ignorance. He questioned the Greek-Athenian establishment and was accused of corrupting the youth. Dr. Juan Vicente Moscoso Carvajal's criticisms would also be considered a threat to the Haitian government.

Dr. Juan Vicente Moscoso Carvajal was well known to Haitian authorities as one of the signatories of the Declaration of Independence of Spanish Haiti on December first, 1821; he was also a former member of the Rebellion of Los Alcarrizos (or the Rebellion of Alcarrizos) in 1824 against the Haitian government. Haitian authorities began to monitor him once again as both the fragility of the Haitian government under President Boyer and his activity against him increased. mulatto and black Dominicans as well as Haitians who'd grown disenchanted with President Boyer were joining movements against the Haitian government. Previously, Dominicans desired a return of their territory to Spain and a united coalition with La Gran Colombia. However, these movements were increasingly united towards the establishment of an independent republic, which was supported by large segments of the Dominican population regardless of class or color.

Dr. Juan Vicente Moscoso Carvajal was widely known as the Dominican Socrates, and his fame and influence upon Dominican intellectuals (including Juan Pablo Duarte and Felix Maria del Monte) motived the Haitian government to consider his exile to Cuba. This only served to motivate his followers to further rebel against the Haitian government. After his exile, Dr. Juan Vicente Moscoso Carvajal became the head of canon and civil law of the Seminario school in Cuba until his death in 1837. Other supporters of Dominican independence were threatened and arrested by the Haitian government, sometimes severely beaten as an example to any Dominican dissenters.

Various groups against Haitian rule arose, and La Trinitaria were rapidly growing in power and influence. Members of La Trinitaria were usually called Trinitarios (or Trinitarians). Julio Manuel Medina was attracted to their message and he sought membership into the group after he witnessed the abuse of Haitian soldiers and the increasing fragility of President Boyer. Marco Aurelio was nervous regarding his brother's activities, and he suspected he was involved with several pro-independent Dominican movements and possibly La Trinitaria. Others also suspected Julio Manuel Medina of involvement in various groups plotting a rebellion against the Haitian government.

As Julio Manuel Medina was walking home one summer night, he was suddenly intercepted by Haitian soldiers and some Dominican support forces. One of the soldiers motioned to one of the Dominicans as he approached Julio Manuel. The Haitian soldier was tall and slender and was of high rank. He spoke in careful, stern Creole and used one of the Dominicans to translate for him: "Excuse me, my Spanish is not good. My name is Jean Dumont and I am the leader of these soldiers. It has come to my attention that you have unfortunately involved yourselves with anti-government groups that are threatening the peace and unity of our independent island. The Haitian government has fought and shed blood to bring freedom and stability to our people, and if our government is threatened by the Europeans, we will use our divisions to reoccupy. At this moment, we live in freedom unlike our island neighbors in the Caribbean, and we should maintain our freedom and serve as an example to the other islands to continue their struggle for independence."

Jean Dumont paused and spoke to his Dominican translator, revealing his name was Ramon De La Cruz. After a private conversation with Ramon, he returned his gaze to Julio Manuel Medina and continued his lecture. "These are difficult times as the world is in embroiled in warfare. Rebellions are rising against the European colonizers while the Europeans fight amongst them-selves for our territory and resources. It is important to note that despite the conflict amongst the European Empires, they still agree on the punishment of the people they colonize in an effort to enrich their respective states, while those of us who are independent of their brutality continue to fight for the maintenance of our liberties. The United States and their leader from New York, President Martin Van Buren, continue to wage war against the Seminoles as the United States attempts to displace tribes from their native lands. The United States is essentially finishing what the Spaniards began as they battle the Seminoles in Florida. The United States is a young nation with no king. However, as we seek to eliminate slavery, they aspire to become an empire just as the English from whom they won their independence from. Haiti participated in the first successful slave revolution—a feat that not even the great Spartacus could accomplish against the Roman Republic. We defeated the French Army of Napoleon Bonaparte and have successfully waged war against the other colonial powers—including the English, who continue to hold the island of Jamaica hostage. We have also aided Simon Bolivar and his people in their struggles for emancipation against the Spaniards. This nation has fought hard against our oppressors and through the leadership of Toussaint Louverture, Dessalines, and President Boyer, we have maintained liberty in this island. This balance is fragile, and now we have reason to believe that you have involved yourself with various groups who threaten this stability."

Julio Manuel Medina carefully listened to Jean Dumont's words until he finished and responded with the aid of Dumont's Dominican translator: "I respect freedom and I am also against the European powers and their colonization. Like you, our people have fought for several centuries since the arrival of Christopher Columbus in 1492. The brave native leaders such as Cacique Caonabo, Cacique Anacaona, and the Taino people battled bravely against the Spaniards as well as the numerous African tribes that arrived in 1501. The Dominicans are now a people, and a culture has formed from the first African slaves, Tainos, and other natives—as well as the Spaniards and other Europeans who the Africans and Tainos fought against. I respect your fight, but I cannot accept the mistreatment of my people. We have not forgotten the atrocities the Haitian Army has inflicted upon the Dominican populace, including those perpetrated in Moca in 1805—the closing of our churches, schools, and university mandated by the Haitian government. The Haitian government has looked down upon Dominican culture and the Spanish language we speak. Dominicans prefer to reestablish our own nation as we did before in 1821; to live in harmony with the Haitians as our neighbors as two nations sharing one island. Haiti has emancipated the slaves, however many of your own Haitian people live under slave-like labor: tied to the fields while President Boyer agreed to pay France 150 million gold francs for its lost colony which is now crippling Haiti. Many yearn for a peaceful resolution, but as the Haitian government continues to weaken through debt, corruption, and violence, we will have no choice other than open warfare."

As Julio Manuel spoke, some of the Dominicans serving for the Haitian Army listened carefully as Ramon De La Cruz translated his words into Creole. Jean Dumont wrestled with his rising anger, attempting to maintain his well-known calm demeanor as he replied, "Haiti's fight against the colonial powers is justified despite the mistakes of our past leaders. I myself do not agree with every choice our prior leaders made, however I stand with Haiti and the blood my people shed to overthrow colonial power. As a military man, my responsibility for the nation of Haiti is even greater than the responsibilities of a civilian. I must carry out my orders and maintain the discipline of the Haitian Army. Part of my mission is to stop any potential rebellion against the Haitian Military and government. Your suspected involvement with La Trinitaria means I must incarcerate you, and your opinions strengthen my belief that you do plan to violently overthrow the Haitian government. Your honesty could both be considered brave and foolish, as you have incriminated yourself." As Jean Dumont completed his statement, he motioned to his lieutenant to apprehend Julio Manuel Medina.

Dumont's lieutenant was Antoine Robespierre: a man who possessed great strength and monumental will. Antoine Robespierre forcefully held Julio Manuel Medina and when he reacted, Robespierre struck Julio several times until he collapsed. Robespierre attempted to strike Julio once more but was ordered by Jean Dumont to stop the beating. Antoine Robespierre angrily exclaimed, "After all these years, Dominicans like these still do not understand our Creole language, even as they have been instructed by our government to learn Creole. How will we be able to have social cohesion if they cannot communicate in our language?"

Julio Manuel Medina was quickly transported to a secret Haitian holding facility near the border of the city of Santo Domingo where other Dominicans were also brought against their will. He was beaten unconscious by several guards only to be awakened in the middle of the night by the desperate screams of Dominican prisoners. Julio Medina did not eat for several days and was sporadically given water to ease his growing thirst. As he anxiously awaited his fate, he thought of Jean Dumont and Antoine Robespierre, who had recently arrived at the holding facility.

Antoine Robespierre shared the same name as the infamous French leader Maximilien Robespierre. Julio's brother, Marco Medina, often spoke about the French Revolution and the various figures involved in French politics; Maximilien Robespierre had been brought up in their conversations many times. Marco Medina had previously spoken of Maximilien Robespierre and his membership in the Estates-General, the Constituent Assembly, and the Jacobin Club. Maximilien Robespierre advocated for the rights of the poor, the abolishment of slavery in the French colonies, Universal manhood suffrage, and was against the use of force and authoritarianism. Maximilien Robespierre opposed dictatorships which stemmed from war and was quoted in 1791 as stating, "If they are Caesars or Cromwells, they seize power for themselves. If they are spineless courtiers, uninterested in doing good yet dangerous when they seek to do harm, they go back to lay their power at their master's feet and help him to resume arbitrary power on condition they become his chief servants."

At the national convention, France was declared the French Republic on the twenty-first of September 1792. After the discovery of a secret cache of 726 documents consisting of King Louis' personal communications, King Louis XVI would be sentenced to execution. Maximilien Robespierre believed King Louis XVI would remain an obstacle for the French Republic if left alive, and he would begin assassinating other political figures he opposed.

Maximilien Robespierre once stated, "Louis was a king, and our republic is established; the critical question concerning you must be decided by these words alone. Louis was dethroned by his crimes; Louis denounced the French people as rebels; he appealed to chains, to the armies of tyrants who are his brothers—the victory of the people established that Louis alone was a rebel. Louis cannot, therefore, be judged; he already is judged. He is condemned, or the republic cannot be absolved."

Despite Maximilien Robespierre's prior beliefs, he soon became feared and autocratic as he led a wave of violence called the "Reign of Terror". Between June 1793 and July 1794, there were over 16,000 official death sentences in France. The Reign of Terror lasted until the fall of Robespierre and his own execution by guillotine on the twenty-eighth of July 1794—after he was declared a tyrant. As Julio Medina thought about the rise and fall of Robespierre, he heard the voice of Antoine Robespierre as he and several other Haitian guards approached his holding cell. One of the Haitian guards entered Julio's cell and struck him in the face, causing him to bleed from his nose and stumble backward. As the guard approached, Julio hit him in his face with a strong blow while avoiding a counterattack and delivering three more punches to the Haitian's stomach, after which he collapsed to the ground. Julio Medina then struck the second guard but was tripped by Antoine Robespierre, who unleashed his anger and fury upon Julio's body as soon as he fell. The other guard was able to recover and join in on the violent beating.

The next morning, Julio awakened to see Antoine looking directly at him, and then he began to speak. "You have some fight, and I respect that. However, I believe you should be executed for your transgressions. The reason you remain alive is that my superiors believe you may have information on other Dominican rebels who have so far managed to remain free from arrest as they continue to plot against the Haitian government. If I were to be perfectly honest, we should not be lenient with Dominican rebels such as you. Haitians are the first people to rise against the weight of oppression and succeed to create our great nation—all of which occurred predominantly on the backs of the African slaves of our land. I sometimes suspect the intentions of those Haitians of mixed heritage who are in positions of power, so you can only imagine the distrust and disdain I have for you Dominicans. Your people are largely of mixed ancestries and have mixed opinions on the those who have oppressed the black people of these islands. I believe many of your people to be of questionable motives and sometimes of weak character in the face of European peoples that seek to destroy us. Perhaps many of you feel some cultural bond with them, but none of them care for both our people. My superiors think we can build a united island with peace and understanding, however I feel that individuals like you and your rebel friends serve to remind the doubtful and convince the ignorant that your true intention is to destroy all we have built."

Slightly annoyed, Julio Medina replied, "Our people have fought against many European powers and will continue to fight those who seek to hurt us. Just as some among us have fought alongside the Europeans, shall I remind you that your own Haitian leaders have also fought alongside Europeans—including the French, who controlled the lands you now call Haiti. Your leaders separated themselves with some joining the Napoleonic French Army who sought to continue slavery, and today your leaders seek to make deals with European powers. I understand that Haiti has to preserve its independence, however many Dominicans are simply asking for the return of our nation, sovereignty, and an opportunity to navigate our own nation and people independently in the global community."

Antoine Robespierre interjected before Julio Medina continued, "Haiti has to do what it can to survive as a free nation after our act of emancipation from France, and people like you are dangerous to the Haitian government because you threaten the very liberty of this nation. Due to your actions and beliefs, I believe it is safe to assume you have poisoned the minds of your friends and family members with the ideas of the Dominican rebels such as the man named Juan Pablo Duarte. You will reveal to me the locations of these rebels, and if you choose not to cooperate you shall be violently encouraged to do so. I will promise you that you will always remember my name if you survive your punishment."

Julio Medina attempted to defend himself, but he was weak from lack of food and water and easily succumbed to the overwhelming strength of Antoine Robespierre as he was beaten viciously for daring to speak against him. Antoine Robespierre sought Julio Medina's friends and family— including his older brother Marco, who he brought into captivity several days later. To the relief of Julio Medina, his brother was taken to the holding facility peacefully—a younger Dominican was carried into captivity in an unconscious state.

The young Dominican was originally from the northern region of the Cibao, and his name was Alonso Kebehi Dos Santos. Alonso's father was of Portuguese and Galician ancestry while his mother's family arrived from the Islas Canarias (or the Canary Islands). The Dos Santos family, largely consisted of mixed and white, poor Dominicans. Alonso's mother Rosa was born in the Cibao region and most of her family arrived during the late 1790s. Rosa's family previously lived in the largest island of Tenerife in the Canary archipelago, and Rosa's father attended the University of La Laguna in Tenerife (founded in 1792). Rosa named her only son Kebehi in honor of the Berber natives called Guanches. Alonso's last name was Portuguese, given to him by his father Ferdinando Dos Santos.

The Dos Santos family suffered various abuses at the hands of Haitian soldiers during the brief reign of Jean-Jacques Dessalines (or Emperor Jacques I) and were once again subject to cruelty at the Haitian Army. Julio

Medina would later learn that one of the Haitian soldiers molested Alonso's female cousin and he retaliated by severely beating two Haitian soldiers. Alonso quickly involved himself in various Dominican rebel groups and began to aggressively call for rebellion. He was accused of involving himself with La Trinitaria and attending La Filantrópica (or The Philanthropic), which spread veiled messages of liberation from Haiti through theatrical plays. Although he desperately attempted to appear so, Alonso Dos Santos was not a cultured man. Nor was he an artistic man, and it was hard to believe he attended La Filantrópica. Because of his actions, Alonso Dos Santos was beaten worse than the other inmates, but he was resilient and almost seemed to welcome death. Alonso Dos Santos' family members were questioned and imprisoned—this included his father Ferdinando Dos Santos, who was brutally beaten into critical condition and devastating the entire family.

Julio and Marco Medina were horrified with the possibility that the rest of their loved ones would join them in captivity, but after further questioning, Marco Medina was released, and Julio remained imprisoned. After several months in captivity, Julio Medina learned through the conversations of the Haitian guards that Juan Pablo Duarte had been located and threatened with exile from the island of Hispaniola. However, the exile or execution of Juan Pablo Duarte would only further galvanize La Trinitaria and the Dominican population against the Haitian government.

CHAPTER 4

LA TRINITARIA & THE OVERTHROW OF PRESIDENT BOYER
(1840)

There was little to celebrate in the Medina household as Christmas and the new year came. Julio was still in captivity, and the rest of the family were under the surveillance of the Haitian government. La Trinitaria, however, was secretly gaining the support of Dominicans within the Haitian Army and joining alliances with liberal Haitians who opposed the rule of President Boyer. The tension was strongly felt by Dominicans within Haitian society as Juan Pablo Duarte and other Trinitarios (or Trinitarians) were soon identified and apprehended by the government. Rumors spread regarding the harsh actions by the Haitian government against Dominican rebels—or suspected Dominican rebels. The Medina family felt these tensions acutely as they were monitored by the government and their spies.

Marco Medina returned to his home, but his younger brother remained in Haitian captivity and Marco's petitions to visit him were continuously denied. Julio's beatings lessened over time, however Julio was gripped with growing anxiety as the Haitian government destabilized and the Dominicans began to increasingly call for open rebellion. Marco Medina resumed his farm work, but instability within society threatened his livelihood as well as the safety of his family. Marco was concerned for his household and his two-year-old baby girl, Catalina Violeta Medina. Anibal Hector Medina, who was now ten years old, was filled with uncertainty as he was warned by his parents to remain indoors—particularly after sunset—and to maintain a small circle of friends. Dominican families were wary of associating themselves with the Medinas, and they limited their interactions with the family. Isolated, the Medinas were aware of the voices calling for independence, including Juan Pablo Duarte's sister, Rosa Protomártir Duarte y Diez—she was hosting various plays to raise funds to support the reestablishment of an independent Dominican state.

Like other Dominican children, Anibal Medina heard whispers regarding Dominican rebel groups like the theatrical plays held by La Filontropica. Many of the performances were held in several neighborhoods within Santo Domingo as well as other cities. Throughout his travels, Juan Pablo Duarte learned how the arts and theater helped increase nationalism amongst the Spaniards and in their efforts against Napoleon Bonaparte and the French occupation of Spain and Portugal. Ironically, the Spaniards aided the French with their invasion only to be betrayed by Napoleon, who subsequently invaded Spain the following year in 1808—which led to the French occupation of the Iberian Peninsula. Spanish rebels would fight against the French Empire and Spanish forces under the leadership of

Napoleon Bonaparte's brother King Joseph-Napoleon Bonaparte of Spain or King Joseph I. King Joseph-Napoleon Bonaparte would be dethroned and Spain would reclaim its independence. Napoleon Bonaparte was later exiled for a second time to the island of Saint Helena after his devastating loss to the Allied Seventh Coalition which defeated him at the Battle of Waterloo; he died in 1821. His brother Joseph Napoleon would reside in the United States and decline an offer from Mexico to rule as their king.

In only a few years, the Trinitarians rapidly gained strength within the Dominican population. Juan Pablo Duarte officially formed La Trinitaria alongside his Dominican supporters on the sixteenth of July 1838 in the city of Santo Domingo. The clandestine meeting took place at the house of Doña Marfa Pérez de La Paz, who was the mother of a Trinitarian named Juan Isidro.

Juan Pablo Duarte carefully thought of his words before he addressed his fellow rebels: "We are convinced that a fusion between Haitians and Dominicans within a single nation is not possible. We are two people from two different cultures, and our destiny is to be independent. Our organization shall be known as La Trinitaria because it will be composed of groups of three. We will place our group under the protection of the Holy Trinity. Our motto is 'God, Homeland, and Liberty'. My friends, we are here for the purpose of revolting against Haitian power to establish ourselves as an independent state which will be named the Dominican Republic. The white cross that our flag carries will tell the world the Dominican people, upon entering the life of freedom, proclaim the union of all races by the bonds of civilization and Christianity. The situation in which we put ourselves is a serious one, and once we take this path, going backwards is impossible. Now, at this moment there is still time to avoid commitment. However, after you decide to be a part of La Trinitaria, it is a lifelong allegiance."

Before Juan Pablo Duarte continued his speech, a few Dominicans interrupted, stating they stood with Juan Pablo Duarte and they ratified the decision to establish the independent state of the Dominican Republic. The other eight Dominicans were Juan Isidro Pérez, Pedro Alejandro Pina, Félix María Ruiz, José María Serra de Castro, Felipe Alfau, Juan Nepomuceno Ravelo, Benito González, and Jacinto de la Concha. Two Dominicans by the name of Francisco del Rosario Sánchez y Matías Ramón Mella would later join La Trinitaria as Juan Pablo Duarte dispatched his group throughout the eastern half of Hispaniola. The message and push for independence rapidly spread as La Trinitaria began to form an alliance with liberal Haitians who sought to overthrow President Boyer.

Secretary Joseph Balthazar Inginac previously attempted to increase Haiti's alliances and seek international recognition. Secretary Inginac supported increased relations with England, and some believed he sought to make Haiti a protectorate of Great Britain—to the dismay of President Boyer. The president was wary of welcoming the British diplomats due to the disrespect displayed by prominent British officials. Joseph Balthazar Inginac also attempted to deepen the relationship with Latin Americans, however Haiti did not participate in the Congress of Panama held in 1826.

The Congress of Panama was also called the Amphictyonic Congress in honor of the Amphictyonic League of Ancient Greece. It brought together representatives from Gran Colombia, Peru, the United Provinces of Central America, and Mexico. Chile and the United Provinces of South America declined to attend the Panama Conference as well as the Empire of Brazil due to its ongoing fight with Argentina. Various politicians within the United States—including those from the southern states—did not want to send delegates, as they still practiced slavery and Latin nations had outlawed this practice. President John Quincy Adams and Secretary of State Henry Clay wanted the U.S. to attend the Congress, but one delegate died enroute while the second (John Sergeant) arrived after the conclusion of the conference.

As the year 1843 approached, Haiti itself was on the brink of civil war. President Boyer moved against Juan Pablo Duarte and several other Trinitarians and exiled them from Haiti as he attempted to maintain power. The leader was now rejected by the Haitian mulatto elite as well as the black Haitian majority. Charles Rivière-Hérard led the rebel conspiracy against President Boyer as he attempted to quell a possible Dominican rebellion. President Boyer's control further weakened when in May of 1842, a devastating earthquake wrecked major cities in Haiti. The capital of Port-au-Prince burned for many days, and the disaster destroyed homes, roads, and businesses. Along the northern coasts of Haiti, seawater flooded the fields and damaged farm areas, further crippling the economy and government. In the past, there were other earthquakes such as during the French Colonial period of 1751 and 1770. Various Haitian groups opposed to President Boyer gained strength while Dominican separatists and nationalists increased their de-mands.

Haitian leaders in Les Cayes formed the Society of the Rights of Man and the Citizen, calling for the end of President Boyer's autocratic rule and inviting the Haitian Military under the command Charles Rivière-Hérard to march towards the capital. The previous governor of the eastern Dominican side of the island (General Maximilien Borgella) and the current governor of Les Cayes did not oppose Charles Rivière-Hérard. President Boyer accepted defeat on March thirteenth, 1843, and afterward secretly fled Haiti aboard an English ship and took the Boyer family to Jamaica. The Haitians adopted a new constitution, and General Charles Rivière-Hérard seized control of Haiti and installed himself as president.

News of President Boyer's defeat quickly spread throughout Haiti and the Dominican population to the east. Marco Medina feared a retaliation by the Haitian authorities and the corrupt members of the military. Julio was released from incarceration, however recent events within the Haitian government frightened both Marco and Julio due to Julio's activities with rebel groups. Despite Marco's wishes, Julio went into hiding to keep his family safe. It would prove to be a wise decision, as the Haitian officer Antoine Robespierre returned to question Julio and the Medina family. Terror swept through Dominican neighborhoods within Santo Domingo as malicious members of the Haitian Military sought to use the political unrest to loot homes and livestock as well as abuse any Dominicans who attempted to fight back.

The Haitian government had previously stripped white landholders and extended these policies towards white and various mixed Dominican were able to keep their lands. However, Haitian Military members once again questioned Dominican landholders—including Marco Medina's employer Romulo Andujar, who was approached by Antoine Robespierre. It was rumored the two got into an argument over the ancestry of Romulo Andujar, who declared he was of mixed heritage.

After stating his Arab, African, and Spanish ancestry, Robespierre scoffed, replying that, "Arabs are the enemies of the African people, both historically and currently." Antoine Robespierre deemed Dominicans to be traitorous to the Haitian government and the Haitian soldiers proceeded to set fire to Andujar's farms and ranches, and quickly incarcerated Romulo Andujar and his relatives.

Several days later, Haitian soldiers located the Medina home and inquired about the location of Julio Medina. Marco walked outside as nervous Dominican neighbors quietly observed. Antoine Robespierre threatened to imprison and kill Marco as his wife and children cried for mercy; he seemed to derive joy from the idea, briefly smiling while he hit Marco, who defended himself from the following strike.

Marco Medina attempted to restrain Antoine as he declared, "I am a working man who has obeyed the laws. I am not a political man, and I do not know the whereabouts of my younger brother. All I desire is peace and a return to peaceful society. I was a supporter of the Republic of Spanish Haiti and even sought peace under Haitian governance, however if peace cannot be maintained, perhaps it will be better if the Haitian government can allow a peaceful coexistence of both cultures with equal opportunities for Dominicans in this government."

Antoine Robespierre angrily replied, "My people have shed blood to keep this land free and the very peace you desire is now threatened because of Dominicans such as your brother who encourages rebellion amongst Haitians." Antoine proceeded to beat Marco Medina publicly for all to see as soldiers looted his home and the homes of other Dominicans within the community. Antoine then threatened Marco with death if he did not provide the location of his brother. Later, as the new year of 1844 approached, Antoine received information from some Dominican sources that Julio Medina had fled to San Cristobal. Against the orders of his superior Dumont Pierre, Antoine Robespierre would travel towards San Cristobal with a group of Haitian soldiers during New Year's Day. However, as Robespierre marched towards San Cristobal, Julio Medina traveled towards Santo Domingo to free the Dominican captives.

The Dominicans led by Julio Medina were heavily armed with weapons as well as intelligence provided by members of the La Trinitaria. Julio learned that several Dominican Military members were ready to defect from the Haitian Army and support the establishment of an independent Dominican state. Wealthy friends of Romulo Andujar also helped provide money and weapons as Julio Medina and other Dominicans infiltrated the secret prison to release the other captives (including Alonso Kebehi Dos Santos) as a firefight began. Several Haitian soldiers were killed as the Dominicans escaped before additional guards arrived. Julio Medina then accompanied the Dominican rebels towards the Medina household and encouraged Marco to flee with his family towards San Cristobal, where they would wait for the Trinitarians to announce the establishment of the new Dominican state.

For several weeks, the Haitian Military committed acts of violence in Santo Domingo, which increased in the month of February. Various Dominican rebels openly called for usage of the Spanish language, reopening churches and schools, and more representation within the government. Meanwhile, the Trinitarians' initial attempt to contact Juan Pablo Duarte to encourage him to return failed. The Trinitarians were unable to procure weapons and financial support from Juan Pablo Duarte, who was exiled in Venezuela. However, they were able to gain support from various separatist Dominican factions, including the conservative Dominicans.

The Pro-French faction was led by Buenaventura Baez and Manuel Valencia, who were members of the Haitian Constitutional Assembly. They believed they could use the help of the French to gain independence, and Buenaventura Baez advocated the French consul Andre Levasseur. The Pro-Spanish Dominican faction sought an alliance with the Spaniards and contacted various officials currently in the islands of Cuba and Puerto Rico. The Trinitarians, how-ever, would become the leading organization advocating for the complete independence of the Dominican people under the free Dominican Republic.

Marco Medina feared for the safety of his family as several weeks passed without any for-mal declaration, but the Trinitarians sent a message to Julio Medina that they were ready to seek the establishment of an independent

Dominican Republic. On the morning of the twenty-fourth of February 1844, the Trinitarians led by Francisco del Rosario Sánchez appeared at La Puerta Del Conde (or the Count's Gate) and proclaimed independence. The Constitution of the Dominican Republic was signed in San Cristobal in 1844, and the city was nicknamed *La Ciudad Benemerita* (or the City deserving of grace). The Trinitarians fired in the air, sending a signal throughout the land that independence was now reestablished, and the nation would now be re-named as the Dominican Republic. The flag was raised, and celebrations began within Santo Domingo and spread throughout the free land.

CHAPTER 5
THE BIRTH OF THE DOMINICAN REPUBLIC
(1844)

The proclamation of independence of the Dominican Republic shocked the Haitian government as President Charles Rivière-Hérard attempted to assuage the Dominican population. President Charles Rivière Hérard attempted to peacefully prevent further rebellion by replacing corrupt Haitian officials and promising to allow Dominicans to openly speak Spanish and practice their culture. However, the idea of an independent state free of the Haitian government now gained the support of powerful regional Dominican leaders, including Pedro Santana. As the Dominicans quickly organized their military, President Charles Rivière-Hérard ordered the Haitian Military to attack the Dominican Republic in the month of March.

While Haitian soldiers evacuated Santo Domingo, the Medina family attempted to travel back towards the capital with other Dominicans during the late afternoon when they were confronted by Haitian soldiers who identified them. They had sent a message to Antoine Robespierre—who was nearby—and he rode to their location to punish the Medina family. Robespierre, however, was unaware that the Dominican faction of the Haitian Military had defected from the Haitian Army in support of the Dominican Republic. In addition, they had forced Jean Dumont to retreat towards Haitian territory, which was reverted by nationalist Dominicans towards the original western borders that existed in Hispaniola. Rumors spread that a possible massacre of Dominicans would occur near the city of San Cristobal as Antoine Robespierre located and apprehended Marco Medina, brutally beating him in front of his family. Anibal Medina was also beaten when he tried to come to the aid of his father. Robespierre ordered the Haitian soldiers to kill all the Dominican captives and burn Dominican villages. Jean Dumont, who finally reached Robespierre, ordered Robespierre to release the captives and join his march towards Haiti. Antoine Robespierre disobeyed Jean Dumont's orders as the Haitian soldiers continued to torture and kill the Dominicans. Antoine Robespierre then turned to Marco Medina and attempted to strike him with his sword. However, as he attempted to land the fatal blow, shots were fired by approaching Dominican forces, making the Haitians retreat. Antoine Robespierre was hit by a bullet from the young Dominican Alonso Kebehi Dos Santos.

Additional Dominican soldiers led by Ramon De La Cruz successfully defeated the Haitian Military and joined Julio Medina, who killed several Haitian soldiers. Antoine Robespierre managed to escape the Dominican counterattack, but Jean Dumont and several Haitian soldiers were wounded and captured. Marco Medina was soon informed that the father of Alonso Dos Santos was arrested once again by the Haitian Military. Ferdinando Dos Santos died after another extensive beating, leaving his widow Rosa depressed and gravely ill. As the sun set and darkness enveloped the newly established Dominican Republic, Alonso Kebehi Dos Santos demanded the death of Jean Dumont and the other Haitian soldiers and appealed to the Dominican onlookers that retribution would be the order of the day. As Alonso Dos Santos attempted to shoot Jean Dumont, Marco Medina advised he should be spared and allowed to retreat towards Haiti.

Alonso Dos Santos angrily replied, "These Haitian soldiers have treated us like animals. They have killed and raped my family members and they have beaten your younger brother. Their brutality has led to the death of my father and my family will be avenged. They displayed no such mercy towards us and the Dominican people. President Boyer ruled this island for twenty-two years and now they replace him with another Haitian hegemon who will once again attempt to reconquer our lands after we have reestablished our independence. If we release Jean Dumont, he will only return leading Haitian soldiers against us in war."

Marco Medina responded, "If we execute these captured soldiers, we will only perpetuate the most negative aspects of Haitian rule that you so detest. We must be an example and reflect the best aspects of the Dominican people. We must represent the ideals of our leaders who made our independence possible. There is a possibility that Jean Dumont will return, and if he returns, we will face him honorably on the battlefield. We will not dishonor ourselves by killing him and his men in a brutal fashion. There are still Dominicans who want to live peacefully with our Haitian neighbors, and if we are able to maintain our independence, we desire a peaceful coexistence and relationship with Haiti."

Alonso Dos Santos responded, "Mr. Medina, with all due respect, the Haitian government does not want peace with the Dominican Republic— even if Dominicans and the Haitian people desire it. The Haitian government will lose a large tax base if they lose the Dominican territory and populace, and they yearn to reconquer the island of Hispaniola—or at the very least expand their borders. Even as they retreat towards Haiti they will murder, loot, and burn down our cities and villages just as they have in the past. This is a decent man, I agree; however, he did not discipline his rogue animalistic soldiers. They will return with a much larger, experienced Army than the young Dominican Republic, and we will fight bravely. However, it makes no sense to let potential enemy combatants flee as they plot against us."

After various discussions throughout the night, the Dominicans agreed to release Jean Dumont and the other Haitians. The Haitian response would be strong and swift as the military regrouped and began preparations to march towards the Dominican Republic.

The Dominican Republic began organizing a small army with General Pedro Santana leading the southern Dominican forces. Within weeks, Dominican civilians joined—including Marco and Julio Medina, who were recommended by Ramon De La Cruz.

As the Trinitarians awaited the return of Juan Pablo Duarte to lead the Dominican Republic in a war against Haiti, they welcomed the arrival of the brothers Ramon and Pedro Santana from El Seibo and appointed General Pedro Santana as the leader of the Southern Dominican Army.

General Pedro Santana was believed by many Dominicans to have been named after Spanish Colonel Pedro Santana, who participated in the Battle of Palo Hincado in 1808—he sought to surpass his namesake in the battlefield. Marco and Julio Medina joined the southern Dominican forces (which numbered over 3,000 soldiers) against the superior forces of the Haitian Army led by President Charles Rivière-Hérard. The Haitian vanguard attacked the town of Azua where Santana had positioned his forces on March nineteenth, 1844. Dominican cannons fired upon the Haitians and ripped through the Haitian fighters, leaving many Haitian soldiers dead as they re-treated and Pedro Santana marched towards the city of Bani to position most of his army closer to the capital city of Santo Domingo.

As General Pedro Santana organized his main army at Bani, he strategically positioned various groups of Dominican guerrilla forces within the mountain terrain of El Numero between Azua and Bani. General Santana placed Dominican leaders—including Ramon De La Cruz—in charge of the Dominican guerillas. Julio Medina stayed with Ramon De La Cruz while the injured Marco Medina traveled with General Santana to Bani. The Haitian Army (numbering over 10,000) marched from Azua towards Bani, where they encountered a powerful attack from the Dominican guerillas, resulting in many Haitian casualties and numerous injuries. Ramon De La Cruz waited patiently as the Haitians suffered the first two waves of Dominican attacks. The Haitians lost several thousand soldiers as they reluctantly retreated as Ramon De La Cruz ordered his men to fire upon the Haitian troops. They attempted to return fire, but as the sun set the soldiers lost visibility and were ambushed by the Dominican guerillas on two fronts, forcing the Haitians to retreat to Azua.

Under the leadership of Fernando Taveras, Dionisio Reyes, and Vicente Noble, the Dominican Army defeated the Haitian Army at Baoruco. Dominican forces numbering a little over 500 men led by General Manuel de Regla Mota and General José María Cabral were able to defeat Haitian troops numbering roughly over 10,000 at the battle of Cabeza de Las Marías and Las Hicoteas near Azua de Compostela. The Haitians lost over

1,000 men and suffered a crushing defeat. At the battle of Santiago, under the direction of General José María Imbert, General Fernando Valerio, and Pedro Eugenio Pelletier, the Dominicans defeated a numerically superior Haitian force of over 15,000 soldiers led by General Jean-Louis Pierrot and General St. Louis. In the third major confrontation during the Battle of El Memiso, Dominican forces under General Antonio Duvergé and General Felipe Alfau defeated the larger Haitian forces led by Colonel Pierre Paul and Colonel Auguste Brouard. The naval superiority of the Dominican Republic was established under the order of Commander Juan Bautista Cambiaso, Captain Juan Bautista Maggiolo, and Lieutenant Juan Alejandro Acosta.

As the days progressed, Ramon De La Cruz informed Julio Medina and the rest of the Dominican guerillas that the Dominican northern Army had defeated the Haitian northern forces led by General Pierrot. The Haitians suffered over 750 casualties while the Dominicans, who in some areas held higher ground, suffered only a few. General Pierrot requested an agreement with the Dominicans to retrieve the Haitian dead and wounded. The Dominicans subsequently released a false report stating that President Charles Rivière-Hérard had perished during the southern battle, leading General Pierrot to retreat towards Haiti. President Charles Rivière-Hérard reluctantly re-treated towards Haiti, where he faced further Dominican attacks while awaiting possible turmoil within the Haitian government. The Dominicans were emboldened as they proved they could defeat the more numerous and experienced Haitian Army in battle.

President Charles Rivière-Hérard quickly traveled back towards Haiti to stop a rebellion against his government, including a black revolt in southern Haiti. The black peasant majority rebelled against the Haitian mulatto elite and formed groups known as piquets due to the long spikes they carried. The piquet rebels were united under former army officer Louis Jean-Jacques Accau, who used them to disrupt the government and control southern Haiti. President Charles Rivière-Hérard was unable to quell the rebellion and he fled to Jamaica; thus, General Guerrier was installed as president. However, President Guerrier would later pass away on April fifteenth, 1845 and President Jean-Louis Michel Pierrot was installed by the Haitian mulatto elite the following day.

President Pierrot—who was previously defeated as a Haitian General during the battle for Santiago—now proclaimed the indivisibility of the island while looking to avenge his previous defeat. The Dominicans were much better prepared compared to the preceding year, and the Haitian advance was halted at both the northern and southern borders. The Haitians were defeated on September seventeenth at the battle of La Estrelleta (led by the black Dominican General José Joaquín Puello and General Antonio Duverge near Las Matas de Farfan in San Juan Province), and a naval attack by the Haitians on December twenty-first was defeated by a Dominican naval counter-attack near Puerto Plata. The Dominicans protected their young nation at the border and patrolled their waters with the aid of several schooners.

The first naval battle between Haiti and the Dominican Republic was previously won by the Dominicans off Tortuguero. The Dominican ships the Maria Chica with three guns (commanded by Juan Bautista Maggiolo), and the Separación Dominicana (or "the Dominican Separation") with five guns (commanded by Commander Juan Bautista Cambiaso) defeated the Haitian brigantine Pandora and the schooners *Le signifie* and *La Mouche*—all with unk guns. On April twenty-third, 1844, the Junta Central Gubernativa authorized to incorporate these three schooners in the newly created Dominican Navy, and Commander Cambiaso was appointed Admiral. The Haitian Military subsequently mutinied when ordered to renew further offenses against the Dominicans.

The Trinitarians resumed their calls for Juan Pablo Duarte's return and they arranged for a schooner to depart for the island of Curacao to transport him to the Dominican Republic and install him as President. The Trinitarians were previously outmaneuvered by the conservatives and Tomas de Bobadilla—a former Boyerist—was elected President of the Junta instead of Francisco del Rosario Sanchez, who remained the leader of the Trinitarians. As the conservatives gained control of the Junta and the Dominican Military, the Trinitarians lost power. When Juan Pablo Duarte arrived several months later, the Trinitarians were able to gain control over the conservatives, installing Francisco del Rosario Sanchez as president. In an effort to erode the power of General Santana, the Trinitarians began to arrange for the installation of Juan Pablo Duarte as General-in-Chief of the Dominican Army and named four prominent Trinitarians into the positions of brigadier and division generals. The situation worsened when Colonel Roca was sent to Azua to replace General Santana. The effort to replace Santana was a failure, as his army mostly consisted of men associated with his family members, friends (compadres), who were loyal only to him— they refused the orders of the Junta Central. General Santana subsequently marched towards Santo Domingo with over 2,000 of his soldiers as his supporters encouraged the Dominican populace to accept him as the true leader of the Dominican Republic. The military commander in Santo Domingo (Commander José Joaquin Puello) was ordered by the Trinitarians to arrest General Santana. However, he refused under pressure by the French consulate.

Juan Pablo Duarte was declared as president of the Cibao region, and the Trinitarians continued to denounce General Santana and proclaim Juan Pablo Duarte as true president of the Dominican Republic. General Pedro Santana nearly lost his life at the hands of the Trinitarian named Juan Isidro

Perez, who compared General Pedro Santana to the tyrant Julius Caesar and likened himself to Brutus—he desired to remove the dictator from his position of power.

While the country was still in disarray, the Dominican Army continued to strengthen and prepare against any potential Haitian offensives. Julio Medina and other soldiers were too preoccupied with sporadic fighting and heightened tensions at the border to bother with politics. Meanwhile, Marco Medina was stationed in Santo Domingo witnessing all the political drama along with his wife and children, who had moved back into their home in the capital. Marco Medina was assigned to a reserve unit stationed in Santo Domingo and observed the political turmoil occurring in the capital city. Marco was overjoyed with the reestablishment of a free Dominican state, however he feared the potential of a Dominican civil war. Marco believed the young Dominican nation should strengthen its military while also strengthening the government by creating a constitution that would promote stability and provide liberty and true representation for the Dominican people.

Santo Domingo was an interesting city surrounded by numerous cattle ranches; most of its food was imported from neighboring San Cristobal. The farmers cultivated many crops, including plantains, yucca, yams, and sweet potatoes. In Bani, the people exploited the natural salt ponds, raised pigs, goats, and cattle, and cut mahogany wood for export. Santo Domingo, Puerto Plata, and Santiago contained large import houses which were important for traders within the Dominican Republic.

Anibal Medina celebrated the independence of the Dominican Republic along with many of the youth who were born under the rule of the Haitian government and never witnessed an independent state. Marco Medina had taught his son about the brief Republic of Spanish Haiti and now Anibal experienced the rebirth of an independent Dominican nation. Many proudly waved the new Dominican flag, and they were taught the meaning of the colors and the importance of the motto, "Dios, Patria, y Libertad" (or God, Homeland, and Liberty). The Dominican flag was designed by Juan Pablo Duarte. Centered by a white cross extending to the edges, it was divided into four rectangles. The white cross symbolized salvation; blue represented liberty, and red symbolized the blood of the fallen Dominican heroes. The top two rectangles were also blue, and the bottom two rectangles were red. The Dominican coat of arms was adopted in 1844, and Juan Pablo Duarte declared all Dominicans of all ancestries including black, white, Asian, Arab, and the majority of mixed-race Dominicans to be emancipated from foreign rule. They were to live as free men and women in the sovereign nation named the Dominican Republic.

The flag was raised and many visitors observed the flag and the new independent land. The Dominican Republic influenced the neighboring peoples of Cuba and Puerto Rico, who remained under Spanish control. The flag of the Dominican Republic was similar to the Trinitarians', which also had a white cross—although the cross did not extend to the edge of the flag, leaving an upper blue half and lower red half. The Trinitarians remained powerful within politics, but they were currently locked in a political battle with the Dominican conservatives.

Anibal Hector Medina was now fourteen years old, and he was joyful as he experienced the open celebrations of Dominican culture expressed in the Spanish language and its various dialects. Anibal was educated under the instruction of his father and desired to further his studies in science and mathematics. Many of the Dominican schools were now reopening along with the universities as the government reversed the laws in place under Haitian rule.

Marco Medina was excited his son would return to school and possibly attend the university in Santo Domingo, where he desired to get a job as a teacher once his duties in the Dominican Military were completed. Marco believed he would soon be relieved from duty due to his injuries sustained during his Haitian detention and battle. The internal turmoil within Haiti also allowed for less threat of attacks and increased stability and peace for the Dominican Republic. Politics were rarely spoken about in the Medina household, however Marco and his family largely agreed with the ideals of Juan Pablo Duarte regarding the establishment of an independent republic. Marco Medina secretly harbored negative views on the Dominican leaders and military figures such as General Pedro Santana. Instead, Marco focused on his military service and the education of his children.

Life in the city of Santo Domingo was interesting for the young Anibal Medina. Santo Domingo was the oldest continuous European city in the Americas, where the first African slaves were brought from West African tribes; where the first African slave revolt occurred, where African slaves as well as African Muslims brought their indigenous faiths. It was also the site where the Africans and native Tainos fought against the Spanish Catholics; where the first Jewish people settled, and where the Tainos, Africans, and later the Spaniards would mix into the people now called Dominicans. Dominican politicians would intentionally misinterpret history to maintain power and arouse their forms of nationalism, however Marco Medina would teach his son Dominican history and the various political leaders he believed would improve society.

Anibal was interested in learning his culture and history; he would joyfully read the history of Spain, West Africa, and the Middle East. Anibal would often ask his father for books to read, eagerly awaiting the end of his father's military services and his potential work at the university. Anibal also enjoyed playing with his friends and his little sister, Catalina Violeta Medina, who was usually with their mother Altagracia. The Medina family were

42

overjoyed with their baby girl, who had been given the middle name Violeta because she was born in the late afternoon when the sun was setting over a violet sky. Anibal hoped war would cease on the island of Hispaniola, and he desired complete independence for the nation. Marco Medina expressed his ideas to his son and wife for the end of warfare and how the government could come to a peace agreement between Haiti and the Dominican Republic so he could return to his true passion of teaching Dominican youth.

To thank them for saving him from captivity and extended torture, Romulo Andujar promised to give Marco Medina and his brother Julio some land. Although Marco desired to teach, he believed these lands could provide his family with an additional source of income. Romulo Andujar also had business connections with many Jewish and European traders in the Dominican Republic and the surrounding Caribbean islands—including a young Irishman born in the island of Jamaica in the city of Kingston named Rory McDonnell. Marco anticipated these possible opportunities after his military duties were completed and he desired for the return of his brother Julio, who was serving in Dominican offensive units at the border.

Julio Medina continued to enjoy the company of women and betting on cockfights. However, he began thinking about marriage and family life. Julio had begun courting a younger Dominican woman from San Pedro de Macoris named Paulina Martinez. A beautiful, twenty-five-year-old woman with brown skin, dark black hair, and hazel eyes, Paulina Martinez was from a middle-class conservative family. Julio Medina maintained a correspondence with her for several months during the war and thought about marrying her as soon as the conflict concluded.

President Jean-Louis Michel Pierrot appointed military ranks on many of the peasants from the Sud Department of Haiti. However, after he appointed Jean-Jacques Acaau to Commandant of the Anse-à-Veau Arrondissement, the peasants revolted and appointed General Jean-Baptiste Riché as president of Haiti.

President Pierrot would also lose another major conflict against the Dominican Republic at the Battle of Beler on November twenty-seventh, 1845 at the Beler Savanna, Monte Cristi Province. Dominican General Francisco Antonio Salcedo and Luitenant José María Imbert defeated Jean-Louis Pierrot and the Haitian forces while three Dominican schooners—the *Separación Dominicana*, *María Chica*, and *Leonor* (led by Admiral Juan Bautista Cambiaso)—blockaded the port of Cap-Haïtien to prevent sea reinforcements from making ground.

Many of the previously exiled Dominican political figures were returning to the nation and information regarding political figures slowly spread as the years continued to pass. Dominicans would soon learn about the death of the first Dominican president of the short-lived Republic of Spanish

Haiti: José Núñez de Cáceres. He had opposed Simon Bolivar while living in Caracas Venezuela and wrote articles in El Constitucional Caraqueño (or The Constitutional from Caracas), El Venezolano (or The Venezuelan), and La Cometa (or The Comet)—a newspaper that harshly attacked Simón Bolívar. He also wrote El Conejo (or The Rabbit), La Oveja y el Lobo (or The Sheep and the Shepherd), El Lobo y el Zorro (or The Wolf and the Fox), La Araña y el Aguila (or The Spider and the Eagle) and La Aveja y Abejorros (or The Bee and Bumblebee). These fables were signed under the pseudonym El Fabulista Principiante, meaning "The First Fabulist".

José Núñez de Cáceres moved to Mexico in the city of Victoria—the capital of Tamaulipas—where he was appointed prosecutor of the Supreme Court. In 1833, he was elected senator of the state of Tamaulipas and became a member of the Mexican Confederation Congress, where he was named Distinguished Citizen of Tamaulipas. In 1834, he was appointed the treasurer of Public Finance and continued to work in various professions until he fell ill and passed away on September eleventh, 1846; he died in Ciudad Victoria, Tamaulipas. José Núñez de Cáceres y Albor continued to write, influenced by various fabulists like Aesop, Phaedrus, Jean de La Fontaine, Samaniego, and Tomás de Iriarte. It was rumored that he was happy with the proclamation of independence of the Dominican Republic.

CHAPTER 6
THE DOMINICAN-HAITIAN WARS
(1848)

In the Dominican Republic, Juan Pablo Duarte went into hiding and was exiled along with his family in 1845 (after General Pedro Santana announced that the Trinitarians were enemies of the Dominican State). General Pedro Santana's control of the government increased as he served as the first president of the second independent Dominican nation: the Dominican Republic. Meanwhile, to the west, Faustin Soulouque would seek to consolidate his control over the Republic of Haiti.

President Faustin-Élie Soulouque replaced President Jean-Baptiste Riché, who was rumored to have been poisoned by his political enemies. President Faustin-Élie Soulouque was a black Haitian leader who took pride in his ancestry and culture; he openly practiced Voodoo. Faustin appeared to be an ignorant and malleable older man by the Haitian elite. However, Faustin Solouque was aware of his enemies and their clandestine intentions. Faustin was born into slavery in Petit-Goâve, Haiti in 1782, and he witnessed and participated in the Haitian Revolution in 1803 against France. The revolution deeply impacted him, and Faustin had a dislike for the Europeans who had enslaved his people and the people of the Caribbean. Likewise, he held a disdain for the higher status held by the Haitian mulattos during slavery and their continued rule as the elite. Faustin was freed in 1793 by decree of Léger-Félicité Sonthonax, the Civil Commissioner of the French colony of Saint-Domingue who had abolished slavery in response to slave revolts in 1791.

Faustin subsequently joined the Haitian revolutionary army when the French attempted to reintroduce slavery in their territory (Saint-Domingue, which would later become Haiti). Faustin would join the Horse Guards under President Pétion in 1810, where he would rise to the rank of colonel under President Guerrier. Faustin reached his highest position in the Haitian Army when he assumed the title of Lieutenant General and Supreme Commander of the Presidential Guards.

After the death of President Jean-Baptiste Riché, the presidential race between General Souffrant and General Paul was close with neither man gaining a majority. This brought Haiti to the brink of a potential civil war and led the Senate to choose the unassuming Faustin. Faustin was often ridiculed by the Haitian elite, and it was rumored that President Jean-Pierre Boyer had once pointed towards him while stating that "if Haiti deteriorated further, even a man like him could rule."

In reality, President Faustin Soulouque was Machiavellian in his pursuit of power and control of Haiti. As the months passed, his intentions became clearer as he began to eliminate his political enemies and increased his autocratic rule. Although President Faustin Soulouque despised the Europeans, he researched their monarchs (including Emperor Napoleon) and believed he could bring an empirical style of rule which would create power and wealth to the nation. As the Haitian mulatto elite began to openly question President Faustin's increasing despotic rule, the leader countered by questioning their loyalty to the nation of Haiti, criticizing their wealth and power over the poor black Haitian majority. President Faustin gained support from the black peasant class by invoking black racial pride, and most importantly by promoting various social programs which would economically uplift the majority of the black Haitian poor class. President Faustin was also a Voodooist and kept as his palace staff bocors and mambos. Voodoo was openly practiced in the capital of Port-au-Prince during his reign as he became the first Haitian president to give the Voodoo belief system partial official religious status in Haiti.

A mambo is a female voodoo priestess and leader in the Voodoo temple who performs healing work and guides others during complex rituals. A notable mambo was Cécile Fatiman, known for sacrificing a black pig in the August 1791 Voodoo ceremony at Bois Caïman, which is believed to have ignited the Haitian Revolution. A bokor is a male and caplata is a female associated with special abilities. This included the creation of people who appeared dead (or zombies). This was due to the use of potions which included various ingredients from plants and those extracted from puffer fish. These people appeared dead and would be mistakenly buried and would later be 'reanimated' to do the work for the bokor. Others believed the bokors to raise the soulless dead from their graves.

As threats to his rule continued, President Faustin began to accuse the mulatto elite of treasonous activities, assassinating Haitian political figures. President Faustin intended to bring peace to Haiti by eliminating any potential rebellion. He developed a secret police force called the Zinglins, who began to arrest, torture, and kill mulatto Haitian political figures or Haitian blacks who openly opposed his rule or were suspected of treason. Faustin also gained supporters from a large portion of the black Caribbean community who supported his ideas and leadership, including many black Americans who opposed ongoing slavery in the southern United States. However, President Faustin's policies became more radicalized, leading to a massacre of the Haitian mulattos in the capital of Port-au-Prince on the sixteenth of April 1848. As news of the massacre spread throughout the Caribbean and the neighboring Dominican Republic, many of President Fustin's supporters turned against him and Dominican nationalists began to further prepare their military for a possible Haitian offensive.

President Faustin married Adélina Lévêquei on December thirty-first of 1847 and adopted her daughter. After he assassinated General Dupuy, his military executed Celigny Ardouin and others, but various enemies of Faustin were able to flee—including Bergeaud and Beaubrun. The black Haitian general Maximilien Augustin (commonly called Similien) was against wealthy black Haitians he believed were a threat to Faustin and the Haitian mulatto elite. President Soulouque made Similien commander of the Palace Guard as well as a terrorist secret police force known as the Zinglins. Similien and his followers in Port-au-Prince continued their attacks on Haitian mulattoes and encouraged the pillaging of their businesses and homes while advocating for the deportation of mulattos from Haiti. Pierre Noir and the black rebels called the piquets attempted to kill the Haitian mulattos and remove them from their lands and businesses as they sought to end their debt owed to France. Foreign European ships patrolling Haitian waters attempted to rescue the mulatto fugitives as the killings continued. Similien was later removed from his position and imprisoned when Faustin received information that he was interested in gaining power and was believed to have collaborated with some embittered members of the Haitian mulatto elite.

As 1849 approached, President Faustin began plans to extend his power and decided he would extend his rule as emperor as petitions spread throughout Haiti. Under threat of violence, many Haitians signed the petition while supporters and nationalists did so willingly. A bill conferring the imperial title of President Faustin Soulouque was passed by the chamber by the Haitian Senate the following day. The president of the Senate then placed the Imperial Crown on the head of the Chief of State President Faustin, and a cross of gold on his buttonhole. Next, he placed around the neck of Empress Adélina Lévêque a chain of great value, after which the shouts of "Vive l'Empereur" echoed throughout the Palace Hall. Exclamations of "Long Live the Emperor!" spread in the Haitian capital and a new Imperial Constitution was adopted, making the Haitian Monarchy hereditary.

Emperor Faustin made his public appearance after the coronation in Port-au-Prince, stating, "Haitians! Let the new era which opens before us be marked by the most complete fusion of hearts. Let it cause all passions to be silent if any still exist among us; and let us all join hands of reconciliation on the altar of the country." Faustin would now rule the Empire of Haiti as Emperor Faustin I, alongside his wife Empress Adélina Soulouque.

Emperor Faustin I adopted the motto of King Louis XIV of France: "I am the state, my will is the law." Emperor Faustin I also used many of the French noble titles while creating a large Haitian nobility and using vast sums from the Haitian treasury to fund his Imperial events. By the Constitution of 1849, the emperor received 150,000 gourdes years, the Empress 50,000 gourds, and 30,000 gourds annually went to the nearest relatives of the Emperor—who included Faustin's three daughters and brother, his eleven nieces and nephews, as well as the Empress' five brothers, three sisters, and parents. Emperor Faustin I proclaimed the island indivisible and quickly named dukedoms while advising his generals to begin the military offensive against the Dominican Republic. Rumors spread amongst Dominicans that Emperor Faustin I also desired to be proclaimed Emperor in the capital city. General Pedro Santana prepared as the Haitian Army began to travel towards the undefined border. Numbering over 10,000 soldiers, they entered the Dominican Republic as General Pedro Santana planned a counter-offensive with roughly 6,000 soldiers.

The drought of 1846 severely limited tobacco production and hurt the Dominican economy as President Pedro Santana tightened his grip on power. President Pedro Santana had previously entered a political conflict with Minister Bobadilla and the Dominican Congress, leading to the resignation of Bobadilla. President Santana subsequently retired temporarily from public office and left for his hacienda in El Seibo. He would be succeeded by President Manuel José Jimenes González—born in Baracoa, Guantanamo, Cuba. He was part of a Dominican exile community that had escaped towards Cuba during the Haitian Revolution. President Manuel Jimenes faced a Haitian offensive that he could not successfully halt until the counter-offensive launched by General Pedro Santana, leading to the presidency of Ramón Buenaventura Báez Méndez. France officially recognized the Dominican Republic as an independent and free nation in 1848 through a provisional treaty. Emperor Faustin I and Haitian officials felt threatened by this treaty as they suspected France would occupy Samaná Bay, which was contested by the United States, England, Spain, and France. Emperor Faustin I marched east and the Haitian Army quickly occupied most of the frontier towns—including San Juan de la Maguana, which became Emperor Faustin's General Headquarters and would lead to the weakening presidency of Manuel Jimenes.

In command of the Dominican Southern Army, General Pedro Santana defeated the Haitians at the mountains of El Numero and later at the crossing of the Ocoa River called Las Carreras. Marco Medina was soon ordered to fight in the upcoming major battle in Bani and would serve under the command of General Santana. Although he was motivated to fight for the Dominican homeland, Marco Medina secretly did not like Pedro Santana and his policies against the Trinitarians. The independence of the Dominican Republic brought about a sense of pride in Marco Medina that he had once felt as a young man during the establishment of Spanish Haiti in 1821. Although Marco appreciated General Pedro Santana's skills on the battlefield, he was against his authoritarianism and his antagonism towards the founding fathers and their relatives. General

Pedro Santana assassinated various Trinitarians and their family members, including María Trinidad Sánchez—the aunt of founding father Francisco del Rosario Sánchez—because she failed to locate other Trinitarians. María Trinidad Sánchez, along with Concepción Bona, Isabel Sosa, and María de Jesús Pina, had designed the flag of the Dominican Republic. Ironically, the military under Santana proudly carried this flag into battle. In 1845, Santana crushed many rebellions, including one in Santa Maria twenty miles west of Santo Domingo involving black families of Haitian descent.

The black revolt in Santa Maria was fomented by Haitian propaganda that the Dominican government would reinstitute slavery. Although Marco Medina was against the Haitian government and their propaganda, he believed open discourse to dispel the Haitian misinformation was more appropriate than the quick, violent response Santana chose. The young black men were to join the Dominican Army and defend the border, however Santana's actions alienated them further. Despite his action in Santa Maria, many black Dominicans ignored the Haitian propaganda and enlisted in the Dominican Army. General Pedro Santana and other Dominican leaders had previously attempted to allay fears regarding the propaganda of the reinstitution of slavery by appointing the black Dominican José Joaquín Puello de Castro and his brothers Gabino and Eusebio to prominent government and military positions. Although the Dominican government was in turmoil, Marco Medina disliked the tyrannical rule of Haiti under Emperor Faustin I. Marco supported the Haitian Revolution and the emancipation of black people from slavery, but he did not support Haiti's authoritarian leaders and the frequent military offensives into Dominican territory. Marco Medina desired a decisive Dominican victory against the Haitians and the establishment of peaceful relations so the Dominican Republic could remove Pedro Santana and establish a more liberal government.

Despite the previous Haitian defeat at El Numero, Emperor Faustin I continued to march forward as General Santana positioned his army at the Ocoa River. Marco Manuel once fought against Haiti and although he was confident, he was anxious to face the Haitian Army led by Emperor Faustin I. Marco's brother Julio Medina, under the leadership of General Francisco Domínguez, fought at the battle of El Numero alongside Ramon De La Cruz and defeated the Haitian Army. However, Emperor Faustin I still had numerical superiority over the Dominicans. As the days progressed, additional Dominican forces arrived at Ocoa—including Julio Medina and Ramon De La Cruz, who revealed that many Haitians died at the battle of El Numero such as Jean Dumont, who had fought bravely. The news of Jean Dumont's death saddened Marco Medina, who viewed him as an honorable soldier who respected law and order and represented the best in Haiti's soldiers as opposed to the cruel and sadistic Antoine Robespierre.

As Marco conversed with Julio regarding their upcoming battle, General Antonio Duvergé Duval arrived to speak to the Dominican soldiers, further raising Dominican morale. Antonio Duvergé was of French ancestry and his family changed their original surname of Duverger to Duvergé to make the name sound more Spanish and less French—they wanted to separate their family from the Haitians. Antonio Duvergè Duvas was born in Mayagüez, Puerto Rico to a French father, Joseph Duverger, and a French-Dominican mother, Maria Duval. As a general, Duvergé was a great tactician. He described his battle tactics with General Pedro Santana, and his leadership helped the morale of the Dominicans even more. They gained confidence and began calling Emperor Faustin I *Rey Falso* and *Falso Rey* (or False King), which quickly spread throughout the camp.

General Pedro Santana addressed the soldiers; it was the first time many of the Dominicans stood close to the General Santana, and it was the first time Marco Medina and his brother were led by him directly. The Dominicans beat the previous Haitian armies, but the Haitian army under Emperor Faustin I was larger and improved. On April twenty-first, 1849, the battle commenced in Bani as the Dominicans opened a barrage of cannon fire on the Haitian frontline. The Haitian Army returned fire and attempted to advance, however as the battle raged into the afternoon, the Haitian Army had seven of their artillery pieces captured. The Dominicans continued to fire from a distance, causing the Haitian center to nearly collapse as Emperor Faustin I ordered the Haitian Army to charge forward. The Dominicans fired on the Haitians and would engage in fierce hand to hand combat as the night progressed.

Marco Medina picked up his machete as the Haitians attacked while his brother Julio wielded a sabre to defend his brother's blind side. The fight was violent and proceeded until morning. Marco was punctured in his right leg and he staggered as he continued to fight until he and was ordered to take a position in the rear. General Antonio Duvergé led a group of Dominican soldiers behind the Haitian flank as General Pedro Santana pushed towards the weakened center of the Haitian Army towards Emperor Faustin I. As the second day of fighting continued, additional Dominican forces arrived and Emperor Faustin I was forced to retreat as the Haitian officers feared his capture or death. Marco Medina was injured and was unable to pursue the fleeing Haitian forces. However, his brother Julio joined the pursuit.

The Haitian army attempted to initially remain within Dominican territory, but they were continuously attacked by Dominican guerillas—including a large force which severely crippled Haitian morale. Alonso Kebehi Dos Santos participated in the violent attacks on the retreating Haitian Army and through fierce determination in battle, would distinguish himself from his Dominican counterparts. Emperor Faustin I and the

Haitian Army were soundly defeated and in retaliation, they burned several Dominican towns as they retreated. Antoine Robespierre nearly lost his life despite the Haitian defeat, and he would later participate in additional atrocities against the Dominican people as the Haitians attempted to destroy various Dominican towns in their retreat through the southern coastal road. The Dominican Navy responded by heavily bombarding several southern Haitian coastal towns as the war came to an end. After the Dominican victory, President Manuel Jimenes was removed from office.

Many Dominicans stated that Manuel Jimenes had a greater passion for cockfighting than governing the Dominican Republic. He was seen as a lackluster leader more interested in personal pursuits; he was not strong in the defense of the Dominican Republic, and many called for a stronger leader to defend the nation. On May twenty-first, 1849, Manuel Jimenes married his second wife Altagracia Pereyra Pérez and would be overthrown several days afterward by General Pedro Santana, leaving the presidency open for Ramón Buenaventura Báez Méndez. Born in the town of Rincón (which was later renamed Cabral) and the son of Pablo Altagracia Báez and Teresa de Jesús Méndez, Ramón Buenaventura Báez Méndez became the third president of the Dominican Republic. He was light-haired and blue-eyed like his father, but also had curly hair and more mixed features which earned him the nickname the Jabao. After the death of his father, Buenaventura Báez inherited his fortune and became involved in Haitian politics during the reign of President Boyer. President Buenaventura Báez learned various languages—including English and French—during his previous studies in Europe, and his involvement in the overthrow of President Boyer earned him a high position as Deputy of Azua within the Haitian Constituent Assembly. President Buenaventura Báez was a Francophile who attempted to remove what he believed was an anti-white bias within the Haitian constitution, and he would seek the annexation of the Dominican Republic to France. President Buenaventura Báez was against the Trinitarians and their liberal ideals and was previously against their independence movement. He doubted the independent Dominican Republic would be able to defeat the numerically superior Haitian forces, but when he observed that the Dominican people supported the Trinitarians, he joined the fight for Dominican independence.

However, as president, he would resume his annexation goals for the Dominican Republic—favoring annexation by the United States, which angered many Dominicans. The United States would soon reject the annexation of the Dominican Republic. During this time Marco Medina retired from the military due to his injuries and applied to teach at the university while his brother Julio remained in the Dominican Army. Alonso Kebehi Dos Santos would also continue to serve in the Dominican military and maintain his faith and full support of General Pedro Santana. Marco

Medina was increasingly angry with General Pedro Santana due to his control over the Dominican government and his continuous actions against various Trinitarians who had also helped him defeat the Haitians in war. Marco Medina respected General Pedro Santana's abilities on the battlefield, but he respected General Antonio Duvergé's strategic abilities as well as his vision for the Dominican Republic. Marco was also upset regarding the incarceration of José Joaquín Puello and the accusation by the French Consul of France—Eustache Juchereau de Saint-Denys—of prejudice against France and harboring anti-white sentiments. José Joaquín and Gabino were sentenced to death by firing squad while their brother Eusebio served a short prison sentence and was reinstated into the military after losing his rank. The actions of General Pedro Santana against the Trinitarians and other liberal Dominicans like José Joaquín Puello angered Marco Medina and other Dominicans.

The vision of both President Buenaventura Baez and General Pedro Santana were pro-Annexionist, which conflicted with the Trinitarians and Marco Medina, who sought to distance himself from politics and the military and return to private life. President Buenaventura Báez lavished great praise upon General Pedro Santana and his victories on the battlefield, bestowing upon him the title of Liberator of the Nation.

A large number of Dominicans supported the Dominican Army in their war against Emperor Faustin I and the Haitian Army and provided weapons and manpower to the increasing Dominican Army. Many Dominicans sought external support as well as political support for the buildup of the Dominican Army and the protection of the border—including a young man from Bani, which the Dominican Republic named Máximo Gómez y Báez. Máximo Gómez supported the Dominican Army and as a teenager, he sought to join the Dominican Army if the Haitians invaded once again.

CHAPTER 7
MÁXIMO GÓMEZ Y BÁEZ
(1850)

Máximo Gómez y Báez was born in Bani, the Dominican Republic on November eighteenth, 1836. The son of a lower middle-class family, he entered a religious seminary, but his instruction was soon interrupted by the Haitian invasions. He supported the Dominican Army in the first military offensives of Emperor Faustin I and would contemplate joining, as it was popularly believed the leader would not honor any potential peace treaties and try to bring the island under his rule once again. Máximo Gómez read about great historical military figures and various European battle tactics as well as the guerilla strategies employed by Dominican generals. Máximo Gómez also studied the Haitian revolution and the uprisings against colonial power in the Caribbean, making a note of which were successful and which were failures.

Máximo Gómez y Báez was aware the recent dissolving of the National Assembly after the French coup d'état staged by the nephew of Napoleon I, President Louis-Napoléon Bonaparte, in December 1851. After taking the throne on the second of December 1852—the forty-eighth anniversary of his uncle's coronation—and reestablishing Universal Suffrage, Louis-Napoléon Bonaparte now ruled as Emperor Napoleon III. King Louis Philippe was previously deposed and replaced by Jacques-Charles Dupont de l'Eure and François Arago, then subsequently the heads of the French Second Republic. These world events helped shape the views of Máximo Gómez y Báez and the possible directions the Dominican Republic could take.

In Spain, the War of the Madrugadores (or the War of the Early Risers) was recently fought between the forces of Spain under Queen Isabella II and her liberal supporters (called the Cristinos or Isabelinos) and the Carlists of Catalonia under General Ramón Cabrera. Queen Isabella II of Spain was born in October of 1830 and was crowned as a three-year-old in 1833. The Carlists opposed the coronation of a child and sought an opportunity to revolt. Isabella II was the daughter of King Ferdinand VII and his niece and fourth wife Maria Christina of Bourbon-Two Sicilies. King Ferdinand VII's brother, Infante Carlos of Spain (also known as Carlos V or Don Carlos) was the first pretender to the Spanish Throne. "God, Country, and King" was the rallying cry of Carlos V and the Carlists as they fought for nationalism, traditionalism, and the Catholic church, which gave rise to Spanish Republicanism. The Inquisition was ended by the regime of Napoleon I's brother Joseph and was also prohibited under the *Progresista* (or Progressive) government. Previous liberal leaders of a coup against Spain were arrested and their leader Rafael del Riego y Flórez was executed. The second Carlist War ended in defeat for the Carlists led by the vengeful General Ramón María Narváez (nicknamed The Tiger of the Maestrazgo) and a victory for the liberal supporters of Queen Isabella II of Spain.

After coming of age, Queen Isabella II of Spain took a more active role in government, however she remained largely unpopular. The Spanish Empire and their famous army were severely weakened by debt, the rise of Napoleon and France, and the increased powers of other Europeans—including Great Britain. The weakening Spanish Empire was not able to keep her Spanish colonies as various Latin American Republics arose after their independence movements.

The United States also employed its Monroe Doctrine which was previously established under the former leader President James Monroe in 1823. This doctrine viewed any European intervention in established American nations negatively. The United States continued to implement the Monroe Doctrine against European colonialism under the current leader President Millard Fillmore. Millard Fillmore became president after the death of President Zachary Taylor. He was against Emperor Napoleon III of France and his attempt to annex Hawaii and was also in conflict with the Southern states and their desire to convert Cuba into an additional slave-owing state. A wealthy Venezuelan-born, former Spanish General of Basque origin named Narciso López de-signed the Cuban flag and recruited several hundred men including Americans, Hungarians, Germans and some Cubans to sail to liberate Cuba. This led to the capture and execution of most of the members of the excursion, including Narciso López. Whoever remained was forced into labor in the Cuban mining camps. Although the expedition of Narciso López was a failure, it briefly united the northern and southern United States against the weakening Spanish Empire. During the internal struggles of Spain and the growth in power of other European rivals and the United States, Spain was only able to maintain control of the islands of Cuba and Puerto Rico under colonial rule in the Americas. President Millard Fillmore also dispatched Commodore Matthew C. Perry to open Japan (ruled by the Tokugawa Shogunate at Edo) to relations with the outside world—by force if necessary.

Máximo Gómez studied the emerging relationship between the world powers in the Caribbean and particularly the Dominican Republic. Despite increasing republicanism in Latin America and Europe, the French would emerge as an empire once again under Emperor Napoleon III. In Latin America, empires existed in Brazil and a short-lived Mexican Empire under the leadership of Emperor Agustín I of Mexico from 1821 to 1823. Mexico would subsequently become a republic like the Centralist Republic of Mexico, which was plagued with internal discords, rebellions, and the

Mexican American War (that the Mexicans called the American Intervention), which would result in the loss of Mexican territory. Texas was among these territories and be-came the independent Republic of Texas which was annexed by the United States in 1846.

The current leader of Mexico was the authoritarian President Antonio López de Santa Anna. He maintained power in Mexico even after his various defeats to the United States— including the Battle of Buena Vista under the leadership of the now deceased Zachary Taylor. President Antonio López de Santa Anna previously stated that he would sell northern Mexican territories to the United States in exchange for safe passage towards Mexico. However, he declared himself president and resumed his war against the United States. The wars created a division within the United States between the slaveholding South who supported the war and additional lands to expand slavery and the Industrial North. Politically, the Democrats largely supported the war while the Whig Party did not. Many notable people opposed the Mexican American war and Manifest Destiny, including Representative Abraham Lincoln and the ex-slave and abolitionist Frederick Douglass.

England was now the world power during the reign of King George III and the defeat of Emperor Napoleon I. England continued to hold various colonies around the world, including India. Although England remained a world power, they suffered significant losses of their colonies in North America. King George IV of the United Kingdom also ruled through wars and internal conflict. His alcoholism and gluttony made him obese and sickly, leading to the reign of King William IV. The reign of King William IV saw the abolishment of slavery in the English colonies through the Slavery Abolition Act in 1833, the Factory Act of 1833 which prevented child labor, and the Poor Law Amendment Act of 1834. The current leader of the British Empire was now Queen Victoria of the United Kingdom of Great Britain and Ireland, while India was ruled by the British East India Company. The British continued to hold colonies in the Caribbean throughout the English-speaking Caribbean, the largest being Jamaica.

Máximo Gómez read extensively about the European partners and their corporate arms which exploited the resources and governments of the colonies in which they established themselves. Máximo Gómez particularly desired a strong military in the defense of the Dominican Republic. The ongoing tensions with the Empire of Haiti to the west immediately threated the autonomy of the Dominican Republic as Emperor Faustin I of Haiti did not honor any treaties and rumors spread he would avenge the previous Haitian defeats. Máximo Gómez studied the European militaries as well as the rebel uprisings against them and implemented them within the Dominican Military. His intelligence and hard work quickly earned him higher rank in the Dominican Army. He would soon distinguish himself in battle when Emperor Faustin I would once again initiate a larger Haitian offensive into Dominican territory.

CHAPTER 8

THE BATTLE OF SANTOMÉ & THE FAILED INVASIONS OF EMPEROR FAUSTIN I OF HAITI

(1854)

Emperor Faustin I of Haiti strengthened his position as leader. However, as head of state he failed to conquer the Dominican Republic in 1849 and 1850—which was his primary goal. Emperor Faustin I saw the elite Haitian mulattos as enemies, and he believed the Haitians should avenge their previous defeats at the hands of the Dominicans. The emperor created an autocratic Haitian government and increased his and his family's power. World leaders held contempt for Emperor Faustin I which was for the most part, racially motivated. Political instability arose within Haiti, however Emperor Faustin I would quickly stop the rebellions against his rule as he prepared the Haitian Army for war and began his offensive against the Dominican Republic.

In 1854, the Haitian Army totaling over 30,000 soldiers marched in three columns into Dominican territory. Despite Haiti's numerically superior army, the Dominicans prepared for the possible Haitian invasion and were equipped with an increased number of soldiers, Dominican youth which provided additional energy and motivation, and a large segment of veterans who were battle-hardened and provided valuable guidance. President Pedro Santana recaptured the presidency of the Dominican Republic as he continued to strengthen his army. In November 1854, two Dominican war ships captured a Haitian war ship and bombarded two Haitian ports, causing significant damage and prompting Anibal Medina to join the Dominican Army. In 1855, four more Dominican war ships sank during a hurricane. However, the Dominicans continued to defend the state as Haitian forces entered their territory.

Due to his degraded physical condition, Marco Medina was unable to participate, but his son Anibal took up arms. Marco Medina did not believe his son should participate in the war, but Anibal's uncle and father's bravery inspired him to join the Dominican Army. The following year, Anibal, along with his Uncle Julio, approached the border under the command of Generals José Maria Cabral and Francisco Sosa. The Haitian Army would be led by General Antoine Pierrot and General Pierre Rivere Garat.

Anibal Medina and his Uncle Julio continued their march northwest to face the Haitian forces. Julio comforted Marco regarding the upcoming battle, stating that confidence and resolve in warfare were vital for survival. Julio Medina had climbed up the enlisted ranks and now served as a leader; he counseled the young Dominicans who never faced combat. Julio was more focused on his military career and life afterwards. He also understood the grave danger of the on-going war for the Dominican Republic as well as for his family. He had more to live for; he had married Paulina Martinez in a wedding ceremony in San Pedro de Macoris in 1852, which produced his young son Carlos Medina.

Anibal and his uncle were under the direct leadership of General José María Cabral, who was born in Ingenio Nuevo, San Cristobal Province in 1816. José María Cabral was from a wealthy Criollo family from Hincha. His father was Juan Marcos Cabral y Aybar and his mother was Ramona de Luna y Andujar, who was the cousin of the Virgins of Galindo. The Virgins of Galindo were young Dominican girls named Ana Maria Clemente Andujar de Lara, Marcela Andujar de Lara, and Agueda Andujar de Lara; they were raped and dismembered outside of the city walls of Santo Domingo. Many believed the perpetrators were Dominican and Haitian civilians, however Dominican officials and citizens who were against the previous occupations blamed the Haitian Military.

As they marched towards Santomé, Anibal felt a growing anxiety. The Haitians were previously defeated by the Dominicans, but Anibal and others believed Emperor Faustin I would be a formidable foe.

Julio Medina calmed his nephew as he stated, "You must believe in your abilities and stand bravely among your fellow Dominican compatriots. I have participated in numerous battles and we have been victorious many times. However, we must learn from our mistakes and celebrate and build upon our previous victories through our victories in upcoming battles. My *sobrino*, I believe you will serve well and with distinction. You will add to our victories against this despot Faustin who calls himself emperor."

Various Haitian forces in other battles were already retreating as the Dominican troops led by General José Maria Cabral arrived at Santomé in the province of San Juan. On a cool morning on December twenty-second, 1855, the Dominicans began their battle against the Haitians near Las Matas. The Haitians started the attack, but they were cut down by Dominican artillery. Many Dominicans also had machetes and engaged the Haitians as they attempted to out-flank them. Dominican firearms overwhelmed the Haitian right flank as the Dominicans rushed forward in fierce hand to hand combat. Anibal fired his rifle from a safe distance towards the Haitian center line while Julio stayed close to his nephew.

The battle was vicious as the Haitian forces were rejuvenated by the impassioned speeches and the bravery of Emperor Faustin I. As the day continued into the afternoon, additional Dominican forces joined the battle and many young Dominican soldiers including Máximo Gómez replenished the Dominican frontline as the Dominicans slowly began to turn the clash in their favor. The Dominicans started to collapse the Haitian center as the Haitian right flank retreated. Anibal Medina and his Uncle Julio continued to fire as the Haitian left flank reinforced the Haitian center line. General

José Maria Cabral ordered the Dominicans to charge the Haitian left flank as the other Dominicans advanced into the enemy army with machetes and lances. Máximo Gómez progressed with a machete in hand, leading the Dominicans forward and cutting through the Haitian left flank which could not fully lend support to the collapsing center.

Sensing the defeat of the Haitians, General José Maria Cabral ordered his remaining forces to attack. Anibal Medina was now thrust into a battle among many injured and dead as he fought Haitians yelling in Creole for reinforcements and Dominicans screaming in Spanish to maintain their offensive. Soon Anibal's blue and white uniform became stained with dirt and blood as he bravely advanced in the defense of the Dominican nation. Máximo Gómez and other Dominicans continued to advance after the left Haitian flank collapsed. Additional Dominican forces rushed towards the Haitian right flank, causing panic among the Haitian soldiers. Anibal fought fiercely alongside his uncle and struck a Haitian soldier younger than himself—probably a sixteen-year-old—in the arm with a machete and blood squirted in his face. The Haitian soldier kicked him back and lunged as he brought down the machete on his shoulder and caused him to fall backward. Another Haitian soldier ran towards Anibal before he was shot by Julio Medina. As Anibal fought, he thought of the brutal treatment perpetrated by Antoine Robespierre against his father and family; he desired to see him dead on the battlefield. The anger towards Haitians such as Robespierre motivated him to fight for his life. Anibal's uncle encouraged him to press on, loudly exclaiming, "Palante! Palante!"

For several hours, the fighting intensified and then the Dominicans gained the advantage as the Haitian center line collapsed. Suffering injuries and facing the possible wrath of Emperor Faustin I, General Antoine Pierrot continued to advance in an effort to encourage the Haitians to no avail—he was struck by a Dominican machete. The Dominicans subsequently reorganized and began firing on the retreating Haitians while General José Maria Cabral ordered his forces to follow the fleeing Haitians and General Francisco Sosa ordered his units to fire on them. As the sun began to set on the bloody day, both General Antoine Pierrot and General Pierre Rivere Garat lay dead on the battlefield. Over 700 Haitians joined them, with many more injured while the Dominicans lost over 200 men with many hurt and disabled. The battle reinvigorated the Dominican Army and increased the belief that Emperor Faustin I would soon face defeat.

The Haitians retreated under the setting sun and the Dominicans pursued them. Anibal received several blows to the face and body as well as a glancing machete strike to his abdomen. Exhausted from battle, Anibal was comforted by the words of his Uncle Julio inspiring him to continue the fight. Anibal and his uncle were informed several days later that the remaining Haitians had retreated to the fortress of Cachimán and then beyond the border, while another Haitian force met defeat on the same day at Cambronal. On Christmas Eve 1855, the Haitians were also bested by the Dominicans at Savana Mula and subsequently were beaten at Ounaminthe. In 1856, the Dominicans were on the verge of victory and Emperor Faustin I began his plans for a larger offensive. He turned his attention to the northwestern region of the Dominican Republic at Sabana Larga in Dajabon. Emperor Faustin I, General Cayemite, and General Prophete would face the Dominican Northern Army led by General Juan Luis Franco Bido, General Pedro Florentino, and General Lucas Peña.

The Battle of Sabana Larga began on January twenty-fourth, 1856. Emperor Faustin I led over 22,000 Haitian soldiers against over 8,000 Dominicans led by General Juan Luis Franco Bido. The battle was violent, but the Dominicans felt victory was close. With Emperor Faustin I personally leading the battle, General Juan Luis Franco Bido encouraged the Dominicans to fight and push forward. Dominican Military leaders attempted to capture or kill Emperor Faustin I, which would deliver a devastating blow to the Haitian Military and state. The battle was disastrous for the Haitians and Emperor Faustin I suffered a humiliating defeat as they retreated. The Dominican forces in the north experienced success in the battlefield and Alonso Kebehi Dos Santos (who was transferred to the northern Dominican Army) fought bravely in the Battle of Sabana Larga, shooting and killing several Haitian soldiers and charging into vicious hand to hand combat.

Anibal Medina and his family were soon informed of the bravery of Alonso Kebehi Dos Santos in the battle of Sabana Larga and the various honors that would potentially be awarded to him—including the promise of a promotion to officer in the Dominican Army. Alonso Kebehi Dos Santos and a Dominican unit also cornered a group of Haitian soldiers led by officer Antoine Robespierre. Antoine Robespierre was confirmed killed towards the end of the battle along with other Haitian officers, severely damaging their upper leadership. Over 1,500 Haitian soldiers were killed in action with many were captured as prisoners of war along with several Haitian artillery pieces.

Recently receiving word his mother Rosa had passed, Alonso Dos Santos was motivated by hatred and revenge against the Haitian Army. Alonso Dos Santos was able to apprehend Haitian prisoners of war and he would enjoy extracting information from them. Some of his victims would offer valuable intelligence regarding the Haitian Army's locations and battle strategies. The Haitian Army that was entrenched in Jácuba near Puerto Plata was also defeated by the Dominicans led by General Florentino and General Peter Lucas Peña as the Haitians continued to fight in subsequent battles that also resulted in victory for the Dominicans.

The Dominicans pursued the Haitians as they retreated and briefly entered Haitian territory as the war came to an end. Emperor Faustin I and the Haitian Army were defeated as the Dominicans pursued a peace treaty encouraged by the French and Spanish. The war against the Dominican Republic became unpopular in Haiti and the Haitian losses in the battlefield undermined Emperor Faustin I's reign. Emperor Faustin I shifted blame towards Haitian commanders who served as scapegoats; political assassinations, executions, and imprisonment of Haitian citizens who threatened his monarchy increased. The Dominican Republic continued to strengthen their military power and Haiti's threats of invasion lowered. Politically, this also endangered the rule of President Santana, who needed the wars and the dangers of Haitian offensives to maintain his power. President Santana and Spanish Consul Antonio María de Segovia were involved in a political struggle which led to the resignation of Pedro Santana; Manuel de Regla Mota y Álvarez assumed the presidency. This lasted several months until the return of Buenaventura Báez.

Kebehi Dos Santos was celebrated throughout the city of Santo Domingo as a hero who had previously suffered under Haitian injustice. Secretly, Kebehi Dos Santos brought the body of Antoine Robespierre (who represented the most brutal aspects of Haitian cruelty) as proof of his death to those who feared and suffered his abuses. Kebehi Dos Santos also displayed the body for Marco and Julio Medina, and they instructed Dos Santos to properly lay the corpse to rest or hand it over to the Haitian government. After much convincing, the cadaver of Antoine Robespierre was returned to Haiti. Anibal Medina wished he was the one who'd punished Antoine Robespierre for his crimes against Dominican civilians and his family. However, Anibal understood Kebehi Dos Santos was one of the few Dominicans who suffered the most under the brutality of Antoine and his companions.

Kebehi Dos Santos found purpose within the Dominican Military and discovered order in a tumultuous society—a direction that contrasted drastically in comparison to his purposeless past. Kebehi Dos Santos was patriotic and found a place for his fierce hatred of Haitians and a solidifying loyalty for Pedro Santana and Dominican conservatism. Rumors of the brutality of Kebehi Dos Santos in warfare spread among the soldiers. Some Dominicans believed that although Kebehi displayed bravery in battle, his behavior towards Haitian prisoners of war and civilians away from the battlefields made him undeserving of the various honors bestowed upon him. Kebehi's dishonorable actions were largely unknown to most Dominicans, and he desired to conceal them. Kebehi was intelligent, and although he understood some of his brutal actions should be hidden from the public, he believed they were necessary against what he viewed as a fierce Haitian force who had a numerically superior army secretly derived some pleasure in what he viewed as vengeance for his people.

Kebehi Dos Santos was invited to the Medina household in Santo Domingo and he arrived several hours earlier than expected in the early afternoon. When he approached the door, Marco Medina noticed him and exclaimed, "*A buen tiempo!*" as he motioned for him to enter. "Please, come in. We are getting ready for dinner." Marco happily stated.

Maria Altagracia Medina was a great cook who'd learned the finest Dominican cuisines from her mother and grandmother. Dinner was rice with some ground coconut and beans with *pernil* (or roast pork shoulder) cooked with various spices including oregano, cilantro, aji, *cebolla* (or onions), *pimientas* (or peppers), and a little tomato sauce because Marco Medina enjoyed tomatoes. After Maria Altagracia began a short prayer, she brought cold *limonada* (or limeade).

Marco initiated the conversation. "We are all blessed at this table to have survived intact through the wars and now enjoy dinner as free men in our free nation. We should establish peace and live for our families now. I am happy to have you as our guest, Kebehi, and hope that God blesses you with a long and fruitful military career."

Kebehi smiled and replied, "I am happy to be with my friends enjoying our dinner together. Although we may have different visions for the direction of our Dominican homeland, I believe we should all come together as Dominicans to confront major obstacles that can hurt our nation. The constant menacing Haitian threats of invasion should be one of our major concerns, especially now as our economic issues make our nation weak."

Altagracia and her daughter Catalina Violeta Medina attempted to change the conversation, but Julio interjected, "I have also faced Haitian hostility and I will soon become a veteran who honorably fought for our nation. The Haitian threat of invasion should not be our primary concern, my friend Kebehi. Instead, our primary concerns should be towards our economic fragility and the creation of a Democratic, inclusive, Dominican government that is free of the corruption that plagues it. The age of the caudillo might have been necessary during times of warfare, however I believe now that era should come to an end. Emperor Faustin is currently facing Haitian rebel groups against his regime, and his failed military invasions have cost Haiti. I would be surprised if the Faustin Monarchy even lasts another five years!"

Kebehi responded by revealing intelligence, stating that Haitian officials were once again plotting another invasion against the Dominican Republic. Kebehi continued, "Perhaps the Dominican Military should invade Haiti and topple the weakened Faustin Monarchy to give the Haitian rebels what they want? The Haitians will create a new government free of autocratic rule and we can ensure the safety and sovereignty of the Dominican Republic."

The conversation slightly irritated Kebehi Dos Santos, and although he'd improved his stoicism, his anger still appeared on his face and in his voice. Marco Medina quickly changed the topic of conservation as they finished their food. Marco Medina then offered some Mama Juana for his family and Kebehi (a classic Dominican drink which allowed rum, red wine, and honey to soak in a bottle with tree bark and herbs). The various herbs were previously used as a tea by the native Tainos and later alcohol was added after the arrival of Cristobal Colón.

The men would share a drink outside on the patio, enjoying the afternoon wind and the shade of the trees which gave the men a much-needed respite from the heat. Various friends arrived at the Medina household and the air was full of Dominican music which would soon lead to dancing. The political talk decreased and gave way to conversations involving neighbors, friends, and ladies. Anibal relaxed as he drank some *romo* (or rum). It slid slowly down Anibal's throat, providing a slight burn that warmed and relaxed him. Candles were lit as well as gas lamps as some of the guests brought instruments like the *tambora* and *guitara* and began playing merengue music.

Marco Medina was a great dancer, and his brother Julio relished playing instruments. Both delighted in the Dominican styles of Salve and Gagá, which were based on West African music. This music originated among the slaves from West African societies that had arrived in the land now called the Dominican Republic. Marco Medina also enjoyed the merengue and various other types of Dominican music which combined Spanish, European, native Taino, and West African influences. Some Dominicans believed the merengue originated from slaves dancing as they cut sugar to the beat of drums while being chained together by one leg, forcing the other leg to be dragged. Others stated a Dominican revolutionary hero was wounded in the leg, making one leg drag and leading others to dance the same way during a party to honor the hero.

Music, like the Dominican culture, was a fusion of the various ancestries which shaped the culture. Some of the young Dominican ladies arrived and began to dance as Julio and some of the men played music. Anibal danced with several of the beautiful morenas and other Dominicans of various complexions from darker tones, light dark, caramel, and fair skinned—all beautiful in their own ways. The atmosphere was festive despite the political uncertainties facing the nation. Maria Altagracia accompanied her husband Marco and Julio Medina's fiancé Paulina Martinez soon joined the festivities. The Medinas were overjoyed with Julio's recent engagement and marriage to his longtime girlfriend; they believed marriage would bring peace and stability to his life.

The Saint-Lot family were also invited to the Medina household. They arrived during the reign of President Boyer and were one of the few families who remained in the neighborhood after the establishment of the Dominican Republic in 1844. The Saint-Lot family arrived as the sun began to set over the Dominican horizon and they were joyously received by their host Marco Medina. The Saint-Lots brought along their young teenage son Raymond, who was born in 1840—four years before the Dominican Republic was declared as an independent nation. The Saint-Lot family were middle-class merchants who had established themselves. Felix Saint-Lot moved with his young wife Nadine to Santo Domingo in 1838. Various Haitian families left during the wars, but passions had calmed, and some Haitians remained within the Dominican Republic. Raymond Saint-Lot spoke Creole and fluent Spanish; he culturally identified himself as a Dominican. The family formed a bond with the Medinas despite how other Dominicans like Kebehi Dos Santos reserved some caution regarding members of the Haitian community; they were often suspected of espionage or violence. As the festivities continued throughout the night, Dos Santos began expressing unfavorable views regarding the Haitian community, prompting Julio Medina to confront him.

Julio took Dos Santos away from the other guests as he quietly yet sternly stated, "The war is over, Kebehi. There is no need to be antagonistic towards the Haitians, especially when we are entertaining our friends. In times of peace, we must display the utmost hospitality, decency, and respect for any foreigners who choose to visit or live peacefully in our nation. We must demonstrate the qualities of what it means to be a Dominican. Even in warfare, we as a people must not devolve to the worst attributes possessed by our enemies, or we will not be any better than they are."

As the festivities continued, Kebehi Dos Santos soon departed to his home, slightly embarrassed at his slight state of drunkenness. Julio soon rejoined his wife as his nephew Anibal continued dancing with several of the beautiful young Dominican ladies. After a few dances, Anibal took a moment of rest as his Uncle Julio announced that he desired to have another child with his wife Paulina.

Everyone celebrated as Marco Medina approached his son Anibal. stating with a smile, "Even your uncle decided to get married. Soon you will have to choose a woman as your wife. Hopefully, you will not wait as long as your uncle."

When the music began once again, Anibal Medina spoke of several of the women he'd previously courted and the women he particularly fancied from Samaná.

As the months passed, the Medina family would celebrate the wedding of Julio and Paulina, and the people of the Dominican Republic were less anxious about the possibility of wars against Emperor Faustin I. As the year 1858 approached, the weakened Emperor Faustin I would face a strong rebel movement led by General Fabre Geffrard, which would put an end to any significant Haitian aggression towards the Dominican Republic. Despite the political turmoil within the Dominican Republic, the Dominican Military proved itself in battle and the sovereignty of the Dominican Republic was secured.

CHAPTER 9

A CONVERSATION ON RACE & THE HISTORY OF THE DOMINICAN REPUBLIC & THE UNITED STATES

(1858)

People filled the streets of Santo Domingo as various leaders were showcased as defenders of the Dominican Republic. Ramon De La Cruz was also honored for his service in the military and retired. Alonso Kebehi Dos Santos was celebrated along with other young Dominicans, including Máximo Gómez. Máximo Gómez was revered for his bravery and intelligence; he was also recommended for the Spanish Military Academy. The Dominican government believed Máximo Gómez could become a great general and strengthen the Dominican Military.

Marco Medina continued his career as a teacher in Santo Domingo, while Anibal pursued his military duties and his interests in ranching and trade. Anibal's sister, Catalina Violeta Medina, attended school and desired to become a doctor. Julio Medina remained in the army and maintained a business relationship with Romulo Andujar. Julio limited his betting at the cockfights and now concentrated on saving money and building a future for his wife and son. Anibal continued his studies and yearned to attend the University of St. Thomas Aquinas, which the Dominican government promised to reopen. Anibal was interested in science and mathematics and read voraciously on the days he did not participate in military exercises. Anibal would also join his Uncle Julio in the ranching and farming business as he sought to own land after his time in the military.

Anibal was patriotic and sought to defend the Dominican Republic. However, he believed that despite the threats from Emperor Faustin I and the Haitian government, the wars between the two nations would soon come to an end. Anibal did not desire to remain in the Dominican Military long-term, as he was not politically associated with many of the officers and the conservative pro-annexation policies of Dominican politicians— including President Buenaventura Baez. Like his father Marco and Uncle Julio, Anibal was aligned with the vision of the original Trinitarians, various Masonic lodges, and other anti-authoritarian and progressive Dominicans who wanted to maintain the Dominican state as an independent republic. Meanwhile, President Buenaventura Baez and other politicians believed the only solution to constant warfare with Haiti and a worsening economy was to annex the Dominican Republic. The fear among many Dominicans spread regarding possible Haitian or American invasions, which only increased President Buenaventura Baez's power.

The United States and Haiti did not recognize the Dominican Republic, while Spain did in effort to regain its declining power in the Caribbean.

Dominican politicians promised that the Dominican Republic would not aid rebel movements against Spain in Puerto Rico and Cuba, however many Dominicans—including Anibal and his family—supported rebel groups against the Spanish Empire. Spanish leaders were wary of losing their authority as rebellions would continue throughout the Spanish territories.

Anibal and many other Dominicans were also alarmed at the increasing imperialistic aims of the United States. The United States' ideology of Manifest Destiny stripped Mexico of its lands and now the United States and various American citizens ventured into Latin America, including William Walker.

William Walker was a southerner of the United States who became president of Nicaragua and planned to conquer the other five Central American states and reintroduce slavery in the enterprise known as filibustering. United States leader, President Franklin Pierce, legitimized President William Walker's regime and angered many Latin Americans. The leader of Costa Rica, President Juan Rafael Mora Porras, and a coalition of Central American armies soon revolted against and defeated President William Walker at The Battle of Roses.

President William Walker was born in Nashville in 1824, and one of his uncles (John Norvell) was a senator from Michigan as well as the founder of the Philadelphia Inquirer. William Walker graduated summa cum laude from the University of Nashville and would later study medicine for a short time at the University of Edinburgh in Scotland and the University of He-delberg in Germany. He would then graduate with a medical degree from the University of Pennsylvania. William Walker would later get involved in three duels with rivals; it was not long after that he began to formulate the idea of conquering Latin American states for his personal slave enterprise.

He initially approached both the Mexican and American governments with the proposal of establishing a colony and developing the Republic of Sonora (similar to the Republic of Texas that was absorbed by the United States). After this failure, William Walker would infiltrate Nicaragua while successfully supporting the Democratic/Liberal Party against the Legitimist/Conservative Party. President Francisco Castellon of Nicaragua helped William Walker circumvent Neutrality Law of the United States. William Walker subsequently removed Francisco Castellon and became president, leading to a war against Costa Rica. President José Santos Guardiola of Honduras sent (Honduran as well as Salvadorian) soldiers under the leadership of the Xatruch brothers. The Hondurans were later nicknamed Catracho and the Salvadoreans were called Salvatrucho, derived from the figure of General Florencio Xatruch. The Costa Ricans and their allies quickly won the battle, forcing the retreat of William Walker, who surrendered to Commander Charles Henry Davis of the United States Navy in 1857. William Walker would later return to Central America, where he would be captured by the British Navy and executed by Firing Squad by the government of Honduras in 1860.

Although slavery was abolished in the English colonies and in the various Latin American states, the Spaniards continued slavery in the territories of Puerto Rico and Cuba. Massive Chinese and Indian indentured servants continued to arrive in the Caribbean and other territories like Guyana. The Dominican people desired to remain independent as the filibustering actions of citizens from the United States and the ideology of Manifest Destiny increased tensions within the Dominican Republic against Yankee Imperialism. Marco Medina often warned his son Anibal about the ancient practice of slavery perpetrated by ancient empires like the Babylonians, the Greeks, the Roman Republic and Roman Empire, the Umayyad and the Abbassid Caliphates, and the current Ottoman Empire. Slaves of various ancestries from European groups like the Slavic people to Africans continued to suffer through slavery.

Marco Medina informed his family about the natives who had first resisted against Spanish colonial efforts in 1492, and the first major African slave revolt against the Spaniards in 1522 by the ancestors of the Dominican people. The resistance continued throughout the Caribbean islands and throughout Central and South America, however the island of Hispaniola and the Dominican Republic maintained their sovereignty—an important fact that Anibal Medina always preserved within his mind and heart as he vowed to support Dominican independence against any foreign invaders.

Anibal Medina intended to remain in the Dominican Military for several more years once he was promised the rank of sergeant. Anibal wanted to settle in San Cristobal after his military career and take ownership of some land promised to him by the Andujar family. His plan was to pursue farming and ranching; to build a solid income for him and his family while developing trading networks with some of his associates (including the Irish-Jamaican merchant named Rory McDonnell). During his time in the military, Anibal had a few relationships with Dominican women, and among them were a beautiful conservative with dark brown skin and almond eyes named Nidia Rosamaria Almonte and a girl with long blonde hair and blues eyes named Athena Carballo (who was named after the Goddess and daughter of Zeus). Anibal's relationship with Athena Carballo soon ended and Athena married another suitor named Salvador Luis Agra.

Anibal Medina turned his attention to a young Dominican woman named Romina Grant. Born in Samaná in the northeastern region of the Dominican Republic, her father was a black American man by the name of Robert Grant and her mother was a Dominican woman from a working-class farming family named Carmen Acosta. Romina spoke fluent English as well as an English Creole that other Dominicans called Samaná English. Anibal's interest in the United States and the various people who lived there attracted him to her and they began to solidify their relationship.

Romina's father lived in New York City as an indentured servant and soon left for Philadelphia. After finding little job prospects and living as a poor, free black man in the United States, he decided to start a new life in Samaná. Robert's ancestors were originally brought as slaves, and although the Southern United States was where most of the slaves currently resided, most of them were sent to work in Long Island. It was the previous Dutch Colony of New Amsterdam now known as New York, which was originally the first territory which brought most of the African slaves through the Dutch West India Company in 1626.

Anibal enjoyed his time with the beautiful Romina and as their relationship blossomed, Romina's father Robert Grant increasingly requested Anibal's company. Robert Grant was an intelligent man who enjoyed his life in the Dominican Republic. He had gained strong business and social ties with Dominicans who welcomed him into the community. They called Robert "Roberto" or "Robby", and would often speak to him regarding his experiences living in New York City. Ironically, unbeknownst to Robert and Anibal, the first non-native immigrant to Manhattan, New York City before the Dutch settlers was a Dominican of Portuguese and African ancestry named Juan Rodríguez.

Juan Rodríguez was born in Santo Domingo; his father was a Portuguese sailor and his mother was an African, which made him the first European, African, Latino, and merchant to settle in what became Manhattan, New York. Though it was not common knowledge, some Dominicans mentioned Juan Rodríguez and the historical relationship between the lands that are now called the Dominican Republic and the United States.

Anibal Medina inquired about Robert Grant's life in New York and the various people that inhabited the city. Robert Grant taught himself how to read and devoured history books. He enjoyed reading about African history and yearned to know more about his ancestry. He learned that New York was the former capital of the United States during the Congress of the Confederation until 1790, when the capital was moved to Philadelphia and shortly afterward to its current location in Washington, D.C. in July 1790. New York City is a diverse city with people originating from a variety of nations and cultures. It now had over a million residents and the opening of the Erie Canal in 1825 under the leadership of Governor DeWitt Clinton established a navigable water route from New York and the Atlantic Ocean to the Great Lakes. This also created a fresh water supply, which helped make New York City the economic capital of the United States. Tammany Hall increased in power, fueled by the influx of immigrants to New York

City—particularly the Irish, who helped elect the Democratic leader Mayor Fernando Wood in 1854. Robert Grant spoke about the Irish, who arrived in increased numbers to New York City during the Great Irish Potato Famine of the 1840s. New York's immigrant populations created a diverse and sometimes tumultuous society even within people of the same groups.

Robert Grant spoke about the Great Fire of New York City in 1835, which occurred during the winter under freezing temperatures. Anibal Medina was curious regarding the winter season and he often questioned Robert Grant about living in New York during those months. The Dominican Republic's diverse topography has the most diverse climates in the Caribbean, including light snow at high altitudes. However, the Dominican nation never experiences the heavy snowfall found in the United States. Anibal yearned to visit the Northeastern United States and found the political divisions between the Northern and the Southern slave-holding states to be interesting as it could possibly lead to a conflict under the weak President James Buchanan. The northern United States recently suffered a large economic collapse involving over fourteen hundred state banks and five thousand businesses while the south remained largely unscathed. Although the weakening of the United States could improve the conditions of Latin America, the European powers still loomed large in the Caribbean and in the Dominican Republic—which was controlled by politicians who continued to seek annexation against the beliefs of the Trinitarians who desired complete independence.

Robert Grant enjoyed his success and did not support the Dominican politicians. He admired the Haitian revolutionaries, which led to the establishment of the first black independent nation. However, as a Dominican he simply desired peace between Haiti and the Dominican Republic. The government of the Dominican Republic remained unstable as the rule of Baez ended. President José Desiderio Valverde Pérez served a short presidency, which was followed by the reinstatement of President Pedro Santana (the caudillo) to the leadership of the Dominican Republic by September of 1858.

Anibal informed Robert Grant about the unique history of the Dominican Republic. It was a nation where the first West African slaves arrived around 1501, formed the first maroons and even formed the first African slave rebellion in 1522 near the city of Santo Domingo (initiated by mostly Jolof Muslim African slaves in the sugar plantation of the son of Cristobal Colón, Don Diego Colón). The people of the Jolof Empire now resided in the colonized areas of Gambia and Senegal. Various colonial powers encroached upon Africa and now the French were colonizing parts of Senegal with England controlling the Gambia. The arrival of the first slaves to the Dominican Republic—along with the first European settlements including the city of Santo Domingo and the intermixing that occurred between Africans, European, Arab, and native and Asiatic groups—deeply interested Robert Grant. In the United States, this level of mixing was not as prevalent, even in the multicultural city of New York.

Robert Grant spoke about the colonies of Plymouth Rock and Jamestown, Virginia established by Great Britain. The Roanoke Colony was created in Roanoke Island by England in North Carolina in 1585 but was lost during the war between Spain and England (or the Anglo-Spanish War from 1585 to 1604). Although the French, Portuguese, and Spanish colonized the Americas first, England's victory over Spain and the disastrous defeat of the Spanish Armada helped increase England's power in Europe as well as the Americas. The London Company established James Fort in Virginia and converted it into James Town in 1619. The Africans originally arrived as indentured servants just like their white counterparts, and the colony remained relatively stable until Bacon's Rebellion in 1676.

Bacon's Rebellion was led by Nathaniel Bacon, who was against the rule of Governor William Berkeley (appointed by King Charles II of England). The Doeg natives attacked the colony as many of the black and white indentured servants desired to expand westward. The indentured servants joined together against the natives, killing many and soon rose against Governor William Berkley. Nathaniel Bacon would later die of dysentery, and the rebellion would fail under the command of Joseph Ingram. The white elite feared the unification of both poor whites and blacks and strengthened the racial caste system under the Virginia Slave Codes of 1705 (signed by the House of Burgesses). The Virginia Slave Codes further stripped the few rights black people possessed and would lead to the perpetual enslavement of black people in the colonies and subsequently the United States.

The separation of blacks and whites increased in the United States. However, Robert Grant was initially surprised to see such a large population of mixed people within the Dominican Republic. The nation primarily consisted of combined races, which would continue into its future with a unique culture formed from various ancestries.

In the United States, Haiti was viewed with admiration by many within the Afro-American community, including some Abolitionists who desired Americans to find freedom within Haiti. Some African Americans also desired to move to the Dominican Republic, which was advocated by some to be a haven for all races within a highly racially blended society. Although there existed a section of Dominican society—particularly the elite—who looked down on the Haitians with disdain, the Dominican community remained less racially hostile than the United States. Some Dominicans— the less educated and the educated elite—actively promoted anti-Haitian hostility, using the recent Haitian invasions to push their agenda.

Robert Grant questioned Anibal's involvement in the Dominican Military, stating, "You have participated in several conflicts against the Haitian Army. May I question you regarding these battles?" He seldom inquired about Anibal's military experience, but he desired to understand more about the young man who proclaimed his love for his daughter and would potentially become his son-in-law.

Anibal replied, "Initially, I was not particularly interested in joining the Dominican Army. However, I felt patriotic duty for my nation in the face of the invasion. I was born during the rule of President Boyer and the Haitian government. My father informed me about the history of our people and our first independence in 1821. We originally named our nation the Republic of Spanish Haiti. Shortly afterward, President Boyer unified the island under his rule, but his autocratic rule brought mixed support from both Haitians and Dominicans. Towards the end of President Boyer's rule, many Dominicans of all racial backgrounds desired the reestablishment of an independent Dominican state. The Trinitarians finally led a united front against Haiti, which led to the Declaration of Independence of the Dominican Republic in 1844. Even my father and those who supported Haiti's revolution against the French Empire decided it was time for us to establish the Dominican nation. Against my father's wishes, I decided to join the Dominican Military when Faustin declared himself emperor and launched multiple offensives into Dominican territory. I participated in the Dominican Southern Army and we won most of the battles against Haiti despite their larger forces. The Haitian failed offensives led some of the soldiers to rise up against Emperor Faustin I, and now his rule is weakened I hope and believe that our two nations can live in peace with mutual respect."

Robert Grant was wary of some Dominicans—particularly various members of the elite and politicians—and he questioned Anibal regarding these topics.

Anibal answered, "My goal is currently to be the best military man I can be. I admire my Uncle Julio and his rise in the Dominican Army. I can say briefly that I support the establishment of the Dominican Republic, but not the policies of annexation supported by our political leaders. We cannot trust the imperialist United States and their ideology of Manifest Destiny. We must be careful of the European Imperialists' aims in the Dominican Republic and the Caribbean. In war, my family has taught me to be smart, safe, and show mercy towards the defeated and civilians. Just as we did not support the most negative of Haitian soldiers during Haitian rule, we must show mercy and compassion in war as well as within the borders of the Dominican Republic."

Robert Grant laughed. "You are a good man, Anibal. Your family has raised you well. Perhaps you do have a possible career in politics when you complete your military duties. I want to inform you that it was the Haitian government that brought me to Samaná and the land now called the Dominican Republic. I have done well for my family here and have found love with my wife in this nation. With the right leadership, the Dominican Republic can truly become unique, made up of different races striving for a better future. However, under the worst of leadership, divisions will arise and will be exacerbated by the Dominican elite to serve their purposes. My life in New York and later Philadelphia has taught me well about corrupt politicians and the evils of division. I hope there is true freedom for the black people in the Dominican Republic and the Caribbean; the slaves that still inhabit Puerto Rico, Cuba, and the United States."

Anibal replied, "Division weakens nations. It has weakened Haiti, which aided us in our revolutionary goals. If we allow division within Dominican society, it will weaken us as well. I am of African ancestry from the first African slaves to arrive in the Caribbean and this hemisphere, so I also agree we should be a society that allows equity for all."

As the men continued to speak, Robert's wife, Carmen Acosta Grant and their daughter Romina joined them. *"Bienvenido a nuestra casa,* Anibal," Carmen exclaimed as she embraced and welcomed Anibal to her home.

Anibal smiled as he kissed Carmen and Romina in cheek to cheek fashion common in the Dominican Republic. "Muchas gracias, Doña Carmen."

Carmen cooked some goat with rice and beans and the smell filled their home and intoxicateded Anibal's taste buds as he waited to eat. Carmen inquired about Anibal's family, including his Uncle Julio's wedding and the recent birth of his daughter, Alejandra Medina. The marriage of Julio and Paulina brought great joy to the Medina household and the Medinas looked forward to additional peace and prosperity in the coming years.

Carmen Grant smiled, quietly stating, "Perhaps your uncle will inspire you to make an official commitment to our daughter." Anibal laughed as Paulina glanced int Anibal's direction.

Anibal replied, "I do enjoy Romina's company, and perhaps if she so desires it, we can make a future together."

After dinner, Anibal excused himself and asked the permission of Robert and Carmen Grant to take a walk with Romina. Robert briefly met Marco Medina and his family to discuss business, and he asked if both families could meet soon for dinner together. This would be a good way for him to gain a better perspective on Anibal; for both families to bond in the case that the relationship between Anibal and Romina became serious. Anibal happily agreed as he and Romina departed into the beautiful afternoon.

CHAPTER 10

PHILADELPHIA LOVE

(1859)

Romina Grant wore a beautiful cream dress with yellow, blue, and red ribbons in her hair. Anibal desired to learn more, and asked, "So your father moved to Philadelphia. What does that name mean?"

Romina replied, "My father says it means 'the city of brotherly love', and it is Greek in origin. Just like Philosophy means 'the love of wisdom'." Anibal quickly made the connection as his father often talked about ancient Greece and Rome. Marco often mentioned the subject of Filosofia (or Philosophy), and it interested Anibal. Romina spoke about the founding fathers of the United States and the importance of Philadelphia during the colonial period.

Romina tried to hide her laughter at Anibal's limited, heavily accented English, but she was impressed he was able to hold a simple conversation. She explained that an English Quaker named William Penn founded the city of Pennsylvania, and that one of the founding fathers named Benjamin Franklin was believed to be a Quaker by the Religious Society of Friends. Benjamin Franklin, however, did not belong to any church and generally believed in God—although various religious groups attempted to claim him as their own. The Quakers and abolitionists of the 1700s desired the end of slavery, and Benjamin Franklin was among them. However, he seldom publicly debated the issue of slavery. The history of the United States aroused curiosity within Anibal and he relished the company of Romina and Robert Grant, who had roots in the Northeastern United States.

Romina was prideful in maintaining her language. She was fluent in the English variation spoken by her community in Samaná. Anibal heard a similar style of English from merchants arriving at the Dominican Republic from some of the English Caribbean islands (including the Jamaican patois). Anibal practiced his English with Romina as they continued to stroll the streets of Santo Domingo when Anibal suggested they ride his horse and take a trip to the beach several miles south. The Medina family lived in northwestern Santo Domingo while the Grant family had relocated further south, closer to the Caribbean Sea.

It was late afternoon when the young couple arrived at the beach. The heat of the day had dissipated, giving way to a gentle breeze that brought with it the pleasant smell of the ocean. The ride towards the beach was quick, and Romina laughed as the wind rushed past and twisted her long black hair. Anibal slowed his horse, taking a rope and tying it to a coconut tree which bent towards the Dominican shoreline as if trying to reach the sparkling water. Anibal helped Romina down from the horse and asked for her hand as they removed their shoes and walked towards the shoreline. The sand felt great underneath Anibal's feet and he smiled to finally have some private time with the woman he loved.

The water briefly touched Anibal's feet as he slowed his pace and quietly spoke. "I really enjoy spending time with you, Romina. It is nice to finally take some leave from the army and to speak to you alone. I think we should be together, and I think our families will get along well."

Romina replied, "Now that the wars are over, what are your plans for the future? You told me before you plan to leave the army soon."

Anibal stopped as he looked at Romina and stated, "Yes, I plan to leave the army soon—especially because I believe Haiti will not threaten the Dominican Republic anymore. The ongoing wars have been costly for Haiti, and their nation might have an impending revolution. I believe our two nations can live in peace and between me and you, I believe it can only help the Dominican Republic. I don't speak openly about this, but I think the resigning of our current leaders and a more Democratic form of government is much needed. My fear is that even after the wars are over, our current leaders will exploit the anger and fear of the Dominican people to keep their grip on power. Nevertheless, I know the Dominican Republic is strong and my duties as a soldier will soon come to an end. I only look forward to my life and future with you. I love you, Romina, and would love for us to start our lives together."

Anibal gave Romina a light kiss and looked into her eyes as he brought her closer, saying, "Te amo, mi Morena." Anibal then gave Romina a deep, long kiss as the sun began to set on the Caribbean horizon. Anibal thought about proposing to Romina, but he did not feel this was the right moment; he wanted their families to spend more time together before his proposal. Anibal also desired to speak to Robert Grant personally to ask for his permission for his daughter's hand in marriage. Anibal walked back towards the coconut tree where he'd secured his horse and asked Romina if she was thirsty. After she said yes, he climbed the tree, picked a couple of coconuts, and unsheathed his machete. Anibal cut the tops and upper sides of the fruits until he opened a small opening in both, allowing them to drink the coconut water. Anibal smiled as the late afternoon sky was littered with the blue and green glow of insects. The lightning bugs brought back memories of a childhood filled with happiness for Anibal—a joy he had not felt so intensely until now.

The coconut water was refreshing and helped quench Romina's thirst. The sound of the Caribbean Sea calmed their spirits, and Anibal informed Romina that it was named after the Carib natives that still inhabited the smaller islands. The Igneri people (the Arawaks of the Windward Islands in the Lesser Antilles) and the Kalina (or Kalinago) people were the Caribs that the Spaniards encountered in those smaller Caribbean islands in 1492.

The Spaniards never fully conquered these smaller Caribbean islands, choosing to settle in the larger Antilles and displacing the majority population of natives that the Spaniards collectively called the Tainos. Romina was interested in her Dominican people and their history, and she inquired about the Tainos and other native groups of the Caribbean. Anibal informed Romina of the various ethnic native groups including the Guanahatabey of western Cuba, the Ciboney (or Siboney) people of Cuba, the Lucayan of the Bahamas and Jamaica, the Macorix people of the Eastern Dominican Republic, and the Tainos. The Dominican Republic was also inhabited by an indigenous Ciguayo people in the Samaná Peninsula of Northeastern Dominican Republic.

Because she herself was born in that region, Romina was particularly curious regarding the Ciguayo of Samaná. As Anibal continued to explain the Ciguayo people, Romina remarked, "A heavenly land we inherited from our ancestors, and I miss the beaches of Samaná in the north—they are different from the Caribbean seas of the southern Dominican Republic. Samaná is such a beautiful place and I enjoyed my childhood there among other English-speaking people. My father and our teachers made sure to teach us of our history and that we maintained our culture within the greater Dominican culture."

Anibal enjoyed the different ethnic groups that contributed to the Dominican Republic, and he desired to travel to other regions. Serving for the army, he was not given any positions in the northern Dominican Republic yet, and he was deeply interested in exploring the different areas there.

As the young couple prepared to return home, she said, "I think you are a good man, Anibal, and you belong to an honorable and great family. I would love to go forward with you in a serious relationship and perhaps build a future with you. I hope these pointless wars will come to an end so we can live in peace, and I will support you whether you stay in the military or not."

The couple finished brushing off most of the sand from their feet and Anibal lifted Romina to the saddle of his horse. Climbing on behind her, he began the short journey back. As they rode to Romina's home, Anibal inquired about what she desired to do with her life. Romina stated she was unsure and after a brief pause, added, "I love English literature and language. perhaps I can be a teacher like your father. I wanted to be a teacher in Samaná, but now that I live in Santo Domingo, perhaps I can find a career teaching English and English literature."

Anibal replied, "Yes, you will surely find Dominicans who wish to learn the English language. Many upper-class Dominicans know several languages, but the working-class Dominicans also have a desire to educate themselves and their children. Learning an additional language can open a larger window of education for them."

Anibal was an avid reader like his father, but he rarely read any English. With Romina, he hoped to improve his English and read literature from the English-speaking world. Robert Grant informed his daughter about various English authors and their writings, including the works of Shakespeare. Robert read some of Shakespeare's tragedies like Hamlet, Othello, and Macbeth. He also shared with Romina comedies including A Midsummer Night's Dream, Twelfth Night, and Love's Labour's Lost. Romina spoke about other English novels of the current Victorian Era, which had given birth to Jane Eyre by Charlotte Brontë and The Pickwick Papers by Charles Dickens. Charles Dickens was the famed author of Oliver Twist, Nicholas Nickleby, A Christmas Carol, and David Copperfield. Romina stated that Charles Dickens was currently writing other novels, however it would be some time before she could hopefully gain access to these more cur-rent novels.

Anibal was interested in reading some of these books, and Romina promised she would gift him some. Romina possessed novels written by authors of the United States like *The Fall of the House of Usher*, *The Premature Burial*, and *The Tell Tale Heart* by Edgar Allan Poe. Other writers Romina introduced to Anibal were Ralph Waldo Emerson, Henry David Thoreau, and authors influenced by Abolitionism like William Lloyd Garrison, Harriet Beecher Stowe, and Frederick Douglass. Anibal smiled with excitement as he made it his goal to improve his English language abilities and learn about the great foreign writers. When they reached Romina's home, Anibal helped her down from his horse and kissed her deeply.

After embracing, Anibal whispered, "*Te quiero, mi amor,*" and brought her to her door.

Romina laughed and teasingly said, "I hope you love me more than any of those other women who fancy you." They both laughed as Romina's parents came to the door and said goodbye to Anibal.

Before Anibal left, Romina brought some books for him—including some short stories from Edgar Allan Poe and a couple of novels by Charles Dickens. Anibal also requested Uncle Tom's Cabin, by Harriet Beecher Stowe as he was inspired by the slave narrative of Josiah Henson titled, The Life of Josiah Henson, Formerly a Slave, Now an Inhabitant of Canada, as Narrated by Himself, which was dictated to former Boston Mayor and abolitionist Samuel A. Eliot. The protagonist of Uncle Tom's Cabin was Uncle Tom, who was based on the life of Josiah Henson and portrayed as a noble character of Christian faith who stood for his beliefs against the antagonist slave master Simon Legree. Although he is beaten to death, Uncle Tom refuses to betray the whereabouts of two escaped slave women. Anibal also purchased the Narrative of the Life of Frederick Douglass, an American Slave, written by the former slave and famous abolitionist

Frederick Douglass. He was aware of Frederick Douglass and some of his travels, but it was the first time Anibal would read his writings. Slavery was established and abolished before Anibal's birth in the land now called the Dominican Republic, and he was interested in understanding the plight of the black people under the current system of slavery in the United States.

Anibal quickly rode north to his home to spend his next few days of leisure with his family. He intended to read as much English and American literature he could and take notes, making sure to learn any English words he did not know.

Anibal would soon celebrate Christmas and New Year's Eve, welcoming the year 1859. When he once again returned to military service, he would learn that his predictions regarding Haitian politics had manifested. Rumors soon spread throughout the Dominican Republic that Emperor Faustin I faced a potent Haitian uprising against his monarchy. The Haitian rebellion now enveloped Haiti and now threatened the Haitian capital of Port-au-Prince. Not long after, Anibal's superiors confirmed that Emperor Faustin I would soon be dethroned, further securing the sovereignty of the Dominican Republic. After several days, the mood in the Dominican Republic was festive when news of the Haitian rebellion led by General Fabre Geffrard proved successful over Emperor Faustin I. The news spread throughout the Dominican populace that the Haitian constitution of 1846 would replace the Haitian Monarchy with the Haitian Republic. Emperor Faustin I abdicated his throne on the fifteenth of January, prompting social instability within Haiti. Faustin Soulouque subsequently fled Port-au-Prince in a small boat, accompanied by his son and two supporters, Ernest Roumain and Jean-Bart. Faustin abdicated his throne and fled to Kingston, Jamaica on the twenty-second of January 1859 along with his family.

Like many other Dominicans, Anibal Hector Medina was excited by the news of Faustin's abdication, and he suspected that Haiti would never militarily threaten the Dominican Republic. Anibal believed that any subsequent Haitian offensive would be met with defeat with the strengthening Dominican Military; the time would soon arrive when a Democratic and inclusive Dominican government would come to fruition. The continuance of caudillo politics in the Dominican Republic should come to an end, but realistically, Anibal worried that his vision would be dampened by President Pedro Santana's continuous grip on power. Even if President Santana was removed from office, Anibalwas concerned another Dominican caudillo would replace him—perhaps Buenaventura Báez or someone else. Nevertheless, Anibal believed the lives of all Dominicans should be improved and the end of the war could help motivate them to rebel against autocratic rule. It was in the best interest of both working-class Haitians and Dominicans to live peacefully without warfare and under intelligent, just leadership. Now Anibal Medina chose to celebrate the end of Haiti's monarchy and hopefully the end of warfare. He Anibal would leave deeper thoughts of the future for another day and enjoyed some rum with his fellow soldiers as he toasted the sovereignty of the Dominican Republic.

CHAPTER 11

THE STORY OF FREDERICK DOUGLASS, NAT TURNER, & THE SLAVE REBELLIONS IN THE UNITED STATES

(1859)

One particularly hot July afternoon, Anibal Medina traveled to the home of Robert Grant. Anibal slowed his horse to a trot as his heartbeat increased. He had excelled in the military, and his superiors stated he was on track to become a sergeant. Anibal made sure to save his money from the military while he worked with his Uncle Julio on obtaining a home with a ranch and farm in San Cristobal. In San Cristobal, he could find a quiet neighborhood for himself and Romina away from the politics of Santo Domingo, yet still close enough for them to visit their families and conduct business.

Julio became a high-ranking sergeant and leader in the Dominican Military, but like Anibal, he considered resigning from the army due to his disagreements with officers and politicians and their policies of annexation. Anibal and Julio both agreed that the Dominican Republic should prepare for European threats, including American presence in the Caribbean, which would most certainly replace the Spaniards and the English. Anibal believed the Dominican Republic was now at a time of peace, which allowed him an opportunity to resign from his military duties and start his life with Romina.

As he approached the Grant home, he gathered his courage and confidently demounted from his horse. Robert Grant's wife and daughter were attending afternoon service at the Catholic Church, giving the two men privacy. Robert Grant approached Anibal and said, "I hope you had a pleasant ride, young man. How are you?"

Anibal replied, "I am doing very well, Mr. Grant." Anibal previously arranged to meet Robert Grant on this particular Sunday, and he eagerly awaited to speak with Anibal, although he had an idea the conversation would be regarding his daughter. Robert Grant welcomed him in and they sat down.

After some brief conversation regarding Anibal's family and career, Anibal looked Robert Grant straight in his eyes and stated, "I love your daughter, and I believe she is the right woman for me. I arranged our meeting today because I wanted to inform you of my intentions of proposing to your Romina and marrying her in the future."

After a long pause, Robert Grant smiled. "I am happy you have informed me of your intentions. When I arrived here, I was nervous about starting my new life. However, my life in New York and Philadelphia was hard with little opportunities. I came to this land where all people live free from slavery and although I did not know the Spanish language, I was able to live in an English-speaking community in Samaná. Eventually, I learned a little Spanish and met my wife and we had our lovely daughter Romina. I have prospered here in the Dominican Republic, and I have made this my country and the people have accepted me and my family as Dominicans— for that I am grateful. My only desire was to find a good, honorable Dominican man for my daughter to marry, and if she accepts your proposal, I will be honored to have you as my son-in-law."

Anibal let out a laugh of relief as Robert Grant concluded his statement and both men embraced. They relaxed now that the main purpose for the meeting was addressed, and Anibal shared his plans for after the military. Robert Grant also offered to assist him in his future endeavors as the conversation began to shift towards the people of the Dominican Republic and the black people of the United States. Anibal was curious regarding the continuing institution of slavery within the Americas, while England had outlawed slavery in 1833 and ended in England's largest Caribbean colony of Jamaica on the first of August 1834. The Spaniards also continued their practice of slavery on their island colonies of Puerto Rico and Cuba.

Anibal read some of Edgar Allan Poe's works during his free time, as well as a little of *Uncle Tom's Cabin* and the writings of Frederick Douglass. Anibal partially read the Narrative of the Life of Frederick Douglass, an American Slave, and he carried this memoir with him. Robert Grant was happy to see Anibal with his book and he began speaking about the famous abolitionist. He stated that Frederick Douglass was born into slavery on a plantation, possibly in his grandmother's cabin, on the eastern shore of the Chesapeake Bay. Frederick Douglass did not know his birthday, although he would claim February fourteenth, 1818. His full name was Frederick Augustus Washington Bailey, and he was given that name from his black slave mother Harriet Bailey. Like the majority of the Dominican population, Frederick Douglass was also of mixed racial background—black, white, and possibly indigenous—and he believed his slave master was his father. In the United States, he was viewed by anti-abolitionists, racists, and southern slave-owners as a negro slave who was uneducated and troublesome.

Frederick's mother died when he was about nine or ten years old while he lived with his maternal grandmother Betty Bailey. Frederik was soon separated from his grandmother and placed at the Wye House plantation, where Aaron Anthony worked as overseer. After the death of Aaron Anthony, Frederick was given to Lucretia Auld, who was the wife of Thomas Auld. Robert Grant explained that Frederick Douglass was sent to Baltimore to provide slave labor for the brother of Thomas Auld, Hugh, and his wife Sophia, who taught Frederick the alphabet. Anibal confirmed that in the autobiographical work he was currently reading; Frederick wrote that Sophia Auld treated him like a regular citizen of the United States. Hugh Auld did not approve of Frederick learning how to read and write, as he believed educated slaves would make miserable slaves who became rebellious and encouraged others to rebel.

Frederick Douglass read numerous political essays, poems, newspapers, and The Columbian Orator—an anthology used in American classrooms to teach students reading and speaking—heavily influenced him on the subject of human rights. After being hired out to William Freeland, Frederick Douglass began instructing slaves how to read and write while teaching the New Testament every Sunday, which infuriated the local slave-owners. As punishment, Douglass was given to a notorious slave-breaker named Edward Covey, who relentlessly beat the sixteen-year-old. Frederick Douglass later fell in love with a free black woman named Anna Murray, and subsequently fled north in 1838 to the Quaker city of Philadelphia, Pennsylvania (which was a free state). Frederick Douglass would visit the home of the abolitionist David Ruggles in New York City, and he married Anna Murray in September 1838 just days before his arrival.

Nathan and Mary Johnson welcomed Frederick Douglass into their home, and he joined the African Methodist Episcopal Zion Church. Its current members included Harriet Tubman and Sojourner Truth. Robert Grant informed Anibal that Frederick Douglass, who was originally named Frederick Augustus Washington Bailey, changed and shortened his name to Frederick Douglass when his host (Nathan Johnson) suggested that he take the surname of a character in the poem The Lady of the Lake. Frederick Douglass gave a speech in Manhattan, New York during his tour as a member of the American Anti-Slavery Society, which greatly inspired many black Americans and white abolitionists. Robert Grant also informed Anibal about Douglass' tours to England and Ireland during the Irish Potato Famine. Douglass spoke with the Irish Nationalist Daniel O'Connell and in England, he met with the English Abolitionist Thomas Clarkson.

Robert Grant was deeply interested in Frederick Douglass and he worked hard to obtain news regarding the famed abolitionist. He made friends with various merchants and some upper-class Dominicans who traveled to the United States to acquire books and other information relating to the state of blacks in America and the abolitionist movement. Frederick Douglass' autobiography (Narrative of the Life of Frederick Douglass, an American Slave), which Anibal was currently reading, circulated in the United States and Europe and gave blacks in America hope that slavery in the United States would soon be abolished. The fight for emancipation and women's rights in the United States deeply interested Anibal Medina, and he desired the same for Puerto Rico and Cuba with a more liberal Democratic Dominican government.

Frederick Douglass also faced constant danger, including a mob attack in Pendleton, Indiana that resulted in a broken hand, leading the Hardy family (local Quakers) to protect him. Through all his hardships, Frederick

Douglass persevered. He would start publishing the abolitionist Newspaper North Star from the basement of the Memorial AME Zion Church in Rochester, New York in 1847. The North Star's motto was, "Right is of no Sex – Truth is of no Color – God is the Father of us all, and we are all brethren." The North Star and the AME Zion Church was opposed to the American Colonization Society, which proposed sending black Americans to Africa. Along with the previous Haitian governments, the American Colonization Society, ironically helped send groups of black Americans to Haiti and Samaná, including Robert Grant's community. Frederick Douglass also supported women's rights, and in 1848, he was the only black person to attend the Seneca Falls Convention (the first women's rights convention) in upstate New York. Elizabeth Cady Stanton asked for a vote for Women's Suffrage and Frederick Douglass stated that he could not accept the right to vote as a black man if women could not also claim that right. Throughout the 1850's, Frederick Douglass met with many abolitionists, including John Brown and George DeBaptiste. Female black Americans like Harriet Tubman helped many slaves escape north towards freedom and after the Fugitive Slave Act of 1850, she helped them escape further north towards British North America or the Canadas. The abolitionist William Lloyd Garrison likened Harriet Tubman to the Prophet Moses, who led the Hebrews to freedom out of Egypt. Sojourner Truth was born into slavery in Swartekill, Ulster County, New York and escaped in 1826. She would win a case against her slave master in 1828 to recover her daughter. Robert Grant stated that Sojourner Truth grew up speaking Dutch in New York and was a champion for women's rights and emancipation.

Anibal questioned Robert Grant regarding the current condition of slavery within the United States. Robert Grant stated there were numerous failed rebellions, and a significant one was led by Nat Turner. Born a slave in Virginia in 1800, Nat Turner's slave master (Benjamin Turner) named him. After the death of Benjamin Turner in 1810, his son Samuel owned him. Nat Turner soon would be called to conduct Baptist services, and he gained many slave followers—as well as whites. On February twelfth, 1831, an annual solar eclipse was visible in Virginia, and Turner envisioned the hand of a black man reaching over the sun. Nat Turner would organize a rebellion against the slave owners on July fourth, the independence of the United States. However, he delayed providing his coconspirators additional time to devise an improved plan of attack. A previous eruption of Mount St. Helens left lingering ash in the air, causing the solar eclipse of August seventh, 1831 to appear bluish-green and giving Nat Turner a sign that the slave uprising should begin. On the twenty-first of August 1831, Nat Turner gathered slaves (including his most trusted allies Henry, Hark, Nelson, and Sam) as well as free men of color, and the uprising began.

This lasted two days. Nat Turner ordered the rebels not to use firearms, but quiet weaponry like blunt instruments, knives, and axes were permitted. The rebels did not discriminate killing white men, women, and children, but after those two days, Nat Turner escaped to the woods. The rebellion alarmed whites in the United States, and Robert Grant stated it reminded him of a smaller-scale version of the Haitian Revolution. Numerous slave owners were once again wary of the growing slave population—only now in the United States—and some whites like Samuel Warner called him "General Nat". Samuel Warner stated that a successful rebellion would lead General Nat to a decimation of the white population similar to what occurred in Haiti, sending widespread fear while Nat Turner continued to evade capture.

Farmer Benjamin Phipps eventually discovered Nat Turner in a hole covered with fence rails. He was arrested and convicted in a court of law; subsequently hung on November eleventh, 1831 in Jerusalem, Virginia. Nat Turner's body was flayed and decapitated, left in public view as an example to other slaves. The state executed fifty-five people believed to have been involved in the uprising while angry white mobs killed over 120 black people who had nothing to do with the rebellion.

Anibal sat silently as Robert Grant informed him of the intricate details of Nat Turner's rebellion and the black struggle in the United States, but finally broke his silence. "I am fortunate to have been born a free man on this island. We have been free for several generations in this land and some families have experienced freedom for many generations. I am also blessed to have fought for the Dominican Republic and earning the right to live freely within our own nation. Perhaps someday freedom will come for your people in the United States."

Robert Grant smiled. "My people are strong, and someday soon, the black people of the United States will be emancipated from the evil institution of slavery. The abolitionists are gaining strength, and there is increasing friction between the Northern and Southern States. Hopefully it will lead to freedom for black people."

Anibal replied, "I hope that day will soon arrive, Mr. Grant. A weakened United States can give us time to strengthen the Dominican Republic and perhaps we can emancipate the people of Cuba and Puerto Rico without their interference."

Robert Grant grinned as he thanked Anibal for a wonderful conversation as well as his honesty regarding his love for Romina. Anibal prepared to depart before the arrival of Carmen and Romina Grant, and as he mounted his horse Robert Grant exclaimed, "Best wishes on your proposal, Anibal!"

CHAPTER 12

THE WORLD POWERS & THE COMPETITION FOR SAMANÁ BAY

(1860)

Anibal was awarded the rank of Sergeant in the Dominican Army by his superiors, who respected his honorable service in Santo Domingo. With this rank came new duties; he was now responsible for other Dominican soldiers and upholding the values of the military, which strengthened under veteran leadership. Máximo Gómez was previously recommended to attend the military academy in Spain, and he learned well from the battle tactics of the Spanish Imperial Army. The Dominican leader President Pedro Santana boasted of an increased roster of experienced generals which were loyal to him. However, despite Haitian promises of non-invasion, President Pedro Santana still held plans to increasingly send envoys to Spain to help fortify the Dominican Republic.

President Fabre Geffrard reduced the Haitian Military in half from 30,000 to 15,000 and in June 1859, he founded National Law School and reinstated the Medical School that President Boyer had begun. The ministers of education Jean Simon Elie-Dubois and François Elie-Dubois established many *lycea* (or secondary schools) in Jacmel, Jérémie, Saint-Marc, and Gonaïves. President Fabre Geffrard was a Catholic, and he implemented measures to renounce the Haitian-Voodoo faith that his predecessor Faustin Soulouque had practiced and elevated. President Fabre Geffrard began plans to destroy various instruments used in Voodoo like altars and drums. Then he started to establish friendly relations with the neighboring Dominican Republic, which he hoped would increase trade between the two nations and revitalize the economy. Despite his disagreements with the former government, President Fabre Geffrard was an abolitionist and he sought to bring African Americans to the nation of Haiti where they could live free from the shackles of slavery.

President Pedro Santana worried about the heightened Haitian activity at the border and the increased Haitian population within the Dominican Republic as these reports arrived from Azua. President Santana was also concerned about his rival Buenaventura Baez and his possible collaboration with Haitians and Dominicans who opposed his regime. Some government officials reported that Baecistas (supporters of Buenaventura Baez) continued to encourage a rebellion in the Dominican south and in the islands of St. Thomas and Curacao. Meanwhile Baez's cousin, General Valentin Ramirez Baez, increased trade with the Haitians in the border. While he vacationed in Europe, General Felipe Alfau received a letter notifying him that President Pedro Santana had appointed him as envoy with the mission of speaking to Queen Isabella II of Spain.

The Dominican government was also troubled by United States' expansion into the Caribbean. These fears materialized when American adventurers landed in April of 1860 on the small rocky islet of Alta Vela, off the southwestern coast of the Dominican Republic. The Americans claimed Alta Vela as territory of the United States and began plans to exploit its guano deposits. After months of protests by the Dominicans and a diplomatic failure between the governments of the United States and the Dominican Republic, the Dominicans responded by sending the war ship La Merced to Alto Velo. The Dominican Navy fought and captured the Americans, imprisoning them in Santo Domingo.

Sergeant Anibal Medina was positioned in the southwestern Dominican Republic along with thousands of other troops who were on high alert for a possible retaliatory attack by the United States. Sergeant Anibal was ordered to report to the area while his uncle remained in Santo Domingo. The Dominican naval victory raised morale as the Americans were captured and transported to the city of Santo Domingo for questioning. Anibal rarely spoke with Dominican sailors, however during the transportation of the American prisoners, he met a few of them—including a young twenty-two-year-old Chinese-Dominican sailor named Valentino Xin.

Valentino Xin was a first generation, native-born Dominican from a small fisherman family that had migrated from Hong Kong, China. He was eight years younger than Anibal, the same age as his sister. Valentino Xin's family were Han Chinese who'd left China. Despite being born in the land now known as the Dominican Republic, Valentino Xin was taught the Cantonese language by his parents, who wanted to preserve their culture. China was currently ruled by the Manchu Qing Dynasty (established in 1636 and began governing China in 1644 after the overthrow of the Ming Dynasty). The Qing Dynasty was founded by the Jurchen Aisin Gioro clan in Manchuria. Nurhaci was originally a Ming Chieftain who began organizing military units called banners and created a union between Jurchen, Mongolians, and Han. Nurhaci's son, Hong Taiji, drove Ming forces out of Liaodong and declared a new dynasty: the Qing. In 1644, peasant rebels led by Li Zicheng conquered the Ming capital, Beijing. Li Zicheng would rule briefly as emperor of the Shun Dynasty, but was defeated at the battle of Shanhai Pass and would die the following year. The Southern Ming and the Revolt of the Three Feudatories (led by Wu Sangui) would continue to rebel for four decades until the Kangxi Emperor defeated them. The Ten Great Campaigns of the Qianlong Emperor from the 1750s to the 1790s would extend Qing control into Inner Asia.

Anibal Medina enjoyed speaking to Valentino Xin and the young Dominican sailor relished talking about his culture and history with Anibal. Valentino Xin was part of a small Chinese Dominican community and although he was an only child, he had a few cousins. Various Chinese people also recently arrived in the Dominican Republic from neighboring Cuba to work in the farms. Valentino Xin joined the navy as he felt it was his patriotic duty to defend the Dominican Republic from increasing foreign aggression. Valentino's first combat mission was the battle at Isla Alto Velo (or Alto Velo Island). He and his fellow sailors first landed on a larger island north of Alto Velo named Beata as his superiors planned their attack. Valentino Xin was part of a secondary unit of sailors ordered to supplement the initial Dominican offensive. The Dominican Navy previously ordered the Americans to evacuate Alto Velo within twenty-four hours on the twenty-third of October 1860. Early the next day, the Dominican ship La Merced easily subdued the Americans with little retaliation as various ships of the Dominican Navy sailed throughout the southern coastline in search of additional ships belonging to the United States.

Under the Guano Islands Act of 1856, the United States claimed numerous small islands, including Navassa within Haitian territory. The United States was able to establish control of Navassa Island under the claim of Captain Peter Duncan on September nineteenth, 1857. President James Buchanan issued an Executive Order upholding the claim for Navassa in 1858. Seeking more territory, the United States would lose their claim of Alto Velo to the Dominican Government in 1860.

It was the first time Valentino Xin had set foot on these islands, and he informed Anibal Medina about the mangrove swamps in the northern region of Beata as well as the beautiful limestone forests. Erosion caused jagged edges called *diente de perro* (or dogtooth). Upon Valentino's arrival to Alto Velo Island, the first Dominican Naval offensive was almost complete with most of the invaders on the highest part of the island over 150 meters above sea level. The Americans were quickly overwhelmed, stripped of their weapons, and transported to Santo Domingo. Valentino Xin described his anxiety and elation after a quick, successful result. Anibal Medina would later receive reports from his superiors regarding the interrogation of the American prisoners in Santo Domingo.

After several weeks, Julio Medina sent a letter to his nephew Anibal regarding the details relating to the attempted occupation of Alto Velo Island by the United States. An act of Congress in 1856 allowed American merchants to claim any land they deemed unclaimed by foreign government. The Firm of Patterson & Murguiendo began work in Alto Velo for several months in 1860. After their capture, a man named Mr. Miller requested to leave one man remaining on the island to inform some of the American merchants who had briefly traveled along with Captain Cimbal to the island of Jamaica aboard the ship Alice Mowe. One of the leaders was a man named Jonathan Elliot, who was also imprisoned and questioned in Santo Domingo. The Dominican Government, along with the Dominican Naval Commander Juan Evertz, countered the claim by the United States, stating that the island of Alto Vela belonged to the Dominican Province of Azua.

After several months, the merchants were slowly allowed to return to the United States after further questioning. Anibal Medina now sought to travel to Santo Domingo and he informed his superiors he would end his military service. Anibal nervously anticipated the annexation of the Dominican Republic to Spain—an act that he believed would bring great disappointment to a majority of patriotic Dominicans. Samaná Bay continued to be contested by the world powers, and the Alto Velo Island ordeal further convinced Anibal Medina that President Pedro Santana would convince his loyalists to annex the Dominican Republic to counter these foreign threats.

In 1854, the previous leader of the United States, President Franklin Pierce, instructed a special agent to initiate an agreement with the Dominican Republic to use Samaná Bay as a Naval Base. The British and Spanish, alongside the Dominican government, would insert a stipulation that the Dominican people would be treated with the same status as White Americans, which helped break down the deal. President James Buchanan did not seek reelection in 1860, choosing to support Vice President John C. Breckinridge over Douglas. President James Buchanan previously lobbied the Supreme Court in support of Dred Scott v. Sandford, which detailed that a negro whose ancestors were imported into the United States, whether enslaved or free, could not be an American citizen and therefore had no standing to sue in federal court. It also described that the federal government had no power to regulate slavery in the federal territories acquired after the creation of the United States. Dred Scott Illinois was an enslaved man who unsuccessfully sued the United States after he claimed that he lived in the Wisconsin Territory for four years, where slavery was illegal and that he and his wife should be granted freedom. The United States Supreme Court decided 7–2 against Scott.

Chief Justice Roger B. Taney had hoped to settle issues related to slavery and Congressional authority by this decision, however it only increased public outrage and deepened sectional tensions between the northern and southern states. Candidate John C. Breckinridge would lose support as his Democratic Party split into rival factions. Southern Democrats walked out of the 1860 Democratic National Convention, while in Baltimore the Democratic Party's northern faction nominated John C. Breckinridge and the Democratic Party's southern Faction nominated Douglas. The Constitutional Union Party, which was composed of mostly conservative members of the Whig Party, nominated John Bell and hoped to prevent the Civil War over the slavery issue. The division helped the new Republic Party nominee Abraham Lincoln win the election. Abraham Lincoln defeated Seward and Chase and ran an anti-slavery campaign within the United States and its territories. He also previously stood against the Mexican American War, and his surprising victory caused anger within the United States. As the sixteenth president Abraham Lincoln caused the breakdown of the Union, southern states seceded the Union forming the Confederate States of America, bringing forth the Civil War.

In the Dominican Republic, President Pedro Santana continued his communication with the Spanish Monarchy, and Queen Isabella II of Spain and various Spanish ministers agreed to obtain a Dominican Protectorate in the Caribbean. President Pedro Santana subsequently decided to annex the Dominican Republic to Spain, which many Spanish officials viewed as a more favorable agreement in order to reestablish Spanish control of the Caribbean. President Santana and his loyal ministers would add several conditions for the annexation of the Dominican Republic. In December 1860, the Prime Minister of Spain (Leopoldo O'Donnell) declared that his government desired to postpone the reincorporation of the Dominican Republic until the outbreak of the United States Civil War. Preoccupied with the Civil War, the United States would not be able to enforce the Monroe Policy.

The Dominican government and the Spanish diplomats agreed that the Spaniards would not reinstitute slavery in the Dominican Republic; they would not consider the Dominican Republic as a territory and therefore, they did not believe Dominican people should be treated as equals. The Dominican and Spanish governments also agreed that the Spaniards would employ a large number of Dominicans to military and civil positions; the Spaniards would amortize all paper currency in the Dominican Republic and recognize all the acts passed by the Dominican government since 1844 as good and valid. President Pedro Santana desired to remain as the leader of the future Dominican territory, and he negotiated in secret alongside his most loyal ministers in order to avoid widespread Dominican Rebellion. President Santana believed if the Spaniards respected his agreements and the Dominican populace were treated as equals, he would prevent Dominican turmoil and establish peace in the Dominican Republic.

President Pedro Santana awarded his most loyal supporters financially and placed his loyalists in high-ranking positions. Alonso Kebehi Dos Santos, a Santana supporter, benefited greatly during the leadership of President Pedro Santana and was appointed as an officer in the Dominican Army. While continuing to maintain his plot from most of the Dominican population, President Pedro Santana began preparing his most loyal supporters for the eventual annexation of the Dominican Republic. Dos Santos would soon take a short leave to Santo Domingo after his appointment as lieutenant in the Dominican Army.

The Medina family soon welcomed Sergeant Anibal Medina and his

Uncle Julio Medina to their family home in Santo Domingo. Anibal Medina and other Dominican soldiers were returning to their families for temporary leave. As the Medina family celebrated the independence of the Dominican Republic in February, Anibal announced he would soon resign from the Dominican Army. Julio decided to remain in the Dominican Army, despite his nephew's opinion that he should retire from service. Anibal believed that Dominican sovereignty would come to an end and did not want to serve in a Dominican Military that would soon serve Queen Isabella II of Spain. Anibal pleaded with his Uncle Julio about resigning from the military as Anibal's fears were soon confirmed: Dominican civilians and military members began to publicly speak out against President Pedro Santana and the possible annexation of the Dominican Republic.

Marco Medina encouraged his son and brother to resign from military service and to not involve themselves in the possible uprising. However, Julio Medina felt the Dominican nation would face the horrors currently experienced in the islands of Cuba and Puerto Rico. Marco agreed with his brother, but he believed the annexation would be short-lived as President Pedro Santana would lose control of his own position and would not be able to maintain a grip on the military.

Marco stated to his son and brother, "The Dominican people are resilient, and they will not accept foreign occupation. We have fought all foreign occupation and our spirit for freedom will give us victory over Spain. I believe in fighting, but I do not think it is the right time to revolt since I think most Dominicans and even a large portion of the Dominican Military remain ignorant of Santana's designs. We need better organization before we challenge Pedro Santana and his Spanish alliance. Most importantly, Julio, you are a family man—and Anibal, you plan on proposing to Romina Grant. Both of you have more than just your own lives to consider. You are responsible for your families."

Both Anibal and Julio agreed with Marco. However, Julio replied, "The fact is that we will not have a life under the yoke of the Spaniards. My duty as a military man is to protect the sovereignty of the Dominican Republic against all who threaten it. What President Pedro Santana is doing should be considered treason to the founding fathers of the Dominican Republic. If the entire military is informed regarding President Santana's plot, then we will be able to depose him and his loyalists and maintain Dominican sovereignty. The Spaniards will not be able to establish rule in the Dominican Republic once the people and leadership are united against them."

Julio was adamant that he could convince other Dominican soldiers to turn against the military leadership. Anibal's mother (Maria Altagracia Medina) also advised Julio to resign to no avail. However, she was happy to discover Anibal's upcoming resignation from the Dominican Military in early 1862.

Other Dominican service members would soon resign or defect, including Anibal's friend Valentino Xin, who was influenced by Anibal's thoughts against President Pedro Santana. Various movements began to publicly rebel against the Dominican government and Spain, and Anibal was unsure whether the annexation plans were completed. However, his fears were confirmed when he heard rumors that Lieutenant Alonso Kebehi Dos Santos revealed the plans of annexation during his stay in Santo Domingo. He frequently vocalized his support for President Pedro Santana and began to openly criticize Dominicans who did not share his beliefs to be against the Dominican state. Marco Medina had previously viewed Dos Santos as cruel due to his despicable actions during the Haitian-Dominican War, and he advised his brother and son to stay away from Dos Santos; he was growing increasingly unstable with power.

Anibal Medina was wary of President Pedro Santana, but he still desired to complete his military duties the following year and marry Romina Grant. Anibal subsequently traveled to the home of Robert Grant and privately proposed to Romina at the same beach he previously professed his love for her. At thirty years of age, Anibal had waited long to marry due to his career, but now felt he was ready to start his family and live a private life away from a segment of military leadership which deeply disappointed him.

Several days later, President Pedro Santana proclaimed the annexation of the Dominican Republic at the Cathedral Plaza on the eighteenth of March 1861. Manifestos were forged and published throughout the nation in an attempt to give the impression that a majority of Dominicans supported the reincorporation of Spain. On the second of May 1861, General José Contreras and a group of his followers (mostly Baecistas) revolted against Spaniards, declaring they would reintroduce slavery in the Dominican Republic. However, they were defeated, and the various leaders were shot. In June, one of the founding fathers of the Dominican Republic, Francisco del Rosario Sanchez, finally arrived from Haiti, but he was ambushed by government forces. Later, he was shot along with other rebel leaders.

Other rebel leaders like General José Maria Cabral were shot but managed to escape while the Catholic Vicar who attempted to organize a rebellion against the Spaniards, Father Fernando Arturo de Meriño, was captured and expelled from the nation. The Dominican Republic was in political turmoil as Spaniards began arriving from Spain, Cuba, Puerto Rico, as Spain tightened their control over the Dominican Republic.

CHAPTER 13

QUEEN ISABELLA II OF SPAIN & THE ANNEXATION OF THE DOMICAN REPUBLIC

(1861)

Queen Isabella II of Spain continued her lengthy rule as her empire increased by the addition of the Dominican Republic and the Civil War of the United States afforded Spain the opportunity to regain their presence in the Caribbean. The Spanish schooner La Amistad was owned by a Spaniard living in Cuba named Don Ramon Ferrer. In June 1839, fifty-three enslaved Mende people from Mendiland Western Africa rebelled and took over the ship, forcing them to sail back to Africa. The ship was heading towards Guanaja, near Puerto Principe, Cuba to deliver the slaves to various Cuban slave plantations. However, the ship would land in Long Island, New York. The United States and Britain prohibited the international slave trade since 1808, however, the ships owners claimed the slaves were born in Cuba and said they were being sold in the Spanish domestic slave trade. The Supreme Court Case the United States v. The Amistad ruled that the slaves were illegally transported and rebelled in self-defense and were to return to Africa. The Africans were aided by funds raised by the United Missionary Society, a black group founded by James W.C. Pennington, who was a Congregational minister and fugitive slave in Brooklyn, New York.

The Spanish Empire continued to have an increasingly difficult relationship with the various European powers and the United States. While facing occupation during the Napoleonic Wars, the Spanish Empire lost the majority of their American colonies. Spain continued to face instability as Queen Isabella II faced political turmoil. The Carlist Wars and the unpopularity of Queen Isabella II would lead to the insurrection of 1854, led by General Domingo Dulce y Garay and General Leopoldo O'Donnell y Jarris. The insurrection overthrew the dictatorship of Luis José Sartorius, First Count of San Luis, bringing the Progressive Party into power. In 1856, Queen Isabella II attempted to form the Liberal Union under the leadership of Leopoldo O'Donnell. Spain would aid France in Asia in the region of Cochinchina starting in 1857 and in Mexico in 1861. In 1860, Queen Isabella II launched a successful war against Morocco (waged by generals O'Donnell and Juan Prim), which increased her popularity in Spain.

The Europeans sought to reclaim their American territories as the United States Civil War raged on and the French intervened in Mexico. The French (led by Emperor Napoleon III) sought to remove Mexican President Benito Juárez and install Ferdinand Maximillian (who was the younger brother of the Austrian leader, Emperor Francis Joseph I) of Austria as Maximillian I of Mexico. President Benito rose to power several years after the overthrow of President Antonio López de Santa Anna, after the Revolution of Ayutla in 1854.

Queen Isabella II also accepted the annexation of the Dominican Republic. The Dominican Republic held symbolic importance for Spain, as it was the location of Santo Domingo, the oldest European city in the Americas as well as the first headquarters of the Spanish Empire in the New World since 1494. The acquisition of the Dominican Republic could help Spain solidify their control of their territories in Puerto Rico and Cuba in the Caribbean as well as aid the Spanish Empire in playing a stronger role in Latin America. Queen Isabella II was often criticized for her politics and her large, robust figure. Some critics disdained her somewhat expressionless face, but a segment of the Spanish government enjoyed her recent territorial gains. Queen Isabella II began sending a large amount of money, arms, and provisions to the Dominican Republic and in May 1861, President Pedro Santana was appointed Captain-General of the province of Santo Domingo. The captain general of Cuba, Francisco Serrano, exercised authority over Pedro Santana; he would appoint Brigadier Antonio Pelaez de Campomanes as second in command.

On August sixth of 1861, a commission was installed in the Dominican Republic called the Junta Clasificadora (or the Classification Board) which analyzed military service records. The Junta Clasificadora began to see many Dominican Military officers who were loyal to Pedro Santana as unqualified in the new Spanish Military in the Dominican Republic. European immigration rose as people arrived from various locations, including Spain and the Canary Islands. Spaniards were increasingly appointed to high military positions in the Dominican Republic, and the Spaniards began sidelining and removing Dominicans from high-ranking military and political posts. In addition, they angered the Dominican population with policies like the policy of bagajes, which required citizens to hand over any work animals to the Spanish Military upon d-mand without any guarantee of compensation. The bagajes policy particularly enraged Dominican peasants from the Cibao region in the Northern Dominican Republic, who heavily depended on their cattle.

The relationship between President Pedro Santana and Spaniards worsened as the Spaniards gradually replaced some of Santana's loyalists from their government positions, and Dominican politics were increasingly controlled by Spanish officials from Cuba and Puerto Rico. Despite sharing similarities in culture, the majority mixed population of the Dominican Republic formed their own identity. The Dominicans were free, and they were angered when the Spaniards reminded them that a large portion of Dominicans would exist as slaves in neighboring Puerto Rico and Cuba.

The Spaniards would negatively impact the Dominican economy, and it appeared the Spaniards would not redeem Dominican paper money which also angered Santana's loyalists. Dominicans who held the paper money were considering sending a commission to Santo Domingo if the Spaniards did not redeem the currency. Queen Isabella II sought to solidify relations with the Dominican Republic and Governor-General Pedro Santana by bestowing upon him the title of Marquess of Las Carreras, in honor of Pedro Santana's previous victory against the Haitians at the Battle of Las Carreras in 1849. Despite Santana's new title, relations between the Spaniards and Dominicans increased with the arrival of Archbishop Bienvenido de Monzon.

Archbishop Bienvenido de Monzon criticized Dominican marriages which were socially acaccepted but rarely were ecclesiastical. He attempted to modify Dominican customs and increase religious marriages in the Dominican Republic while criticizing the Dominican clergy, which Archbishop Bienvenido de Monzon believed had minimal contributions to the Church. The Dominican clergy was angered by Dominican freemasonry—although they lacked the anti-monarchical and anti-clerical characteristics found in Spain, Italy, and other Latin American countries. Nevertheless, the Masonic Lodges in the Dominican Republic were ordered to close. These actions angered the Dominican people and the Masonic Lodges increased their support for a return of Dominican Republicanism and the eviction of the Spaniards from the Dominican Republic

Puerto Ricans and Cubans who continued to exist and suffer under the institution of slavery viewed the annexation of the Dominican Republic as a disappointment while the growing rebellion gave them hope. Marquess of Las Carreras Pedro Santana was perceived a traitor to the Dominican Republic and Dominican sovereignty. Pedro Santana's feared image as a dictator quickly deteriorated as his power was reduced and he realized he was just another administrator in the greater ambitions of the Spanish Empire in the Caribbean.

Many Dominican Military members were placed into reserve units while the leading military positions were filled with increasing numbers of Spaniards. The Dominicans were often not allowed to wear the same uniform as the Spaniards as the Dominican people were being reduced to second-class citizens in their own country. Some Dominicans who accepted Spanish control in the Dominican Republic maintained their positions in the military, including Alonso Kebehi Dos Santos, who kept his rank of lieutenant.

As the Dominican elite continued to lose power, Lieutenant Alonso Dos Santos aligned himself with the Spanish authorities. Lieutenant Alonso Dos Santos supported President Pedro Santana and believed the Spaniards would honor the conditions set in place by his government. Spanish officials enjoyed Lieutenant Dos Santos' loyalty and fierce determination to maintain the Spanish annexation and possibly extend the borders of the Dominican Republic westward. The Spaniards began to plan the reclamation of territory that the Spaniards previously lost to the French, and they needed the support of men like Dos Santos.

The Haitian government was unsettled with the return of the Spaniards to the island of Hispaniola and Haitian officials began plotting against them. President Fabre Geffrard continued to develop the Haitian educational system and economy while placating the peasants by once again selling state-owned lands. He also improved the schism with the Catholic Church while eliminating the aspects of Voodoo he viewed negatively. President Fabre Geffrard was an abolitionist, and he held a state funeral for the white abolitionist John Brown, who was hanged for leading an armed insurrection against the government of the United States in 1859.

President Fabre Geffrard also collaborated with the Scottish-born journalist and anti-slavery activist James Redpath. The immigration campaign was reinstated when President Fabre Geffrard desired to bring African Americans to Haiti and sponsored James Redpath's Haytian Bureau of Emigration in the United States. James Redpath wrote various works, including Talks with Slaves in the Southern States, Echoes of Harper's Ferry, and A Guide to Hayti. James Red-path believed the emigration of educated African Americans to Haiti could improve Haiti as well as ease racial relations within the United States. In the meantime, President Abraham Lincoln, who believed that freed slaves could have trouble adjusting to American citizenship, could combine freedom for slaves and social harmony with mass deportation.

Haiti was granted diplomatic recognition by the United States after the secession of the slave-owning Southern states while the British and Spaniards supported the Confederacy. The Spanish and British territories of Cuba, Puerto Rico, the Bahamas, and now the Spanish controlled Dominican Republic also supported the Confederacy, while Haiti and the Caribbean island of Danish St. Thomas supported the Union. However, President Fabre Geffrard became increasingly autocratic as racial divisions escalated between the elite mulatto Haitians and majority black Creole-speaking Haitians. President Fabre Geffrard also increased animosity between Haitians of the Catholic and Voodoo faiths as his rule continued. Various plots against him continued including the failed plot of Faustin I's Minister of the Interior, Guerrier Prophète and the failed plot of General Legros when he tried to take over the weapon storage but was imprisoned. Etienne Salomon currently gathered Haitian peasants in an effort to overthrow President Geffrard. President Geffrard was now actively attempting to interfere in Dominican affairs by sup-porting Dominican guerrillas against the Spanish Empire in an attempt to protect the Haitian border and keep the Spaniards from the island of Hispaniola. In 1861,

Spain gave Haiti an ultimatum to stay out of Spanish affairs in the Dominican Republic and President Fabre Geffrard agreed to the Spanish terms—which deeply humiliated and angered the Haitian population, which believed the exiled Faustin would never agree to the demands of a colonial power.

The Dominican Republic became a pivotal territory in the Caribbean for the Spanish Empire as the Spaniards indirectly supported the Confederate States of America in the ongoing United States Civil War. The reign of Governor-General Don Pedro Santana Y Familia, First Marquis of Las Carreras, was slowly coming to the end as the year 1862 approached. Pedro Santana suffered from depression caused by the previous deaths of his fiancé (María del Carmen Ruiz) and his twin brother (Ramon), who did not survive the Dominican revolution of 1844. Added to his turmoil were his failed marriage to the wealthy Micaela Antonia del Rivero—the widow of Miguel Febles—and now his weakening position as leader of the Dominican Republic. Pedro Santana became sick and planned retirement alongside his current wife Ana Zorrilla.

The increasing power of Spain in the Dominican Republic troubled many Dominicans as minor rebellions became more frequent. Julio Medina began planning with Dominican rebels within the military as well as civilian plotters to gather the names of Dominican enlisted men and officers who desired to quickly restore the independence of the Dominican Republic. Julio Medina desired to help bring freedom once again to the Dominican people. He planned to rejoin his wife and son and looked forward to possibly having another son or daughter after the war of restoration was over. Anibal Medina did not share his uncle's goals of undermining Spanish rule within the Dominican Military and planned to retire in April of 1862; he could not bear to serve in the Dominican Army under the Spaniards. Anibal Medina believed he was not protecting the sovereignty of the Dominican Republic but aiding an occupying Spanish force. He secretly denounced Pedro Santana and would plan to wear his military uniform at his upcoming wedding with Romina Grant. After the wedding, Anibal Medina sought to aid the Dominican rebellion as a Dominican veteran and civilian.

CHAPTER 14

HOLY MATRIMONY

(1862)

Anibal Hector Medina traveled to his family home in Santo Domingo and the Medina family rejoiced when they were informed of the wedding several months before. Marco smiled proudly at his son and looked forward to his retirement from the military the following month. Friends and family from Santo Domingo and throughout the Dominican Republic who could attend the wedding made their way to the Medina home in the previous days. The mood was festive despite the ongoing turmoil in the country.

Marco Medina was now sixty years of age while his wife (Maria Altagracia Medina) was fifty-five, and their love was stronger than ever as their family was happy and increasingly successful. Marco Medina was also joyous as he expected the Dominican government to reopen the University in Santo Domingo as soon as the country stabilized. Julio Medina was also present, along with his wife Paulina and nine-year-old son Carlos. Carlos Medina was a strong boy and looked like he would surpass his father's five-foot ten frame as an adult. Robert Grant and his wife Carmen were there, anxiously awaiting the marriage ceremony. Anibal's sister Catalina Violeta, who was now twenty-four years of age, was in attendance along with Anibal's close friends—including Valentino Xin.

The Haitian Saint-Lot family had grown close to the Medina family and were also invited. Felix Saint-Lot, his wife Nadine, and their son Raymond arrived early and they ate various Dominican foods prepared for them and the rest of the guests. The Medina family chose to have a Catholic wedding for Anibal and Romina. They exchanged vows before their family and friends, which numbered nearly 100 people. Anibal was dressed in his ceremonial Dominican Army uniform displaying his rank of sergeant. Anibal was proud to wear it, despite his political differences with Pedro Santana and his loyalists. Romina Grant wore a beautiful long white dress which accentuated her beautiful deep caramel skin. Her father Robert Grant donned a black suit and walked his daughter down the aisle. Anibal appeared striking in his military uniform as he showcased a large smile as soon as he caught a view of his soon-to-be wife. To Anibal, his uniform represented his values and the future he desired for the Dominican Republic as a sovereign, successful nation. It symbolized his and his family's sacrifice and patriotism for the Dominican Republic against all internal and external enemies.

After the priest confirmed their marriage, Anibal whispered, "*Te amo mas que la Luna y las estrellas,*" (or "I love you more than the moon and the stars") and gave Romina a deep, passionate kiss as if he only had that last chance to kiss her. Romina felt intense love when Anibal stated his feelings and they embraced after their kiss.

The guests laughed and some of the ladies—including Anibal's mother and Romina's mother—cried while some of the men attempted to keep their tears to themselves. The celebrations started shortly afterward in the early afternoon; the children played, and the adults danced to the sound of Dominican music until their legs grew tired. They laughed and rejoiced and ate until their bellies were full. After the wedding, Anibal removed his military uniform in favor of casual clothes and the newlyweds danced as the late afternoon approached.

Anibal spoke with many of the guests, including his father, who embraced him as he joyously said, *"Mi Hijo! Que Dios te cuide y te proteja a ti y a tu mujer. Estoy muy orgullosa de ti, Anibal,"* (or "My Son! May God keep you safe and protect you and your lady. I am very proud of you, Anibal"). Marco proudly sent many blessings to Anibal and Romina as he continued to embrace him while offering his son some rum.

Anibal held his mother Maria who was crying as she thanked his son for choosing such an honorable woman from a great family. Maria Medina had grown close to Robert Grant and his wife Carmen; she was impressed with the successful life he had made for himself and his family in the Dominican Republic. Maria slowly learned about Robert Grant and his upbringing in New York and the painful stories of the slavery still ongoing within the United States. This also occurred in Cuba, and Puerto Ricans reminded the Medina family as well as others why Dominicans should rebel against the Spaniards and swiftly reestablish their independence.

Anibal spoke to Robert and Carmen Grant, who were very excited about the marriage. Robert Grant was honored to welcome Anibal Medina to their family, and he was happy to join a great Dominican family with good morals and respectability. Romina Grant was now Romina Grant de Medina, and her excitement expressed itself in her large smile and her increased sociability. Romina Grant de Medina (or Romina Medina, as she was usually called) embraced her parents as her father let out a few tears, surprising Romina, who had never witnessed her stoic father cry despite his hard life. Romina began to shed tears of joy alongside her parents and Anibal's mother, who also embraced her.

Anibal approached his new friend Valentino Xin, who was wearing his Dominican Naval uniform and sitting around several young ladies and members of Anibal's family, including his sister Catalina Violeta. Valentino Xin brought several Chinese dice and board games like Go and Chinese Dominoes, which interested many and attracted children who wanted to learn how to play. Chinese Dominoes was brought to Italy by missionaries in China and later to the Americas; now the modern version of dominoes had deviated from the Chinese version. Valentino Xin informed the wedding guests that the ancient game was believed to have been first played in Ancient Egypt or Ancient China during the Song Dynasty and possibly earlier. Valentino Xin also explained that during the Tang Dynasty, people began using paper money—a possible byproduct of block-printing—and the subsequent Song Dynasty was believed to have been the first government to have issued paper currency. Valentino Xin captured the attention of various Dominicans interested in the history of the Far East while impressing his female admirers, who gathered around him and as consequence aroused secret feelings of jealousy within Catalina. Valentino was jovial and funny, making all the young ladies and men laugh with his relating to his time in the military and his family.

Anibal jokingly stated as his sister laughed, "Be careful with Valentino. This man is a smooth talker."

Catalina replied, "I didn't know your friend was such a great storyteller, *hermano.*"

Valentino Xin told stories about his father's life in China and their arrival to the Dominican Republic, leaving most of their family behind. It was a rarity for Chinese to arrive in the Dominican Republic from China, as many Chinese laborers came to Puerto Rico and Cuba as well as other islands in the Caribbean.

Valentino Xin explained his appreciation of being born free from abuse and indentured servitude like his fellow Chinese in the other Caribbean islands. Valentino Xin was born during the reign of President Boyer and supported the independence of the Dominican Republic. When questioned about why he volunteered to enter the Dominican Navy, he quickly replied, "I was born here and learned Spanish as my first language and identified as a Dominican. When independence was declared, I supported this nation during the subsequent wars against Emperor Faustin 1 and joined the Dominican Navy shortly afterward. My father was a fisherman and merchant in China and he always speaks about his love for the sea as he continued to fish in the Dominican Republic. I grew to love the sea myself, and I believed in the Navy I could better serve this nation and its sovereignty. In China, the minority Manchu people are the elites under the Qing Dynasty. The other ethnic groups, including the Han Chinese like me and my family, are socially below them. Although the elites of various ethnic groups occupy high positions in the Qing government, the Manchu have imposed their culture upon the rest of Chinese society. My father wore the imposed Manchu styled haircut called the queue—a high shaved forehead and a long-braided ponytail that all Chinese people have today, including some recent Chinese arrivals here in the Dominican Republic. My family loves the freedom here, and although I am a minority in the Dominican Republic, my family and I are accepted as Dominicans. We have faced no animosity and have been welcomed by overwhelming support by our fellow Dominican people." Everyone laughed and embraced Valentino Xin, a man who proudly chose to serve his nation.

Valentino next spoke about the Eight Banner System which was imposed by the Qing-Dynasty, placing the Manchu people as the elites of China. The Eight Banner System was an administrative and military system where the Manchus had their own elite banners while the Mongol and Han had their own as well. The Han Chinese formed the Green Standard Army which recruited from various areas including areas of mostly Hui people that mostly belonged to the religion of Islam. During the Revolt of the Three Feudatories from 1673 to 1681, the Manchu Generals were shamed by the better-performing Han Green Standard Army against the Ming Loyalists, prompting the Kangxi Emperor to task Generals Sun Sike, Wang Jinbao, and Zhao Liangdong in leading the Green Standard Army until the revolt was stopped. The White Lotus Rebellion was a secret religious society which led impoverished people in a tax protest that began in 1794 and was stopped in 1804. An earlier rebellion called the Red Turban Rebellion took place in 1352 and occurred against the Mongol-Yuan Dynasty and was also led by a White Lotus Society. The White Lotus Society demanded the return of Han Chinese-led Ming dynasty and promised the return of the Buddha. Valentino Xin spoke about the weakening of the Qing Dynasty and the ongoing Taiping Rebellion which began in 1850 and was led by a Christian man who had convinced his followers he was the brother of Jesus Christ.

Due to the instability in China, Valentino Xin was overjoyed that he was born in the Dominican Republic. However, he feared continuing warfare against the Spaniards. Like many of his compatriots like Anibal Medina and his family, Valentino Xin secretly supported the Dominican rebellion while others like Julio Medina began to publicly speak against the Spanish annexation. Valentino voiced his dismay to Anibal, but Marco warned Valentino to keep his opinions to himself while he continued to serve in the Dominican Navy. Marco Medina believed that Dominican popular support for the growing rebellion was not yet strong enough to counter the ever-increasing powerful Spanish presence in the Dominican Republic. Valentino Xin agreed with Marco, however he privately informed Julio Medina he would support him if he decided to form a coalition of Dominican Military who would challenge Spanish power in the nation.

The wedding celebrations continued for several days while Anibal and Romina took a private vacation together to enjoy their new marriage. The festive mood would only last several days for the Medina family. They soon learned that Lieutenant Dos Santos, along with a young German-Dominican captain named Ricardo Hoffmann, had arrived in Santo Domingo. Captain Ricardo Hoffman was born in the Cibao region to a German merchant and his Dominican wife. He trained in the Spanish

Military Academy, rising quickly in rank and only several years older than Lieutenant Dos Santos. Encouraged by Captain Hoffman, Lieutenant Dos Santos traveled to Santo Domingo searching for enemies of President Pedro Santana and the Spanish annexation.

Lieutenant Dos Santos harassed those that he believed to be Dominican rebels as well as those he suspected to be Haitian collaborators against the government. Julio Medina was approached by Lieutenant Dos Santos and Captain Hoffman and questioned regarding the Spanish annexation and his possible support of the Dominican rebels.

Wearing a slightly noticeable smile, Lieutenant Dos Santos stated, "I was informed about your nephew's wedding. I want to congratulate you and offer you and your family my blessings. For the first time in many years, we are now able to maintain stability and security for Dominican people. You have served honorably in the Dominican Army, rising to a high position and where you are respected by many Dominicans. Your brother Marco also served honorably during the war for our independence. We experienced economic fragility in the face of constant invasion, but now we will be strong and economically sound. I feel that these rebellions and possible discontent within the military will only serve to fracture this nation once again and bring turmoil for the Dominican Republic."

Julio Medina stood silent for a brief moment as he slowly responded, "Lieutenant Dos Santos, we have fought honorably together for this nation. However, we should not call our land the Dominican Republic because we are not currently a republic, but a territory that belongs to Queen Isabella II and the Spanish Empire. We experienced economic problems before, but we still suffer today living in a land that is no longer ours. I serve President Pedro Santana, however I am not sure if I serve him or the Queen of Spain. I will serve as honorably as I can for the Dominican people just as we did before, but we must be careful as many of us are now being put into reserve units while more Spaniards arrive to the island. How long will you last as an officer alongside Captain Hoffman? I suspect the Spaniards will not keep their agreement with Pedro Santana and our government and we may devolve into the same situation that the people of Puerto Rico, Cuba, and the rest of the Caribbean are now facing. They bestowed Pedro Santana the title of the First Marquis of Las Carreras, but the Spaniards that arrived here do not respect their agreements—just as the first Spaniards who arrived here on this land with the Italian Cristobal Colon in 1492 also did not. You speak of freedom but the Spaniards in Cuba and Puerto Rico are actively supporting the Confederate States of America who want to maintain slavery in the United States. We are Dominicans that have lived as free men and women for several generations. Dominicans have freedom and honor in their hearts, and anything less than that will not be supported. As a representative of the military, I believe we will serve honorably but we should be careful to serve only those that are honorable."

Captain Hoffman laughed, but Lieutenant Dos Santos appeared angered by Julio Medina's statement. "We must serve honorably and not be traitors to our land. Dominicans will maintain their freedoms and we shall expand Dominican territory and improve our economy and stability. We have stopped any possible Haitian invasion and we now are able to improve our society, economically strengthen this nation, and bring order and prosperity to Dominican society."

Julio Medina replied, "We have fought together as rebels and as military men against Haitian brutality. I understand your anger at the Haitian Military, who killed and tortured your family, just as they tortured me and those I hold dear. You must remember these are not all Haitians, but the corrupt few who sought to take advantage of their power. I fully believe in our ability to de-feat any Haitian offensives in our land without the help of Spain or any foreign power. Our abilities on the field of battle have proven that we are able to fight off an invasion. As Dominicans, we must be gracious in victory and we must not hurt the weak and innocent or we will become the very worst of the people that you despise."

Angered, Lieutenant Dos Santos raised his voice as he warned Julio Medina of possible rebels living within the Dominican Republic and the commitment they had as soldiers. Julio became incensed, but he decided to quickly finish the conversation that had begun to turn into an argument and return home. Anibal and his would be informed about the argument between Julio and Lieutenant Dos Santos. Marco advised his sons to avoid the lieutenant, whom he believed was mentally troubled since the horrific violence the Dos Santos family experienced. It was a mental instability that Marco confirmed when Dos Santos previously returned to Santo Domingo with the rotting corpse of his sworn enemy Antoine Robespierre. What Lieutenant Dos Santos saw as a triumphant moment, Marco Medina and many others viewed this as deeply troubling and outside of their morals. Marco Medina also understood that Lieutenant Dos Santos' brutality and loyalty were used by the Spaniards to enact their darkest of deeds.

As the months passed, the growing rebel activity within the Dominican Republic concerned the Spaniards. Governor-General Pedro Santana was physically sick and lost his motivation to lead as his image of a great Dominican leader quickly faded and the pitiful reality that he was simply a puppet established itself in his mind. Governor-General Pedro Santana was unable to mitigate the growing concerns of Dominican rebellion. Soon, Governor-General Pedro Santana would be accused of inaction against the Dominican rebels and was subsequently removed from his position. On July twentieth, 1862, Felipe Ribero y Lemoine would assume the office of Governor-General of the Dominican Republic. The subsequent fall of Pedro Santana only encouraged the Dominican rebels as they began to plan a great war against the Spaniards.

CHAPTER 15

EL CHINO & THE IRISHMAN

(1862)

In April 1862, Anibal Hector Medina resigned from the Dominican Military. He completed his duty and sadly said goodbye to the young soldiers who looked up to him. Although he attempted to keep his motivations a secret, rumors spread regarding his anti-Santana views and how he felt about Spanish occupation, which polarized the Dominicans who were aware of them. Some soldiers privately sided with the Dominican rebels, ashamed to serve under the weakened Pedro Santana. This shame increased when Pedro Santana resigned from his role as a puppet for the Spaniards and during a time when all vestiges of Dominican sovereignty were non-existent. Under the leadership of Governor-General Felipe Ribero y Lemoine, Dominicans began to publicly denounce the Spaniards. Governor-General Domingo Dulce y Garay, First Marquis of Cas-tell-Florite of Cuba was an abolitionist, however he continued to send Spanish troops to the Dominican territory as he continued to follow the military orders of Queen Isabella II.

Anibal Medina continued to encourage his Uncle Julio to resign from the Dominican Military after he was moved to a Dominican reserve unit and then to the Cibao. Anibal suspected that the Spaniards desired to remove Julio Medina from his influential role in the southern faction of the Dominican Army to the north in order to restrict his influence. Santana's loyalists and pro-Spanish forces numbering roughly 12,000 would remain mostly in the southern Dominican Republic, where they solidified their loyalties to the Spanish government against any possible Dominican rebellion in the south. The Spaniards continued to arrive and remove Dominicans from positions of power throughout the Dominican Republic.

Valentino Xin grew frustrated with the abuse within the Dominican military as members who voiced concern over the unjust rule of the Spaniards were reprimanded and suspected as potential collaborators with rebels. Valentino Xin heard rumors of some of his friends punished for voicing anti-Spanish opinions, while other Dominicans apprehended civilians who spoke about various abuses perpetrated by the Spaniards. Tales of Dominican brutality against other Dominicans deeply disappointed Valentino Xin as he sunk into despair and pondered his role in the navy, which conflicted with his personal convictions.

Valentino Xin was dismayed when he discovered that Julio Medina was transferred to the Cibao region and placed in a Dominican reserve unit with reduced responsibilities. He believed if the Spaniards could easily remove a respected leader in the Dominican Army such as Julio Medina, then lower enlisted members such as himself were insignificant. Valentino thought they effectively sidelined Pedro Santana, so it would make sense the Dominican people would become second class citizens in their own country after they sacrificed their lives to establish independence. Valentino Xin observed an increasing number of Spanish merchant and war ships arriving from Cuba, Puerto Rico, and now Spain. Many believed that the proud Dominican people would soon be placed under the same conditions of servitude that the Cubans and Puerto Ricans were experiencing.

Valentino desired to speak to Julio or Anibal to understand Julio's plan of action against Spain. He believed he did not have enough support among his fellow sailors to rebel against the naval commanders and he requested to not renew his current obligations to the navy. Valentino traveled to Santo Domingo, where Anibal and Romina were making plans to move to San Cristóbal to their new farm and ranch (given to them by the Andujar family). Valentino Xin arrived at the Medina home one morning near noon to find Anibal, Romina, and Marco Medina, along with several other guests like Robert Grant. Anibal made several trips between Santo Domingo and San Cristobal, as he was establishing his new life after the military with his wife.

There were several merchants present, including a Jamaican-Irishman named Rory McDonnell. McDonnell was in a joyous mood as he announced that he'd recently married a young Jamaican woman named Abigail. Rory described her as a beautiful, slim woman with a deep brown complexion and dark, enchanting eyes. Rory celebrated the marriage of Anibal and Romina as the two men discussed their future lives as husbands.

Anibal Medina desired to focus on ranching and farming full-time; he wanted to extend his business into the central Dominican Republic, and with the help of Rory, possibly Jamaica. Anibal quickly improved his English and completed most of the books given to him by Romina. Rory admitted he was slightly nervous about the annexation of the Dominican Republic; he believed it would cause turmoil in the country—an anxiety he also experienced in Jamaica as the black Jamaicans were being mistreated by the English government. Rory was angry towards the European colonial powers, particularly England, which had terrorized his ancestors in Ireland and continued to treat the Irish badly.

Despite Valentino's disapproval of the ruling Ming minority under the Qing Dynasty, he was dismayed at the increasing aggression of European powers that desired to carve up China to extract her resources. Valentino spoke about the First Opium War in 1840, when the British Empire defeated China as Queen Victoria of England forcefully delivered opium to the population, causing drug addiction and the breakdown of the Chinese family and society. The First Opium War led to the Treaty of Nanking in 1842, which led to the period of the Unequal Treaties. Valentino stated that the Treaty of Nanking granted Great Britain indemnity and extraterritoriality to Britain, opened five treaty ports to foreign merchants and ceded his family's hometown of Hong Kong.

Valentino Xin stated that a trade imbalance was created as the demand for Chinese products increased in Great Britain for silk, porcelain, and tea as European silver flowed into China through the Canton System. The British East India Company attempted to stop the trade imbalance by increasing the flow of Indian opium into the Chinese coasts, paying middlemen to import and creating increasing numbers of opium addicts in China. The Daoguang Emperor rejected the proposals to legalize and tax opium by appointing Viceroy Lin Zexu, who banned the drug. Valentino's parents still had a copy of a previously published open letter (1893) from Viceroy Lin Zexu to Queen Victoria which read:

We find that your country is sixty or seventy thousand li from China, yet there are barbarian ships that strive to come here for trade for the purpose of making a great profit. The wealth of China is used to profit the barbarians. That is to say, the great profit made by barbarians is all taken from the rightful share of China. By what right do they then in return use the poisonous drug to injure the Chinese people? Even though the barbarians may not necessarily intend to do us harm, in coveting profit to an extreme, they have no regard for injuring others. Let us ask, where is your conscience?

Valentino Xin informed Anibal, Marco, and Rory that the most recent Second Opium War from 1856 to 1860 was between the Qing Dynasty and the combined power of the French and British Empire, leading to the defeat of the Qing Dynasty and the Treaty of Tientsin. The United States aided the imperial European powers against China, further weakening the Qing Dynasty. Various Chinese indentured servants and those who were free of their labor contracts who'd arrived in the Dominican Republic told the other Chinese of more treaties which opened up eleven additional ports in China—including Newchwang, Tamsui (or Taiwan), Hankou, and Nanjing—while foreigners were able to walk freely and sail their ships on the Yangtze River. China was also to pay France and Britain over six million taels of silver as they further opened China to Great Britain, France, Russia, and the United States.

After the end of slavery in the British West Indian territories, the West Indian sugar colonies attempted to replace forced labor with emancipated slaves and families from Ireland, Germany, Malta, and Portuguese from Madeira. Increasing numbers of Chinese indentured servants began arriving in Cuba in 1847 and later as Chinese society destabilized, and the British Empire started bringing Chinese contract laborers as thousands of Han people came from Hong Kong, Macau, and Taiwan to various Caribbean islands like Jamaica, Trinidad, and British Guyana. Like Valentino Xin, the

Chinese who arrived introduced their religion of Buddhism to their territories. European colonialism continued to bring people from across their global territories to the Caribbean. Through the information spread by merchants and diplomats, Valentino as well as other Dominicans also knew the British Empire had acquired India several years prior in 1858, now calling it the British Raj. In November 1844, British India mandated the transportation of Indian indentures to different territories—including Jamaica, Trinidad, and Demerara (now Guyana). The first ship named the Whitby carried Indian indentures to British Guyana on the fifth of May 1838; as of May 1845, Indian laborers arrived aboard the Fatel Rozack to Trinidad, and the ship Maidstone transporting Indian workers landed at Old Harbour Bay, Jamaica. Further Indian laborers would be transported to Trinidad in 1851 and Jamaica in 1860.

Rory McDonnell confirmed the arrival of the Chinese on the island of Jamaica, stating the new various groups of people could improve his business. The main issue was the political unrest found throughout the Caribbean islands and the potential for war in the Dominican Republic. Rory McDonnell spoke about the plight of the Irish under English domination and the movement for Home Rule (or Irish independence) from England. He told them about the Scottish hero William Wallace and his fight against King Edward I.

Ireland fell into a political conflict between the Catholics and Protestants during the Glorious Revolution. The controversial historical figure, Lord Protector Oliver Cromwell signed the execution of King Charles I and ruled as a dictator of the Republic of England (or the Commonwealth of England); he was greatly involved in the expulsion of the Irish people he deemed undesirables.

While a myriad arrived voluntarily as indentured servants from the fifteenth to eighteenth centuries, many of the Irish, English, Scots, and Welsh prisoners were transported for forced labor in the Caribbean to work off their term of punishment. Rory's parents both arrived from Ireland searching for a better life, but in Jamaica his father Dylan briefly joined a group of English pirates. He was killed by the Spaniards when Rory was a small child, and his Irish mother Aideen later died from a disease when he was a teenager, leaving the young Rory to learn how to survive on his own. As Irish Catholics, Rory's family was subjected to discrimination among the British Protestant population in Jamaica. Robert Grant confirmed it was the same for Irish in the United States and stated that some Irish sided with the slaves and were abolitionists like Daniel O'Connell. However, many Irish people in the United States stood against the black Americans and desired to maintain slavery.

The golden age of piracy was over, as it was not as lucrative as in generations past. Rory spoke about the age when pirates were very rich and formed their own society in cities like Navassa in the Bahamas and Port Royal Jamaica before the city was destroyed in a natural disaster in 1692. Rory talked about the English pirates that made a fortune attacking and stealing from the Hapsburg Spanish ships as well as those who later formed their societies free of all imperial powers. Rory spoke of Sir Francis Drake, William Kidd, Bartholomew Roberts (or Black Bart), Henry Every, the Irish female pirate Anne Bonny, Francois l'Olonnais, the infamous Edward Teach (or Blackbeard), and Calico Jack. Valentino Xin named Asian pirates like Chen Zuyi, who terrorized the Asian sea during the Ming Dynasty until his defeat at the hands of Admiral Zheng He, Cheung Po Tsai, and the female pirate Ching Shih. They all laughed as they agreed that the pirates were only stealing from larger empires who stole at a grander level.

Marco Medina interjected, "These European imperialists have been stealing from the natives of these lands for hundreds of years—particularly the Spaniards who have been terrorizing this island since 1492."

Marco commented that the Spaniards occupied many of the Caribbean islands and after the English took Jamaica, they named Port Royal as the capital until its destruction—when they chose the city of Santiago de la Vega as the capital and renamed it Spanish Town. The historical evidence of Spanish brutality and expansion in the Caribbean further encouraged Anibal Medina to believe the Spaniards would not regain their former territory of the Dominican Republic and that the Dominican people deserved independence once again. Romina insisted Anibal remained by her side, however she understood that raising a family under Spanish domination was not ideal. Her children should be born free in the Dominican Republic.

The men continued to discuss their plans for the future while Valentino Xin revealed he did not want to serve as a sailor in the Dominican Navy. Marco and Anibal persuaded him to remain in the navy until he completed his duties or until the outbreak of the war against Spain. Rory promised the Medina family financial and armed support, but he stated that he must stay with his young wife in Jamaica as the tensions between the Jamaican government and the black population worsened. The situation for the Medina family became grim when in late January of 1863, they received information that several Dominican generals and senior enlisted men had attempted to leave their positions in the military and forcefully move against Spanish bases. This would lead to the imprisonment and deaths of all of those involved—including Julio Medina, who was held captive and stripped of his rank.

Julio's family tried to contact him to no avail and the corrupt Spanish government would not release him, leading Anibal Medina to recruit other Dominicans against the annexation in a northern journey to the Cibao to locate his uncle. Anibal faced his sad mother and wife, who pleaded for him to remain in Santo Domingo until further information regarding Julio was revealed. However, Anibal continued to plan his trip to the Cibao in an attempt to gain information. After several days, he received support from his father and with tears in his eyes, Robert Grant advised Anibal to fight for his nation and live.

Grant freely stated, "You are Dominican just like me and my family, and the Dominican people have fought bravely against all invasions and lived as free men and women while my people in the United States remain enslaved. Do not allow the same fate for your people. Dominance by a foreign power is unbecoming for Dominicans because you have all tasted generations of freedom. To be subjugated would be even more of a disappointment for the Dominican people than people who have only known of slavery from birth."

Robert Grant planned to remain with the Medina family to defend them in case the Spaniards or Dominican Spanish loyalists desired to question them. Upon hearing this unsettling news, Valentino Xin promptly defected from the navy and joined Anibal Medina and his group as the Dominican rebellion grew and the Spaniards began to lose several battles against them.

CHAPTER 16

PRESIDENT ABRAHAM LINCOLN, THE EMANCIPATION PROCLAMATION, & THE AMERICAN CIVIL WAR

(1863)

Abraham Lincoln joined an anti-slavery party called the Republicans and his subsequent election caused a deepened polarization among the people of the United States. Previously, Lincoln had attempted to dissuade the possibility of a civil war with his House Divided Speech in 1858. He was a man of conviction who towered above most, but he secretly suffered mentally throughout his life. Nevertheless, Abraham Lincoln led his Republican party to victory through the most violent and politically divided times of the young United States. The southern states separated themselves from the Union, declaring President Jefferson Davis as the leader of the Confederate States of America, and moved their capital to Richmond, Virginia.

President Abraham Lincoln grew up on the western frontier in Kentucky and Indiana and was largely self-taught. As a young man, he served in the Illinois Militia and was promoted to captain during the Black Hawk War of 1832. Led by a Sauk war chief named Black Hawk, the war was against a coalition of Sauks, Meskwakis, and Kickapoos (called the British Band) that crossed the Mississippi River into Illinois from Iowa Indian territory. The Menominee and Dakota tribes supported the United States, resulting in a victory for their forces. The war would influence the policy of Indian Removal, which pressured native groups to sell their lands and move west of the Mississippi. Although he gained leadership experience while other notable figures served during the war—including Winfield Scott, Zachary Taylor, and Jefferson Davis—Abraham Lincoln never participated in combat. He would later become a lawyer and enter politics.

Twenty-three-year-old Captain Lincoln experienced scalped and mangled corpses and other atrocities committed during the battle of Stillman's Run. Captain Lincoln also assisted in the burials after the Battle of Kellog's Run and later wrote, "I remember just how those men looked as we rode up the little hill where their camp was. The red light of the morning sun was streaming upon them as they lay head towards us on the ground. And every man had a round red spot on top of his head, about as big as a dollar where the redskins had taken his scalp. It was frightful, but it was grotesque, and the red sunlight seemed to paint everything all over. I remember one man had on buckskin breeches."

Captain Abraham Lincoln stood at a height of roughly six feet four inches and was athletic and popular among the company he commanded.

His experiences as a captain and lawyer would influence him as president.

Early in Lincoln's political life in the House of Representatives, he supported the Whig candidate and war hero Zachary Taylor. However, after his election, President Taylor remembered Abraham Lincoln's disapproval of the Mexican American War and offered him the governorship of the Oregon Territory in order to remove him from the expanding state of Illinois. Abraham Lincoln declined, later reentering politics. He was also a pragmatist, stating that President Zachary Taylor was the only electable Whig candidate and that a vote for former President Martin Van Buren would divide the anti-slavery vote and possibly lead to the election of the Democrat Lew-is Cass. Born in Kinderhook, New York, President Martin Van Buren was known as Old Kinder-hook and would use the fad term O.K. (or okay), meaning "all correct" in his campaign for reelection to stand for "Old Kinderhook". The Boston abbreviation was used for other terms, including OFM (which meant "our first men"), GT (for "gone to Texas"), and SP (meaning "small potatoes"). Despite the popularization of the slang term O.K., President Martin Van Buren would lose his reelection campaign in 1840.

President Abraham Lincoln warned the south, stating, "In your hands, my dissatisfied fellow countrymen, and not in mine, is the momentous issue of civil war. The government will not assail you... You have no oath registered in Heaven to destroy the government, while I shall have the most solemn one to preserve, protect and defend it."

The Confederates struck first on April twelfth, 1861, firing on Union troops at Fort Sumter and forcing them to surrender. This was the start of successive Confederate victories against the Union as Abraham Lincoln attempted to turn the tide of the Civil War through capable Union generals. President Abraham Lincoln quickly expanded his powers, imposed a blockade on all the Confederate shipping ports, and after suspending habeas corpus, he would arrest all suspected Confederate sympathizers.

General John C. Frémont, the former Republic presidential nominee, declared martial law in Missouri, which dictated any citizens found bearing arms would be court-martialed and shot; slaves of those who aided the rebellion would be freed. John C. Frémont was a controversial figure who had previously led army expeditions that resulted in the deaths of many non-hostile indigenous villages. In 1846, Frémont and his army returned to California and pushed the formation of the California Battalion. His military advice led to the capture of Sonoma and the formation of the Bear Flag Republic. Frémont served as the Military Governor of the California Republic, which only lasted several days until it was incorporated into the United States on July ninth, 1846. As the current commander of the Union's Western Army, Frémont would issue an edict freeing all the slaves. However, his growing autocratic rule and decreasing communication with

Washington, D.C. led to his removal from his position by President Abraham Lincoln.

John Frémont would defeat the Confederates at Springfield, delivering the only Union victory against the Confederates in 1861. President Abraham Lincoln also expanded his power, taking control of Washington, D.C. and Maryland while seizing prominent figures—including a third of the Maryland State Assembly. Supreme Court Justice Roger Taney ruled it was unconstitutional for President Abraham Lincoln to suspend habeas corpus. Federal troops soon imprisoned various people, including a prominent Baltimore newspaper editor named Frank Key Howard (Francis Scott Key's grandson) after he criticized Lincoln in an editorial for ignoring the Supreme Court Chief Justice's ruling.

President Abraham Lincoln was also wary of European powers and their support for the Confederacy; he left most foreign policy decisions to Secretary of State William H. Seward. President Jefferson Davis of the Confederate States of America desired to establish a strong relationship with Great Britain through Cotton Diplomacy, erroneously believing Great Britain desired cotton from the Confederacy for its industries. However, Great Britain highly valued grain and not cotton, as Great Britain had large quantities of the latter. James M. Mason was sent to London as Confederate minister to Queen Victoria, and John Slidell was sent to Paris as minister to Napoleon III. Both Great Britain and France refrained from recognizing the Confederate States of America because recognition meant loss of American grain, exports, investments in securities, and a potential invasion of Canada and other North American colonies. Many of the British working class opposed the Confederacy, while only part of the British elite publicly supported the Confederate cause.

Relations between the Union and Great Britain soured in 1861 during the Trent Affair when a Union war ship under Captain Charles Wilkes (the USS San Jacinto) fired upon the Royal British merchant ship the Trent, which was carrying Confederate commissioners James M. Mason and John Slidell. The Trent was boarded, and the Confederates were imprisoned. The relationship between the Union and Great Britain improved, and the Trent Affair led to the Lyons-Seward Treaty of 1862—an agreement to prohibit the Atlantic slave trade by using the Union and Royal Navies.

President Abraham Lincoln desired to bring the Civil War to a quick end and General Winfield Scott devised the Anaconda Plan to win the war with as little bloodshed as possible, arguing that a Union blockade of the main ports would weaken the Confederate economy. However, the Civil War continued with confederate leader General Robert E. Lee winning several major battles against the Union. President Abraham Lincoln began to consider the emancipation of all slaves except in the border states within the Union. Freeing all slaves could deliver an advantage to the Union, and he would wait for a decisive victory before making the announcement. On the thirtieth of August 1862, at the Second Battle of Bull Run (or the Battle of Antietam), under the leadership of Union Major General, John Pope's Army of Virginia defeated General Robert E. Lee and the Confederacy.

The Battle of Antietam was the bloodiest one-day battle in United States history; it halted General Robert E. Lee and his Confederate forces from invading Maryland and his retreat towards Virginia. There were over 22,720 casualties in a single day—almost the same amount of losses that had shocked the nation at the two-day Battle of Shiloh five months earlier. Various generals died during this conflict, including Major Generals Joseph K. Mansfield, Israel B. Richardson, and Brigadier General Isaac P. Rodman on the Union side, and Brigadier Generals Lawrence O. Branch and William E. Starke on the Confederate side. Confederate Brigadier General George B. Anderson was shot in the ankle during the defense of the Bloody Lane, dying a few months later after an amputation.

President Abraham Lincoln traveled to the location of the Battle of Antietam as he prepared to proclaim the emancipation of the slaves. on New Year's Day 1863, Proclamation 95 (or the Emancipation Proclamation) was an Executive Order issued by President Abraham Lincoln which turned all slaves to free status within Confederate territory while keeping slavery in the bordering Union slaveholding states. President Abraham Lincoln understood that he did not have authority over the four slave states that were not in rebellion which included Kentucky, Maryland, Delaware, and Missouri, and so those states were not named in the Proclamation. The nearly 500,000 slaves in the aforementioned states were later freed by separate state and federal actions. Also specifically excluded by name were some regions that were controlled by the Union Army.

About three and a half million of the four million slaves were freed and encouraged to enlist in the Union Army. President Abraham Lincoln maintained conserving the Union, however after the Emancipation Proclamation, he saw an opportunity to combine both the efforts of the emancipation of the slaves and the Union war cause in a method that would result in a victory for the Union Army and the preservation of the United States. Runaway slaves who had escaped to the northern states and were held as "contraband" by the Union Army were immediately released. The Proclamation was denounced by Copperhead Democrats who opposed the war and advocated restoring the Union by allowing slavery. While running for the governorship of New York, Horatio Seymour stated, "A proposal for the butchery of women and children, for scenes of lust and rapine, and of arson and murder, which would invoke the interference of civilized Europe."

War Democrats who supported the Union saw the Emancipation Proclamation as a viable military tool against the South and worried that opposing it might demoralize troops in the Union Army. The rival Democratic factions would soon cause a split in the Democratic Party. General Ulysses S. Grant observed that the Proclamation, combined with the usage of black soldiers by the Union Army, profoundly angered the Confederacy. In a letter that General Grant wrote to President Abraham Lincoln, he stated, "The emancipation of the Negro is the heaviest blow yet given to the Confederacy." Some Confederates believed the Emancipation Proclamation would anger southerners and increase enlistment in the Confederate Army. The Confederacy fiercely protected its slavery economy (or its Peculiar Institution), which many Confederates believed was different from the harsh slave systems in other parts of the world.

President Abraham Lincoln also minimized the probability of direct English intervention in the Civil War as the momentum increased in favor of the Union. Thousands of black Americans celebrated on the day of the Emancipation Proclamation, including a young nine-year-old boy named Booker T. Washington, who stated, "As the great day drew nearer, there was more singing in the slave quarters than usual. It was bolder, had more ring, and lasted later into the night. Most of the verses of the plantation songs had some reference to freedom. ...Some man who seemed to be a stranger (a United States officer, I presume) made a little speech and then read a rather long paper—the Emancipation Proclamation, I think. After the reading, we were told that we were all free and could go when and where we pleased. My mother, who was standing by my side, leaned over and kissed her children, while tears of joy ran down her cheeks. She explained to us what it all meant, that this was the day for which she had been so long praying but fearing that she would never live to see."

President Abraham Lincoln suffered from bouts of depression which was exacerbated by the recent death of his son William Wallace. However, Lincoln remained focused on bringing victory for the Union and preserving the United States. The First Lady Mary Todd, who demonstrated increasingly erratic behavior and bad spending habits, contributed to Lincoln's commitment to his work in ending the Civil War. Frederick Douglass desired to meet the president to speak to him about the ills facing black people. Frederick Douglass' main concern was the abolition of slavery through the law. He previously disagreed with President Lincoln, writing in 1860, "Mr. Lincoln opens his address by announcing his complete loyalty to slavery in the slave States... He is not content with declaring that he has no lawful power to interfere with slavery in the States, but he also denies having the least "inclination" to interfere with slavery in the States. This denial of all feeling against slavery, at such a time and in such circumstances, is wholly discreditable to the head and heart of Mr. Lincoln. Aside from the inhuman coldness of the sentiment, it was a weak and inappropriate utterance."

Frederick Douglass quickly changed his view on President Abraham Lincoln after the Emancipation Proclamation and began recruiting black people to enlist in the Union Army, stating, "Once we let the black man get upon his person the brass letter, the U.S., and let him get an eagle on his button, and a musket on his shoulder and bullets in his pocket, there is no power on earth that can deny that he has earned the right to citizenship."

However, problems emerged between President Abraham Lincoln and Frederick Douglass once again as the segregated black Union soldiers experienced inequality—including unfair pay with white Union soldiers receiving thirteen dollars a month with no deductions, while black soldiers received only ten dollars per month, from which three dollars were held back as a clothing deduction, which yielded a net pay of only seven dollars. Frederick Douglass also spoke against how black Union soldiers were treated during war and the addition of the Confederate policy, as decreed by Jefferson Davis and the Southern Congress, which treated captured black soldiers not as prisoners of war, but as insurrectionary runaways to be re-enslaved or even executed.

Frederick Douglass disagreed with other abolitionists because he did not fully support John Brown's rebellion and emancipation by force. However, his support among abolitionists increased during the Civil War. On the morning of August tenth, 1863, Douglass, accompanied by Kansas Republican Senator Samuel C. Pomeroy, went first to the War Department to meet with Secretary of War Edwin M. Stanton, who offered Douglass a commission as an army officer to aid his efforts in recruiting black soldiers. Frederick Douglass witnessed a long line to meet the president. Thinking he would wait a half a day, to his surprise, he was asked to see the leader of the United States within two minutes. When Frederick Douglass approached President Abraham Lincoln, he began to introduce himself, but the President stopped him and smiled, stating, "You need not tell me who you are, Mr. Douglass; I know who you are; Mr. Seward has told me all about you."

Frederick Douglas spoke to President Lincoln about the unequal treatment of black Union soldiers, the conditions of black people in society, and the treatment of black prisoners of war. The meeting went well as the two men discussed a multitude of issues, and President Lincoln promised that he would make equal pay for black and white Union soldiers. However, he stated that these issues would take some time as he gradually persuaded Northerners to accept black Union soldiers. President Lincoln also signed General Order 233, stating that, "For every soldier of the United States killed in violation of the laws of war, a rebel soldier shall be executed; and for each Union soldier enslaved by the enemy or sold into slavery, a rebel soldier shall be placed at hard labor on the public works and continued at such labor until the other shall be released and receive the treatment due to a prisoner of war." Frederick Douglass and President Abraham Lincoln had admiration for one another despite their differences, and Douglass would meet with Lincoln several more times while resuming his duties to recruit black Americans for the Union.

President Abraham Lincoln also had to deal with an Irish riot in Lower Manhattan in New York City. After new laws passed by Congress that year to draft men to fight in the ongoing American Civil War, many working class Irish men and men of Irish descent resented that wealthier men could afford to pay a $300 commutation fee to hire a substitute and were spared from the draft. The Irish were also angry towards black people competing for work and soon it turned into a racial riot as the Irish attacked black communities, resulting in the deaths of over 120 black people. After New York Police could not subdue the mobs, President Abraham Lincoln diverted several regiments of militia and volunteer troops after the Battle of Gettysburg to control the city. Angry crowds ransacked or destroyed numerous public buildings, including two protestant churches, various abolitionist, black sympathizer, and black homes, and the Colored Orphan Asylum at 44th Street and Fifth Avenue, which was burned to the ground. After three days, what came to be known as the New York City Draft Riots were stopped as President Abraham Lincoln quickly returned his focus to the Civil War.

The Confederacy was beginning to weaken as the months progressed with some southerners disassociating themselves from Confederate ideology and deserting from the Confederate Army. Many poor whites saw the war as southerners being sacrificed in the battle to conserve wealthy slave owners and the political elite. A man named Newton Knight defected from the Confederate Army after the passage of the Twenty Negro Law, allowing large plantation owners to avoid military service if they owned twenty slaves or more (with an additional family exempted from service for each additional twenty slaves). Newton Knight was also informed that his brother-in-law Morgan was abusing Knight's children. In October 1862, Newton Knight went AWOL. After his imprisonment and abuse, he began to actively fight against the Confederate Army. Newton Knight gained the following of other white southerners, including escaped black people who opposed Confederate classism and slavery. While living in Jones County of Mississippi, Knight would establish the Free State of Jones and the Knight Company would engage in skirmishes with Confederate forces. Newton Knight would lead multiple raids, with one skirmish taking place on December twenty third 1863 at the home of Sally Parker (a Knight Company supporter). It left one Confederate soldier dead and two badly wounded.

Other southern slaves would escape from the southern states and join the Union Army. Robert Smalls freed himself along with his family and several others and escaped by commandeering a Confederate transport ship (the CSS Planter) in Charleston harbor on May thirteenth, 1862. He sailed it from Confederate-controlled waters to the U.S. blockade and at twenty-three years old, Robert Smalls became a hero in the north and participated in various naval battles for the Union. In June 1863, David Hunter was replaced as commander of the Department of the South by Quincy Adams Gillmore. With Gillmore's arrival, Smalls was transferred to the quartermaster's department. Robert Smalls was the pilot of the USS Isaac Smith, and later was put in charge of the Light House Inlet as a pilot. On December first, 1863, Smalls was piloting the Planter under Captain James Nickerson on Folly Island Creek when Confederate batteries at Secessionville opened. Nickerson fled the pilothouse for the coalbunker, and Smalls refused to surrender, fearing that the black crewmen would not be treated as prisoners of war and might face execution. Smalls bravely entered the pilothouse and took command of the boat, steering her to safety. For this, he was reportedly promoted by Gillmore and made the acting captain of the Planter. Robert Smalls was encouraged to enter political life as a Republican.

In July 1863, the Gettysburg Campaign was the largest battle between the Union and Confederate forces, ending in a victory for the Union and the defeat and subsequent retreat of General Robert E. Lee and his Confederate forces (General Robert E. Lee suffered over 27,000 casualties). The Confederacy continued to lose battles as President Jefferson Davis proved to be a weak leader. President Jefferson Davis could not lead the Confederacy with the same authority as President Abraham Lincoln led the Union, and Davis continuously feuded with Confederate governors while giving preferential treatment to his friends. President Davis could not work with those who disagreed with him, particularly as the Confederate Army began losing repeated engagements and civil matters became less of a priority for him.

President Abraham Lincoln delivered the Gettysburg Address at the dedication of the Soldiers' National Cemetery in Gettysburg, Pennsylvania, on the afternoon of Thursday, November nineteenth, 1863. Lincoln spoke about his desires to preserve the Union and described the Civil War as a struggle not just for the Union, but also for the principle of human equality. The speech was a resounding success and it emboldened the Union Army as President Abraham Lincoln gathered increasing support. He desired to bring an end to the Civil War and rebuild the United States., as well as to put an end to the encroaching European powers in the Caribbean and Latin America.

With the help of the hacendados (or the conservative elite of Mexico), Emperor Napoleon III of France successfully placed his younger brother as Emperor Maximillian I of Mexico, bringing Hapsburg rule once again to

Mexico. Union leaders began plans to support the indigenous working-class Mexican leader Benito Pablo Juárez García against Emperor Maximillian I. The Empire of Brazil was stable, and their military was strong under the reign of Emperor Dom Pedro II and remained strong after their victory in the Platine War—although they were on the verge of warfare once again with their Latin American neighbors.

Though the Mexicans defeated the French at the Battle of Puebla on May fifth, 1862, they were not able to win the war as the Second Mexican Empire was established in 1863. In the Caribbean, the Union was surrounded by the English Caribbean islands and the Spanish islands of Cuba and Puerto Rico, which supported the Confederacy while Haiti helped the Union forces. The Haitian leader President Fabre Geffrard increased his autocratic rule while executing his political rivals and criminals.

In 1863, a six-year-old girl was killed by Voodoo practitioners in a gruesome fashion. Geffrard ordered a deep investigation and a public execution was to be held in February of 1864 after four men and four women were convicted for abducting, murdering, and cannibalizing a twelve-year-old girl. This case became the famous Affaire de Bizoton and it negatively impacted the Voodoo religion within Haiti, the Dominican Republic, and around the world. As President Fabre Geffrard continued to remove what he viewed as some of the more backward practices of Voodoo, he continued to face rebellions against his leadership. After the betrayal of Aimé Legros by his own rebel troops and his execution, other Haitian rebel groups plotted against President Fabre Geffrard. The leader obeyed the Spanish demands of non-interference in the Dominican Republic, which only served to anger the Haitians. As the months passed, Dominican rebel activities occurred against the Spaniards. The Dominican and Spanish War was about to begin.

CHAPTER 17

EL GRITO DE CAPOTILLO & THE PROVISIONAL DOMINICAN GOVERNMENT OF PRESIDENT JOSÉ ANTONIO SALCEDO

(1863)

In early February of 1863, in the southwestern town of Neiba, a group of over fifty Dominican rebels attempted the assault of the local military commander, but it was quickly put to an end. The attack was part of a larger plot against the Spaniards, directed by Dominican General Santiago Rodriguez located in the town of Sabaneta. The new rebellion included the entire rebel population of the Cibao and was to begin on February twenty-seventh, the anniversary of the Dominican Republic. On February twenty-first, the plan was discovered by Spanish authorities, but the Spaniards were repelled by Dominican rebels and forced to retreat. The Spaniards recuperated and stopped the Dominicans who fled westward, where they began to plan a large-scale attack on the Spaniards from their current base of Dajabón. The Spaniards frantically searched for Dominican rebel leaders while abusing Dominicans and forcefully removing Haitians.

Anibal Hector Medina arrived at the Cibao in early July 1863 along with several other Dominicans—including Valentino Xin—in search of his Uncle Julio. Anibal rode north on horseback as he carefully gathered intelligence. Dominican rebel activity had increased as Dominicans publicly demanded the return their sovereignty. Rumors spread regarding the defection of various prominent generals in favor of the rebel cause for Dominican restoration. Rebel groups established secret gatherings and housed other Dominicans sympathetic to the rebellion. Anibal inquired about the location of his uncle and was informed that his group was being held in the city of Santiago de los Caballeros. This would be the first time Anibal Medina would travel there, and he would need the help of Dominican rebel groups to locate the secret location of the prisoners.

El Cibao (or the Cibao) is named after the Taino word Cibao, meaning, "rocky land". The city of Santiago de los Caballeros (or Saint James of the Knights) refers to the Hidalgos de la Isabela, a group of knights who had come from La Isabela city to stay in Santiago. The city is also called Santiago *de los treinta Caballeros*, or Saint James of the Thirty Knights. Upon their return to Spain, the Knights lodged a formal complaint before the king stating that their horses had been unfairly commissioned as beasts of burden and their weapons had been appropriated by the Columbus brothers (Diego and Bartolomeo Colon). The original colony was founded in Jacagua in 1495 but the settlement was later destroyed by an earthquake it was moved to its current location in 1506. An earthquake in 1562 forced the survivors to settle on land belonging to Petronila Jáquez of Minaya, adjacent to the Yaque del Norte.

After months of traveling mostly at night and living in rebel homes attempting to not arouse the suspicions of paranoid Spanish officials, Anibal and Valentino arrived at the city of Santiago de los Caballeros in June of 1863. Anibal and his party were provided with armaments and supplies by Andujar and other Dominican rebels. Anibal was amazed at the beauty of Santiago and the fertile lands of the Cibao, out of which substantial wealth was cultivated for the Dominican people. Throughout his travels, he had witnessed the full majesty of the Cordillera Central, which ended in San Cristobal in the south and formed the highest mountain range in the Caribbean. Anibal believed that the Cordillera Central could be an ideal location to launch guerrilla attacks on the Spaniards in the upcoming war. The people of the Cibao were a wide mixture originating from Spain, the Canary Islands, West Africa, and contained small populations from East Asia and other European states like France and Germany. As the Caste system was relieved, most of these various groups mixed, creating the Dominican people of the Cibao.

Anibal and Valentino were welcomed in the home of a liberal Sephardic Jewish-Dominican man named Moisés Aponte and his wife Josefina while some of the other Dominican rebels stayed at nearby homes that also supported the rebellion. Josefina Aponte was a slender woman a few years younger than Moisés, who was graceful with dark brown skin and white hair that majestically flowed to her hips. Josefina was a Christian woman who respected her husband's Jewish faith, and they shared a long, mutually respectful relationship. Josefina and Moisés Aponte were against Pedro Santana's annexation policy and supported the Dominican rebels. Moisés Aponte received substantial intelligence regarding the imprisoned Dominican Military men who spoke out against the Spaniards. He was over seventy years old and his family was among the Jewish people who left Spain during the 1700s. Moisés Aponte had a large tobacco field and he sold to the European market—predominantly Germany. Moisés Aponte was worried about the increasing Spanish discrimination against the majority mixed population, their killings, and abuses of masons, Muslims, Jews, and Protestants. The abuse by the Spaniards led him to support the Dominican rebellion as he desired the return of Dominican autonomy and the tolerance and peace he enjoyed during the previous independence of the Dominican Republic.

Moisés Aponte informed Anibal that the Sephardic Jews were named for the Hebrew word Sefaraddim, which were a Jewish ethnic group from Spain and the Iberian Peninsula. The Jewish people in Spain suffered after the Reconquista (or The Reconquest) in 1492 when the Catholic Monarchs, Ferdinand, and Isabella completed the conquest of Granada. The Sephardic Jews were subsequently expelled from Spain by the Alhambra Decree (or the Edict of Expulsion), which ordered the expulsion of practicing Jews from the Kingdoms of Castile and Aragon and its territories and possessions by July thirty-first of 1492. Many conversos (Jews) who converted to Christianity were threatened to remain New Christians and prohibited from reverting to Judaism while many others were exiled. A converso who secretly practiced Judaism was called a *judaizante* (or a Judaizer) as well as a *marrano* (or swine). Meanwhile, Muslims who converted to Catholicism were called Moriscos, and although they practiced Catholicism, they were all subject to expulsion.

The Jewish people traveled to Northern Africa—Algeria and Morocco—and the Ottoman Empire. Sultan Bayezid II sent out the Ottoman Navy under the command of Admiral Kemal Reis to Spain in 1492 to evacuate Jews and Muslims safely to Ottoman lands. Sultan Bayezid II granted the refugees permission to become citizens while ridiculing the conduct of King Ferdinand II of Aragon and Queen Isabella I of Castile for expelling a class of people that were beneficial as subjects in Spanish society. Sultan Bayezid II also issued a *firman* (a royal mandate) that Spanish refugees within Ottoman territories should be welcomed and accepted. Chief Rabbi Moses Elijah Capali influenced Sultan Bayezid II to help the Jewish refugees, and Moisés Aponte made sure that Anibal and Valentino understood that he was named after him as opposed to the prophet Moses of the Bible.

Moisés Aponte also informed Anibal that many Jews escaped before 1492 to a location controlled by the Ottoman Empire in the Near East that encompassed Anatolia, the Levant and Egypt, and the Balkans in Southeastern Europe. Moisés Aponte's family mostly fled to various places in what is now called the Americas towards places in the Caribbean like Curacao, the United States, and the Dominican Republic. Most of Moisés Aponte's children now lived in New York City and Florida, while his youngest son David remained in the Dominican Republic to take over the family business. As the men continued to speak, a light rain began to fall and Moisés Aponte gave them rum and cigars. Anibal rarely smoked, but to calm his anxiety and enjoy the conversation, he accepted the cigar.

Moisés Aponte continued, "The Jewish people have suffered throughout our history— at the hands of many including the Babylonians, Romans, and the English who also had an Edict of Expulsion issued by King Edward I of England in 1290, expelling all Jews. Although some of the earliest Jews who first arrived with Cristóbal Colón participated in the horrors that the Spaniards committed on the Tainos of this land, many of the Jews—including my family—always worked for the safety of all Dominican people and participated alongside patriots to maintain Dominican sovereignty and peace. This is the reason I support the Dominican rebels against the Spaniards. Despite some economic and political issues, my family and I were allowed to practice our religion freely. Although in my old age I cannot fight, I will provide material and financial support to help restore the Dominican Republic once again; we are all Dominicans fighting for a common cause."

As the sun began to set, Anibal questioned Moisés Aponte regarding the status of his Uncle Julio and the others and whether there were any plans to liberate them. To the relief and disappointment of Anibal, his Uncle Julio was still alive. However, he was informed that some of the other military men were executed while Julio was transported north to Puerto Plata, where the Spaniards advised that he be transferred to Cuba so as not to arouse anger from the Dominican population. Moisés Aponte told Anibal and Valentino that General Santiago Rodriguez crossed into Haitian territory and was receiving funding and arms from Haitian supporters while other rebel groups were currently planning additional attacks on Spanish installations. When Anibal Medina spoke about Lieutenant Dos Santos, Moisés informed him that he was recently promoted to the rank of captain and that Captain Dos Santos had become even more brutal than the Spaniards.

Moisés stated, "That man—if I can call Captain Dos Santos a man—represents the most horrendous of Dominicans. A Dominican who only serves himself and betrays his own people, believing an erroneous ideology only to excuse and manifest the darkest thoughts of his broken soul."

Moisés enlightened Anibal and Valentino with detailed accounts of Captain Dos Santos killing and torturing with reckless abandon, molesting innocent women in the countryside, probably leaving behind bastard children.

Moisés Aponte promised he would send word to various rebel groups regarding Anibal's advance towards Puerto Plata. He also gathered financial support from Dominicans of all racial backgrounds—including weapons from Dominican-German families like Wagner and Schmidt, which greatly put Anibal's mind at ease as Dominicans of all backgrounds were supporting the rebellion. Moisés Aponte's wife prepared a meal of rice and beans with cow tail for her guests before they departed, wishing them good luck.

Anibal, Valentino, and their party were reinforced with more Dominican rebels as they approached the outskirts of the city of Puerto Plata. The Dominicans rode mostly at night as they interacted with other rebel groups, one of which revealing the location of Julio Medina. They encouraged Anibal to attack the prison at night and catch the Spaniards off guard. As Anibal pre-pared for the attack on one hot, rainy night in late July, he realized some of the Dominican prisoners had attacked their guards and decided to take the initiative. The Spaniards turned to fire but were quickly overwhelmed by Anibal and the Dominican rebels. Anibal and Valentino fought ferociously as they believed Captain Dos Santos was somewhere among the Spaniards. The battle continued all night, aided by a young black Dominican named Facundo who fought with immense bravery and intelligence. After the prison burned to the ground, over fifty Spanish soldiers lay dead along with ten Dominicans who sided with the Spaniards and a few Spanish soldiers who were captured. In fear for his life, one of the Spaniards stated that Captain Dos Santos was nearby but possibly fled back towards Santiago de los Caballeros.

Anibal and the rebels searched the bodies of the Dominican prisoners and gathered all Spanish Military documents. Although they were excited over their victory, sadness soon overwhelmed Anibal as he discovered the body of his Uncle Julio, dead with a gunshot wound to the back of the head. He had been executed and was not able to join the initial attack on the Spaniards with the other prisoners. Grief overwhelmed Anibal as he held the body of his uncle while tears rapidly flowed down his face. Valentino attempted to console Anibal, who was devastated. Anibal could not remain in Puerto Plata and he and the other rebels carried the body of Julio Medina towards Santa Cristobal and the house of Moisés Aponte.

As Anibal and his men carried Julio's body and escaped Puerto Plata, the Spanish government stated that Dominican rebels attacked the prison and the prisoners died while attacking the guards. It was an obvious lie by the Spanish government in an effort to maintain their weakening grasp on the Dominican people. However, Dominican public opinion was mostly anti-Spaniard, and the incident in Puerto Plata would only worsen their image. When Anibal finally reached the home of Moisés Aponte, his sadness was replaced by intense indignation. Facundo also aided Anibal in connecting with rebel groups as August approached, and he revealed that his parents and family were murdered by the Spaniards after his father Solomon retaliated. The Spaniards abused the women in his family and soon executed them in secret while he was able to escape certain death. Anibal revealed his deep anger for the Spaniards and the Dominicans who had aided them as well as his desire to avenge his uncle's execution. Anibal longed to bring his uncle's body to Santo Domingo, but he decided to leave him near Moisés Aponte's home as it appeared the war against the Spaniards would begin.

On August sixteenth, 1863, a new group under the leadership of Santiago Rodríguez made a daring raid starting from the city of Dajabon, raising the Dominican flag on Capotillo hill. The group included Santiago Rodríguez, Captain Eugenio Belliard, Segundo Rivas, Alejandro Bueno, Pablo Reyes, Juan de la Mata Monción, José Angulo, San Mézquita, Tomás de Aquilino Rodríguez, José Cabrera, Sotero Blan, Benito Monción, and Juan de la Cruz Alvarez. El Grito de Capotillo was declared, and quickly other rebel groups throughout the northern Dominican Republic organized into large-scale warfare. Throughout the nations, they sprang up against the Spaniards and began the Spanish Dominican War.

Anibal, Valentino Xin, and Facundo joined a major Dominican rebel group, and Valentino Xin was informed that his older cousin Pancho El Chino arrived at the town of San Ignacio de Sabaneta in Santiago. Pancho El Chino and a large Dominican force were gathering under the leadership of General Gregorio Luperón, who had arrived from Monte Cristi. The battle, unfortunately, resulted in a Spanish victory as General Gregorio Luperón and his forces retreated to the mountains of La Vega to regroup and plan additional attacks. Anibal and Valentino discussed whether to leave for La Vega or report to other regions that were ready to engage the Spaniards. Valentino Xin made the decision to travel to La Vega to assist his cousin and serve under General Gregorio Luperón. Within days, Dominican officers encouraged rebels to report to a large rebel force gathering to attack the Spaniards at their installation Fortaleza San Luis.

Anibal and Facundo soon joined a large Dominican rebel alliance which swelled to over 6,000 men from all over Santiago. As a united front, they descended upon Fortaleza San Luis (or Fort San Luis) near the Yaque del Norte River, which was held by over 800 Spaniards. The Spaniards previously sent four infantries under the command of Colonel Ramon de Portal y San-to Domingo to occupy Fort San Luis, and Anibal was fueled by anger and believed that Captain Dos Santos might be there. The Dominicans attacked the fort with extreme force, fighting with passion against the overwhelmed enemy. Close to four hundred Spaniards attempted to fire upon the Dominicans, however the Spaniards were quickly surrounded and vicious hand to hand combat ensued. Anibal Medina cut down several Spaniards with his sabre as he rode his horse into the Spanish lines. He turned around to give himself some distance and began firing, hitting the Spaniards in their legs, torsos, arms, and chests. The screams of agony and gunfire were so loud that it could seemingly be could be heard miles away. The Spaniards attempted to send messengers to get reinforcements, but many of them were cut down. Facundo remained close to Anibal as they took turns successfully firing into the Spanish lines and the fight raged on throughout the day.

The Spaniards fought as best they could before they began to retreat towards Fort San Luis, which was soon surrounded by Dominican forces as the Spaniards defended it from within. Various Dominican leaders including General Gaspar Polanco Borbón joined the attack. Fort San Luis had a row of huts sheltered with yagua palm leaves which soon caught fire and encouraged General Gaspar Polanco to set fire around Fort San Luis as he declared a war of *sangre y fuego* (or blood and fire) to capture Fort San Luis and Santiago. The fires spread to the surrounding town and devastating smoke and flames engulfed its borders as the Spaniards continued to defend the fort. Dominican revolutionaries from La Vega, Moca, Puerto Plata, San Francisco de Macoris, and Cotui prepared to send reinforcements to counter the Spanish reinforcements arriving in Santiago. Anibal, Facundo, and hundreds of Dominican rebels were tasked with eliminating the arriving Spanish troops with heavy gunfire as Fort San Luis continued to be encircled.

On September thirteenth, 1863, an armistice was signed whereby the remaining Spaniards were allowed to leave the city of Santiago while some were held for questioning. Fort San Luis was now occupied by Dominican rebel forces, which began spreading in larger operations to attack, capture, and defend Santiago and the surrounding towns. However, General Gaspar Polanco followed the defeated Spaniards towards the towns of Carril, and Limón caused numerous Spanish casualties as he pursued them towards Puerto Plata. There, he continued to engage the Spaniards in vicious battle, weakening Spanish morale as they took massive losses in the field of battle.

On September fourteenth, 1863, General José Antonio Salcedo y Ramírez established a Provisional Dominican Government, declaring himself as president of the Dominican Republic. President José Antonio Salcedo y Ramírez and Vice President Benigno Filomeno de Rojas now led the Provisional Dominican government. Pedro Santana was publicly denounced as a despot and a traitor to the Dominican Republic, which fueled the passions of the rebels. To the elation of most Dominicans who sought to end the recent annexation, the Spanish government under Captain-General Felipe Ribero y Lemoyne was declared an unlawful occupation of the Dominican Republic. Provisional President José Antonio Salcedo benefited from the capable leadership of his supporters, including a young man named Ulises Hilarión Heureaux Leibert.

President José Antonio Salcedo or Pepillo was born in Madrid, Spain from Creole parents of Spanish heritage who moved from Santo Domingo to Spain in the year 1815. Dominican leader General Gaspar Polanco was against the leadership of General José Antonio Salcedo and his military decisions, which he saw as misguided and foolish—including his decision to grant an armistice to the remaining Spaniards. General Gaspar Polanco was a brave, proud man who served with distinction, and his older brother (Juan Antonio Polanco) served alongside Benito Monción and Pedro Antonio Pimental as they pursued the defeated Spanish leader Brigadier General Manuel Buceta at the battle of Capotillo in August 1863. General Gaspar Polanco continued to successfully lead his rebel army against the Spaniards while secretly planning to remove President José Antonio Salcedo as he intended to establish a stronger rebel leadership. Despite their differences, both men concentrated their forces to attack the Spaniards. The fires raged in Santiago as open battles against the Spaniards continued while the Dominicans began to force them into a temporary retreat from several towns. The Spaniards were able to maintain control of Azua, El Seibo, Hato Mayor, and Higüey, but it was weakened by constant Dominican guerilla attacks. The Spaniards could not fully control these towns except for a pass into the Cibao called El Sillon de la Viuda. The Dominican Provisional Army now sent rebels to block the path of Spanish reinforcements there as well.

Spain appointed Carlos de Vargas Machuca y Cerveto as Captain-General, but he was unable to defeat the Dominican rebels. Dysentery, Malaria, and frequent vomiting plagued the Spanish troops, resulting in over 1,000 deaths each month. This threatened to break the Spanish morale as the war continued. Thousands of sick and wounded Spanish troops were transported to the Spanish colonies of Cuba and Puerto Rico while the Spaniards began to send more reinforcements from Cuba and Puerto Rico. Anibal and Facundo remained in the Cibao along with Facundo for several months until late November of 1863, when Anibal requested that he return to Santo Domingo to protect his family and continue his fight in the southern rebellion. Anibal sent a message to Valentino Xin that if he so desired, he should join him in the south where General Pedro Santana was located. Anibal believed that Captain Dos Santos might have joined the forces of General Santana. Promising to return to Santiago to retrieve the body of his Uncle Julio after the war was over, Anibal, Facundo, and other Dominicans rode towards Santo Domingo to join the southern Dominican rebellion.

CHAPTER 18

THE DOMINICAN WAR OF RESTORATION

(1864)

Anibal Hector Medina returned to the city of Santo Domingo, where he promptly joined a local Dominican rebel unit. Due to his reputation as a good leader, Anibal was appointed to the rank of sergeant once again. To his relief, he found Romina and his family safe. Marco Medina also stated that the German-Dominican Ricardo Hoffmann was in Santo Domingo and was recently appointed colonel. Also, Captain Dos Santos and Colonel Ricardo Hoffmann had arrived at the Medina home in October of 1863 and proceeded to harass them, accusing the family of being rebel sympathizers and questioning them about Anibal's whereabouts. Marco sadly stated that the Saint-Lot family were apprehended by Captain Dos Santos and Dominicans allied with Spain and accused of being Haitian plotters against the government. Raymond Saint-Lot, who had retaliated against the Spaniards and their allies, was brutally beaten by Captain Dos Santos personally and would have been killed if it not for various Dominican families who pleaded for their safety and spoke against the claims of Captain Dos Santos. Marco Medina and other Dominicans stated that the Saint-Lot family were of utmost moral character and never participated in any rebel activities against General Pedro Santana and the local southern Spanish authorities. After several weeks, Raymond Saint-Lot was released to his family. However, Marco stated that he feared Captain Dos Santos would seek revenge against the Saint-Lot family, the Medina family, and any others he believed were rebel sympathizers.

Anibal informed his family regarding the death of Julio Medina, and he told his widow Paulina, who was devastated by the news. Marco was deeply saddened by the loss of his brother, and he worried about the repercussions that son and family would suffer at the hands of the vengeful Captain Dos Santos. The Medina family were forced to mourn in secret so as not to arouse further suspicion from the Spanish authorities and the conservative Dominicans who remained loyal to Spain. It was an immensely torturous experience for the Medina family as they mourned, however it served to instill a raging anger and determination within Anibal, who sought to return the honor of his family and the independence and respect for the Dominican people.

Anibal informed his father about his contributions to the defeat of the Spaniards at Fort San Luis as well as the Spanish defeat at Santiago. He also revealed his participation in the war and the evidence that he had recovered proving Captain Dos Santos was part of the Dominican officers who colluded with the Spaniards in the capture and imprisonment of Dominican

Military members—including Julio Medina. The captain had recommended imprisonment and torture as well as the possibility of extradition of Julio Medina to the authorities in Cuba.

Anibal feared for the safety of his wife and family and encouraged his father to seek shelter in one of the many homes of the Andujars. Anibal also sought to encourage his father-in-law Robert Grant to join his family in safety along with his wife while he patrolled Santo Domingo and San Cristobal with the increasing rebel forces in the south. Soon, Captain Dos Santos would discover Anibal Medina's involvement in the rebellion, and he would retaliate against his family. Anibal would begin to engage the forces of General Pedro Santana in the south as the Dominican revolutionary forces continued to fight the Spaniards with great leadership—including Dominican commanders Gaspar Polanco, Gregorio Luperón, Santiago Rodríguez, Benito Monion, Pedro Antonio Pimentel, and the young leader Ulises Espaillat. General Gregorio Luperón was highly popular and attracted the friendship of non-Dominican nationalists like the Puerto Rican nationalist Dr. Ramón Emeterio Betances. The Dominican rebels would receive support from Haitians, Cubans, Puerto Ricans, and other nationalists who were against European hegemony in the Caribbean. The Spaniards countered with Lieutenant-General José de la Gándara y Navarro. The Military Governor, Commander-in-Chief, and now Lieutenant-General José de la Gándara y Navarro of the province of Santiago de Cuba dispatched Spanish troops aboard the ship the Isabella II towards Puerto Plata in 1863. Now he advanced and attempted to control Santo Domingo and San Cristobal.

Anibal and Facundo continued to lead their rebel groups in the outskirts of Santo Domingo against a resurgent Spanish force. The fighting was vicious, but it encouraged Dominicans to continue joining the rebellion and inspired Puerto Rican and Cuban nationalists living among the Dominican people to fight as well as fight for the independence of Cuba and Puerto Rico from the Spanish Empire. Anibal understood the importance of aid from Cuban and Puerto Rican nationalists who were unable to declare independence in their respective islands. Cuba once attempted to follow the example of Haiti and establish their own Black Republic in 1844, but their plan failed. Puerto Ricans were also inspired by the ideas of Simón Bolívar, who sought the liberation of Latin America from Spain and the creation of a Federation of Latin America Nations. Brigadier General Antonio Valero de Bernabé was also known as the Liberator from Puerto Rico. He had trained in the Spanish Military and previously fought to liberate Spain and expel Napoleon Bonaparte. Later, General Antonio Valero de Bernabé would serve Simón Bolivar against the Spaniards in Colombia, Peru, and Panama and would die in 1863. The Spaniards attempted to maintain control of Cuba, however instability increased as indentured Chinese servants at times would engage in conflict with black Cuban slaves as well as with the Spaniards—which coincided with growing Chinese suicide rates. To counter the Spaniards, who had experienced similar turmoil in the islands of Cuba and Puerto Rico, the Spanish Empire brought increasing numbers of poor Spanish laborers to Cuba and Puerto Rico, attempting to mitigate the rebellious spirit in their lands. Despite the Spaniards' attempts to control Cuba and Puerto Rico, nationalism and Latin American unity continued to be strong as the Puerto Ricans and Cubans were encouraged by the Spanish and Dominican War.

Anibal traveled to the outskirts of Santo Domingo, where he joined a large rebel group which participated in guerrilla raids against the Spaniards and attempted to cut off the supply lines into Santo Domingo. The clashes were mostly successful, with Anibal and Facundo participating in devastating attacks upon the forces of General Pedro Santana as they lost morale and they were now regarded as traitors to the Dominican people. As the weeks continued, the demoralized General Pedro Santana and his army fell into disarray as communications between himself and his superiors quickly broke down. Anibal and the Dominican rebels increased their attacks as the Spaniards sent additional troops towards Santo Domingo.

In March 1864, General Pedro Santana received orders from the Governor of Santo Domingo (General Vargas) to concentrate his forces in Santo Domingo in compliance with the orders from Madrid, Spain. General Pedro Santana rebuked the orders and was admonished by his Spanish superiors. General José de la Gandara soon replaced Governor-General Carlos de Vargas Machuca y Cerveto, and General Pedro Santana was soon relieved from his position in May 1864. Most of the Dominican leadership under General Santana were replaced by Spaniards, and the disgraced Pedro Santana was ordered to report to Spanish authorities in Cuba. Pedro Santana became uncooperative with the Spaniards and on June fourteenth, 1864, he died suddenly, and rumors of suicide spread amongst the Dominican populace. Pedro Santana's body was quickly buried the following day at the courtyard of the Ozama Fortress next to the Torre del Homenaje (or the Tribute Tower) to avoid the desecration of his corpse by those who considered him a traitor. Pedro Santana died with no legitimate children and he left properties to his nephews, godchildren, and stepchildren. He also included a pension to his disabled brother Florencio and his aunt Dominga Familia.

With the death of Pedro Santana, Dominican liberals, rebels, and even some former supporters soon joined the movement for independence. Many peasants continued to enlist in the rebel forces while others fought independently to reestablish Dominican independence from the Spaniards. Dominican elders, women, and children who did not directly fight against the Spaniards provided shelter for the wounded and food for the rebels.

For several months, Anibal and Facundo led attacks throughout Santo Domingo and the surrounding towns, killing many of the Dominicans loyal to Spain as well as several Spanish leaders, devastating the Spaniards' hold on the south. Governor-General José de la Gándara y Navarro soon traveled back north towards Monte Cristi to negotiate an armistice with President José Antonio Salcedo and the Provisional Dominican Government as the Spaniards continued losing thousands of soldiers through war and disease. President José Antonio Salcedo sent a commission to Monte Cristi in order to negotiate the armistice, but the talks quickly failed as both sides desired the surrender of the other.

As the war continued, President José Antonio Salcedo quickly fell out of favor with the Dominican elite of the Cibao region. He grew increasingly frustrated with insubordination of Dominican rebel leaders and threatened to resign while speaking positively of the former caudillo and former President Buenaventura Báez, which angered the Cibaeño elite as President Buenaventura Báez threatened their business interests. Buenaventura Báez also angered many Dominicans, as he was living a life of luxury in Spain while receiving a government subsidy and had the honorary rank of field marshal. President Salcedo's willingness to negotiate with Governor-General José de la Gándara y Navarro and the Spaniards as well as his mistakes on the battlefield also angered many of the rebels and rebel leaders—including General Gaspar Polanco, who was increasingly recognized as Generalissimo. President Salcedo subsequently sent a second commission to Monte Cristi to negotiate with the Spanish government, which further increased his unpopularity among the Dominican rebel leaders. Although Vice President Ulises Francisco Espaillat remained a popular figure with the Dominican rebels and was a respected and intelligent man, the leadership of President Salcedo was now widely unpopular among Dominican rebel leaders.

On October fifteenth, 1864, President Salcedo sent a message to his wife who lived in Guayubín with the young soldier Ulises Heureaux. Later, Ulises Heureaux returned from Santo Domingo in order to assist the provisional government. That same day, President Salcedo was surprised by rebels against his government and captured him and several other provisional government leaders who were loyal to General Gaspar Polanco. President Salcedo was assassinated after he was refused entry into Haiti to live in exile, and General Gaspar Polanco assumed the Presidency, establishing autocratic rule and demanding a more aggressive war against the Spaniards. President Gaspar Polanco soon named Ulises Heureaux as his vice president while his cabinet would include Máximo Grullón Salcedo y Silverio Delmonte in the position of Interior Commission and Police, and the poet Manuel Rodríguez Objío in the Foreign Relations Commission.

President Gaspar Polanco issued his manifesto to his followers and the

Dominican people. It circulated throughout the Dominican Republic and beyond its borders. The Manifesto was called "The Peace", and stated that only full independence for the Dominican people would be allowed:

"GOD, COUNTRY, AND LIBERTY! Gaspar Polanco, General of Division, President of the Provisional Government.

"MANIFESTO.

"The general will of the people and the unanimous acclamation of the liberating army have chosen me to fill the first magistracy of the State, disavowing the authority which was exercised for one year by General José Antonio Salcedo. The salvation of my country for some time demanded a reform, and only under the pressure of this conviction I determined to lead the movement which brought it forward, free from all personal ambition.

"I wish that the popular election for the Presidency should not have fallen upon me; and if I have submitted to it, I have done so only to give a proof of my obedience to the sovereign will of my fellow citizens, accepting it as a new sacrifice for their sake, and ready to confirm this truth the day on which the National Convention will meet, before which I shall surrender the power with which I have been invested.

"The whole nation well knows the causes that, have led to the deposition of General Salcedo, for in no other way his presence in the Government could have spread so general a discontent. But I cannot refrain from mentioning them, both for my own satisfaction and for the purpose of saving the Dominicans from any unjust stigma they may be branded with by their enemies.

"For some time, the glorious Restoration initiated on the 16th of August, for the purpose of expelling Spanish despotism from our soil, had lost the vigor of the first days. To the incredible victories, to the portentous deeds of arms, had succeeded discouragement and inaction, while such a state of decay animating the hopes of our enemies, was inducing them to conceive the possibility of conquering us. And it could not be otherwise, for the first magistrate of the nation, always distant from the seat of Government, was unadvisedly destroying its best measures and annulling them without regard.

"Such conduct, occasioning embarrassment, difficult to be surmounted, constantly obstructed the match of the revolution, and while there existed an executive in the field and another in the capital, there was, in reality, no Government at all. General Salcedo thought, also, that he would deserve the title of magnanimous in tolerating the excesses of the Spaniards, whilst this culpable tolerance, when energy was a duty, caused the weakening of public spirit; thus, involuntarily constituting himself a candidate of a reaction which, although it could not be successful, might place the country in great danger.

"His thirst for popularity frequently moved General Salcedo to make abundant issues of paper money, always opening the will of his colleagues in the Government for the purpose of buying at a high price the goodwill of a few, thus increasing the discredit of our currency, and totally destroying the basis of our financial system. Always persisting in the idea of annulling the acts of his colleagues, he destroyed the Government created on the 14th of September 1863, by popular elections, because, in the exercise of its faculties it, had continued the sentence of death which the court-martial had pronounced against a convicted and confessed traitor—thus constituting himself as supreme dictator of the nation, without consulting its will.

"He arbitrarily created a cabinet, and assuming the rights of a people who fight for their liberty, curtailed this and misled the national opinion; but his dictatorship, careless of the administration of public affairs and to ally absorbed in his personality, was leaving to crumble little by little, the grand work of the 16th of August, while he was indulging in frivolous amusements and pleasures, which stained the dignity of the people whose representatives he had ignored. The present representatives of the Spanish Government, who, In view of so many blunders, came to conceive the possibility of a diplomatic and military surprise, initiated negotiations of peace, and General Salcedo, anxious for it, sent a commission to Monte Christi composed of Generals A. Deatjen, Julian D. Curiel, Pablo Rajol, Pedro A. Pimentel and Colonel M. R. Objto. A few conferences were held with Lieutenant-General Don José de la Gandara, whose bad faith, detected by the commissioners, caused them to stop short all negotiation and return to the Dominican camp, giving the cry of alarm.

"General Salcedo, lulled by the hopes of peace, had completely neglected the cantons near Monte Christi; and although the attitude of the people and the echo of that alarm induced him to publish a warlike allocution, he conceived, nevertheless, the idea of sending another committee, which, while it showed his weakness towards the enemy, would humiliate the national dignity. In the midst of these delays and negligence, he was surprised by this popular movement, which occasioned his downfall, and the Patriots, reassured by this act, are again animated by that revolutionary vigor which the circumstances demand. I have cheerfully endeavored to direct them, convinced of the necessity of such a reform; by it, the Dominican nationality has been insured; it has given now guarantees of triumph to our cause; it has saved our liberty. Should Spain insist on her purpose of subjugating the people I represent, and war becomes inevitable, greater will be our glories. If she desires peace, the road to it is clear.

"The Dominicans repel her dominion; let her desist in her desire to force it upon them. My presence in the Government is the expression of the national mind, which has no object but the expulsion of a common enemy, and the reestablishment of order, vigor, the economy in the finances, regularity and method in the service, activity, and perseverance in the work of restoration upon which the Dominican people have decided.

"I believe I have performed my duty in making this exposition and announcing my program. Let the impartial world be the judge of the facts.

"Santiago, October 15, 1864, A. D., 21st of the Independence, and 2d of the Restoration."

By November 1864, Anibal received information regarding the overthrow of President Salcedo, which was confirmed by various rebel leaders. Anibal did not particularly agree with some of the decisions of President Salcedo, and he disagreed with any Dominican leader who proposed annexation. However, he was not particularly fond of President Polanco Gaspar either. Anibal was aware of rumors that President Gaspar desired to only grant top positions to his friends and family and planned to monopolize the tobacco industry in favor of his friends. President Gaspar Polanco was widely derided as an illiterate hothead; although he was brave in battle, he would sometimes fail in his objectives because of his lack of planning.

Anibal was very focused on war and only wanted to concentrate on Dominican politics after the Spaniards were defeated. After several raids against the Spaniards, one particular afternoon, Anibal and Facundo defeated and captured Spaniards in western Santo Domingo. The intelligence gathered from the frightened captured Spaniards revealed that Captain Dos Santos and Colonel Ricardo Hoffmann were retreating eastward towards the town of San Cristobal. Anibal received intelligence that over 2,000 Dominican soldiers loyal to Spain and over 4,000 Spanish soldiers were retreating from a failed battle against General José María Cabral y Luna. San Cristobal was the birthplace of General Cabral and many rebels were loyal to him in the town. Anibal realized that this was an opportunity to face his most hated enemies in battle, and he and Facundo raced towards San Cristobal along with over 4,000 Dominican rebels.

Anibal attempted to notify various rebel leaders, yet many of them were focused on President Gaspar's plan to attack Spanish bases in the northern Dominican Republic, including Monte Cristi. The rumored attack appeared to be rushed and not tactically sound, but Anibal desired a Dominican victory if President Gaspar Polanco attempted the offensive. Anibal decided to act alongside Facundo as a major victory in San Cristobal would potentially break the morale of the Spaniards. As Anibal arrived near San Cristobal, he sent messengers to inform the rebels in Santiago to join in the attack.

As the Spaniards entered San Cristobal, Captain Dos Santos and Colonel Richard Hoffman were finally identified among the occupying Spanish forces. Anibal feared that Captain Dos Santos had discovered his involvement in the rebellion and would soon exact revenge on his family. Anibal feared that even if Captain Dos Santos was unaware of his involvement, he would receive information from escaped Spanish prisoners or any Spanish soldiers who escaped death at the battle for Fort San Luis. A decisive victory and the death of Captain Dos Santos would alleviate his most immediate concerns. Anibal and the rebels decided to strike during nightfall to surprise the Spaniards. A few rebels infiltrated San Cristobal and stayed with the local community. Anibal's home, farm, and ranch were constantly monitored by his family members, the Andujars, and sometimes Robert Grant. However, through the volatile recent events, only members of the Andujar family would maintain Anibal's property.

The Spaniards began to abuse the local Dominican people of San Cristobal, taking their food and animals. Anibal wanted to strike soon, before his own house was reached by Captain Dos Santos. The day before the battle, the rebels remained in hiding outside of San Cristobal as Anibal began to address his friends and young rebels who fought with him:

"The Spaniards are losing this war and with our victory, we will further cripple the Spaniards and those Dominicans who continue to aid the enemy in our lands. What is most shameful is that Dominicans under the leadership of Pedro Santana invited this abuse under the false premise of stability and protection from invasion and warfare with our neighbors to the west. My fellow Dominican compatriots, even if Pedro Santana was correct, do you all not believe we would have stopped any invasion just as we have done in our past? Why should we listen to people who do not believe in the Dominican people, many of whom participated in the very wars for Dominican independence?

"We were victorious against far superior numbers of a seasoned Haitian Army. Despite our tumultuous experiences with the Haitian government and their military in the past, some Haitians are now helping us in our war against the Spanish Empire and the Spanish loyalists in this island. Santana used Dominican fears of invasion and the hatred that some of us have against our neighbors for his gain, and now his supporters are using the same tactics for their political aims to preserve their power. Their tactics have once again subjugated the Dominican people under Spanish rule and we can agree that this is not acceptable by most Dominicans."

The Dominicans were joyous and motivated by Anibal's speech, and he looked each man in the eye as he continued, "My fellow Dominicans, Pedro Santana is dead! His dictatorship is over, yet many of his followers continue to fight for a lost cause. I do not know what your political ideologies or motivations are, but we must all agree that we want to once again defeat the Spaniards from our nation and destroy their hegemony in the Caribbean once and for all. We will encourage our Cuban and Puerto Rican brothers and sisters to take our revolution as an example, just as they have been inspired by our previous revolts, to create a free and sovereign nation once again. We are a people that have been formed from Europeans, Africans, and the natives that have survived within us—and now joined by other people from Asia. One of these Asians I call a friend to me and my family.

"We are also a people of mostly Roman Catholic faith, but our Dominican Jewish and Muslims as well as our Arab populations have also joined us simply as a united Dominican people to restore our independence so we can once again call ourselves a republic. We have had our differences amongst Dominican people, however we have largely maintained our unity as Dominicans, and it is of vital importance that we maintain our strength. We will defeat the Spaniards and their loyalists here in San Cristobal. We will defeat José de la Gándara y Navarro, who claims to be the Governor-General of our Dominican nation. I refuse to call ourselves a territory of Spain, and we all have lived as free Dominicans in a sovereign nation. Because of this, I believe we will swiftly bring about our independence and restore the independence of the Dominican Republic. We will fight for ourselves, our people, our wives and children, our families, and our survival! We will defeat Queen Isabella II and the Spanish Empire and restore the honor of the Dominican people and once again establish the Dominican Republic."

Facundo and the rebels were highly excited after Anibal's speech as they began to prepare the attack on San Cristobal. As the strategy was formulated, Facundo jokingly stated to Anibal, "Hermano, you should become a politician after the war is over."

Anibal cracked a rare smile and laughed as he stated, "I will avenge the death of my Uncle Julio, and you will avenge the death of your parents."

The two men embraced as rebels infiltrated San Cristobal to prepare the people for the upcoming battle. Several Dominican women took up arms while others provided food, shelter, and arms for the rebels. As the months passed, increasing numbers of Dominican women joined the rebellion as Dominican victories increased.

As night fell, the Dominican rebels split into two groups; one would attack the Spaniards and the Santana loyalists from the front while another would approach from the right. The Spaniards were concentrated in western San Cristobal, and some Dominican rebels began silently killing any Spaniards who were alone or sleeping. The infiltration continued for several hours until the assault began with Dominican rebels lining up in formation and firing upon the Spaniards, surprising them as they scrambled for their weapons. The Dominicans continued to fire upon the Spaniards in successive rounds, using their own weapons and arms captured from the thousands of dead Spaniards from previous battles. Anibal then sent a message to his friend Facundo, who was with the other Dominican rebel to attack on the enemy's right flank.

As the Spaniards began to return fire, Facundo and his rebels shot at them from the right flank and near the rear. Most of the men led by

Captain Dos Santos were killed as they began to retreat. The fight quickly turned into fierce hand to hand as the Dominican rebels used their sabers and bayonets to cut down the remaining Spaniards. Attempting to retreat westward, the Spaniards were attacked by Dominican peasants who used anything they could find—guns, machetes, sticks, and stones. The battle continued throughout the night, resulting in the decisive victory for the Dominican rebellion with less than 1,000 Spaniards remaining. Over 500 Spaniards escaped westward, leaving less than 500 Spaniards and some Dominicans loyal to Santana remaining near the western border of San Cristobal.

Anibal Medina located Captain Dos Santos as the sun began to rise in the Dominican sky. Anibal and Facundo mounted their horses and pursued the Spaniards and Captain Dos Santos towards the western border of San Cristobal, where they were soon pinned down and desperately fired upon the approaching Dominican rebels. Captain Dos Santos identified Anibal Medina and attempted to fire upon him, but he missed his mark. Anibal dismounted from his horse, took cover, and returned fire. Captain Dos Santos and some of the Spaniards retreated into a nearby *conuco* lined by rows of plantain trees. Anibal was now close to Captain Dos Santos, the man who could bring further destruction to his family. It was necessary to capture or kill him at this moment; he was too dangerous to be left alive. Anibal and his fellow rebels returned fire and quickly approached Captain Dos Santos and the remaining Spaniards.

Captain Dos Santos stated, "My suspicions regarding your involvement with the rebels are now confirmed. I previously received a report that you participated in the battle of Fort San Luis, and you are very fortunate that I did not find that information earlier. Your family betrayed Pedro Santana and aided rebels and Haitians who sought to destroy our peace and stability. Pedro Santana was trying to save this country and bring security during an economic crisis."

Anibal shot Captain Dos Santos in the right leg and he fell. Facundo fired upon the Spaniards attempting to rescue their leader, killing two and injuring several as additional Dominican forces quickly arrived.

Anibal approached Captain Dos Santos as he stated, "My family has fought right alongside you. My uncle was imprisoned with you. My family always aided you because of the pain you experienced in your youth, and I also fought alongside my uncle against the Haitian Army. We always stand for the independent Dominican Republic, however you decided to support Pedro Santana and Spanish annexation. Pedro Santana and his supporters willingly allowed Spain to reoccupy this nation once again. In the eyes of most Dominicans, Pedro Santana and his supporters are traitors to the ideas of Juan Pablo Duarte and the Trinitarios who fought hard to establish Dominican sovereignty."

Anibal and Facundo shot the remaining Spaniards who were with Captain Dos Santos, as Captain Dos Santos replied, "We were attempting to avoid another invasion by the Haitians. You have not seen the intelligence we received as many of their politicians were once again planning another invasion even after Emperor Faustin was overthrown. We were suffering an economic disaster and although we previously defeated the Haitians, additional wars would have further weakened our nation. Their culture is one of disorder, and they were threatening to destroy us under their policies. They have embraced the most negative aspects of Voodoo. Fabre Geffrard has punished those who have perpetrated the most abhorrent violence through their practices and attempted to stabilize his nation, yet that nation continues to suffer from political disorganization and rebellion—something that Pedro Santana sought to avoid. We are Dominicans and we were to be treated as equals to the Spaniards. We are a free people and we were not to be subjugated to slavery like the Cubans and Puerto Ricans."

Anibal replied, "The Spaniards, who were invited back by Pedro Santana, would never treat Dominicans as equals. Any occupying force usually will see themselves as superior to the people they control. Although Haitians are predominantly of African descent, I must remind you that the first Africans slaves who arrived in 1501 eventually became Dominicans. Our culture is a combination of Africans, Spanish, and other Europeans, and the Tainos and various groups native to this island and the Caribbean. We can never disrespect or degrade any of these people because all of them have contributed to the culture that became Dominican. We can equally point out the negatives of any culture. Perhaps there are some negative extremists who practice Voodoo, but I can equally say the same regarding the Spanish Inquisition and the abuses of the Jewish and Islamic people in Spain; the Catholic Church's role in the abuses of the native Tainos and Africans here in the Dominican Republic and throughout Latin America. Look at what the Spaniards did to the Taino leaders like Anacaona and Hatüey, who fled this island towards Cuba and were burned alive. Cacique Enriquillo fought a war against the Spaniards from 1519 to 1533 and only managed freedom for his people for a short time until the Spaniards dishonored their agreement soon after Cacique Enriquillo's death.

"The Spaniards have broken their agreements with the native people of this land and the rest of the Caribbean and Latin America. There were good Catholics who fought for the rights of the natives and Africans, but the Catholic Church mostly followed the imperial actions of Spain. I fought against the Haitian army just like I would fight against any invading army. My uncle fought in many wars as well—and served honorably—and you helped imprison him, which led to his execution. You have dishonored yourself by imprisoning Dominican patriots and supporting Pedro Santana, even as most of the Dominican people are against the annexation. Pedro Santana understood his decision would be largely unpopular, which led him to annex the Dominican Republic in secret. Santana was a despot and although he was effective as a general, many of his political decisions remain unpopular with Dominicans. Now the Spaniards who control this nation decide foreign policy in their favor and just like the English, they are currently supporting the Confederacy. As Dominicans, we cannot allow the Spaniards to continue to control our society and dictate our foreign policy. We shall put an end to Spanish rule."

Captain Dos Santos was visibly angered as Anibal continued, "The mostly black Haitian population faced an even worse existence under the French than we did by the early 1800s, and their large numbers and experienced leaders enabled them to fight and defeat the French. The black people were always treated the worst under the system of slavery and caste, which is important to understand. I never agreed with many of their leaders, and their decision to invade our territory—particularly after we declared independence in 1844. However, that is no excuse for Pedro Santana to annex our nation. The Dominican people deserve independence and freedom in the sovereign Dominican Republic."

Facundo attempted to attack Captain Dos Santos while he focused on Anibal, but Captain Dos Santos turned and shot Facundo in the chest and he fell face-first in the mud. The shooting was sudden and surprised both Facundo and Anibal.

Anibal ducked behind a tree as Captain Dos Santos stated, "I understand, and I agree with much of what you have to say, Anibal. I never meant for Julio Medina to be killed. I suspected he would rebel against the government and lead others to defect from the military and cause chaos. I only recommended that Julio Medina be imprisoned and removed from the military. The Spaniards decided to send him and the others to Cuba to face punishment and when it was discovered that Julio Medina was plotting to kill the Spaniards and escape from jail, he was executed. However, Dominican rebels—including you—were already near the jail when the execution occurred. I only demanded justice and fought against the Haitian leaders who desired to invade and take control of the Dominican Republic. You speak about black people being mistreated and brutalized, and I ask you what about my family? My family is mostly white Dominican and a group of Haitian soldiers killed them and violated the females. My family has been ruined and suffered the brunt of Haitian brutality. They had nothing to do with the French and their mistreatment of the Haitians. The Haitian government intended to erase our culture and prohibit our Dominican Spanish language. Pedro Santana intended to protect this country and your rebellion helped weaken his position. Now the Spaniards are in open warfare with the people of the Dominican Republic. It was not an ideal decision for Pedro Santana to allow the Spaniards to return, but it was a pragmatic one.

Captain Dos Santos continued after a brief pause, "Remember, that through Pedro Santana's leadership the Dominican Military was quickly able to counter and defeat the Haitian offensives in Dominican territory! Remember it was Pedro Santana and his strategic brilliance in battle that allowed the Dominican Republic to defeat Emperor Faustin's and the Haitian invasions in our nation. If we allowed weak leaders like President Manuel Jimenes, the Dominican Republic would have been conquered by Haiti and forced under a more disastrous situation than the earlier Haitian occupation under Boyer. You speak about Pedro Santana being a despot, however if you defeat the Spaniards all you will have will be despots for many generations. Or worse, you will have regionalism once again and disorder in the Dominican Republic with a powerful military and political figures controlling their respective regions in the nation. You may have one of the current Dominican caudillos taking control of the nation, or perhaps Buenaventura Báez will return once again to take control of the Dominican Republic."

Anibal Medina shouted, "You fool! The Spaniards were always against us! Pedro Santana and his followers allowed Spain to regain control of this country while the United States is preoccupied with their Civil War and allowed them to solidify the Spanish Empire in the Caribbean. Spain will lose this war, and our victory will encourage the Cubans and Puerto Ricans to declare their own independence as well. Pedro Santana was an opportunist and so are you. You will now join Pedro Santana as a traitor to the Dominican Republic."

Anibal Medina rushed towards Captain Dos Santos and both men fired almost simultaneously as Captain Dos Santos attempted to get up. Anibal hit Captain Dos Santos in the stomach as he returned fired, striking Anibal in the lower right arm. Captain Dos Santos fell once again in extreme as blood poured out of his mouth and stomach.

Anibal yelled, "Where is Colonel Richard Hoffman?" However, Captain Dos Santos was unable to respond as he writhed in agony. Anibal aimed at Captain Dos Santos' head, intending to kill him and end this ongoing tragedy. He looked into Captain Dos Santos' eyes as he began to laugh.

"Cobarde! You are not man enough to kill me and look at me in my eyes while I am on the ground. I believe it is a misplaced sense of morality or a self-righteousness that renders the Medina men to be bad decision-makers. Dominicans like me are pragmatic and realists; we are forced to do the undesirable hard work that led to the strengthening of this nation while others like you point their fingers at us after the wars and political battles are over."

Anibal decided it was best to imprison Captain Dos Santos and learn the location of the other Spaniards and Colonel Hoffman, as he believed the war would soon be over. While he slowly backed away, he noticed his friend Facundo was struggling to get up and he began to walk towards him.

Suddenly, Anibal Medina heard Captain Dos Santos yell, "Que viva Pedro Santana!"

As Anibal turned around, he heard a loud shot that surprised him. Anibal raised his firearm and turned to see Captain Dos Santos dead with a shot to his chest. His eyes widened and his heart raced as he took in Captain Dos Santos dying on Dominican soil, a man in his mid-forties with grey hair littering his carefully combed hair, blood soaking his clothes as he breathed his last breath. Anibal realized that his friend Facundo killed Captain Alonso Kebehi Dos Santos, thus saving his life. Captain Alonso Kebehi Dos Santos lay in the dirt with his mouth and eyes open, a shocked expression on his face as he acknowledged the Spanish collapse and realized his life was now coming to an end. Anibal thought about the possibility that Alonso Kebehi Dos Santos was relieved to know he would die and would not live an agonizing life after the trauma inflicted on his family.

Anibal quickly embraced his friend Facundo, thanking him for his decisive action. Facundo laughed. "Anibal, please tell me you were not going to let that vile man live."

Anibal just shook his head and laughed as the rest of the rebels arrived at the scene. However, Anibal quickly fell into sadness as Facundo passed away the following day from his injuries. Facundo was buried in San Cristobal and the Dominican rebels honored him for his bravery in battle. Anibal would often think of Dos Santos' last words and the reality that Pedro Santana's leadership helped deliver Dominican victories in the battlefield, but he remained critical of Pedro Santana's leadership.

The fight against Spain was necessary for the freedom of the Dominican people as well as the restoration of honor and respect that the Dominicans deserved. The war against Spain was successful, but the Dominicans would suffer a major defeat. Anibal would later be informed that President Gaspar Polanco led a failed offensive in Monte Cristi in December 1864. He was soon overthrown by a movement which included his own brother General Juan Antonio Polanco, Pedro Antonio Pimentel, and Benito Moncion. In January 1865, Benigno Filomeno de Rojas was appointed the President of the Dominican Republic.

Gaspar Polanco was accused of tyranny and involvement in Salcedo's assassination. The provisional junta issued several decrees, lowering the war taxes that the government of Gaspar Polanco was collecting from the tobacco producers. They stated that the 1858 Constitution of Moca would be enforced until a national convention could be held on February twenty-seventh. The newly elected President Benigno Filomeno de Rojas launched an investigation regarding the assassination of President Salcedo, and the

Dominican government continued to wage war on the Spanish positions throughout the country.

CHAPTER 19

THE DOMINICAN VICTORY OVER THE SPANISH EMPIRE & THE RESTORATION OF THE DOMINICAN REPUBLIC

(1865)

President Benigno Filomeno de Rojas and Vice President Gregorio Luperón continued to wage war against Spain. The Dominican rebels confronted the Spanish forces as the Dominican people fended off the Spanish offensives. Governor-General José de la Gándara y Navarro won a decisive battle at Monte Cristi but was failing to properly take control of the county as the Dominican rebels harassed the Spaniards and broke their supply lines. Disease crippled the Spanish Military as many Dominicans once loyal to Spain began to defect from the military. The overwhelming majority of Dominicans did not desire a negotiation with the remaining Spanish troops and demanded only full expulsion and encouraged the rebels to continue their efforts.

Some Cubans and Puerto Ricans also aided the rebels and as Dominican victory seemed imminent, the Dominican fight encouraged Cuban and Puerto Rican nationalism. Some joined Anibal Medina and the rebel group as they returned to patrol the outskirts of Santo Domingo, including a young Puerto Rican Jíbaro and nationalist named Miguel Diaz. Jibaro was a Taino word, meaning "people of the mountain" (now referred to the lower-class mixed population often of a darker complexion). Some Jibaros were also poor whites who came to work the land owned by the hacendados (or wealthy elite criollos). Anibal was aware of some books which mentioned the Jibaro like the Coplas del Jíbaro (or Couplets of the Jibaro) written by a Puerto Rican poet from Arecibo, Miguel Cabrera (1820) as well as the book El Gibaro (or The Jibaro) written by Dr. Manuel Alonzo in 1849.

Miguel Diaz was a slender mixed Puerto Rican with a black father and a mixed light-skinned mother. Miguel Diaz was born in central Puerto Rico in the municipality of San Juan Bautista de Barros—a region located in the Central Mountains range inhabited by the Taino indigenous people called the Jatibonicu (their leader was Cacique Orocobix). Miguel Diaz was inspired by the voices of Puerto Rican nationalists and in 1860, at the age of fifteen, he arrived at Mayagüez months after Dr. Betances, who returned from Europe and was mourning the death of his young love María del Carmen (nicknamed Lita. Dr. Betances). He would begin wearing a dark suit, sporting a long, unkempt beard and a Quaker hat. Their marriage was supposed to occur on May fifth, 1859 in Paris, but Lita fell sick with typhus and died at the Mennecy house of Dr. Pierre Lamire—a friend from Betances' medical school days. Dr. Betances would subsequently write a poem in French called La Vièrge de Boriquén (or The Boriquén Virgin), which was influenced by his love for Maria del Carmen in the writing style of Edgar Allan Poe.

The Spanish governor of Puerto Rico, Fernando Cotoner, threatened Betances with exile, but he returned to Mayagüez in 1859 and established a successful surgery and ophthalmology practice. Even his opponents—including the pro-monarchy journalist José Pérez Morís—regarded Dr. Betances as the best surgeon in the island. Miguel Diaz spoke about Dr. Ramón Emeterio Betances' close relationship with Dominican general and political figure Gregorio Luperón. Dr. Betances stayed in Puerto Plata during the Dominican War against Spain, aiding the Dominican rebellion. Upon his return to Puerto Rico, Dr. Betances and Ruiz would help establish the Hospital San Antonio, which provided healthcare for the poor and opened on January eighteenth, 1865. Ruiz was a Freemason who invited Betances to join his lodge, named the Logia Unión Germana or the German Union Lodge in nearby San Germán, Puerto Rico and advocated for the building of secondary schools which the local Spanish government rejected for fear of the school creating an educated Puerto Rican population which could foment rebellion against the Spaniards.

Miguel Diaz observed the Dominican war against Spain and was deeply inspired. Skinny as a reed but strong as an ox, Diaz carried the enthusiasm of his youth and the will to fight. He talked about the poor health conditions and lack of education in Puerto Rico as well as a devastating cholera epidemic in the 1850s when he was a boy. Miguel Diaz also spoke enthusiastically of a Puerto Rican man named Dr. Ramón Emeterio Betances, who along with four other doctors, was in charge of taking care of over 24,000 residents in Mayagüez, Puerto Rico. Dr. Ramón Emeterio Betances was also an abolitionist who spoke about the horrid conditions of black Puerto Rican slaves. Puerto Rico had less than 600,000 people, with about fifty-one percent being white and close to forty-nine percent being people of color—mixed or mulattos and mestizos—as well a small percentage of other groups including Asians.

The Secret Abolitionist Society was founded by Dr. Ramón Emeterio Betances and was also supported by his friend, the abolitionist Segundo Ruiz Belvis. In Mayagüez, Segundo Ruiz Belvis established his law practice and was named Justice of the Peace and elected for city council, which made him responsible for the wellbeing of the slave population as well as the management of the city's funds. Segundo Ruiz Belvis began plotting how to free the slaves there and bring independence to Puerto Rico.

Miguel Diaz informed Anibal that Segundo Ruiz Belvis left for Spain in early 1865 to appear in Madrid, Spain at the Cortes Generales (or the bicameral legislature of the Kingdom of Spain) to advocate for the abolition of the slaves. Anibal understood that certain defeat awaited Spain at the hands of the Dominican rebel army, which would put pressure on the Cuba and Puerto Riccan governments. These developments energized Anibal and encouraged him to further push against Spanish occupation and drive the Spaniards from the Caribbean.

After weeks of successful raids on Spanish troop installations, Anibal finally took a short leave to see his family. Many had slowly begun to return home, and Robert Grant and his wife had made the journey safely. Romina returned to the Medina home in Santo Domingo soon after Anibal went to the Andujars' residence. Anibal believed the war was coming to an end by the middle of February 1865, as the Spaniards did not initiate any further major offensives and began retreating to mostly to the northern coastline of the Dominican Republic. He felt relieved in the arms of his wife, and at night they spoke about their future together.

As they kissed, Romina quietly said, "I love you, Anibal, and we have spent little time together since the beginning of this war. I respect and understand your fight against the Spaniards, and I am happy that this conflict seems to be coming to an end, but we need to move forward with our lives and start our own family."

Anibal replied, "I am sorry I have been away from you for long periods of time, but I never wanted our children to experience the humiliation of a brutal occupation. Many Dominicans have once again sacrificed and shed blood for the freedom of this nation and all I want is to help the rebels win this war."

Romina responded, "People have children through the best of times and through the worst of times. People have continued to live their lives throughout the most of difficult times in history. I will always support you in whatever you decide to do. I just want the best for our families, and I believe we should move forward in life no matter the outcome of the war."

Anibal looked deep into the eyes of his wife and slowly said, "Yes, I will fight for this country, but I will also fight for our family and for us. I love you, Romina."

Anibal kissed Romina passionately and she smiled as she noticed that despite his mental stress, the war had made a positive impact on his body. Anibal was strong, more agile, and leaner with larger muscles and better health. Anibal relaxed as rebels guarded the Medina home and the Dominicans were close to restoring the nation. After many months, he made love to his wife.

The Spaniards had capable generals still serving them, such as the feared General Máximo Gómez. The general matched the ferocity of the Dominican rebels in battle as he mastered the "Machete Charge" and applied everything he had learned in Spanish Military school and combined it with his previous experiences as a Dominican soldier in the war against Haiti. General Máximo Gómez was impressed with the courage of the rebels, and he soon grew dissatisfied with the violence perpetrated against the Dominican people. He soon planned to leave the Spanish Military; he did not believe in their ongoing war against the Dominicans, who only desired independence. In the month of March, the Spaniards attempted to negotiate with the Dominican government and General Máximo Gómez turned against them, believing in the cause for Dominican independence as well as the independence for Cubans and Puerto Ricans.

Many Dominicans believed that with continued Spanish losses, leaders like General Máximo Gómez would soon defect to support the rebels. As the month of July approached, many Dominicans defected from the Spanish Army and actively supported the restoration of the Dominican Republic. General Máximo Gómez and his family did not want any more Dominican blood to be shed, and he soon left for Cuba. Many of the Spaniards did not wish to fight or lose their lives in what they now believed was a lost cause. The Spanish people also did not desire to continue the war against the Dominicans and began to protest their government.

On March third, 1865, Queen Isabella II of Spain signed the annulment of the annexation. The Spanish government was informed that the United States Civil War would soon come to an end as the Confederates were on the verge of surrender. Thus, Queen Isabella II and her advisors believed it would be fruitless to continue a losing fight against the Dominicans. The United States would continue the Monroe Doctrine, and Queen Isabella II's advisors believed Spain should focus on its two remaining colonies in the Americas: Cuba and Puerto Rico.

On March twenty-fourth, 1865, Pedro Antonio Pimentel was chosen to be President of the Dominican Republic with Benigno Filomeno de Rojas serving as Vice President. President Pimentel designated a war council to try Gaspar Polanco and his cabinet. Anibal observed the retreat of the Spanish soldiers as the war continued. By late April 1865, some rebels returned to the southern Dominican Republic after completing their duties in the Northern Dominican Army—including Anibal's friend Valentino Xin, who had joined the Dominican patrols in Santo Domingo. Spanish troops continued to be harassed with some accounts of Dominican abuses against prisoners, but most Dominicans allowed the Spaniards to quickly evacuate Dominican territory.

Anibal Medina began to concentrate on the upkeep of his home in San Cristobal and helping his family fix their house in Santo Domingo. The structures had received minimal damage, while many towns throughout the Dominican Republic were destroyed. Some of Anibal's cattle died despite the Andujar family's attempts to feed and shelter them. Most of Anibal's crops were still intact, and he began to tend to his farm while spending less time with the Dominican rebels as he reorganized his business and his family.

After spending time with his own family, Valentino Xin traveled to the

Medina home to meet a hero's welcome. Everyone was excited to see him and hear his stories from his battles in the Cibao—including Anibal's sister Catalina, who warmly embraced Valentino as he smiled.

Valentino jokingly said, "So, you thought of me while I was away, querida."

Catalina laughed as she replied, "Of course I did, and I am glad you arrived back safely."

They both laughed as they embraced. Catalina enjoyed Valentino's sense of humor even through hardship; he was also intelligent, which set him apart from other suitors. Valentino believed Catalina started to like him as much as he liked her, and he contemplated speaking to Anibal and his parents before he began courting her. After approaching Maria and Marco Medina, they assured Valentino they approved of a relationship between him and their daughter.

Valentino Xin remained in Santo Domingo, helping organize the Medina household and providing help to Anibal on his farm and ranch. Valentino also aided the Medina family by focusing on fishing along the southern Dominican coastline and providing his income to support them. He described the various military engagements he was involved in which were highly successful, such as several offensives led by General Gregorio Luperón in Puerto Plata. Gregorio Luperón was able to successfully lead campaigns throughout the Cibao region. Valentino also spoke of the Dominican campaigns which failed, like the one commanded by former President Gaspar Polanco. The battles were bloody and violent with some Dominicans distinguishing them-selves in battle—including Valentino's older cousin, Pancho El Chino. Pancho El Chino received adulation from the cibaeños, and through his fame received the attention of many Dominican women—including a young lady he met in La Vega. Valentino encouraged Pancho to relocate to Santo Domingo with him, however Pancho decided to remain in the Cibao, where he intended to start a family.

By the month of June, many Dominicans had learned about the annulment of the annexation. José de la Gándara y Navarro was no longer the Governor-General, and the Dominicans were informed that he left the nation the month prior. Many of the rebels would join the Dominican Military while the peasants who aided them went back to working their lands and rebuilding their homes. Dominican flags were raised and they celebrated their independence once again.

Spanish troops quickly evacuated the reestablished Dominican Republic. They were allowed to leave peacefully while some Dominicans yearned to continue their fight— particularly the Cubans and Puerto Ricans who participated in the war and desired to rid themselves of the Spaniards in their lands. Miguel Diaz understood that many of these Spaniards leaving the Dominican Republic would now help occupy Puerto Rico and become his enemy if a war broke out. He spoke to Anibal about his desire to stay in Santo Domingo for several years until Puerto Rican nationalist leaders initiated a war for independence and Anibal and his family agreed to help the young man.

Miguel Diaz was excited about the Dominican victory over Spain, and news spread throughout Cuba, Puerto Rico, and the Caribbean. Spanish failure to maintain the Captaincy General of Santo Domingo and suppress Dominican rebellion reached Europe and the rest of the Americas. All major warfare was completed, save a few skirmishes between angry Dominicans and Spaniards, allowing Anibal Medina to plan his return to the town of Santiago de los Caballeros to the home of Moisés and Josefina Aponte. Anibal wanted to bring his Uncle Julio's body to Santo Domingo so he could have a proper funeral surrounded by the Medina family— including his widow Paulina and their twelve-year-old son Carlos. Miguel Diaz and Valentino Xin agreed to accompany Anibal to the Cibao.

In August 1865, Anibal Medina, Valentino Xin, and Miguel Diaz returned to Santo Domingo to bring home the body of Julio Medina. A beautiful Catholic funeral was held as many of his friends arrived to mourn his death and celebrate his life as one of the patriots for the fight for Dominican independence. The Saint-Lot family also joined the funeral, along with Raymond Saint-Lot, who was recovering after Dominican physicians treated his injuries. Marco Medina spoke about his younger brother Julio and their childhood together as he recounted sharing the key moments of Dominican history with Julio like the birth of the Republic of Spanish Haiti in 1821 and the arrival of the Haitian Military to the capital soon after in 1822. Marco talked about Juan Pablo Duarte, the Trinitarians, and the reestablishment of the nation renamed the Dominican Republic in 1844. He spoke fondly of his brother and their participation in the Dominican Army against Haiti and their leader Emperor Faustin I as well as Julio's subsequent participation in the rebellion against Spanish occupation. Marco briefly mentioned Juan Pablo Duarte and his desire to become the first President of the Dominican Republic; there was a possibility that with his leadership, the Dominican War of Restoration would not have occurred. Most of all, Marco expressed his love for his brother and the pride he felt in his participation in liberating the nation one last time.

Paulina spoke about Julio and her love for him as well as his need to focus more on his family after the war was over. She elaborated on her desire for all those responsible for her husband's death to be brought to justice. Paulina also expressed her pride in her husband and Anibal as well as all the rebels who fought to liberate the Dominican nation. The Saint-Lot family briefly spoke, thanking the Medinas and other Dominican families who had protected them from the violent Spaniards and the Dominican auxiliaries who constantly harassed them. Anibal Medina embraced

Raymond Saint-Lot, who informed him that the elusive Colonel Ricardo Hoffman aided the now deceased Captain Dos Santos in his capture and beating; he promised justice would be delivered.

Anibal stated that he respected his uncle and was inspired by him and his father to join the Dominican Army and later fight as a rebel against the Spaniards. The family continued to celebrate Julio Medina's life and Anibal promised to help his uncle's widow and son. The Medina family soon joined the independence celebrations throughout Santo Domingo and the rest of the nation. The Dominican Republic was restored, however political instability quickly followed after a coup d'état that replaced President Pedro Antonio Pimentel with the liberal President José María Cabral on the fourth of August 1865.

On August sixteenth of that same year, President José María Cabral declared the Restoration of the Dominican Republic and the Second Republic of the Dominican Republic as nationwide celebrations erupted once again. The war was devastating for the Spanish Empire: by some estimates, they lost 20,000 to 30,000 soldiers to disease with close to 11,000 killed in action or wounded. Dominican-Spanish auxiliaries lost roughly 10,000 to battle and disease. Overall, approximately 4,000 rebels were killed while the Spaniards lost roughly 51,000 soldiers along with their 12,000 Dominican auxiliaries. Various diseases that plagued the Spaniards were an important factor in the Dominican victory, just as it once had been for the Haitians against the French in 1804. José de la Gándara y Navarro returned to Spain, where he was offered the position of Governor-General of the Philippines. Governor-General José de la Gándara y Navarro would govern the Philippines until June 1869. He would later publish the Historia de la Anexion y Guerra de Santo Domingo (or the History of the Annexation and War of Santo Domingo).

The last Spanish soldiers evacuated the Dominican Republic and fled towards Spain and the nearby colonies of Cuba and Puerto Rico. President José María Cabral would remain in power until he was replaced by President Pedro Guillermo y Guerrero, who was appointed by Provisional Government Junta of the Dominican Republic. President Pedro Guillermo was born in Media Chiva in the municipality of Hato Mayor del Rey (or the Great Herd of the King) of Hato Mayor Province. The municipality derived its name because it was previously the largest herding area in the island of Hispaniola for King Carlos I of Spain (or Holy Roman Emperor Charles the V) in the sixteenth century. It was founded in 1520 by Francisco Dávila as land that was dedicated to cattle and agriculture. President Pedro Guillermo had three children; two daughters who passed away and a young son named Cesáreo Guillermo Bastardo. President Pedro Guillermo ruled until the arrival of the polarizing Buenaventura Baez, who would become President of the Dominican Republic on the eighth of December 1865.

Anibal Medina did not approve of Buenaventura Baez, however he had other concerns as his wife Romina confirmed that she was with child in August 1865.

As the Medina family celebrated, Miguel Diaz informed Anibal that he would remain in Santo Domingo until 1866, when he planned to return to his native Puerto Rico. Miguel asked whether Anibal would support him and other Puerto Rican nationalists during the time of Puerto Rican rebellion, and Anibal agreed that he would aid in the fight for Puerto Rican independence with any money he could. However, Anibal resigned from the Dominican rebel forces and declined a readmittance into the military with a higher rank in favor of developing his household and livelihood.

Many encouraged Anibal Medina to once again enter the Dominican Military, but Romina wanted her husband to retire from armed combat and dedicate himself to family life. Marco Medina was also informed of the passing of his father Jairo Antonio in his home in the central Dominican Republic. Jairo Antonio Medina died happy to know the Dominican Republic was independent once again, but he lived in sadness after the recent passing of his wife (Epifania Alvarado de Medina) just one year prior. The Medina family mourned the loss of both Jairo Antonio Medina Montemayor and Epifania Medina, who both lived a quiet life. The Medina family's lands and homes remained largely intact as opposed to other regions of the Dominican Republic, which were devastated by warfare. Anibal was happy as their child would be born in the free Dominican Republic—a nation that had once again survived a foreign invasion and occupation.

As the months passed, Anibal and other Dominicans were informed that the Civil War in the United States was over. In 1864, President Abraham Lincoln appointed Ulysses S. Grant commander of all Union armies. General Grant would eventually conquer Virginia as Union General Sherman defeated the Confederate Generals Joseph E. Johnston and John Bell Hood. The fall of Atlanta on September second, 1864 guaranteed the reelection of Lincoln as president. President Abraham Lincoln of the Republican Party (under the temporary name of the National Union Party) defeated the Democratic nominee, the former General George B. McClellan. Letters poured in congratulating President Abraham Lincoln in his reelection and continued fight against the Confederacy. President Lincoln employed several secretaries to handle his mail. The US Ambassador in London, Charles Francis Adams, decided to forward a letter by Karl Marx titled the "Address" to Washington. Karl Marx previously wanted to move to Texas and supported the Union cause and the emancipation of the slaves, as opposed to many in the European elite who held favorable views towards the Confederacy. Karl Marx and Abraham Lincoln developed a friendship and sometimes exchanged letters and shortly after becoming the first northern president to win reelection he read the letter by Karl Marx which stated:

Address of the International Working Men's Association to Abraham Lincoln, President of the United States of America

Presented to U.S. Ambassador Charles Francis Adams

"Sir:

We congratulate the American people upon your reelection by a large majority. If resistance to the Slave Power was the reserved watchword of your first election, the triumphant war cry of your reelection is Death to Slavery.

From the commencement of the titanic American strife the workingmen of Europe felt instinctively that the star-spangled banner carried the destiny of their class. The contest for the territories which opened the dire epopee, was it not to decide whether the virgin soil of immense tracts should be wedded to the labor of the emigrant or prostituted by the tramp of the slave driver?

When an oligarchy of 300,000 slaveholders dared to inscribe for the first time in the annals of the world, "slavery" on the banner of Armed Revolt, when on the very spots where hardly a century ago the idea of one great Democratic Republic had first sprung up, whence the first Declaration of the Rights of Man was issued, and the first impulse given to the European revolution of the eighteenth century; when on those very spots counterrevolution, with systematic thoroughness, gloried in rescinding "the ideas entertained at the time of the formation of the old constitution", and maintained slavery to be "a beneficent institution", indeed, the old solution of the great problem of "the relation of capital to labor", and cynically proclaimed property in man "the cornerstone of the new edifice"—then the working classes of Europe understood at once, even before the fanatic partisanship of the upper classes for the Confederate gentry had given its dismal warning that the slaveholders' rebellion was to sound the tocsin for a general holy crusade of property against labor, and that for the men of labor, with their hopes for the future, even their past conquests were at stake in that tremendous conflict on the other side of the Atlantic. Everywhere they bore patiently the hardships imposed upon them by the cotton crisis, opposed enthusiastically the proslavery intervention of their betters—and, from most parts of Europe, contributed their quota of blood to the good cause.

While the workingmen, the true political powers of the North, allowed slavery to defile their own republic, while before the Negro, mastered and sold without his concurrence. They boasted it the highest prerogative of the white-skinned laborer to sell himself and choose his own master; they were unable to attain the true freedom of labor or to support their European brethren in their struggle for emancipation, but this barrier to progress has

150

been swept off by the red sea of civil war.

The workingmen of Europe feel sure that, as the American War of Independence initiated a new era of ascendancy for the middle class, so the American Antislavery War will do for the working classes. They consider it an earnest of the epoch to come that it fell to the lot of Abraham Lincoln, the single-minded son of the working class, to lead his country through the matchless struggle for the rescue of an enchained race and the reconstruction of a social world.

Signed on behalf of the International Workingmen's Association, the Central Council:

Longmaid, Worley, Whitlock, Fox, Blackmore, Hartwell, Pidgeon, Lucraft, Weston, Dell, Nieass, Shaw, Lake, Buckley, Osbourne, Howell, Carter, Wheeler, Stainsby, Morgan, Grossmith, Dick, Denoual, Jourdain, Morrissot, Leroux, Bordage, Bocquet, Talandier, Dupont, L.Wolff, Aldovrandi, Lama, Solustri, Nusperli, Eccarius, Wolff, Lessner, Pfander, Lochner, Kaub, Bolleter, Rybczinski, Hansen, Schantzenbach, Smales, Cornelius, Petersen, Otto, Bagnagatti, Setacci;

George Odger, President of the Council; P.V. Lubez, Corresponding Secretary for France; Karl Marx, Corresponding Secretary for Germany; G.P. Fontana, Corresponding Secretary for Italy; J.E. Holtorp, Corresponding Secretary for Poland; H.F. Jung, Corresponding Secretary for Switzerland; William R. Cremer, Honorary General Secretary."

The Civil War continued to be successful for the Union and President Abraham Lincoln in 1865; Union Major General John Schofield defeated Confederate General Hood at the Battle of Franklin, and Union George H. Thomas dealt General Hood a massive defeat at the Battle of Nashville, effectively destroying Hood's army. In desperation, the Confederates in their ongoing losing war debated the use of black soldiers, which was deeply rejected by most southern politicians and soldiers who desired to maintain slavery. Confederate newspapers such as the Georgian Atlanta Southern Confederacy were opposed to arming black men, writing in January of 1865, "Such an act on our part, would be a stigma on the imperishable pages of history, of which all future generations of Southrons would be ashamed. These are some of the additional considerations which have suggested themselves to us. Let us put the negro to work, but not to fight." Many Confederates—including R. M. T. Hunter and Georgian Democrat Howell Cobb—were against the arming of slaves. Howell Cobb stated that African Americans were untrustworthy and innately lacked the qualities to make good soldiers; using them would cause many Confederates to quit the army. Robert E. Lee later wrote the Confederate Congress, encouraging them that the idea would take serious traction and on March thirteenth, 1865, the Confederate Congress passed General Order 14 by a single vote in the Confederate Senate. This led to the formation of several black Confederate units who were not involved in a major battle. Most black people were forced to serve in the Confederate Army, but the slaves who were able to escape to live as free men. A large majority of black men, however, joined Union forces, delivering devastating defeats.

Confederate General E. Lee attempted to regroup at the village of Appomattox Court House in Virginia, but Union General Grant surrounded the Confederates and General Lee decided that the fight was now hopeless, surrendering his Army of Northern Virginia on April ninth, 1865 at the McLean House. The war to establish The Confederate States of America and the songs which would honor that nation including "God Save the South," and "The Bonnie Blue Flag" had now come to an end. The Civil War was devastating to the psyche of the people of the United States; it had ripped apart friends and family members, and by some estimates, there were about 828,000 Union casualties and 864,000 Confederate casualties. The traumatic Civil War was now over, and President Abraham Lincoln's popularity increased as he began rebuilding the United States and continued the policy of Reconstruction.

Five days after the surrender of General Robert. E Lee, Abraham Lincoln was assassinated by John Wilkes Booth on Good Friday, April fourteenth, 1865, while he attended a play at Ford's Theatre as the American Civil War ended. He died hours later. Booth was later killed by Sergeant Boston Corbett on April twenty-sixth, 1865. An actor and Confederate spy, Booth was angered when President Abraham Lincoln proposed voting rights for black people. Abraham Lincoln's Vice President Andrew Johnson became President of the United States.

Dominicans were not surprised when they heard news of the Union victory against the Confederacy; many celebrated the emancipation of slaves in the United States. On June nineteenth, 1865, the abolition of slavery was announced in the State of Texas and many former slaves read Abraham Lincoln's Emancipation Proclamation. The day was celebrated as Juneteenth Independence Day (or Freedom Day) throughout the former Confederacy of the southern United States. The slaves there were now emancipated, and they joined the free black people of the Caribbean and Latin America.

Slavery continued in the Spanish colonies of Cuba and Puerto Rico and as Anibal Medina began to build his family's wealth, he and other Dominicans fought for the independence of the Cuban and Puerto Rican people. Anibal felt it was a travesty of human rights that slavery continued in the last two remaining Spanish colonies of Cuba and Puerto, even as the United States emancipated their slaves. Anibal believed the government of the Dominican Republic should put pressure on the Spanish colonial governments of Cuba and Puerto Rico. The Dominicans should contribute arms, money, or directly join revolutionary groups in both islands if they so desired.

The European powers continued to exploit the United States Civil War to infiltrate Latin America—particularly Napoleon III, who returned the Hapsburg Dynasty to Mexico when the younger brother of the Austrian emperor Francis Joseph I declared himself Emperor Maximillian I of Mexico on the tenth of April 1864. In France, Napoleon III began great public works, including the reconstruction of Paris and monuments dedicated to historical figures. Among them was a seven-meter-tall monument of Vercingétorix—the leader who united various Gallic tribes in Gaul in a failed war against Julius Caesar from 58 BCE to 50 BCE. Surprisingly, Emperor Maximillian I implemented various liberal reforms that his opponent Benito Suarez also supported; land reforms, religious freedom, and extending the right to vote beyond the Mexican land-holding class. In an effort to bring peace to Mexico, Emperor Maximillian I offered Benito Suarez amnesty and the position of Prime Minister, which Juarez refused. Emperor Maximillian I invited ex-Confederates to Mexico in a series of settlements called the Carlota Colony and the New Virginia Colony while many of Suarez loyalists were executed after the Black Decree.

Antonio López de Santa Anna—who lived in exile in Jamaica, Cuba, the United States, Colombia, and Saint Thomas—traveled to New York in the 1850s with the first shipment of chicle, introducing the base of what would become chewing gum to the United States. Santa Anna intended chicle to be used for buggy tires, but like many of his business ideas, he failed to convince U.S. tire manufactures and would return to Mexico in 1865 to offer his services against the French. He was denied entry by Benito Juarez and Santa Anna would leave Mexico once again.

Benito Juarez continued their resistance against Emperor Maximillian I and the Mexican Empire, and by 1866, Napoleon III withdrew his troops to Europe to face the threat of Chancellor Otto von Bismarck and the Prussian Military. Emperor Maximillian I was advised to abdicate and under duress, he often retreated to his hacienda to spend time with his Mexican mistress and devote much of his time to the study of insects. When the Mexican Republican press discovered Maximillian I playing with bugs, they nicknamed him "The Great Dreamer" and published negative propaganda against the Emperor.

Anibal supported the nationalistic movements of the Latin American people and was informed regarding the ongoing Mexican war between President Benito Juarez and Emperor Maximillian I. However, he was wary regarding the United States' support of President Benito Juarez and their goals in Mexico and Latin America if Emperor Maximillian I was defeated. Anibal was excited about the future of the Caribbean and the end of the

Civil War in America, but like many Dominicans, he worried about the future imperialistic aims of the United States.

CHAPTER 20

JAMAICA & THE MORANT BAY REBELLION

(1866)

Rory McDonnell was overjoyed when he was informed that the Spainards had been defeated and the Dominican Republic was restored. Many Jamaicans suffering under English discrimination quietly supported the victory. Rory McDonnell celebrated along with his wife Abigail and they prayed for the freedom of the Cuban and Puerto Rican people. However, Rory was unable to return to Santo Domingo as the conflict began. Slavery was abolished in Jamaican on August first, 1834, and blacks outnumbered whites thirty-two to one but only 2,000 out of 436,000 black people were eligible to vote during the election of 1864. Black Jamaicans who were mostly poor could not pay the high poll taxes and they were disenfranchised. The black people of Jamaica continued to be discriminated against and experience a low standard of living.

Rory McDonnell was residing in eastern Kingston, Jamaica with his wife Abigail and their baby daughter Aileen when civil arrest erupted in Morant Bay in St. Thomas-in-the-East. Jamaica was suffering an economic downturn and the black Jamaicans suffered due to crop damage by floods, through cholera and smallpox epidemics, and later a long drought. The unrest would manifest in a massive protest in Morant Bay led by a black Jamaican Baptist deacon and activist. Paul Bogle was advocated for the poor black Jamaicans and criticized the leadership of Governor Edward John Eyre. Peter Bogle formed a friendship with the biracial or creole wealthy landholder named George William Gordon.

George William Gordon was elected as a representative of St. Thomas-in-the-East parish in The House of the Assembly. One of eight children born to a Scottish planter named Joseph and a black slave named Ann Rattray, George William Gordon was a determined young man who taught himself how to read, write, and perform simple accounting. George William Gordon had a correspondence with English evangelical critics of colonial policy and also established a Native Baptist church, where Paul Bogle was a deacon. George William Gordon allied himself with liberals who were against the Jamaican Colonial Government and in May 1865, he secretly attempted to purchase an ex-Confederate schooner with the intention of ferrying arms and ammunition to Jamaica from the United States of America.

Eyre was born in Whipsnade, Bedfordshire in England before his family relocated to Hornsea, Yorkshire, England. After Grammar school, Eyre moved to Sydney, Australia. Previous European explorers settled in Australia—including the Dutch Willem Janszoon in 1606—and Australia was subsequently named New Holland. In 1770, British explorer Lieutenant James Cook charted the east coast of Australia and favored the colonization of Botany Bay (now renamed Sydney). The British established the first European settlement in 1788 as a Penal Colony, and their arrival was devastating to the indigenous Australian people, who were killed by settlers and died from foreign diseases. Other English explorers would arrive in Australia, including John Eyre, who previously transported 1,000 sheep and 600 cattle by land from Monaro, New South Wales to Adelaide and sold them for a large profit. John Eyre led the expedition with John Baxter and three Aborigines, however two of the Aborigines attacked John Baxter and took most of the supplies. John Eyre and an Aborigine named Wylie survived when they observed a French whaling ship the Mississippi under the command of an Englishman (Captain Thomas Rossiter) at a bay near bay near Esperance, Western Australia (which John Eyre renamed Rossiter Bay).

With his profits, John Eyre funded his expedition to the interior of Australia. Together with his Aboriginal companion Wylie, Eyre was the first European to traverse the coastline of the Great Australian Bight and the Nullarbor Plain by land from 1840 to 1841; it was an almost 2000-mile trip to Albany, Western Australia. From 1848 to 1853, John Eyre served as lieutenant-governor of New Munster Province in New Zealand under Sir George Grey. In 1854, John Eyre was governor of several Caribbean island colonies and became the Governor of Jamaica. Governor Eyre was supported by the Jamaican white elite, but he became unpopular with the black Jamaican majority and their advocates like George William Gordon.

Gordon sympathized with the plight of the descendants of the slaves in Jamaica and desired to uplift them in society. He and Governor John Eyre disliked each other, and they were fierce political opponents. George William Gordon wrote that Governor Eyre would not pass reforms, which would result in a second bondage of the poor Jamaican people. Governor Eyre angrily stated that George William Gordon was, "The most consistent and untiring obstructer of the public business in the House of Assembly." George William Gordon responded by saying, "He is devoid of justice and humanity."

In 1865, Dr. Edward Underhill, Secretary of the Baptist Missionary Society of Great Britain, wrote a letter to the Colonial Office in London describing the poor state of Jamaica's masses. Governor John Eyre was aware of the letter, and he immediately tried to deny its statements. Jamaica's poor blacks learned of the letter and began organizing in "Underhill Meetings". Peasants in Saint Ann parish subsequently sent a petition to Queen Victoria asking for Crown lands to cultivate, stating they could not find land for themselves. The letter was sent to Governor Eyre first and he added additional commentary. Queen Victoria later stated that the poor should simply work harder without offering any solution. Paul Bogle led black Jamaicans towards the Jamaican capital city of Spanish Town, where they sought an audience with Governor Eyre. Governor Eyre quickly refused to meet with Paul Bogle and the poor black Jamaicans, angering them further.

On the seventh of October 1865, a black Jamaican was put on trial at the Morant Bay Court House, then imprisoned for trespassing on an abandoned sugar plantation. The people spoke against this miscarriage of justice, and one man named James Geoghegan was approached by police to be removed from the courthouse for protesting the unjust verdict. As the police pursued James Geoghegan, a fight erupted and two policemen were beaten with sticks and stones. The following Monday warrants for the arrest of several black Jamaicans were issued. On the eleventh of October 1865, hundreds of Jamaicans marched towards the Morant Bay Court House. A local inexperienced militia was attacked with various objects and they opened fire on the protestors in a bloody clash that resulted in twenty-five deaths. The Jamaican white elite feared an insurrection by black Jamaicans and their allies as they believed a possible white massacre would occur in Jamaica similar to the one after the Haitian Revolution.

Governor John Eyre sent troops under Brigadier-General Alexander Nelson to stop the rebels and capture Paul Bogle. Fearful of the panic and unrest in Jamaica, Governor Eyre became increasingly autocratic as he coerced the House of Assembly to pass constitutional reforms that brought the old form of government to an end and allowed Jamaica to become a Crown Colony with an appointed rather than elected legislature. Before dissolving itself, the legislature passed laws to deal with the recent emergency, which included sanctioning martial law and increased Governor John Eyre's power. Governor John Eyre ordered troops under Brigadier-General Alexander Nelson to hunt down the poorly armed Jamaican rebels and bring Paul Bogle back to Morant Bay for trial.

Rory McDonnell feared for the black Jamaicans who were now in danger of government retaliation. Government troops began attacking the rebels as well as innocent Jamaicans who were not involved with the protest. Some of Abigail's family members were activists who spoke against the government of Governor John Eyre and some were suspected to be involved in the resistance movement led by Paul Bogle. Paul Bogle was highly intelligent and eloquent and was able to motivate the poor Jamaicans. He was a slender man, strong with focused eyes; as the situation in Jamaica worsened, he remained stoic and courageous in his advocacy for the Jamaican poor against the colonial government. As violence spread throughout Jamaica and particularly Morant Bay, Rory McDonnell could do little, as he was responsible for his wife and baby daughter.

Government troops began attacking the suspected rebels and over 439 black Jamaicans were killed while 354 people—including Paul Bogle—were arrested and later executed without a proper trial. Paul Bogle was killed the day after his capture. Representative George William Gordon was accused of treason and later imprisoned and transported from Kingston to Morant Bay; within two days, Representative Gordon was tried for high treason by court-martial without due process of law, sentenced to death, and executed on the twenty-third of October 1865. This caused an uproar in Jamaica and England.

English liberals including John Stuart Mill spoke against the brutality of Governor John Eyre and created The Jamaica Committee, which called for Eyre to be tried for his abuses. English liberals who joined The Jamaica Committee included, John Bright, Charles Darwin, Frederic Harrison, Thomas Hughes, Thomas Henry Huxley, Herbert Spencer, and A. V. Dicey. Other notable members of the committee were Charles Buxton, Edmond Beales, Leslie Stephen, James Fitzjames Stephen, Edward Frankland, Thomas Hill Green, Frederick Chesson, Goldwin Smith, Charles Lyell, and Henry Fawcett. Countering the Englishmen that called for the trial of Governor Eyre was Thomas Carlyle. He started the Governor Eyre Defense and Aid Committee, which included John Ruskin, Charles Kingsley, Charles Dickens, Lord Cardigan, Alfred Tennyson, and John Tyndall. Cases against Lieutenant Brand and Brigadier Abercrombie Nelson were presented to the Central Criminal Court, but the grand jury declined to certify them.

Many Jamaicans understood that Governor John Eyre would not receive any serious penalties for his crimes, so they continued to protest. Governor John Eyre was soon replaced by Sir Henry Knight Storks, who was appointed Governor of Jamaica on the twelfth of December 1865. The replacement of John Eyre was not the desired justice for the hundreds of Jamaicans who had lost family members during the rebellion. In early 1866, Rory McDonnell was able to travel to Morant Bay and to his relief, discovered that Abigail's parents survived the rebellion. However, a few of Abigail's family members sustained injuries and Rory supported their medical expenses.

To Rory's surprise, his friend Anibal Hector Medina and his nephew Carlos traveled to Kingston, Jamaica in March of 1866. Anibal informed Rory about the recent birth of his son in December of 1865, who he named Raul Saladin Medina. Anibal chose the name Saladin after An-Nasir Salah ad-Din Yusuf ibn Ayyub, who was the first Sultan of Egypt and Syria and the founder of the short-lived Ayyubid Dynasty. Anibal read about Saladin and his leadership in the war against the Crusader forces led by King Richard I of England known as "The Lionheart" and his conquest of Jerusalem. Anibal respected Saladin; he displayed compassion by allowing the Christian and Jewish inhabitants to continue living freely in Palestine and Jerusalem after the Battle of Hattin in 1187, when he wrested control of Palestine, as opposed to the Crusaders who massacred the Muslims after their previous conquest.

Rory congratulated Anibal as both men spoke about the Morant Bay rebellion, which shocked Jamaica and the Caribbean. Rory was impressed with Anibal's improved English and introduced him to his wife Abigail and their baby daughter Aileen. Anibal formerly presented his nephew and spoke about the successful Dominican War of Restoration and the establishment of the Dominican Second Republic. Rory was excited for Anibal, however he lamented the state of affairs in Jamaica. Anibal had quickly recuperated most of his losses and now began to experience a good profit. He promised to financially support Rory McDonell and his family as they attempted to recover from the vicious rebellion the previous year.

Abigail eased Anibal's feelings as he informed him and her husband of the strength of the Jamaican people and spoke about Queen Nanny, leader of the Jamaican Maroons. Queen Nanny was born into the Asante people and after she escaped slavery in Jamaica, she led escaped slaves into successful confrontations against the English. Queen Nanny and the English agreed to a peace treaty and Queen Nanny established Windward Maroons of Nanny Town. However, it was destroyed after the first Maroon War in 1734. Another Maroon leader, Captain Cudjoe, also had a peace treaty with the English, establishing freedom for the Leeward Maroons. Abigail reminded Anibal and her husband about the perseverance of the Jamaican people.

Some of Rory's neighbors arrived at the McDonnell home in Kingston, including the Sharmas, who were an Indian family that had previously came to Jamaica as indentured laborers. The Sharma family belonged to the Hindu religion, which interested Anibal since he had only read about it in books. Jaspal and Anjali Sharma were eager to meet Rory's Dominican friend he often spoke about. The Sharma family had arrived from the Awadhi region of the declining Mughal Empire in 1846, while other Indians arrived from the Bhojpuri region and others came from Southern India. Like all Indian indentures, the Sharma family were paid less than the former black slave laborers. Their fundamental cultural and linguistic difference as well as their tendency not to mix with the local population caused both blacks and British to look down on them. They were often harassed with the term coolie, which referred to their worker status. However, they worked hard and had a positive outlook as they embraced a Jamaican culture they desired to be part of. The Sharma family also had an intelligent young girl named Anoushka about the same age as Carlos, who enjoyed Jamaica and its people, and she spoke in the local Jamaican Patois. Anoushka identified as a Jamaican and quickly made friends beyond her Indian community.

During his stay, Anibal enjoyed some Jamaican jerk food. The word "jerk" is said to come from charqui, a Spanish term of Quechua origin for jerked or dried meat. The food was prepared by poking the meat with holes so flavor could more easily be absorbed. Abigail informed Anibal that jerk food was developed after black Coromantee slaves escaped into the mountains and joined the local Tainos in Jamaica. The ethnic Akan or Coromantee slaves fled from their Spanish slave masters when the English took Jamaica from the Spaniards in 1655. The slaves formed maroons and developed ingredients using local herbs and spices, including Scotch bonnet pepper, cloves, cinnamon, scallions, nutmeg, thyme, garlic, brown sugar, ginger, salt, and allspice (also called pimento). These were used on the meat and slowly cooked in a pit fire. Anibal savored the jerk chicken and pork and during their stay, they also enjoyed the jerk seasonings applied to fish, shrimp, shellfish, beef, sausage, and lamb. The Sharma family also added their spices from India such as curry powder. It was the first time Anibal tasted the flavor of curry, and he was delighted. Carlos Medina relished the curry and asked his uncle if they could take some of this food to the Dominican Republic.

Anibal also enjoyed the Jamaican johnnycake, a cornmeal flatbread which is believed to have originated from the indigenous people of what is now the eastern United States. Rory introduced Anibal to a drink made from seaweed called Irish Moss. The beverage was brought to Jamaica by the Irish immigrants and was now appearing on the Jamaican shore. The drink was prepared by Abigail with about a pound of Irish Moss mixed with some gum Arabic, nutmeg, water, milk, and some other ingredients. Rory joked with Anibal that he would have more children after he finished the drink. As night approached, the Sharma family spoke about their life in India under the declining Mughal Empire, which was under the control of the British East India company and was now the British Raj and directly ruled by Queen Victoria.

The Mughal Empire was a Muslim dynasty with Turco-Mongol Chagatai roots from Central Asia. After it was founded in 1526 by Babur, who defeated Sultan Ibrahim Lodi he brought an end to the Delhi Sultanate. The Mughal Emperors had significant Indian Rajput and Persian ancestry and claimed direct descent from both Genghis Khan (the founder of the Mongol Empire), his son Chagatai Khan, and Timur the Turco-Mongol conqueror who founded the Timurid Empire. The Sharma family explained that the Mughal Empire reached its zenith during the reign of Emperor Akbar The Great. The Mughal Empire developed and employed the use of gunpowder in warfare along with the Ottoman Empire and Safavid Persia, and Emperor Akbar I also used rockets. The empire flourished in sciences, but Anibal was informed that the decline of the Mughal Empire occurred as the British East India Company took control in 1757, after the Battle of

Plassey when Mir Jafar (the new Nawab of Bengal) was enthroned by Robert Clive. In 1773, the British East India Company established a capital in Calcutta and appointed its first Governor-General, Warren Hastings, becoming directly involved in governance. After the Indian Rebellion of 1857, the British reorganized the army, the financial system, and administration in India through the Government of India Act 1858, creating the British Raj.

Jaspal was saddened with the affairs of his homeland. However, he was happy he was not there during the rebellion and only desired to have a safe place to raise his daughter Anoushka—although the recent events of the Morant Bay Rebellion deeply worried him. Carlos spent most of his time in Jamaica playing and speaking with Anoushka, who he found attractive. Carlos never saw a girl with the shade of brown skin that Anoushka had; neither had he ever encountered one with lovely long dark hair that reached her waist. Anibal observed Carlos' growing attraction for Anoushka and noticed how much fun the girl was having with his nephew. Carlos also spent some time teaching Anoushka the Spanish language, which deeply interested her. Towards the end of their brief stay, Anibal jokingly promised to return to Jamaica so he might see Anoushka again.

Anibal and Carlos Medina enjoyed their time in Jamaica. However, Anibal had to quickly return to San Cristobal to take care of his young son. After two weeks, he came back to the Dominican Republic, where he soon learned about the unrest in Puerto Rico as nationalists prepared to move against the Spanish Colonial Government. Anibal desired to speak to Puerto Ricans living in Santo Domingo regarding the situation. As he prepared to aid Puerto Rican revolutionaries, his friend Valentino Xin and his sister Catalina had a wedding in Santo Domingo. The ceremony was a great event that brought many friends and family to the Medina home as Valentino Xin and Catalina Medina were finally united in marriage. In 1868, when Valentino Xin and Catalina Violeta Medina de Xin were about thirty years of age, they had their first son, Alvaro Xin Medina, and a daughter in 1870 named Luna Xin Medina (nicknamed Chinita). The celebrations lasted several weeks as the Medina family continued to grow, and Valentino Xin helped the farm and developed his own fishing business on the beaches of Santo Domingo. The Saint-Lot family also celebrated the wedding of their son Raymond to a Dominican woman named Julia Márquez from Macorix, in the Eastern Dominican Republic.

CHAPTER 21
EL GRITO DE LARES & DREAMS OF A BORICUA REPUBLIC
(1868)

Anibal Hector Medina was optimistic when Dominican leader President Buenaventura Báez was ousted from power on the twenty-ninth of May 1865. President Buenaventura Báez was brought to power by a junta of generals, which prompted a national convention to write a new constitution that, as expected, ended up merely a copy of the Constitution of December 1854. The convention also reorganized the money as a public debt that President Buenaventura Báez had borrowed from the firm of Jesurum & Zoon in Curacao to cover the expenses of the political movement that returned him to power. The reign of terror continued against all liberal politicians and progressives that were in alliance with the Dominican Blue Party as well as any outspoken independents who threatened the government of President Buenaventura Báez. Despite his unpopularity throughout the country, the title of Great Citizen was bestowed upon President Buenaventura Báez.

Various generals opposed President Buenaventura Báez and the Red Party, including the brothers Benito Ogando Timoteo and Andres Timoteo as Generals Gregorio Luperón and General José Maria Cabral continued their revolution against the leader. In Haiti in 1865, the light-skinned mulatto Major Sylvain Salnave began his takeover of the north and Artibonite part of Haiti while speaking against President Geffrard's subservience towards the Spanish occupation of the Dominican territory. He reopened old wounds between the people of Northern, Western, and Southern Haiti and brought foreigners into Haitian internal politics. The Haitians were also angered that President Fabre Geffrard involved the British with the internal affairs of Haiti. President Fabre Geffrard, who had witnessed his reign come to an end, quickly disguised himself and his family members and fled to Jamaica in March 1867.

President Buenaventura Báez allied himself with the Haitian leader President Sylvain Salnave, who provided him with aid. President Sylvain Salnave also agreed to capture and surrender Dominican rebels to the government. President Buenaventura Báez informed the United States that he was willing to sell the bay and peninsula of Samaná for $1,000,000 in gold and $100,000 in arms and munitions. In return, he requested the United States send him three battleships. President Buenaventura Báez then sent his Curacaoan associate Abraham Jesurum to the United States to seek a loan. His efforts were to no avail, as he was soon overthrown and replaced by the military triumvirate of Pedro Antonio Pimentel, Gregorio Luperón, and Federico de Jesús García, which resulted in the presidency of

José María Cabral.

President José María Cabral was shortly ousted from power and replaced with President Manuel Altagracia Cáceres, who was subsequently replaced by a junta of generals—José Antonio Hungría, Francisco Antonio Gómez Báez, and José Ramón Luciano y Franco. During the junta of generals, many Dominican government officials and citizens supported the Puerto Rican Revolution and continued aiding the Puerto Rican nationalists before President Buenaventura Báez returned to power on May second, 1868. President Sylvain Salnave of Haiti was eventually overthrown in a coup by his eventual successor, President Nissage Saget. Salnave was tried for treason and executed in 1870. The instability in Haiti caused complicated alliances between political figures within the Dominican Republic who had their own ideologies and aspirations.

In 1865, the central government in Madrid, Spain set up the Junta Informativa de Reformas de Ultramar (or the Informative Board on Overseas Reforms) to review complaints from provincial representatives. The Puerto Rican delegation was freely elected by those eligible to vote— which were male Caucasian property owners—in what was one of the first exercises of political openness in Spain. Separatist Segundo Ruiz Belvis was elected to the junta, representing Mayagüez. However, many Puerto Ricans who supported Spanish control were horrified. To the frustration of many abolitionists—including José Julián Acosta—the junta had a majority of mainland Spain-born delegates who would vote down almost every measure they suggested, including the abolition of slavery and autonomy for Puerto Rico. When the junta members returned to Puerto Rico, they met with local community leaders at the Hacienda El Cacao in Carolina, in early 1865. Segundo Ruiz invited Dr. Ramón Emeterio Betances to attend. After listening to the voted down measures by the junta, Dr. Ramón Emeterio Betances stated, *"Nadie puede dar lo que no tiene,"* or "You can't give away what you don't own"—a phrase he used often when referring to Spain's unwillingness to grant Puerto Rico or Cuba any reforms.

Dr. Ramón Emeterio Betances and Segundo Ruiz Belvis founded the *Comité Revolucionario de Puerto Rico* (or the Revolutionary Committee of Puerto Rico) on January sixth, 1868 from their exile in the Dominican Republic. Betances authored several Proclamas, (statements) attacking the exploitation of the Puerto Ricans by the Spanish centralist system and called for a revolution. After his exile in St. Thomas in 1867, Betances wrote Los Diez Mandamientos de los hombres libres (or The Ten Commandments of Free Men), which were directly influenced by the Declaration of the Rights of Man and of the Citizen. It was adopted by France's National Assembly in 1789, which contained the principles that inspired the French Revolution. The poet Lola Rodríguez de Tió, who was inspired by Dr. Ramón Emeterio Betances's quest for Puerto Rico's independence, wrote the patriotic lyrics to the tune of *La Borinqueña*—Puerto Rico's national anthem.

The Ten Commandments of Free Men stated:

"Puerto Ricans. The government of Mme. Isabella II throws upon us a terrible accusation. It states that we are bad Spaniards. The government defames us. We don't want separation, we want peace, the union with Spain; however, it is fair that we also add conditions to the contract. They are rather easy, here they are:

The abolition of slavery

The right to vote on all impositions

Freedom of religion

Freedom of speech

Freedom of the press

Freedom of trade

The right to assembly

Right to bear arms

Inviolability of the citizen

The right to choose our own authorities

These are the Ten Commandments of Free Men.

If Spain feels capable of granting us, and gives us, those rights and liberties, they may then send us a General Captain, a governor... made of straw, that we will burn in effigy come Carnival time, as to remember all the Judases that they have sold us until now. That way we will be Spanish, and not otherwise.

If not, Puerto Ricans – HAVE PATIENCE! for I swear that you will be free."

In January 1868, the independence leader Dr. Ramón Emeterio Betances urged Mariana Bracetti to knit a revolutionary flag the Trinitarios used. In 1844, the first flag of the Dominican Republic was raised by the founding members of the Trinitarios: Juan Pablo Duarte, Francisco del Rosario Sánchez, and Matías Ramón Mella. This directly influenced the Revolutionary Flag of Lares, and the Puerto Rican revolutionaries added a white star. Eduvigis Beauchamp Sterling was named Treasurer of the revolution by Betances, and he provided Mariana Bracetti with the materials for the Revolutionary Flag of Lares. The flag was divided in the middle by a white Latin cross, the two lower corners were red, and the two upper corners were blue. A white star was placed in the upper left blue corner. According to many Puerto Rican revolutionaries, the white cross stood for the yearning for homeland redemption, the red squares represented the blood poured by the heroes of the rebellion, and the white star in the solitary blue square symbolized liberty and freedom.

The Revolutionary Committee named twelve of their members as generals: Manuel Rojas (Commander-in-Chief of the Liberation Army); Andrés Pol, Juan de Mata Terraforte Joaquín Parrilla, Nicolás Rocafort,

Gabino Plumey, Dorvid Beauchamp, Mathías Brugman, Rafael Arroyo, and Francisco Arroyo, (Generals of Division); Pablo Rivera (Cavalry General), and Abdón Pagán (Artillery General). The plan was set in motion as numerous Puerto Rican nationalists residing in the Dominican Republic planned to return to Puerto Rico and join the rebel cells throughout the island.

On September twentieth, Francisco Ramírez Medina held a meeting at his house to discuss the insurrection, which was planned and set to begin in Camuy on September twenty-ninth. The meeting was attended by Marcelino Vega, Carlos Martínez, Bonifacio Agüero, José Antonio Hernández, Ramón Estrella, Bartolomé González, Cesilio López, Antonio Santiago, Manuel Ramírez, and Ulises Cancela. Cancela instructed Manuel María González to deliver all the acts and important papers of the meeting to Manuel Rojas.

The Dominican government—particularly under the leadership of Blue Party members—

supported Ramón Emeterio Betances, allowed him to recruit a small army, and gave him a ship containing weapons. However, when the ship was about to sail, the Spanish government made its move and prohibited its departure from Dominican territory. Where the ship was anchored in Saint Thomas, authorities boarded the vessel and confiscated its cargo. Gregorio Luperón and other Dominicans continued to support the Puerto Rican nationalists as rebels changed the date of the revolution to occur earlier.

The revolution began in the town of Lares on September twenty-third. Some 400 to 600 rebels gathered on that day in the hacienda of Manuel Rojas, located near Pezuela on the outskirts of Lares. Rojas and Juan de Mata Terraforte led the rebels as they reached the town of Lares by horse and foot around midnight. Many of the rebels were escaped black slaves who were particularly motivated to defeat the Spaniards and end slavery in Puerto Rico. The rebels were also made up of nationalists as well as poor and middle-class Creoles who were dissatisfied with their lack of economic opportunities. The Puerto Ricans looted stores, captured *peninsulares* (Spaniards born in Spain), and took over city hall. The rebels soon entered the town's church and placed the revolutionary flag of Lares on the High Altar. The Republic of Puerto Rico was proclaimed at 2:00 a.m. local time under the presidency of Francisco Ramírez Medina at the church.

The initial uprising in Lares was soon called El Grito de Lares (or The Cry of Lares). President Francisco Ramírez Medina was the leader of the Republic of Puerto Rico and he appointed various government officials: Aurelio Méndez (Minister of the Interior), Manuel Ramírez (Minister of State), Celedonio Abril (Minister of the Treasury), Federico Valencia (Minister of War), Clemente Millán (Minister of Justice), Bernabé Pol (Secretary to the President), and Manuel Rojas (Commander in Chief of the

Liberation Army). President Francisco Ramírez Medina also introduced the Libreta (or notebook) system. The Libreta system required workers to carry on his person a notebook which stated the type of job they held and who employed him. Anyone who was able to work and did not carry a Libreta was subject to imprisonment. President Francisco Ramírez Medina also ordered the liberation of all Puerto Rican slaves who had joined the rebellion.

Miguel Diaz was involved in a rebel cell located in Mayagüez, and he and about 100 others quickly arrived at San Sebastián del Pepino to join the rebellion under Command Manuel Rojas. The Spaniards quickly responded by sending troops from San Juan, Mayagüez, and Ponce, devastating the Puerto Ricans. Miguel Diaz was motivated and focused during the battle, shooting some of the Spaniards and using his machetes in close combat. However, the Puerto Rican militia was effective and managed to break the rebel forces and send them into a retreat. Miguel Diaz felt strong pride as he fought for the declared Republic of Puerto Rico, but he was shot in the chest and died as rebel forces fled towards Lares. Upon an order from the governor Julián Pavía, the militia soon rounded them up. Within two days, the insurrection was over.

Over 475 rebels—including the leader of the Arecibo cell, Dr. José Gualberto Padilla, Manuel Rojas, and Mariana Bracetti—were imprisoned in Arecibo, where they were tortured and humiliated. On November seventeenth, a military court imposed the death penalty for treason and sedition on all the prisoners. In Madrid, the intellectual Eugenio María de Hostos and other prominent Puerto Ricans were successful in interceding with President Francisco Serrano, who also led a revolution against the monarchy in Spain. The reign of Queen Isabella II ended after La Gloriosa (or the Glorious Revolution), which was inspired by a previous rebellion in 1866 led by General Juan Prim until he was defeated by Prime Minister Leopoldo O'Donnell.

Liberals and Republican exiles made agreements at Ostend in 1866 and Brussels in 1867, which led to a major uprising—this time not just to replace the Prime Minister with a Liberal, but to overthrow Queen Isabella II. The Republicans desired to remove the monarchy and begin the Spanish Republic. When generals Prim and Francisco Serrano denounced the government, much of the army defected to the revolutionary generals upon their arrival to Spain. Queen Isabella II made a brief show of force at the Battle of Alcolea, however her loyal moderado generals (or moderate generals) under Manuel Pavia were defeated by General Serrano. Queen Isabella II subsequently was exiled to France, where she lived at the Palacio Castilla in Paris.

After the previous Crimean War and the death of Prime Minister Leopoldo O'Donnell in 1867, the Spanish Empire was weakened as control of the government passed to Regent Francisco Serrano against Baldomero Espartero's dictatorship. The Cortes (or the Spanish Legislature) rejected Republicanism and soon the Spaniards placed the liberal Italian Prince Amadeo of Savoy on the Spanish throne in November 1870. Amadeo was the second son of Victor Emmanuel II of Italy, and when Isabella II abdicated in 1870, he ruled as Amadeo I of Spain. The liberal Spanish government now offered some reforms in Puerto Rico and in effort to appease the tense atmosphere in Puerto Rico, the incoming governor José Laureano Sanz dictated a general amnesty early in 1869. Juan Ríus Rivera, who previously befriended Betances and was studying law in Spain, learned about the failed uprising in Puerto Rico and traveled to the United States, where he immediately went to the Cuba Revolutionary Junta and offered his services.

There were few minor uprisings after the failed Grito de Lares in the towns of Las Marías, Adjuntas, Utuado, Vieques, Bayamón, Ciales, and Toa Baja. Juan de Mata Terreforte, who fought alongside Manuel Rojas, was exiled to New York City. He joined the Puerto Rican Revolutionary Committee and was named its Vice President and the members of the committee adopted the Flag of Lares as the flag of Puerto Rico. The committee was founded on January eighth, 1867 and was composed of Puerto Rican and Dominican patriots with the goal of creating a united effort by Cubans and Puerto Ricans to win independence from Spain.

Trying to appease the already tense atmosphere on the island, the incoming governor José Laureano Sanz dictated a general amnesty early in 1869 and all prisoners were released. However, Betances, Rojas, Lacroix, Aurelio Méndez, and many others were sent into exile. Anibal Medina was notified of the failed rebellion in Puerto Rico and attempted exile of the various rebel leaders. President Francisco Ramírez Medina was also captured and possibly exiled, but many Puerto Ricans speculated that he was secretly assassinated. Anibal was desperate to get information regarding his friend Miguel Diaz, and he was subsequently notified in March 1870 of his death in the city of San Sebastián del Pepino, the day after El Grito de Lares. Anibal mourned his friend's death and prayed for the Puerto Rican people, who he regarded as brothers and sisters. He continued to support Puerto Rican nationalists, however it appeared a Puerto Rican revolution would not occur as it had in Cuba, which was currently embroiled in an ongoing war.

The Cuban revolution began on October tenth, 1868, when sugar mill owner Carlos Manuel de Céspedes and his followers proclaimed independence, beginning the uprising against Spain. The Cuban rebel leaders included Carlos Manuel de Céspedes, Antonio Maceo Grajales, and the Dominican Máximo Gómez. The Cuban rebels were also supported by Puerto Ricans, Mexicans, and Dominicans who desired to see the

Caribbean free from Spanish control. Anibal comforted himself knowing that the Dominican, Cuban, and Puerto Rican fighting spirit would soon defeat the Spaniards.

Anibal and many Dominicans were also informed about the defeat of Emperor Maximillian I and the French in Mexico. Mexican Empress Carlota returned to Europe, seeking assistance for Maximillian's regime in Paris, Vienna, and in Rome from Pope Pius IX. Emperor Maximillian I enjoyed the support of the elite Mexicans Conservatives and the Catholic Church, however the excesses of his court—including using over 700 bottles of wine every month—angered the majority of Mexicans and his forces were soon overwhelmed. Maximilian continued to fight with his army of 8,000 loyalists. Withdrawing in February 1867 to Santiago de Querétaro, he sustained a siege for several weeks, but on May eleventh he decided to escape through the enemy lines. His plan was sabotaged by Colonel Miguel López, who was bribed by the Republicans to open a gate and lead a raiding party with the agreement that Maximilian would be allowed to escape. The Republicans captured the Emperor on May sixteenth and he was sentenced to Court-Martial, which ruled execution by firing squad. Many monarchists and other prominent figures including liberals Victor Hugo and Giuseppe Garibaldi pleaded Juarez to spare the life of Maximillian, but he refused due to the Mexicans who had lost their lives. He wanted to send a message that no foreign power would occupy Mexico. Prince Felix Salm-Salm and his wife masterminded a plan and bribed the jailors to allow Maximilian to escape execution. However, Maximilian did not agree with the plan because he believed that shaving his beard to avoid recognition would ruin his dignity if he was recaptured.

The sentence was carried out in the Cerro de las Campanas at 6:40 a.m. of the nineteenth of June 1867, when Maximilian and Generals Miramón and Mejía were executed by firing squad. In Spanish, Maximilian stated, "I forgive everyone, and I ask everyone to forgive me. May my blood, which is about to be shed, be for the good of the country. Viva Mexico! Viva la independencia!" The Republic of Mexico was soon restored under President Benito Juarez. Anibal was excited by the developments in the Caribbean and Latin America, but he chose to remain in the Dominican Republic.

Anibal would settle into family life and his business as Romina was once again with child. The Medinas were also overjoyed when the university was established once again in Santo Domingo and Marco Medina was soon employed as a professor in 1870. In 1866, the *Instituto Profesional* (or Professional Institute) was created by José Gabriel Garcia and Emiliano Tejera in Santo Domingo. Marco Medina often spoke about the first university of the Americas in Santo Doming, the Regia y Pontificia Universidad de Santo Thomás de Aquino (or Royal and Pontifical

University of St. Thomas Aquinas). It had been created in 1538 but closed under Haitian rule in 1823. Marco was once again joyful, and it motivated Anibal to seek higher education at the university; he wanted to learn mathematics—particularly the calculus made famous by Isaac Newton—as well as various sciences.

CHAPTER 22

LOS ROJOS, VERDES Y AZULES: THE DOMINICAN SIX-YEARS WAR

(1874)

The two major parties which now battled for control of the Dominican Republic were the Partido Azul (the Blue Party) and the powerful Partido Rojo (the Red Party). The Blue Party was nicknamed Los Bolos (or the Tailless) and the Red Party was nicknamed *Los Coludos* (or the Sharks). Anibal supported the Blue Party and their leader Gregorio Luperón as opposed to the Conservative Red Party and their current leader, President Buenaventura Báez. By 1868, Dominicans began to rebel against the government. President Buenaventura Báez continued to maintain a correspondence with the United States, proposing to annex the Dominican Republic. Since the end of the Civil War, the thirteenth amendment was passed, abolishing slavery and involuntary servitude except as punishment for a crime. The fourteenth amendment addressed citizenship rights and equal protection of the laws and was proposed in response to issues related to former slaves following the American Civil War and guaranteeing clientship for all persons born within the United States. The fifteenth amendment prohibits the federal and state governments from denying a citizen the right to vote based on that citizen's "race, color, or previous condition of servitude". Interestingly, the fifteenth amendment created a split within the women's suffrage movement over the amendment denying women the right to vote on account of sex.

The Democrat President Andrew Johnson embarked on a national tour, promoting his executive policies and seeking to destroy his Republican opponents. Congress passed the Tenure of Office Act, which restricted President Andrew Johnson's ability to fire cabinet members. However, when President Johnson attempted to fire Secretary of War Edwin Stanton, he was impeached by the House of Representatives and narrowly avoided conviction in the Senate and removal from office. President Andrew Johnson also had a tumultuous relationship with various black leaders, including Frederick Douglass. After the Emancipation Proclamation and the end of slavery, black people continued to be disenfranchised by various laws enacted—particularly in the south—known as the Black Codes. The Black Codes restricted the freedom of African Americans and forced them to work in a labor economy based on low wages or debt. Northern states including Ohio, Illinois, Indiana, Michigan, and New York enacted Black Codes to discourage free blacks from residing in those states and denied them equal rights, including the right to vote, the right to public education, and the right to equal treatment under the law.

On February seventh, 1866, Frederick Douglass headed a delegation of black men who met with President Johnson at the White House. Johnson lectured the black men about a "war of races" if the Black Codes were repealed, and black men were given the right to vote. As Frederick Douglass left, he stated within earshot of President Andrew Johnson, "The president sends us to the people, and we go to the people." Privately, President Andrew Johnson was angered by Frederick Douglass and said, "Those damned sons of bitches thought they had me in a trap! I know that damned Douglass; he's just like any nigger, and he would sooner cut a white man's throat than not." President Andrew Johnson would not receive the Democratic nomination and Ulysses S. Grant became President of the United States in March 1869.

President Ulysses S. Grant leaned towards the "radical" faction of the Republican Party, which disfavored allowing ex-Confederate officers to retake political power in the south and emphasized equality, civil rights, and voting rights for the freed people or former slaves. President Grant also created the Department of Justice, used the military to enforce laws in the former Confederacy, and prosecuted the Ku Klux Klan. He also appointed Jewish Americans and African Americans to prominent Federal offices. In foreign Affairs President Grant began his presidency by settling the Alabama Claims against Great Britain which was complex grievances and depredations committed against American shipping during the Civil War by the Confederate cruiser CSS Alabama that was secretly purchased in England. To ease the relationship between the United States and Great Britain, President Grant refrained from recognizing Cuban rebels who were fighting for independence from Spain.

President Ulysses S. Grant's settlement of the Alabama claims was undermined by his attempt to annex the Dominican Republic. In early April 1869, Colonel Joseph W. Fabens (an emissary of President Buenaventura Báez) met with Secretary of State Hamilton Fish and presented a lavish proposal for Dominican Republic annexation. Secretary Hamilton Fish brought up the matter of Dominican annexation at a cabinet meeting, but it was disregarded. Given instructions by Secretary Hamilton Fish to investigate the government, natural resources, people, and economy, in July 1869, President Grant sent Babcock to the Dominican Republic. President Grant believed that the annexation of the Dominican Republic would improve the strategic power of the United States in the Caribbean, increase natural resources, and serve as a haven for African Americans.

President Grant instructed Secretary Hamilton Fish to draw up two treaties: one for Dominican annexation and another for the lease of Samaná Bay. In January 1870, President Grant visited Senator Sumner's home to gain his support for annexation, however the two men fell into a bitter dispute and the treaties failed to pass. The Foreign Relations Committee rejected the treaties by a five to two vote and President Grant had to personally lobby senators on his own. Despite President Grant's efforts, the Senate defeated the treaties by a 28 to 28 vote with nineteen Republicans joining the opposition. President Grant subsequently chose three neutral parties, with Fredrick Douglass to head the commission. The Senate remained opposed, leading President Grant to remove Sumner's friend and Minister to Great Britain John Lothrop Motley while his allies in the Senate deposed Sumner of his chairmanship. The Dominican Annexation was deeply embarrassing for President Grant, and he chose not to move forward with the matter.

Many Dominicans—including Anibal Medina—were deeply angered by the Red Party and President Buenaventura Baez. Anibal did not fully support members of the Blue Party, but he strongly opposed the Red Party president, who he believed disrespected thousands of Dominican rebels who fought and died to establish the independent Dominican Republic. Anibal wanted the Dominican Republic to remain a sovereign nation and believed in the removal of the Spanish Colonial Governments in Puerto Rico and Cuba. Anibal was angered with President Grant and his attempts to annex the Dominican Republic with the agreement of President Buenaventura Baez. However, he supported the policy of bringing a small number of black Americans who agreed to come to the Dominican Republic.

Robert Grant agreed with bringing African Americans to the Dominican Republic only if they chose to come. He was now accepted as a Dominican and believed that African Americans could escape severe racism in the United States by living in the Dominican Republic. Despite some xenophobia felt by some Dominicans, Robert Grant believed black men in America faced worse circumstances. Robert Grant informed Anibal regarding the development of the African American settlement in West Africa.

The American Colonization Society believed African Americans might have better opportunities in Africa. The African Americans formed a colony and declared their independence in 1847, however the United States recognized the Republic of Liberia on February fifth, 1862 during the Civil War. Between January seventh, 1822 and the American Civil War, more than 15,000 freed and free-born black people who faced legislated limits in the U.S. and 3,198 Afro-Caribbean people relocated to the settlement. Joseph Jenkins Roberts—a wealthy, free-born African American from Virginia who settled in Liberia—was elected as first president and the Republic of Liberia modeled their flag after that of the United States. Interestingly, the African Americans brought their own culture and sidelined the natives, and the previous colonial settlements of the African Americans were raided by the Kru and Grebo tribes from their inland chiefdoms. After the declaration of independence, the Americo-Liberians would develop a small elite that controlled political power, and the indigenous tribesmen were excluded from birthright citizenship.

Uprisings began within the Dominican Republic in 1868 against the Red Party and President Buenaventura Baez. A fraudulent referendum on annexation by the United States was held in the Dominican Republic on the nineteenth February 1870, however the annexation would not occur. After 1870, the rebellion against President Buenaventura Baez intensified. During the Civil War, Anibal Medina was informed regarding the location of Ricardo Hoffmann. Anibal learned he was jailed after going into hiding in 1867. He supplied documents to Dominican Military, which identified Ricardo Hoffman and implicated him in crimes throughout several Dominican towns during the Restoration War. Ricardo Hoffmann was stripped of his rank and awards and jailed shortly until he was released in January of 1870 and was allowed to work for the Red Party after President Buenaventura Baez assumed power.

Ricardo Hoffman's release deeply angered the Medina family, but Anibal was encouraged by Romina to avoid getting embroiled in that matter. Anibal now had a second son (born in 1870) who he named Alejandro Homero Medina after Alexander the Great and the Greek story-teller Homer—he wanted to keep his family's tradition of naming their children after notable historical figures. Anibal dedicated his time to his wife and children as he continued to improve his business. He longed for the defeat of the Red Party but was not interested in involving himself in the violence associated with the movements against it. However, he desired to fund certain Blue Party members.

Politically and socially, the Cibao and the southern Dominican Republic functioned almost like two different nations. In Santo Domingo and the southern Dominican Republic, the economic base were mahogany and hardwoods, which they traded mostly with England, Curacao, and Saint Thomas, while the economic base of the Cibao was tobacco. Puerto Plata directed their trade towards Hamburg, Bremen, and Saint Thomas. President Buenaventura Baez lived for many years off the profits from the extensive mahogany forests he had inherited from his father. Campesinos (or farmers) and people living in the countryside planted the tobacco. Among them were Dominican women who cured and packed the tobacco, and also owned animals that transported it to towns and ports. The entire process required the labor of many farmers and their families, muleteers, peons, rope, bag manufacturers, merchants, financiers, and trade brokers. Tobacco helped strengthen the Blue Party and finance the rebellion.

As mahogany production faltered, tobacco profits supplied Gregorio Luperón with a steady flow of credit from the merchants of the Cibao and Saint Thomas. Many of the Cibaeños welcomed liberal ideas from Europe, including equality and freedom. The mahogany industry slowed down while agriculture flourished, which favored the Blue Party because the economy focused more on agriculture instead of the exploitation of forests. However, timber would be taken in the northwest in the Yaque River Valley, where the timber was shipped through Montecristi. President Buenaventura Baez was forced to seek foreign loans, which weakened the Dominican economy further, and soon began embezzling treasury funds to keep their political machine running.

Cubans who arrived from the war were not supported by President Buenaventura Baez and were sometimes mistreated. However, by 1872, President Buenaventura's government was weakening against the Dominican rebels under Gregorio Luperón. Anibal Medina and other Dominicans who supported Gregorio Luperón welcomed the Cubans into the Dominican Republic. Most Cubans remained in the northern Dominican Republic, where they married Dominican women and formed families. Towns like Puerto Plata benefitted greatly from the presence of Cuban professionals, businessmen, and intellectuals. Cubans also invested in land, developed railroads, and established sugar cane plantations and modern sugar mills that used steam power. Cubans also brought the sport of baseball to the Dominican Republic, which quickly grew in popularity.

By 1873, President Buenaventura Baez and his government were in serious trouble. The Dominican people had developed their cultural identity as a racially mixed, predominantly Catholic people who were experienced in warfare after defeating the Haitians and Spaniards. The Dominicans differentiated themselves from Haitian culture and the Spaniards, and now they were fighting the United States and their Anglo-Saxon and Protestant cultural elements. The Dominicans were primarily fiercely nationalistic and desired to defeat President Buenaventura Baez. Anibal Medina and other liberal Dominicans living in the southern Dominican Republic financially supported rebel youth in their continued attacks against the army of President Buena-Ventura Baez. By the second of January 1874, President Buenaventura Baez was ousted from power after his defeat in the Six Years War. Ignacio María González Santín was the founder of the Partido Verde (or the Green Party) and would become the interim president of the Dominican Republic in 1874.

The Green Party was part of the Movimiento Unionista (or the Unionist Movement) in the Dominican Republic. The Green Party was also known as los Rojos desteñidos (or the faded Reds) due to the previous membership of President Ignacio María González to the Red Party. President Ignacio María González opposed the annexationist policies of Buenaventura Báez and canceled the Buenaventura Báez agreements with the Samaná Bay Company, recovering Dominican control of Samaná Bay and the Samaná peninsula. President Ignacio María González also pushed to strengthen the economic relationship between Haiti and the Dominican

Republic while setting policies to define the Haitian-Dominican border and legalize trade between the borders to collect taxes for the Dominican Unionist Government.

The subsequent years became politically unstable in the Dominican Republic as various presidents briefly took control. President Manuel Altagracia Cáceres was followed by the Council of Secretaries of State, which included Pedro Tomás Garrido Matos, José de Jesús Eduardo de Castro Álvarez, Pedro Pablo de Bonilla y Correa-Cruzado, Juan Bautista Zafra y Miranda, Pablo López Villanueva, and Jacinto Peynado y Tejón. President Ignacio María González returned briefly before resigning and was fooled by President Marcos Antonio Cabral, who married the daughter of Buenaventura Baez, Altagracia Amelia Báez Andújar.

The political atmosphere in the Dominican Republic was chaotic, however Anibal Medina enjoyed the loosening grip of the Red Party and welcomed change. Some merchants associated with Moisés Aponte traveled to Santo Domingo, where they informed the Medina family regarding the status of Ricardo Hoffman. He had been contracted by the Red Party and was involved with embezzling and plotting against members of the Blue Party. During the final year of the rebellion against President Buenaventura Baez, several Red Party members were killed. Ricardo Hoffman was among them, who was shot and killed along with some of his accomplices in the town of San Ignacio de Sabaneta in Santiago. News of his death finally put the Medina family at ease as the Red Party continued to weaken.

President Buenaventura Báez returned to power on the twenty-seventh of December 1876. However, by 1878, he was ousted once again and exiled to Puerto Rico. President Ignacio María González and the Green Party resumed control of the Dominican government, celebrating the deal with Haitian leader President Michel Domingue and the cessation of the border conflict and the recognition of independence and sovereignty of the Dominican Republic by the Haitian government. President Michel Domingue asked for a loan from France as Haiti's economy continued to suffer under the weight of corruption, and he would arrest Generals Brice and Pierre Monplaisir Pierre. President Michel Domingue was criticized for his financial policies and took refuge in the embassy of the United States. He resigned on April fifteenth, 1876 and went into exile to Kingston, Jamaica, where he died a year later. Septimus Rameau, the man who wielded real power in Haiti, was soon accused of the executions of the Haitian generals and was assassinated in the streets of Port-au-Prince.

In the Dominican Republic, President Ignacio María González granted licenses to foreign companies for the production of textiles, soaps, chocolate, coffee, and other items. He enjoyed support from members of the Blue Party and liberal Dominicans who opposed the Red Party. President Ignacio María González organized the Dominican Military and was proclaimed *Encargado Supremo de la Nación por la voluntad de los Pueblos* (or the Supreme Commander of the Nation for the will of the Peoples), which distanced and angered the liberal members of the Blue Party and alienated members of the Green Party. As the economy worsened and the autocratic nature of the Presidency of Ignacio María González increased, members of the Blue Party quickly turned against him and he was ousted from power as the Green Party was crippled, giving way to the return of the major two parties: Red and Blue. The Blue Party now positioned itself to become the strongest political party in the Dominican Republic.

Among those who served as president was Ignacio María González, and the Council of Secretaries of State included José María Cabral Joaquín Montolío. President Cesáreo Guillermo of the Red Party would assume leadership, followed by Ignacio María González, who was ousted by a coup, and then the Superior Leaders of the Revolutionary Movement (Ulises Heureaux and Cesáreo Guillermo). President Jacinto del Rosario de Castro followed the Council of the Secretaries of State—Cesáreo Guillermo, Alejandro Angulo Guridi, and Pedro María Aristy. President Cesáreo Guillermo of the Red Party returned to power once again in February of 1879, but rebels once again demanded his removal.

As the Red Party began to fragment, exiles from Puerto Rico and Cuba were openly welcomed to the Dominican Republic. Cubans were followed by American, German, and Italian investors who began to control the sugar industry. As the Azules came to power with the help of tobacco, the tobacco industry began to lose to the sugar market and the intellectual Pedro Fran-cisco Bono advised that the neglect of the tobacco industry and the support of the sugar industry would jeopardize the social wellbeing of the nation. Pedro Francisco Bono believed the rise of the sugar would strip Dominican peasants in the south from their land converting a mass of working-class without a future. After traveling throughout Europe, Gregorio Luperón decided to close his business in Puerto Plata and began several plantations of sugar cane, coffee, cacao, and other fruits, intending to sell his products to the New York market. Gregorio Luperón and the Blue Party quickly gained strength and he would begin to form his provisional government in Puerto Plata.

By 1879, President Gregorio Luperón and the Blue Party would finally defeat the Red Party and lead the Dominican Republic. President Gregorio Luperón appointed the powerful military leader General Ulises Hereaux as the government delegate in Santo Domingo and the southern and eastern regions of the Dominican Republic. Anibal and the Medinas celebrated the victory, and Anibal was joyous and found himself happy with the leadership of President Gregorio Luperón. However, he understood that the stability of the Dominican Republic remained fragile, even with one of his favorite leaders occupying the nation's highest office.

Throughout the rise of the Blue Party, Anibal continued to make trips to Jamaica to ensure his friend Rory McDonnell and his family were safe. After the Morant Bay Rebellion the McDonnell family quickly recovered their financial losses and Rory repaid Anibal, giving him extra money and helping him establish trading partnerships in Jamaica.

Anibal's nephew Carlos, who often traveled with him to Jamaica, developed a romantic relationship with Anoushka Sharma and by 1874, they were married. Carlos and Anoushka were married in Kingston, Jamaica in a Hindu ceremony and Carlos returned to live with Anoushka in Santo Domingo. Carlos continued to teach Anoushka Spanish, and she learned the language quickly as she formed relationships with other Dominican women in the neighborhood. Carlos and Anoushka had their first son in 1875—named Krishna Medina Sharma—as Carlos prepared to enter the new military academy at Fort San Luis, which was rebuilt from the ashes of the previous Dominican War of Restoration. Carlos became a great cadet and graduated as an officer in the Dominican Military several years later as he honored the life of his late father Julio. In 1877, Carlos would have his second child; a daughter named Priya Medina Sharma.

Marco was excited for his son Anibal and encouraged him to attend classes at the university once his children were a little older.

Marco stated, *"Mi Hijo,* like you, I am overjoyed with President Gregorio Luperón and the victory of the Blue Party. I also support many of their ideas. However, we must be cautious with political parties. Frequently, the positions of the political parties may change, and the party you support may shift and have the very same problems the party you oppose has. We are against authoritarianism and governments that exploit their people. We both desire a fair and more economically and socially advanced Dominican Republic, but we as Dominican people must always fight for our rights no matter the person who occupies the presidency. The Dominican Republic has suffered from regional strongman, and no matter which party is in power now or in the future, it will take great motivation by the Dominican people to lessen political abuses and men who choose profits and exploit their own people. Be careful with false prophets, my son. Most importantly, your priority should always be your wife and your children. Your mother and I will soon be part of history, and you and your children will be the future."

CHAPTER 23

THE RISE OF PRESIDENT ULISES HEUREAUX

(1880)

President Gregorio Luperón was born on the eighth of September 1839 in Puerto Plata to his father and mother, Pedro Castellanos and Nicolasa. His parents owned a ventorrillo (or a small business) that sold foodstuffs, including piñonate, a local delicacy made of sweetened pinenut kernels that the young Gregorio and his siblings sold on the street to support their family. At about the age of fourteen, Gregorio began to work for Pedro Eduardo Dubocq, an owner of a major company specializing in wood. Gregorio displayed a strong work ethic and determination, and he was soon promoted to a management position. An avid reader, Gregorio had a passion and curiosity for learning. Mr. Dubocq observed Gregorio's interest in reading and invited him to his personal library, where he would spend most of his non-working hours studying.

Gregorio Luperón developed into an intelligent young man and he was fiercely nationalistic. He briefly landed in jail after a political fight with the Red Party, and then escaped the authoritarian regime of President Buenaventura Báez to Haiti and subsequently the United States. In 1864, he joined the rebellion against the Spaniards and was granted the rank of general. General Gregorio Luperón was a great military strategist and his ideas motivated the rebels, leading him to become a notable member of the Blue Party—which had finally taken control of the Dominican Republic— and this led to his presidency at the age of forty. President Gregorio Luperón welcomed the exiles of Puerto Rico and Cuba and supported the Cuban war against the Spaniards, however the Cuban War soon resulted in a victory for the Spaniards and their continued presence in Cuba and Puerto Rico. President Luperón was informed about the specific details of the war, and although he was disappointed with the outcome, he knew Spanish control of the Greater Antilles would come to an end.

The Cuban Revolutionary War (which was called The Ten Years' War) ended in victory for Spain in 1878. Most of the Spanish casualties were due to yellow fear—a type of natural, unintentional biological warfare that plagued the Spanish and English and aided the Cuban rebels. However, the Cubans suffered more casualties during the War. President Gregorio Luperón analyzed the Guerra de los Diez Años (the Ten Years' War). In Cuba, lax enforcement of the slave trade ban resulted in a dramatic increase in the importation of African slaves—estimated at 90,000—from 1856 to 1860. This occurred despite a strong abolitionist movement in Cuba and rising costs among the slave-holding planters in the east. New technologies and farming techniques made large numbers of slaves unnecessary and expensive. Some preferred hiring Chinese immigrants as indentured workers in anticipation of slavery ending.

Before the 1870s, more than 125,000 mostly male Chinese were recruited to Cuba, where many married white, mulatta, and black Cubans. Some Chinese purchased black female Cuban slaves and subsequently married them. In May 1865, Cuban Creole elites placed four demands upon the Spanish Parliament: tariff reform, Cuban representation in Parliament, judicial equality with Spaniards, and full enforcement of the slave trade ban. Cuba would soon erupt in warfare after nationalists rose against the Spaniards after they made their demands. The Revolutionary Committee of Bayamo was later founded by Cuba's wealthiest plantation owner in Eastern Cuba, Francisco Vicente Aguilera. In 1868, Aguilera freed all 500 of his slaves, which was considered an illegal act under Spanish law in effect in Cuba at that time. He joined ranks along with many of his slaves to retake the city of Bayamo from the Spanish. The rebellion against the Spaniards spread throughout eastern Cuba as Carlos Manuel de Céspedes called on men of all races to join the fight for freedom. The Demajagua flag, which is similar to the Chilean flag, was used to represent the Cuban rebels.

Carlos Manuel de Céspedes raised the new flag of an independent Cuba and rang the bell of the mill to celebrate his proclamation. This manifesto was signed by Carlos Manuel de Céspedes and fifteen others which stated, "Our aim is to enjoy the benefits of freedom, for whose use, God created man. We sincerely profess a policy of brotherhood, tolerance, and justice, and to consider all men equal, and to not exclude anyone from these benefits, not even Spaniards, if they choose to remain and live peacefully among us. Our aim is that the people participate in the creation of laws, and in the distribution and investment of the contributions. Our aim is to abolish slavery and to compensate those deserving compensation. We seek freedom of assembly, freedom of the press and the freedom to bring back honest governance; and to honor and practice the inalienable rights of men, which is the foundations of the independence and the greatness of a people. Our aim is to throw off the Spanish yoke, and to establish a free and independent nation…When Cuba is free, it will have a constitutional government created in an enlightened manner."

Cespedes returned Máximo Gómez to his command as other young commanders like Antonio Maceo Grajales, José Maceo, Calixto García, Vicente Garcia González, and Federico Fernández Cavada rose in rank. Federico Fernández Cavada was born to Emily Howard Gatier (an American from Philadelphia) and Isidoro Fernández Cavada (a Cuban). A diplomat, Federico Fernández Cavada was an officer in the Union Army during the American Civil War, and he was assigned to the Hot Air Balloon unit of the Union Army, sketching what he observed of enemy Confederate positions and movements. He was later assigned by the United States government as counsel to Cuba and subsequently resigned, joining the Cuban rebels along with his brother Adolfo after the outbreak of war. He was commissioned as Commander-in-Chief of all the Cuban forces, and he became known as General Candela (or General Fire) because of his battle tactic of burning and destroying Spanish property. Federico Fernández Cavada was soon captured at Cayo Cruz in the northern coast of Camagüey by the Spaniards when he attempted to leave for the United States to seek military support for the Cuban Liberation Army. He was tried and sentenced to execution by firing squad on July first, 1871 while George Gordon Meade, Daniel Sickles, and Ulysses S. Grant attempted to obtain his release. Federico Fernández Cavada's last words were, "*Adios Cuba, para siempre*," or "Goodbye Cuba, forever."

Antonio Maceo Grajales was the son of a Venezuelan farmer and dealer in agricultural products named Marcos Maceo and an Afro-Cuban woman of Dominican descent named Mariana Grajales y Cuello. Antonio Maceo Grajales had a dark complexion and through his bravery and leadership during the Ten Years' War, he was given various nicknames by the Cuban rebels like *El Titan de Bronce* (or The Bronze Titan) and *El Leon Mayor* (or the Greater Lion). Antonio Maceo Grajales was quickly promoted to lieutenant colonel, and over five years later he was promoted to brigadier general. However, Antonio Maceo Grajales was denied a promotion to major general due to his working-class origins and the color of his skin. Antonio Maceo Grajales was particularly inspired by the Dominican strategist Máximo Gómez and his implementation of the machete as a war weapon as a substitute for the Spanish sword, which was quickly adopted by Antonio Maceo and his troops.

General Arsenio Martínez Campos led the Spaniards to victory against the Cuban Liberation Army and he previously aided in the stabilization of Spain. The general had supported the coup d'état led by Manuel Pavía, fought against Carlist forces, and subsequently led the Valencian Army against the forces of Alicante and Cartagena. King Amadeo I of Spain abdicated the throne after several assassination attempts and Alfonso, the son of the exiled Isabella II, would become King of Spain as Alfonso XII of Spain in 1874. This would bring about the Bourbon Restoration, which stabilized Spanish society and allowed the Spaniards to concentrate on foreign policy—including the defeat of the Cuban rebels. By the end of The Ten Years' War, the Spaniards under the leadership of Arsenio Martínez Campos and subsequently Blas Villate, Count of Balmaceda, would proceed with a brutal campaign of ethnic cleansing called The Rising Flood of Valmaseda.

The Assembly of Guáimaro resulted in the dismissals of Céspedes and Quesada in 1873 and regional divisions within the Cuban rebel army began to weaken it. The Spaniards exploited regional divisions as well as fears that the slaves of Matanzas would break the fragile relationship between whites and blacks. The Spanish changed their policy towards the Mambises (or the Cuban guerrillas), offering amnesties and reforms. In charge of applying the new policy, General Arsenio Martínez Campos arrived in Cuba and it took him almost two years to convince most of the rebels to accept the Pact of Zanjón, which was signed on February tenth, 1878 by a negotiating committee. The provisional government convinced Maceo to give up, and with his surrender, the war ended on May twenty-eighth, 1878.

The same year, Calixto García—who was one of the few revolutionary leaders who did not sign the Pact of Zanjón—issued a manifesto against Spanish rule of Cuba. In 1879, another Cuban revolution was led by him and in New York, Garcia organized the Cuban Revolutionary Committee with others. Among the prominent leaders were José Maceo (the brother of Antonio Maceo), Guillermo Moncada, and Emilio Nuñez. The revolutionaries lacked experienced leaders, ammunition, weapons, and foreign allies. The Cuban people were physically and mentally tired from the Ten Years' War, and in Western Cuba, most of the revolutionary leaders were arrested. The rest were forced to capitulate throughout 1879 and 1880, and by September 1880, the rebels were defeated. This war would be named The Little War.

In 1880, the Spanish legislature abolished slavery in Cuba and other colonies in a form of gradual abolition where former slaves worked as indentured servants for several years. However, their pay was so low that the freed man could barely support himself. President Gregorio Luperón learned about Antonio Maceo Grajales and Major General Calixto García Íñiguez's voyage to New York, as well as their plots for another war against the Spanish colonial government in Cuba. He was informed about José Julián Martí Pérez, who was currently residing in Guatemala; he had also signed the Pact of Zanjón. José Marti returned to Guatemala and published his book Guatemala, and he also collaborated with Afro-Cuban Juan Gualberto Gómez, who was planning a black Cuban revolution against the Spaniards. President Gregorio Luperón was excited that slavery was abolished in Puerto Rico in 1873—and with the recent abolition of slavery in 1880 in Cuba. However, as he left the leadership of the Dominican Republic, he continued to fight for its sovereignty and the end of Spanish colonial rule.

On September first, 1880, a Dominican priest and politician named Fernando Arturo de Meriño y Ramírez would become president of the Dominican Republic. Ulises Heureaux served as Interior Minister, and he began to gain influence over the other cabinet members as he maintained his military power. President Fernando Arturo de Meriño temporarily supported constitutional procedures to stop various followers of Buenaventura Baez, who attempt to foment unrest. However, he abided by the two-year term established by Gregorio Luperón and handed over power to Ulises Heureaux on September first, 1882. President Ulises Heureaux and Vice President Casimiro Nemesio de Moya now led the Dominican Republic as the Blue Party continued to solidify their strength within politics.

By 1884, the ruling Blue Party had no clear successor who enjoyed majority Dominican support. The leader of the Blue Party (Gregorio Luperón) supported General Segundo Imbert, while President Ulises Heureaux backed the candidacy of General Francisco Gregorio Billini. President Ulises Heureaux assured Luperón that he would support General Imbert should he win the election, but he had stuffed the ballot boxes in critical precincts, ensuring that General Billini won. After his election on September first, 1884, President Billini resisted Heureaux's efforts to manipulate and use him as a puppet. Ulises Heureaux responded by spreading rumors that Billini had decreed a political amnesty so he could conspire with ex-president Cesáreo Guillermo against Gregorio Luperón's leadership of the Blue Party. This created a political crisis in the Dominican Republic, leading to President Billini's resignation on May sixteenth, 1885. He was succeeded by Vice President Alejandro Woss y, under whom General Ulises Heureaux expanded his power. In 1885, Ulises Heureaux would suppress the Revolución de Cesáreo (or Cesareo's Revolution), which was led by the ex-president, General Cesáreo Guillermo.

Cesareo was soon hidden by his political supporter in Villa Sombrero and was later found and executed on the November eighth, 1885 in the province of Azua de Compostela. Gregorio Luperón was delighted when his nemesis was captured and executed, and he supported the reelection of Ulises Heureaux in 1886. Ulises Heureaux would reclaim the presidency in 1886, however the rigged elections would lead supporters of Casimiro de Moya to plan a revolt against President Ulises Heureaux which failed. President Heureaux began to further solidify his powers by inviting Red Party as well as Blue Party members into political positions. These actions angered many Blue Party members, including Gregorio Luperón, who was soon exiled by President Ulises Heureaux. Heureaux forced Congress to pass constitutional amendments that abolished the barrier against Presidential reelection, eliminated direct elections, and created a network of secret police and informants to avert rebellions.

By 1888, the Dominican Republic was under the dictatorship of President Ulises Heureaux, and he any politicians he could not manipulate were forced into exile or assassinated. Anibal Medina and his family were saddened by the autocratic rule as the more liberal wing of the Blue Party continued to protest President Ulises Heureaux. Anibal remembered his father's words and was highly dismayed when the president exiled Gregorio Luperón. However, Anibal's younger son Alejandro Homero Medina viewed President Heureaux favorably on some issues like the increased stability of the Dominican Republic and the modernization of the nation. Anibal disagreed with Alejandro regarding the state of the nation, but despite his anger, he did not publicly denounce the government and decided it was best to concentrate on his family.

Despite the authoritarian regime of President Ulises Heureaux, by the year 1890, the Medina family experienced great success in business and were able to steadily rise to the upper middle-class. Anibal was also a co-owner of a small sugar plantation and factory in San Cristobal, which brought him considerable profits. The Medina family's improved standing in Dominican society allowed them to focus on intellectual pursuits. Anibal thought about his life and how time passed so quickly. His nephew Carlos was now thirty-eight years old and had risen to the rank of colonel in the Dominican Army. His son Krishna was now fifteen years old and his daughter Priya was thirteen. Krishna aspired to join the military as well, while Priya wished to become a mathematics teacher.

Anibal previously studied at the University in Santo Domingo while his oldest son Raul Saladin Medina was twenty-five years old and studying architecture. Anibal's younger son Alejandro Homero Medina was now twenty years of age and enjoyed writing stories and he had also joined the military academy at Fort San Luis. Anibal and Romina were now sixty years of age and enjoying life. Marco was now eighty-eight and had and recently retired as a professor at the Professional Institute in Santo Domingo. Marco Medina only desired the continued success of his family and in the affairs of the world and the final defeat of Spain in Cuba and Puerto Rico.

Marco was well pleased with the bravery Dominican warriors displayed in the wars for independence. He was also extremely proud of his family. One night when he was alone with Anibal, Marco revealed the detailed reasons for his son's name.

While the two men drank some rum, the proud father informed his son, "I named you Hector after the Trojan hero and heir-apparent to the Trojan Throne Prince Hector—a character from the story of the Illiad. I enjoyed reading about all the heroes and although Achilles has become one of the most well-known, I believe that Hector is the greatest son of King Priam of Troy and Queen Hecuba. He is one of the greatest heroes in Greek and Roman mythology. Hector challenged the best Greek warriors to one on one combat and even fought the mighty Ajax to a stalemate. Although he later lost and died at the hands of Achilles, Hector is remembered as a courageous man who was also noble, peaceful, intelligent, a loving son, brother, leader, friend, husband and father. I favored Hector over his brothers Helenus and Paris. During the Middle Ages, Hector was named as one of the Nine Worthies among the pagans Alexander the Great and Julius Caesar, the three Jews Joshua, David, and Judas Maccabeus, and the three

Christians King Arthur, Charlemagne, and Godfrey of Bouillon. The qualities displayed by Hector are some of the qualities I hoped you would display as a man, and I am proud to say that you have surpassed my expectations."

Marco Medina smiled and drank some more rum as he continued, "I also named you after a great leader and military strategist, the Carthaginian General Hannibal Barca. The Roman Republic was establishing itself as a major power by defeating and surpassing the Etruscans, the Samnites, and the Greek kingdom of Syracuse. During the Second Punic War, General Hannibal Barca marched his army and war elephants into the Iberian Peninsula, over the Pyrenees and the Alps and subsequently occupied large areas of Italy for fifteen years. General Hannibal Barca won battles in Trebia, Lake Trasimene, and Cannae. After he was driven from Italy, he returned to Carthage and suffered defeat against the forces of Scipio Africanus at the battle of Zama in Northern Africa."

Anibal likened the attack on Carthage and Hannibal's struggles with Numidia in Northern Africa to the Mexican leader General Santa Anna and his return to defend against unrest during the war with the United States.

However, Marco disagreed, stating, "General Santa Anna led a brave fight against the United States, but General Hannibal Barca threatened the very existence of Rome."

Marco Continued, "Hannibal Barca successfully ran for the office of sufet and he enacted political and financial reforms to enable the payment of the war indemnity imposed by Rome. This angered the Carthaginian aristocracy and Hannibal Barca fled to the Seleucid court, where he acted as military advisor to Antiochus III the Great during his war against Rome. Antiochus met defeat at the Battle of Magnesia and Hannibal fled once again and lived in the Kingdom of Armenia. Later in the court in Bithynia, Hannibal was betrayed to the Romans and committed suicide by poison. It is believed Hannibal stated, 'Let us now relieve the Romans of their fears by the death of a feeble old man.' You see, my son, Hannibal Barca was a great and feared leader as well as military strategist. In my opinion, the important message I gathered from Hannibal's life was not only his skills on the battlefield and in politics, but the resiliency of the Romans. They would later become members of the Roman Empire, and he demonstrated the lengths an empire would go to defeat an enemy; they were legendary and respected by the people. Even as an old man, Hannibal was a dangerous figure to the Roman power. This is a lesson for anyone who seeks to be a leader and carry their people to greatness against their enemies."

They embraced as they enjoyed their spirits under the Dominican night sky.

The United States quickly grew into the world's largest industrial nation. The First Industrial Revolution shifted production from artisans to factories, while the Second Industrial Revolution pioneered an expansion in organization, coordination, and the scale of the industry aided in the advancements of technology and transportation. Built by nationally oriented entrepreneurs with British money and Irish and Chinese labor, The First Transcontinental Railroad provided access to previously remote expanses of land. New technologies arose like the Bessemer process and open-hearth furnace as well as communication tools such as the telegraph and telephone, which allowed corporate managers to coordinate across great distances. The corporations grew in power and industrialists—including Andrew Carnegie, John D. Rockefeller, and Jay Gould—who would be known collectively by their critics as "robber barons". The robber barons held great wealth and power, leading President Rutherford B. Hayes in 1888 to note in his diary that the United States ceased being a government for the people and was now replaced by a "government of the corporation, by the corporation, and for the corporation."

In the fast-growing industrial sector, wages were about double the level in Europe, but the work was harder with less leisure. Economic depressions swept the nation from 1873 to 1875 and 1893 to 1897, with low prices for farm goods and heavy unemployment in factories and mines. Immigration increased rapidly with over 85 to 90 percent arriving from Europe and received at the port of New York City (and after 1892 at Ellis Island). New York and other large cities along the east coast received the Jewish, Irish, and Italian populations, while many Germans and Central Europeans moved to the Midwest, obtaining jobs in industry and mining. At the same time, many French Canadians migrated from Quebec to New England. While Europeans were accepted, many Chinese were not and the Chinese Exclusion Act of 1882 denied entry to Chinese immigrants and caused many in the United States to flee to Puerto Rico, Cuba, Dominican Republic, and other Latin American nations.

Many labor unions arose in the United States, including The Noble Order of the Knights of Labor in 1869. Originally a secret, ritualistic society organized by Philadelphia garment workers, it was open to all workers, including African Americans, women, and farmers. The Knights grew slowly until they succeeded in facing down the railroad baron Jay Gould in an 1885 strike, which increased membership to over 500,000. American Federation of Labor (AFL) rose after the fall of The Noble Order of the Knights of Labor, but rather than open its membership to all, the AFL—under the former cigar-makers union official Samuel Gompers—focused on skilled workers and slowly the AFL drifted away from its previous socialist views. There were various strikes like the Great Railroad Strike in 1877, the Haymarket Riot in 1886, and the strike by the Amalgamated Association of Iron, Steel, and Tin Workers in 1892 at the Carnegie's steel works in Homestead, Pennsylvania. 300 Pinkerton detectives fired upon the rioters, killing ten people and leading to the intervention of the United States National Guard.

The United States Military was combatting rebellions and revolts such as the ones led by the native leaders Geronimo and Red Cloud. Goyaałé meant "the one who yawns", but he was renamed Geronimo by the Mexicans and was involved in both the Apache Mexican conflict and the Apache United States conflict. Geronimo surrendered for the last time to Lieutenant Charles Bare Gatewood, an Apache-speaking West Point graduate. Geronimo was later transferred to General Nelson Miles at Skeleton Canyon, just north of the Mexican American boundary. Maȟpíya Lúta (or Red Cloud) was one of the important leaders of the Oglala Lakota. Allied with Lakota and Arapaho bands, the battles involving the Northern Cheyenne against the United States Army between 1866 and 1868 were collectively called Red Cloud's War. In December 1866, the Native American allies attacked and defeated a United States unit in what the whites would call the Fetterman Massacre (or the Battle of the Hundred Slain), which resulted in the most U.S. casualties of any plains battle up to that point. Captains Frederick Brown and Fetterman followed the decoy Crazy Horse into an ambush, resulting in eighty-one deaths for the United States and fourteen for the Allied Native American forces. Red Cloud was transferred to a reservation and in 1884, he, his family, and five other leaders converted and were baptized as Catholics by Father Joseph Bushman.

The United States experienced a continued worsening in race relations and by 1876, many states—particularly in the south—began to implement Jim Crow Laws, which sought racial segregation in the United States. Despite racial mixing by various historical figures (including Thomas Jefferson, who was believed to have fathered six mixed-race children with his slave Sally Hemings), ideas of white racial purity continued to manifest in violence and within the politics of the United States. Many also debated the idea of the One Drop Rule, which was the social and legal principle of racial classification that any person with even one ancestor of sub-Saharan African ancestry (or "one drop") was considered black. In 1865, Florida passed an act that both out-lawed miscegenation and defined the amount of black ancestry needed to be legally defined as a "person of color". The act stated that "Every person who shall have one-eighth or more of negro blood shall be deemed and held to be a person of color."

Jim Crow was a racist term for black people and the phrase "Jim Crow Law" can be found as early as 1892 in the title of a New York Times article about Louisiana requiring segregated railroad cars. Some believed the Jim Crow Laws' origins were from a song called "Jump Jim Crow", performed as a caricature of blacks by white actor Thomas D. Rice in blackface (which first surfaced in 1832). The song was used to satirize the populist policies of

President Andrew Jackson. The rising popularity of Thomas D. Rice and his performances in blackface led to Jim Crow becoming a pejorative expression meaning "negro" by 1832.

In 1895, the former Democratic Representative George D. Tillman of South Carolina stated, "It is a scientific fact that there is not one full-blooded Caucasian on the floor of this convention. Every member has in him a certain mixture of...colored blood...It would be a cruel injustice and the source of endless litigation, of scandal, horror, feud, and bloodshed to undertake to annul or forbid marriage for a remote, perhaps obsolete trace of Negro blood. The doors would be open to scandal, malice, and greed."

These racial ideas in the United States were not found in the same fashion within the Caribbean and Latin America. However, as Spain and the other European powers lost influence in the Americas and the United States increased its hegemony, these different ideas between Latin America, the Caribbean, and the United States would intertwine, sometimes resulting in misunderstandings and violence.

CHAPTER 24
UNITED STATES MINISTER RESIDENT TO HAITI FREDERICK DOUGLASS
(1893)

Frederick Douglass and Anna had five children: Rosetta, Lewis Henry, Frederick Jr., Charles Remond, and Annie, who passed away at the age of ten. Charles and Rosetta Douglass helped produce his newspapers, and his oldest son Lewis Henry was a typesetter at The North Star and Douglass' Weekly. Lewis was a veteran of the United States Civil War, joining the Union Army in 1863. Charles Remond Douglass was the first African American to enlist in the military in New York during the Civil War and served as one of the first African American clerks in the Freedmen's Bureau in Washington, D.C. Frederick Douglass enjoyed a long marriage to his first wife Ann despite his personal relationships with other women—including a British abolitionist named Julia Griffiths and a German abolitionist named Ottilie Assing. After Anna died in 1882, Douglass married again to Helen Pitts in 1884, a white suffragist and abolitionist from Honeoye, New York.

In 1855, Frederick Douglass wrote two more autobiographies which were My Bondage and My Freedom, and he even published a fictional work called The Heroic Slave in 1853. After the Civil War, Douglass remained an active campaigner against slavery. Powerful paramilitary groups like the White League and the Red Shirts, both active during the 1870s in the Deep South, worked to disenfranchise people of color and would disrupt elections in their effort to install Democratic politicians. They operated as the military arm of the Democratic Party, disrupting elections and leading to Democratic control of the southern states. Frederick Douglass proposed the annexation of the Dominican Republic would be good for the United States, and Grant believed annexation would help relieve the violent situation in the south and allow African Americans their own state.

During a visit to the Dominican Republic, Frederick Douglass spoke well of the Dominican nation, describing Dominicans as black people, white people, and a large mixed population of various ancestries that had lived as free people in general peace. He stated that the Dominican Republic was where, "You feel your full stature of manhood." In his opinion, the Dominican Re-public was a country; a biracial paradise of an island that had witnessed the birth of White Christian Civilization and the first resistance to slavery and colonialism in the Americas. The Annexation of the Dominican Republic failed due to racist whites in the United States as well as the fierce determination of the people for the Dominican Republic to remain an independent, sovereign nation.

The famous abolitionist Frederick Douglass was appointed the president of the Reconstruction-era Freedman's Saving and Trust Company (or the Freedman's Savings Bank). The Freedman's Savings Bank was a private corporation chartered by the U.S. government to encourage and guide the economic development of the emancipated African American communities after the Civil War. After the Panic of 1873 and a series of increasingly speculative investments caused them to go into debt, the banks failed. This caused a depression in the United States and Europe. During the next decade, Congress established a program to reimburse depositors up to 62 percent of their savings, however many depositors never received any compensation, which led to a deep mistrust of banking institutions by many in the black community.

At the 1888 Republican National Convention, Douglass became the first African American to receive a vote for President of the United States in a major party's roll call vote. Frederick Douglass also became the first African American nominated for Vice President of the United States as the running mate on the Equal Rights Party ticket and Vice Presidential nominee of Victoria Woodhull. On the first of July 1889, after he took up residence in the White House, the Republican President Benjamin Harrison appointed Frederick Douglass to be the United States' Minister Resident, Consul-General to the Republic of Haiti, and Chargé d'affaires for Santo Domingo in 1889. However, he resigned in 1891. Frederick Douglas would speak at the World's Columbian Exposition in Chicago 1893, which celebrated the 400th anniversary of Christopher Columbus' arrival to the New World in 1492. Chicago beat New York City, Washington, D.C., and St. Louis for the honor of hosting the affair.

The effort to power the event with electricity took place during the War of currents between Thomas Edison and his Direct Current (or DC) and Nikola Tesla and his Alternate Current (AC). Part of the space occupied by the Westinghouse Company was devoted to demonstrations of electrical devices developed by Nikola Tesla, including a two-phase induction motor, generators to power the system, as well as the Egg of Columbus—a metal egg which was used to explain the principles of the rotating magnetic field model. This was also the first demonstration of wireless power transfer. Many spoke at the World's Columbian Exposition— including Frederick Douglass, who addressed to the crowd the nation of Haiti and the leaders which led the Haitian Revolution against Napoleon's French Army:

"No man should presume to come before an intelligent American audience without a commanding object and an earnest purpose. In whatever else I may be deficient, I hope I am qualified, both in object and purpose, to speak to you this evening.

"My subject is Haiti, the Black Republic; the only self-made Black Republic in the world. I am to speak to you of her character, her history, her importance, and her struggle from slavery to freedom and to statehood.

I am to speak to you of her progress in the line of civilization; of her relationship with the United States; of her past and present; of her probable destiny; and of the bearing of her example as a free and independent Republic, upon what may be the destiny of the African race in our own country and elsewhere.

"If, by a true statement of facts and a fair deduction from them, I shall in any degree promote a better understanding of what Haiti is, and create a higher appreciation of her merits and services to the world; and especially, if I can promote a more friendly feeling for her in this country and at the same time give to Haiti herself a friendly hint as to what is hopefully and justly expected of her by her friends, and by the civilized world, my object and purpose will have been accomplished.

"There are many reasons why a good understanding should exist between Haiti and the United States. Her proximity; her similar government and her large and increasing commerce with us, should alone make us deeply interested in her welfare, her history, her progress, and her possible destiny."

Frederick Douglass continued with his speech and the following statement gathered the loudest applause. "In just vindication of Haiti, I can go one step further. I can speak of her, not only words of admiration, but words of gratitude as well. She has grandly served the cause of universal human liberty. We should not forget that the freedom you and I enjoy today; that the freedom that eight hundred thousand colored people enjoy in the British West Indies; the freedom that has come to the colored race the world over, is largely due to the brave stand taken by the black sons, of Haiti ninety years ago. When they struck for freedom, they built better than they knew. Their swords were not drawn and could not be drawn simply for themselves alone. They were interlinked with their race and in striking for their freedom, they struck for the freedom of every black man in the world."

Anibal and Robert Grant would later discuss Frederick Douglass and his speech at the World's Columbian Exposition. They conversed about the assassination of Chicago Mayor Carter Harrison Sr. by Patrick Eugene Prendergast. They spoke about his various events within the United States, including events regarding technological advancements like Nikola Tesla and his alternating current. Anibal wondered when the Dominican Republic would light up the Caribbean night sky under the power of electricity. These discussions would soon lead Anibal Medina to plan a trip to a place that had always fascinated him: New York.

CHAPTER 25

THE ANTILLEAN CONFEDERATION

(1895)

The Paraguayan War (or the War of the Triple Alliance) between Paraguay and the Triple Alliance of Argentina, the Empire of Brazil, and Uruguay ended in total defeat for Paraguay. However, the Empire of Brazil continued its decline. This began after Emperor Dom Pedro II had no male heir (his two sons had died), leaving his daughter Dona Isabel as the only successor. Dona Isabel was not eager to be a monarch, and Emperor Dom Pedro was increasingly uninterested in the affairs of his empire. Many officers favored a Republican dictatorship, which they believed would be superior to the liberal Democratic monarchy. In Rio de Janeiro, a group of military officers of the Brazilian Army led by Marshal Deodoro da Fonseca staged a coup d'état without the use of violence, deposing Emperor Pedro II and the President of the Council of Ministers of the Empire, the Viscount of Ouro Preto. A provisional government was established that same day, the fifteenth of November, with Marshal Deodoro da Fonseca as President of the Republic and head of the interim Government. Emperor Dom Pedro II ruled as a neutral monarch, however while Pedro II was receiving medical treatment in Europe, the parliament passed the Golden Law which Princess Isabel signed on the thirteenth of May 1888, which completely abolished slavery in Brazil. Soon, the ultraconservatives pushed for the establishment of a republic. On November fifteenth, 1889, the Republic of Brazil was declared.

In the United States, Mark Twain's 1873 novel The Gilded Age: A Tale of Today satirized an era of serious social problems masked by a thin gold gilding in the United States. It was a time of great economic growth. Samuel Langhorne Clemens—famously known by his pen name Mark Twain—was born in Florida, Missouri in 1835. Steamboat pilot Horace E. Bixby took Mark Twain on as a cub pilot to teach him the river between New Orleans and St. Louis. Mark Twain studied the Mississippi, learning its landmarks, how to navigate its currents effectively, and how to read the river and its constantly shifting channels, reefs, submerged snags, and rocks. Piloting also gave him his pen name: "Mark Twain" was the leadsman's cry for a measured river depth of two fathoms (or feet), which is safe water for a steamboat. Mark Twain served for two weeks in a Confederate militia, later writing the sketch The Private History of a Campaign That Failed, which described how he and his friends had been Confederate volunteers for two weeks before disbanding.

Mark Twain was now a famous writer who wrote many novels: The Prince and the Pauper, A Connecticut Yankee in King Arthur's Court, The

American Claimant, Pudd'nhead Wilson, The Adventures of Tom Sawyer, Adventures of Huckleberry Finn, and Tom Sawyer Abroad. Mark Twain spoke often about this age of economic growth and the start of the Progressive Era. He was an abolitionist who stated that the Emancipation Proclamation "Not only set the black slaves free but set the white man free also." In addition, he stated that Chinese and other non-whites did not receive justice in the United States. However, his feelings regarding Native Americans were mixed and nuanced. Mark Twain also advocated for labor movements and in a speech to the Knights of Labor he stated, "Who are the oppressors? The few: The King, the capitalist, and a handful of other overseers and superintendents. Who are the oppressed? The many: the nations of the earth; the valuable personages; the workers; they that make the bread that the soft-handed and idle eat."

In the 1860s and early 1870s, Mark Twain spoke out strongly in favor of American interests in the Hawaiian Islands; he viewed a United States war against Spain as a worthy cause. William Randolph Hearst was born to millionaire mining engineer, goldmine owner, and U.S. senator George Hearst, who had served from 1886 to 1891 and his wife Phoebe Apperson Hearst. In 1887, William Randolph Hearst took over management of the San Francisco Examiner, which his father received in 1880 as repayment for a gambling debt, and hired talented writers such as Ambrose Bierce, Mark Twain, Jack London, and political cartoonist Homer Davenport. In 1895, with the financial support of his mother, William Randolph Hearst bought the failing New York Morning Journal, hiring writers like Stephen Crane and Julian Hawthorne. The paper entered a circulation war with Joseph Pulitzer, the owner and publisher of the New York World. William Randolph Hearst then hired Pulitzer's former employees, including Richard F. Outcault (the inventor of color comics) and all of Pulitzer's Sunday staff as well.

William Randolph Hearst began publicizing sensationalist stories that earned him large profits, including ones regarding the Spanish government in Cuba. These works galvanized the people of the United States into supporting a conflict between them and Spain. As the war was close to erupting in Cuba, William Randolph Hearst increased his publication of these articles that people called Yellow Journalism. While the United States government began planning for a possible war against Spain, William Randolph Hearst became a strong ally who provided valuable pro-war propaganda.

The European powers were currently concentrating their attention on the colonization of Africa. By 1870, about ten percent of Africa was directly controlled by European powers and in 1884, the Berlin Conference regulated European colonization and trade in Africa. The Berlin Conference saw the rise of the German Empire and its chancellor Otto von

Bismarck, who was succeeded by Chancellor Leo von Caprivi and was himself succeeded by the current leader: German Emperor Wilhelm II. The partition of Africa continued while the Spanish Empire desperately attempted to maintain control in Cuba and Puerto Rico.

In the Dominican Republic, citizens anxiously awaited the events in Cuba. The Spaniards' weakening hegemony in the Caribbean served to solidify the idea of the Confederación Antillana (or the Antillean Confederation). Proposed by Dr. Ramón Emeterio Betances, the Antillean Confederation sought to unify the people of the Spanish Caribbean with a strong regional entity that would seek to preserve the sovereignty and wellbeing of Cuba, Puerto Rico, and the Dominican Republic. The idea was strongly supported by many intellectuals, including Eugenio María de Hostos (known as El Gran Ciudadano de las Américas or The Great Citizen of the Americas), Gregorio Luperón (hero of the Dominican Restoration War), José Martí (also known as The Apostle of Cuban Independence), and José de Diego. These ideas quickly spread in the Dominican Republic, and Anibal Hector Medina became one of the strongest supporters of the Antillean Confederation.

Dr. Ramón Emeterio Betances previously fled to New York City in April 1869, where he again joined Basora in his efforts to organize Puerto Rican revolutionaries into additional activities that would lead to independence. Betances lobbied the United States Congress successfully against an annexation of the Dominican Republic—requested in a vote by a majority in a referendum in 1869. Betances traveled to Jacmel, Haiti in 1870 at the request of its then-president, Jean Nissage-Saget, who supported Betances' support for a liberal Dominican government. While in New York, Betances wrote and translated numerous political treatises, proclamations, and works that were published in the newspaper La Revolución (or The Revolution) under the pseudonym *El Antillano* (or The Antillean One). Betances spoke about the need for natives of the Greater Antilles to unite into an Antillean Confederation.

Betances had some disagreements with a fellow Puerto Rican named Eugenio María de Hostos. A Puerto Rican educator, philosopher, intellectual, lawyer, sociologist, and novelist, Eugenio María de Hostos was a Puerto Rican independence advocate. Hostos traveled to Peru, where he lived from 1870 to 1873, and he helped develop the country's educational system and spoke against the harsh treatment of the Chinese people in Peru. Hostos taught at the University of Chile and gave a speech titled "The Scientific Education of Women" in which he talked about governments permitting women in their colleges. Soon after, Chile allowed women to enter its educational system. Hostos subsequently traveled to Argentina, where he proposed a railway system connecting Chile and Argentina, which was accepted. In 1875, Hostos went to the Dominican Republic and founded the first Normal School (or Teachers College) in Santo Domingo and introduced advanced teaching methods, which was opposed by the Catholic Church because Hostos was against religious instruction in the educational process. Hostos responded calmly and constructively to the Catholic Church and in 1876, he traveled to Venezuela and married Belinda Otilia de Ayala. Their maid of honor was the Puerto Rican poet, abolitionist, women's rights activist, and Puerto Rican independence advocate Lola Rodríguez de Tió. In 1879, when the first Normal School was finally inaugurated, Hostos was named director and he helped establish a second Normal School in the city of Santiago de los Caballeros.

Salomé Ureña (the daughter of Dominican writer Nicolás Ureña de Mendoza and Gregoria Díaz de León) would marry the Dominican political figure and writer Dr. Francisco Henríquez y Carvajal in 1880. With the help of her husband, she started the first center of higher education for Dominican women called Instituto de Señoritas (or the Institute for Ladies) in 1881. Within five years, the first six female teachers had graduated from the institute, including Mercedes Laura Aguiar, Leonor M. Feltz, Altagracia Henríquez Perdomo, Luisa Ozema Pellerano, Catalina Pou, and Ana Josefa Puello. Salomé Ureña was an inspiration to many Dominican girls through her various works, including her sad poems like *En horas de angustia* (In Hours of Anguish), patriotic writings such as *La Patria* (The Motherland), *Ruinas* (the Ruins), as well as *Mi Pedro* (My Pedro, which was dedicated to her son), *La llegada del invierno* (The Arrival of the Winter), and Steven, where she talks about the Dominican Republic, her family, the plants and flowers, and the island itself.

José de Diego y Martínez supported unity among the people of the Greater Antilles as well as the Antillean Confederation. Born in Aguadilla, Puerto Rico in 1866, José de Diego y Martínez was the son of Felipe de Diego Parajón (a Spanish Army Officer from Asturias, Spain) and Elisa Martínez Muñiz (a native of Puerto Rico). He studied at the Aguadilla Elementary School before he was sent to Spain to finish his education at the Instituto Politecnico de Logroño. While in Spain, José de Diego attended the University of Barcelona to study law and collaborated with the newspaper El Progreso (or Progress), founded by fellow Puerto Rican José Julián Acosta y Blanco. El Progreso attacked the political situation in Puerto Rico, which led him to leave the University of Barcelona and Spain and return to the island of Puerto Rico. José De Diego set up his law practice in Arecibo and was the founder of La República (or The Republic). José de Diego and Román Baldorioty de Castro founded the Autonomist Party in 1887. Members of the party, Luis Muñoz Rivera and Rosendo Matienzo Cintrón, formed a committee which ultimately convinced the Spanish governor in the island (Práxedes Mateo Sagasta) to support the idea of autonomy for Puerto Rico within the Spanish Kingdom.

The idea of an independent Cuba and the formation of the Antillean Confederation was also supported by José Julián Martí Pérez. José Marti worked as a poet, essayist, journalist, translator, professor, and publisher. He was very politically active, and he was an important revolutionary philosopher and political theorist. José Marti wrote in a wide range of genres and published a serialized novel, poetry, essays, and four issues of a children's magazine named La Edad de Oro (or The Golden Age) in 1889. His prose was extensively read and influenced the modernist generation, especially the Nicaraguan poet Rubén Darío, whom Martí called "my son" when they met in New York in 1893.

José Marti founded and wrote for two newspapers in Cuba: *El Diablo Cojuelo* (or The Limping Devil) and La Patria Libre (or The Free Fatherland), which established his political commitment and vision for Cuba. In Spain, he wrote for La Colonia Española (or The Spanish Colony), in Mexico for La Revista Universal (or The Universal Magazine), and in Venezuela for Revista Venezolana (or the Venezuelan Magazine)—which he founded. In New York, he contributed to the Venezuelan periodical La Opinión Nacional (or The National Opinion); in Buenos Aires, he wrote for La Nación (or The Nation); while in Mexico, he published with La Opinion Liberal (or The Liberal Opinion); and in America, he wrote for The Hour. Volume two of his *Obras Completas* (Complete Works) includes his famous essay Nuestra America (or Our America), which touched on various topics regarding Spanish America. José Marti also noted that after Cuba, his interest was directed mostly to Guatemala, Mexico, and Venezuela.

José Marti was also a translator who fluently spoke English, French, Italian, Latin, and Classical Greek so he could read classical works in their original form. In New York, José Marti translated several books for the publishing house of D. Appleton and did a series of translations for newspapers. José Marti soon joined the Cuban rebels against the Spaniards and presented the Manifesto of Montecristi, which outlined the policy for Cuba's war of independence which state that the war was to be waged by blacks and whites alike. Participation of all blacks was crucial for victory, and Spaniards who did not object to the war effort should be spared; private rural properties should not be damaged, and the revolution should bring new economic life to Cuba. Antonio Maceo Grajales demanded that highest command should be in the hands of Gómez, which was approved without reservation by the Delegate of the Cuban Revolutionary Party José Martí. In Costa Rica, gun in hand, Antonio Maceo faced another attempted assassination by Spanish agents at the exit of a theatre. It ended with a fatal result for one of the aggressors.

Near the confluence of the rivers Contramaestre and Cauto, José Martí was killed at the Battle of Dos Ríos on May nineteenth, 1895. Gómez had recognized that the Spaniards had a strong position between palm trees, so he ordered his men to disengage. Martí was alone and seeing a young courier ride by, he said, "*Joven, a la carga!*" Meaning, "Young man, charge!" José Marti was usually dressed in a black jacket and riding a white horse, which made him an easy target for the Spanish. His body was buried by the Spaniards and later exhumed after the they realized it was the corpse of José Marti. His death was a blow to the Cuban revolutionaries, however the rebels continued to fight. Maximo Gómez was designated General in Chief of the Cuban Liberation Army, and Maceo was named Lieutenant General.

Anibal Medina was very interested in the events in Cuba and he spoke of his support of the Antillean Confederation with his family. Antonio preferred the ideas of Betances and disagreed with Hostos on some points. Betances conversed with various political leaders, which helped him to include Haiti in the alliance of the Dominican Republic, Puerto Rico, and Cuba. Betances al-ways remembered the embarrassment he and his family withstood in Puerto Rico. While Ramón was in France, his father sought to change the family's registration from the mixed race to the white or Caucasian classification of families in Cabo Rojo. The process, when successful, entitled the requester to further legal and property rights, and it would also allow his daughter Ana María to marry José Tió, who was a Caucasian. In the case of Betances' father, the process lasted two years and was formalized in 1840, which exposed the family's lineage and religious affiliations to the public and embarrassed them all. Since he was the first to acknowledge that he and his entire family were not *blancuzcos* or whitish, but *prietuzcos* or blackish, Betances was annoyed by the process and mocked it in his letters.

Ramon Betances took pride in his African ancestry and saw a revolutionary people that broke the yoke of slavery and French rule in the Haitians. Betances also admired the Dominican revolutionaries who fought and defeated the Spaniards in 1865. Although Haiti was a French and Creole-speaking nation, Betances believed that the Haitian revolution was of great im-portance to the Caribbean and throughout Latin America and was essential to the ideals of the Antillean Confederation. Ramon Betances argued against various supporters of the Antillean Confederation regarding the Haitian Revolution. He partially agreed with his opponents that the leadership of both Emperor Jacques I and Boyer were authoritarian, however he viewed the Hai-tian leader and first President of Haiti Alexandre Pétion as an ideal representation of Republican leadership. Ramon Betances respected the Cuban revolution and was disappointed that Puerto Ricans did not believe in revolution and supported minor reforms and annexation.

Ramon Betances stated, "The African blood from these sons of the desert, just like the Latin blood from the French, ended up planting the seeds of freedom in American soil; a freedom that the United States denied for so many years and which Spain continues to deny, to that race which is capable of so much sacrifice. The more oppressed a nation is, the more blood is required to conquer its freedom."

Betances would make speeches during his stay in Haiti, and at a Masonic Lodge in Port-au-Prince in 1872, he stated, "The Antilles now face a moment that they had never faced in history; they now have to decide whether 'to be, or not to be'. Let us unite. Let us build a people, a people of true Freemasons, and we then shall raise a temple over foundations so solid that the forces of the Saxon and Spanish races will not shake it, a temple that we will consecrate to Independence, and in whose frontispiece, we will engrave this inscription, as imperishable as the Motherland itself: "The Antilles for the Antilleans"

Despite his involvement in battles against the Haitians, Anibal Medina believed that with the right government, both Haiti and the Dominican Republic could coexist in peace and be an example for the other Caribbean islands. Anibal was angry at the political leaders in Haiti and he fought bravely for the Dominican Republic, but he understood the brutality of war and he did not want his children and future grandchildren to live that way. Anibal agreed with Ramon Betances and desired independence for the people of Cuba and Puerto Rico and a union between Haiti, the Dominican Republic, Cuba, and Puerto Rico. He supported the idea that the Greater Antilles should be free of Spain and the Antillean Confederation would maintain peace in the Caribbean through mutual respect and cooperation.

Anibal Medina also respected Eugenio Maria de Hostos, who he had briefly met in 1879 during the inauguration of his Teachers College in Santo Domingo. Anibal would meet Eugenio Maria de Hostos several more times after his nephew Alvaro Xin was enrolled in the Teachers College in 1886. It was a proud moment for the Medina family as well as Alvaro Xin's parents, Catalina Xin and Valentino Xin.

CHAPTER 26

GENERALISSIMO MÁXIMO GÓMEZ & THE SPANISH AMERICAN WAR
(1898)

On December seventh, 1896, in the vicinity of Punta Brava and accompanied only by his personal escort, Antonio Maceo Grajales advanced into the farm of San Pedro. When they attempted to cut a fence to facilitate the march of horses through those lands, they were detected by a Spanish column, which opened intense fire. Antonio Maceo was hit by two shots: one in the chest and another that broke his jaw and penetrated his skull. His companions could not carry him because of the intensity of the firefight and Maceo's size. The only rebel who stayed by him was the son of Máximo Gómez, Lieutenant Francisco Gómez (known as Panchito), who faced the Spanish column for the purpose of protecting Antonio Maceo's body. After being shot several times, the Spaniards killed Gómez with machete strikes, leaving both bodies abandoned and not knowing the identities of the fallen.

Various uprisings began in Oriente, Cuba and in other locations like Santiago, Guantánamo, Jiguaní, San Luis, El Cobre, El Caney, Alto Songo, Bayate, and Baire. The uprisings in the central part of Cuba such as Ibarra, Jagüey Grande, and Aguada lacked coordination and failed. The leaders were captured, some of them deported and some executed. By 1897, the rebels began to lead successful offensives in eastern Cuba as they planned to move to western Cuba. Spanish General Valeriano Weyler reacted to the rebels' successes by introducing terror methods: periodic executions, the mass exile of residents and forced concentration of them in certain cities or areas, and destruction of farms and crops. General Weyler's actions reached their height of terror on October twenty-first, 1896, when he ordered all countryside residents and their livestock to gather within eight days in different fortified areas and towns occupied by his troops where he had them executed. Estimates stated that Cuban civilian losses totaled 155,000 to 170,000, representing nearly ten percent of the total population.

The Cuban rebel force of 3,000 defeated the Spanish in various encounters, including at the Battle of La Reforma, and forced the surrender of Las Tunas on August thirtieth. The Cuban Mambises—named after the black Spanish officer Juan Ethninius Mamby, who had joined the fight for Dominican independence in 1846 in Santo Domingo—was now defeating the Spaniards in Central and eastern Cuba. The Spanish government in Madrid decided to change its policy towards Cuba and replaced General Weyler. It also drew up a colonial constitution for Cuba and Puerto Rico and installed a new government in Havana. With over half of Cuba out of Spanish control, the rebels did not accept the new Spanish constitution.

Following the death in combat of Major General Ignacio Agramonte y Loynáz in May 1873, Gómez assumed the command of the military district of the province of Camaguey and its famed Cavalry Corps. Máximo Gómez participated in the two previous Cuban revolutions and between both conflicts, he held odd jobs in Jamaica and Panama—including supervising the laborers' brigade during the construction of the Panama Canal—while remaining an active player for the cause of Cuban independence. In 1875, Máximo Gómez was shot in the neck while leading an offensive in eastern Cuba, which led him to wear a kerchief around his throat to cover the bullet hole he plugged up with cotton. Máximo Gómez sold most of his personal belongings to finance a rebellion in Puerto Rico and volunteered to lead any troops if such an opportunity occurred. However, in 1887, the Puerto Rican revolt never came about; the Spanish government recalled Palacio from office to investigate charges of abuse of power.

An exiled veteran of El Grito de Lares and Vice President of the Cuban Revolutionary Committee in New York City, Juan de Mata Terreforte previously adopted the Grito the Lares Flag (modeled after the Trinitarian Flag) as the flag of Puerto Rico until 1895, when a new flag of Puerto Rico was unveiled. The design was influenced by the Cuban flag and was adopted by the fifty-nine Puerto Rican exiles of the Cuban Revolutionary Committee. The new Puerto Rican flag consisted of five equal horizontal bands of red (top and bottom) alternating with white; a blue isosceles triangle based on the hoist side bears a large, white, five-pointed star in the center. This new flag was first flown in Puerto Rico on March twenty-fourth, 1897, during the Intentona de Yauco (or the Attempted Coup of Yauco), which was the second and final major revolt against Spanish colonial rule in Puerto Rico.

Máximo Gómez rose quickly through the ranks, becoming Generalissimo of the Cuban Army. The Generalissimo would suffer his second and last wound in 1896, fighting in the rural areas outside Havana while completing a successful invasion of western Cuba. Generalissimo Máximo Gómez was shot twice during fifteen years of guerrilla warfare against a Spanish enemy far superior in manpower and logistics. In contrast, his most trusted officer and second-in-command, Lieutenant General Antonio Maceo y Grajales, was shot twenty-seven times in the same span of time—number twenty-six had been the mortal wound. Despite the losses of many capable commanders, Generalissimo Máximo Gómez continued to cripple the Spanish Army in Cuba. Generalissimo Máximo Gómez began a policy of torching sugar cane haciendas and other strategic agricultural assets. He personally abhorred the idea of burning the product of poor Cuban workers of more than 200 years, however he believed it was a necessary given the state of misery most of these laborers still experienced. He stated, "Bendita sea la tea!" or "Blessed be the torch!"

Generalissimo Máximo Gómez and his machete charge struck fear into the Spaniards as the Cubans were on the verge of victory. After hostilities increased with the United States, the Spaniards became desperate. The United States and Spain were now heading towards a major conflict as the people of the Dominican Republic, Cuba, and Puerto Rico continued to plot against Spain.

The sinking of the USS Maine (ACR-1) caused widespread outrage as the Cuban and Spanish War raged on. Originally classified as an armored cruiser, the USS Maine was built in response to the Brazilian battleship Riachuelo and the increase of naval forces in Latin America. The USS Maine resembled the British ironclad Inflexible and was comparable to Italian ships. Her two-gun turrets were staggered en échelon rather than on the centerline, with the fore gun sponsored out on the starboard side of the ship and the aft gun on the port side. The ship also had two inverted vertical triple-expansion steam engines, mounted in watertight compartments and separated by a fore-to-aft bulkhead with a total designed output of 9,293 indicated horsepower.

In January 1898, the USS Maine was sent from Key West, Florida, to Havana, Cuba to protect U.S. interests during the Cuban War of Independence. Three weeks later, on the night of the February fifteenth, an explosion on board USS Maine occurred in the Havana Harbor. investigations revealed that more than five long tons (5.1 t) of powder charges for the vessel's six and ten-inch guns had detonated, obliterating the forward third of the ship. The remaining wreckage rapidly settled to the bottom of the harbor. Most of Maine's crew were sleeping or resting in the enlisted quarters when the explosion occurred. A total of 260 men lost their lives and there were eighty-nine survivors—eighteen of whom were officers like Captain Sigsbee; their quarters were in the aft portion of the ship. On the twenty-first of March, the U.S. Naval Court of Inquiry in Key West declared that a naval mine caused the explosion.

The rival newspapers The New York Journal owned by William Randolph Hearst and New York World's Joseph Pulitzer participated in Yellow Journalism as they sensationalized the news of the explosion of the USS Maine. William Hearst announced a reward of $50,000 "For the conviction of the criminals who sent 258 American sailors to their deaths". The New York World also indulged in similar misinformation, insisting continually that Maine had been bombed or mined, although privately Pulitzer stated that, "Nobody outside a lunatic asylum" really believed Spain had sanctioned the Maine's destruction. Political pressures from the Democratic Party pushed the administration of the Republican President William McKinley into a war he had wished to avoid.

The Spaniards requested to end their war against the Cuban rebels so they could join forces against the United States. On March fifth, 1898, the

Captain-General of Cuba—Ramón Blanco y Erenas—proposed that Generalissimo Maximo Gómez and his Cuban troops join him and the Spanish Army against the United States. Blanco appealed to the shared heritage of the Cubans and Spanish, promising Cuban autonomy if they helped fight the Americans.

Captain-General Blanco stated, "As Spaniards and Cubans we find ourselves opposed to foreigners of a different race, who are of a grasping nature...The supreme moment has come in which we should forget past differences and, with Spaniards and Cubans united for the sake of their own defense, repel the invader. Spain will not forget the noble help of its Cuban sons, and once the foreign enemy is expelled from the island, she will, like an affectionate mother, embrace in her arms a new daughter amongst the nations of the New World, who speaks the same language, practices the same faith, and feels the same noble Spanish blood run through her veins."

Generalissimo Máximo Gómez refused the offer of Captain-General Blanco as the Spanish American War began. The war opened in the Caribbean and the Pacific regions as United States troops fought Spain in their colonies of Cuba, Puerto Rico, the Philippines, and Guam. Various generals leading the United States Army in Cuba assisted Generalissimo Máximo Gómez and General Demetrio Castillo Duany, who collaborated with Admiral Sampson on board the battleship New York in the landing of American troops. Under the command of General Demetrio Castillo Duany, the Cubans captured Siboney and thus reduced the risk during the disembarkation of the Americans.

Regular Spanish troops were mostly armed with modern charger-loaded, 7 mm 1893 Spanish Mauser rifles and using smokeless powder. The high-speed 7×57mm Mauser round was termed the "Spanish Hornet" by the Americans because of the supersonic crack it caused as it passed overhead. Other irregular troops were armed with Remington Rolling Block rifles in .43 Spanish, using smokeless powder and brass-jacketed bullets. The U.S. regular infantry was armed with the .30–40 Krag–Jørgensen—a bolt-action rifle with a complex rotating magazine. Both the U.S. regular cavalry and the volunteer cavalry used smokeless ammunition. In later battles, state volunteers used the .45–70 Springfield, which was a single-shot black powder rifle.

On July first, a combined force of about 15,000 American troops in regular infantry and cavalry regiments—which included Theodore Roosevelt and his Rough Riders, the 71st New York, the 2nd Massachusetts Infantry, and 1st North Carolina, and rebel Cuban forces—attacked 1,270 entrenched Spaniards in dangerous Civil War-style frontal assaults at the Battles of El Caney and of San Juan Hill outside of Santiago. Spanish troops were able to halt the American advance after their defense of Fort Canosa, however during the night Cuban soldiers used successive series of trenches (or raised parapets) toward the Spanish positions. Once completed, these parapets were occupied by U.S. soldiers and a new set of excavations went forward.

The Battle of Santiago de Cuba on July third was the largest naval engagement of the Spanish American War. It resulted in the destruction of the Spanish Caribbean Squadron also known as the Flota de Ultramar (or the Spanish Overseas Fleet). American forces destroyed and grounded five of the six ships. Only one Spanish vessel, the new armored cruiser Cristóbal Colón, survived. 1,612 Spanish sailors who were captured—including Admiral Pascual Cervera y Topete—were sent to Seavey's Island at the Portsmouth Naval Shipyard in Kittery, Maine, and were confined at Camp Long as prisoners of war from July eleventh until mid-September. Soon, many of the United States troops withdrew from Cuba due to many casualties—mostly because of diseases like Yellow Fever, which also left about seventy percent of the U.S. forces unfit for service.

In Puerto Rico, twelve U.S. ships commanded by Rear Admiral William T. Sampson attacked Puerto Rico's capital, San Juan. The damage was minimal, however the Americans established a blockade in the city's harbor, San Juan Bay. On June twenty-second, the Spanish cruiser Isabel II and the destroyer Terror delivered a Spanish counterattack but were unable to break the blockade and the Terror was damaged on July twenty-fifth, when 1,300 infantry soldiers led by Nelson A. Miles disembarked off the coast of Guánica.

The first organized armed opposition occurred at the Battle of Yauco. At the Battle of Fajardo, the United States was forced to retreat on August fifth, 1898 by the Spanish-Puerto Rican forces under Pedro del Pino. The United States would recover and participate in various battles—including the Battle of Guayama, the Battle of Guamaní River Bridge, the Battle of Coamo and Silva Heights and finally at the Battle of Asomante. At the Battle of San Germán, the United States forced the Spaniards to retreat to Lares. The United States quickly advanced through the Puerto Rican interior as Spain was on the verge of losing Cuba and Puerto Rico.

Many Spanish officers and soldiers were angered by their former colonial subjects who aided the United States, including Julio Cervera Baviera, who served in the Puerto Rican Campaign and wrote a pamphlet about Puerto Ricans which stated, "I have never seen such a servile, ungrateful country. In twenty-four hours, the people of Puerto Rico went from being fervently Spanish to enthusiastically American...They humiliated themselves, giving in to the invader as the slave bows to the powerful lord." This pamphlet angered the people and he was challenged to a duel by a group of young Puerto Ricans for writing it.

In the Philippines, the United States engaged in a successful war against the Spanish Colonial Government. Magellan explored the Philippines and soon lost his life against the forces of Chief Lapu-Lapu of Mactan Island at the dawn on the twenty-seventh of April 1521. In 1565, King Philip II of Spain directly controlled the Philippines (which was now the Captaincy General of the Philippines). The first battle was in Manila Bay, where on May first, Commodore George Dewey and the U.S. Navy's Asiatic Squadron aboard USS Olympia defeated a Spanish squadron under Admiral Patricio Montojo in just a few hours. The Germans expected an American defeat, but the United States continued to win battles against the Spaniards. Commodore Dewey transported Emilio Aguinaldo—a Filipino leader who had led a rebellion against Spanish rule in the Philippines in 1896—from exile in Hong Kong to the Philippines to rally more Filipinos to support the United States against the Spanish colonial government. Emilio Aguinaldo's forces soon controlled the provinces of Bulacan, Cavite, Laguna, Batangas, Bataan, Zambales, Pampanga, Pangasinan, and Mindoro, and had laid siege to Manila. On June twelfth, Aguinaldo proclaimed the independence of the Philippines. American forces captured the city of Manila from the Spanish in the Battle of Manila, which marked the end of the cooperation between Filipinos and America when the United States prevented them from entering the captured city of Manila.

In Haiti, the reign of the popular leader President Tirésias Simon Sam was coming to an end after the Lüders affair in 1897. Emile Lüders was a mixed man of German and Haitian parentage who came to the aid of his employee Dorléus Présumé, who was suspected of theft and approached by Haitian police. Emile Lüders was at his business Écuries Centrales (or the Central Stables) in the city center of Port-au-Prince when he physically assaulted a Haitian policeman, leading to his arrest along with Dorléus Présumé. After being sentenced to one month's imprisonment, Emile Lüders decided to appeal to the Correctional Tribune, which led to the intervention of the German chargé d'affaires Count von Schwerin, who sought the protection of a small German community numbering close to 200 people who were mostly coffee traders. When U.S. minister Powell insisted for the release of Emile Lüders, President Tirésias Simon Sam freed Emile Lüders, who left Haiti for Hamburg. However, the conflict continued however when on the sixth of December 1897, two German war ships—the SMS Charlotte and the SMS Stein—were anchored in the bay of Port-au-Prince and Captain Thiele of the Charlotte sent a written ultimatum to President Tirésias Simon Sam. They required a formal apology to the German Government, $20,000 in compensation, a twenty-one-gun salute to the German flag, and a reception in honor of Count von Schwerin. If the Haitian government disagreed with the terms the Germans threatened to open fire upon Port-au-Prince and the presidential palace. President Tirésias Simon Sam, who was only given four hours to decide, raised the white flag to signal agreement to the terms. The angry Haitian population who felt dishonored by their leader soon demanded his resignation, including the editor of the Haitian newspaper L'Impartial, who published, "You are invited to attend the funeral of young Haiti, cruelly assassinated by President Tirésias Augustin Simon Sam. The funeral procession will leave the mortuary, located at the National Palace, to give itself to the court of Berlin. Port-au-Prince, December sixth, 1897." President Tirésias Simon Sam would later resign on May twelfth, 1902.

In Guam on June twentieth, a U.S. fleet commanded by Captain Henry Glass consisting of the protected cruiser USS Charleston and three transports carrying troops to the Philippines entered Guam's Apra Harbor. Captain Glass was ordered to proceed to Guam and capture it. Charleston fired a few cannon rounds at Fort Santa Cruz without receiving return fire. Two local officials stated they were unaware of the Spanish American War as fifty-four Spanish infantrymen were captured and transported to the Philippines as prisoners. No U.S. forces were left on Guam, but the only U.S. citizen on the island, Frank Portusach, told Captain Glass he would monitor Guam until the United States returned.

Spain was previously weakened by Emperor Napoleon III of France and later during the Dominican Restoration War in 1865. These defeats eroded Spain's image as a world power and the Spanish American War delivered a devastating loss to King Alfonso XIII. On August twelfth, 1898, the Protocol of Peace was signed in Washington, D.C. between the United States and Spain. The Treaty of Paris was signed in Paris on December tenth, 1898 and was ratified by the United States Senate on February sixth, 1899. The United States gained Spain's colonies of the Philippines, Guam, and Puerto Rico in the treaty, and Cuba became a U.S. protectorate and the went into effect on April eleventh, 1899 with Cubans participating only as observers. Spain retained some of its overseas holdings: Spanish West Africa (or Spanish Sahara), Spanish Guinea, Spanish Morocco, and the Canary Islands. In Cuba, Generalissimo Máximo Gómez was supported by the majority to become the nation's first President after the establishment of the Republic of Cuba and his popularity increased in the Dominican Republic and Puerto Rico. Máximo Gómez retired in 1898 to a villa outside of Havana.

The Medina family were happy to see the end of the Spanish Empire in the Caribbean and Dominicans celebrated their continued sovereignty. The Dominican Republic experienced some political turmoil after the assassination of President Ulises Heureaux in Moca, the Dominican Republic on July twenty-sixth, 1899. Before traveling to Santiago, President Ulises Heureaux—who had previously taken the title of Pacificador de la Patria (or the Peacemaker of the Homeland)—decided to spend time with his compadre Jacobo de Lara and was joined by Carlos Maria Rojas, Lucas Guzman, and others. The signal was given to attack the dictator and a shotgun blast grazed President Ulises Heureaux, causing him to stumble backward and pull out and fire his revolver. Other coconspirators joined as President Ulises Heaureax retreated, where he fell next to a tree and was shot nine times.

The dictatorship of Ulises Heaureax undertook many ambitious projects to modernize the Dominican Republic, including the electrification of Santo Domingo, the construction of a bridge over the Ozama River, and the initiation of inland rail service on a single-track line, linking Santiago to Puerto Plata. However, despite the modernization of the Dominican Republic, the nation was close to bankruptcy. It was revealed that as the mounting public debt made it impossible for President Ulisis Heureaux to maintain his political machine; he increasingly relied on secret loans from the San Domingo Improvement Co., sugar planters, and local merchants. President Ulises Heureaux began printing large amounts of paper currency that were called by Dominicans *las papeletas de Lilís* (or the paper ballots of Lilís), which heightened Dominican inflation and caused the bankruptcy of numerous merchants. President Ulises Heureaux increased his spy network and used the telegraph to coordinate his political events, private meetings, and the maintenance of his regime. Many of his political opponents and anyone he viewed as a threat including Joaquín Campo and Eugenio Generoso de Marchena were captured or killed. By the time of Heureaux's assassination, the Dominican national debt exceeded $35 million, which was estimated at fifteen times the annual Dominican budget. President Wenceslao Figuereo soon succeeded Heureaux.

Anibal Hector Medina was happy as his oldest son Raul Saladin Medina was married in 1894 to a schoolteacher from San Juan de la Maguana named Julieta Garcia. Raul Medina was now an architect who was working on various projects in Santo Domingo and the southern Dominican Republic, and the couple would have two children. Named after the famous Taino leader Cacique Caonabo, Julieta gave birth to a boy in 1895 named Agustin Caonabo Medina Garcia. They would also have a daughter in 1897 named Amelia Medina Garcia.

Alejandro Homero Medina was a young lieutenant in the Dominican Army with a promising career. In 1897, Alejandro also married to a Dominican woman of Arab descent from Santiago named Anastacia Shadid. Anastacia Shadid de Medina was from a poor Syrian family that had migrated from the Ottoman Empire. The Arabs were a small community that had been increasingly arriving from Syria, Lebanon, and Palestine. Anastacia was a smart, hardworking, and frugal woman who helped Alejandro and the Medina family with their finances. Anastacia would give birth to a daughter in 1898 named Fatima Medina Shadid and a son in 1900 named Imran Medina Shadid. Marco and Maria Altagracia Medina were deeply thankful because they never believed they would live long enough to witness the birth of their great-grandchildren.

Carlos Medina retired from the Dominican Military with full honors as a Brigadier General, but he continued to work in the military as a civilian. Carlos and Anouska Medina continued to have a happy marriage while their daughter Priya was studying advanced mathematics and his older son Krishna decided against joining the military and went to school to study law. Carlos and Anoushka Medina would sometimes visit Kingston, Jamaica to meet with Rory McDonell and the Sharma family. They would also on occasion visit Rory's daughter Aileen, who was now married with her own family.

However. the joyous mood of the Dominican people was tempered as many understood that the United States would most likely become a major Empire in Latin America and the Caribbean. Dominicans also understood that the country's economy was now largely under the control of the United States. The Medina family were also preoccupied with the rapidly declining health of the family matriarch, Maria Altagracia Medina, who soon passed away in November of 1898. Marco and Anibal remained at the bedside of Maria for many months. She told her husband she thanked God every day she had met such a wonderful husband and often talked about her beaming pride for Anibal and his wife and children. Her death deeply impacted Anibal and Marco, and Anibal informed his wife Romina that he had only seen his father cry four different times throughout his life and the most was during the death of his mother. Funeral services were soon held for Maria and the family spoke often of their memories of her.

As time went by, Anibal and the Medina family would experience happiness in business and in the developments in the Dominican Republic and the Caribbean. Anibal and many Dominicans were proud when they learned that Máximo Gómez was offered the honor of being the first President of the Republic of Cuba in 1901. The Generalissimo refused the presidential nomination and expected to win unopposed, mainly because Máximo Gómez disliked politics and even after forty years of living in Cuba he strongly felt that being Dominican born, he should not be the civil leader of Cuba. Despite his refusal to become the first president of Cuba, many Dominicans were honored by his contributions to the Dominican War of Independence and the Cuban Revolution.

CHAPTER 27
NEW YORK
(1902)

President William McKinley, who led the United States to victory in the Spanish American War, was assassinated six months into his second term in September 1901 by the anarchist Leon Czolgosz. Inspired by a speech from the anarchist Emma Goldman in Cleveland, Leon Czolgosz was encouraged to shoot President William McKinley twice in the abdomen at the Temple of Music—a concert hall and auditorium built for the Pan-American Exposition in Buffalo, New York. Doctors removed the first bullet and were unable to find the second, however President McKinley's health seemed to improve. Doctors did not know about the gangrene which grew in the walls of President McKinley's stomach, which poisoned his blood and led to his death several months later on September fourteenth, 1901. Vice President Theodore Roosevelt rushed back and took the oath of office as president in Buffalo and Czolgosz was quickly found guilty of murder and executed by electric chair.

President McKinley's security was nervous due to the assassination of King Umberto I of Italy in 1900 by anarchists. King Umberto I was hated particularly by leftists for his colonial expansion into the Horn of Africa and the gaining of Eritrea and Somalia—despite his defeat at the hands of Emperor Menelik II and the Ethiopian Empire at the Battle of Adowa in 1896. In 1882, he approved the Triple Alliance with the German Empire and Austria-Hungary. The other European powers were expanding their empires as they continued to carve Africa. President Theodore Roosevelt and the United States defeated the Spanish Empire in the Americas and gained Cuba and Puerto Rico as well as Guam and the Philippines.

Many black people regarded President McKinley as a friend to the black community as he required the War Department to commission black officers above the rank of lieutenant. McKinley also toured the south in late 1898, promoting sectional reconciliation. He also toured the Tuskegee Institute of black educator Booker T. Washington and visited Confederate memorials. President Theodore Roosevelt spoke about solidifying the social fabric of the United States and became the leading figure of the Progressive movement as he championed his Square Deal. These domestic policies that promised average citizens fairness, breaking of trusts, regulation of railroads, and pure food and drugs. President Theodore Roosevelt made conservation a top priority, and he established new national parks, forests, and monuments to preserve the nation's natural resources. In foreign policy, he focused on Central America, where he began construction of the Panama Canal during the ongoing Colombian Thousand Days' War.

In the Dominican Republic, there was political turmoil as the Council of Secretaries of State led the nation. Its members were Tomás Demetrio Morales, Arístides Patiño, Enrique Henríquez y Alfau, Jaime R. Vidal, and Braulio Álvarez. The People's Revolutionary Governing Junta subsequently led the Dominican Republic—their members were Mariano Cestero, Álvaro Logroño, Arístides Patiño, and Pedro María Mejía. A Red Party member once again became President of the Dominican Republic named Horacio Vásquez.

Anibal was happy when he was informed that Raymond Saint-Lot and his wife Julia had settled in the new city of La Romana in the eastern Dominican Republic. The Medina family were doing well as the Dominican Republic received new people from the surrounding Caribbean islands. After the Dominican Restoration War in 1865, many black immigrants from Turks and Caicos settled in Puerto Plata and immigration from the Anglo-phone Caribbean increased during the late 19th century. Many immigrants arrived from the islands of the Bahamas, the Turks, Saint Kitts and Nevis, Dominica, Antigua, Anguilla, St. Vincent, Montserrat, Tortola, St. Croix, St. Thomas, Martinique, and Guadeloupe. Many of these islanders traveled to the Dominican Republic to work on the railroad connecting the city of Santiago to Puerto Plata and other construction projects as the industrialization of the Dominican Republic increased. These immigrants predominantly settled in Puerto Plata, and later La Romana and San Pedro de Macorix. The people of these English-speaking islands enriched the culture of the Dominican Republic and brought their own cultures, which included different styles of cooking and the popular johnnycake (which soon changed to become the Dominican style johnnycake, which was called *yaniqueques* or *yanikeke*. However, they are made with flour, baking powder, butter, and water, and are typically deep-fried). These migrants brought various Protestant denominations into the Dominican Republic which led to the establishment of the Anglican Church, in 1897 in San Pedro de Macorís. The cocolos also brought the sports of cricket and boxing to the Dominican Republic, but would soon abandon cricket and adopt baseball—although some of their cultural practices were absorbed by the larger Dominican culture. Introduced to the Dominican Republic in the 1870s, baseball remained the most popular sport and its popularity would grow rapidly in the 1900s. The Afro-Caribbean people of the Bahamas would also contribute to the Gullah culture of the people in Georgia, South Carolina and the Sea Islands, who developed their own Creole language similar to Jamaican Patois and Bahamian Creole (commonly known as Gullah language or Geechee).

Anibal spoke to his father about traveling to New York and Marco informed his son to be wary of the United States but encouraged him. The Spanish American War helped establish the United States as a world power and they would seek to reinforce the Monroe Doctrine in Latin America and the Caribbean.

Marco looked to his son Anibal and stated, "My son, empires come and they go. When empires die, others replace them. In the case of the Americas, the major power is now the United States. After the fall of the Persian Empire, the Greek Empire arose with Alexander the Great, and after the end of the Hellenist Age, the Roman Empire rose and fell; then the Western European Empires arose. Ironically, the tribes that are the ancestors of the Northern and Western Europeans were considered barbarians by the Roman Empire. Now the end of the Spanish Empire in the Americas has created a vacuum and the United States is the empire that will soon spread throughout the Americas. The dictator is dead, but the Dominican Republic is still not politically stable. It is necessary that Dominicans take it upon ourselves to unite and fix our nation so we can conserve our sovereignty and dignity as a people."

Anibal Medina and his wife Romina soon departed by ship to New York. The couple arrived in late October 1902. Anibal had never experienced such cold weather before, but he and his wife bought long coats to make their stay more comfortable. New York City was a sight to behold. One of the first things Anibal and Romina saw was the Statue of Liberty at Bedloe's Island. Anibal learned that the Statue of Liberty was designed by the sculptor named Frédéric Auguste Bartholdi and built by Gustave Eiffel. The statue was dedicated on October twenty-eight, 1886. The Statue of Liberty was inspired by French law professor and politician Édouard René de Laboulaye, who stated in 1865 that any monument raised to U.S. independence would be a joint project of the French and U.S. peoples. Made of copper, the Statue of Liberty was mostly brown with areas of green due to oxidation. The torch-bearing arm was previously displayed at the Centennial Exposition in Philadelphia in 1876, and in Madison Square Park in Manhattan from 1876 to 1882. Joseph Pulitzer helped complete the statue by starting a drive for donations to finish the project, which attracted over 120,000 contributors. This amazing statue portrayed the figure of a robed woman representing Libertas, a Roman liberty goddess. She holds a torch above her head with her right hand, and in her left hand she carries a *tabula ansata* inscribed in Roman numerals with "JULY IV MDCCLXXVI" (or July fourth, 1776), the date of the Declaration of Independence.

Anibal spoke with people from different regions of the world and he was amazed when he visited Manhattan and saw the carriages transporting people around the city. Anibal and his wife were astonished when they observed the electrical grid system manifest into the widespread lighting of the Manhattan streets and skyline that could be witnessed from afar. Anibal enjoyed the various beers and a fountain drink called egg cream, which contained neither eggs nor cream. Egg Cream consisted of milk, carbonated water, and flavored syrup which was typically chocolate or vanilla. The drink was believed to have originated from Eastern European Jewish immigrants in New York City. Some New Yorkers informed Anibal there was a popular drink during the 1880s that was made with chocolate syrup, cream, and raw eggs mixed into soda water, while in poorer neighborhoods, a less expensive version of this treat was created called the egg cream. While eating frankfurters (or hotdogs) that Anibal bought for him and his wife at two cents apiece, the couple spoke about how the electrical grid could one day expand to light up the entire city of Santo Domingo.

The numerous electric cars that transported customers from place to place fascinated Anibal. The electric car had various advantages over the steam and gasoline engines, including no vibrations; it was extremely quiet compared to its competitors. The electric cars did not emit smoke or backfire frequently as did gas-powered cars. They were also ready to go when the driver sat in the car. The gas-powered cars that needed to be cranked by hand as well as the steam-powered variety sometimes took over forty minutes to start in the winter months. Manhattan was a city filled with people, trolley cars, trains that ran overhead, buildings close together that rose high like sets of teeth throughout Manhattan, and kids playing outside while working-class families and the wealthy walked amongst each other. Anibal was informed that New York City in the summer months was a sight to behold with more people in the streets and the laughter of children as they played stickball and other games.

Throughout several weeks, Anibal and Romina traveled to Central Park, City Hall, Union Square, and Coney Island in Brooklyn. They also visited Grand Army Plaza and the other boroughs using train systems and motor vehicles. The couple also visited the Bronx and saw the extensive farmlands. The town of Morrisania was created from West Farms in 1855. In 1873, the town of Kingsbridge was established within the former borders of Yonkers, and the whole territory east of the Bronx River was annexed to the city in 1895—three years before New York's consolidation with Brooklyn, Queens, and Staten Island. Anibal was happy to see the cottage of Edgar Allan Poe in the Bronx and enjoyed his brief visit. Various New Yorkers also informed Anibal about extensive subterranean tunnels that would be called the New York subway system. The subway would be opened in several more years, providing transportation for millions of New Yorkers during all four seasons. Anibal learned about the people of different ancestries, including the black American people who spoke about various black leaders and their philosophies.

Anibal enjoyed the music which motivated the people of this great city. Native groups like the Lenape Native Americans played music before New York was New Amsterdam, and the Dutch and English would bring their music to this part of the world as well. In the 1830s, New York City rose to become one of the most important cultural centers of the United States. Minstrel shows—comic and musical acts performed by whites in blackface—spread across the country, which would later leave a negative legacy in the artistic history of the United States.

New York became the home of the New York Philharmonic (formed in 1842), the Professional Yiddish theater (1882), the Metropolitan Opera House (1882), and Carnegie Hall (1891). Now the music scene in New York was filled with African Americans and Jewish influences, with Jazz music rising to prominence. Jazz was created by the African American communities of New Orleans, and developed from blues and ragtime. Anibal also enjoyed the theatrical performances of Broadway. He and his wife saw the musical A Chinese Honeymoon, a musical comedy by George Dance, with music by Howard Talbot and additional music by Ivan Caryll and others.

Anibal was curious about visiting other regions of the United States, but he was wary of the southern United States that locals called "dixie". Anibal was informed regarding the Mason-Dixon line, which was surveyed between 1763 and 1767 by Charles Mason and Jeremiah Dixon in the resolution of a border dispute involving Maryland, Pennsylvania, and Delaware in Colonial America. The Mason-Dixon line was currently the demarcation of four U.S. states, forming part of the borders of Pennsylvania, Maryland, Delaware, and West Virginia. The Mason-Dixon line also symbolized a cultural boundary between the North and the South or dixie. During the Civil War, the Union Army was referred to as Yanks or Yankees and subsequently, all people of the United States were called Yankees by foreigners. Anibal noticed some cultural differences between the northern and southern United States, and although they thought about visiting the south, he and his wife did not want to visit the southern states as they considered the violent racism of the former Confederacy to be backward. However, they realized the northern states had a subtler form of racism. They desired to visit Florida and possibly Louisiana later, when racial divisions decreased.

During his stay in New York, Anibal learned about various black leaders in the United States, including Booker. T Washington and W.E.B. Du Bois. Booker T. Washington was born into slavery in 1856 in Hale's Ford Virginia and became an educator, author, orator, and advisor to presidents. As lynchings reached a peak in 1895, Booker T. Washington gave a speech known as the Atlanta Compromise, which called for black progress through education and entrepreneurship.

W.E.B Du Bois was born in Great Barrington, Massachusetts, and he grew up in a relatively tolerant, integrated community. After completing graduate work at the University of Berlin and Harvard, he soon became the first African American to earn a doctorate. In addition, he became a professor of history, sociology, and economics at Atlanta University, where he would publish The Philadelphia Negro, the first case study of a black community in the United States. W.E.B was an established sociologist, historian, civil rights activist, Pan-Africanist, author, writer, and editor.

Anibal bought several books including The Adventures of Tom Sawyer and The Adventures of Huckleberry Finn written by Mark Twain. He also bought a children's book titled The Wonderful Wizard of Oz, written by Lyman Frank Baum, and a copy of a book titled *Ben-Hur: A Tale of the Christ*, written by a former Governor of New Mexico and a former United States Minister to the Ottoman Empire Lew Wallace. Additionally, he purchased Treasure Island, or the mutiny of the Hispaniola (or simply Treasure Island), written by Scottish author Robert Louis Stevenson in 1883. Anibal was also interested in fantasy and science fiction books written by H.G. Wells like The Time Machine, The Wonderful Visit, The Wheels of Chance, The Invisible Man, The War of the Worlds, The First Men in the Moon, and The Island of Doctor Moreau. He also chose some the works of the French novelist Jules Verne: Tribulations of a Chinaman in China, Twenty Thousand Leagues Under the Sea, and Journey to the Center of the Earth. Anibal decided he would read these books on his voyage back to the Dominican Republic. In mid-December 1902, after he and Romina experienced snowfall for the first time, they departed back to the Dominican Republic.

CHAPTER 28

QUISQUEYA

(1905)

Anibal and Romina arrived in the Dominican Republic in January 1903. The couple was happy to return to Santo Domingo as they prepared to move to their home in San Cristobal. Anibal and the Medina family would later attend the funeral of Eugenio María de Hostos on August eleventh, 1903 in Santo Domingo. Eugenio María de Hostos died at the age of sixty-four, and he desired his body to remain in the Dominican Republic permanently and reinterred in Puerto Rico only when the land was fully independent. Eugenio María de Hostos wrote his own epitaph, which stated, "I wish that they will say: In that island (Puerto Rico) a man was born who loved truth, desired justice, and worked for the good of men."

Anibal was informed of various world events, including the death of Queen Victoria in January 1901. Queen Victoria spent the Christmas of 1900 at Osborne House on the Isle of Wight suffering from rheumatism in her legs and clouded vision from cataracts. She died surrounded by her family members, including her eldest grandson, Emperor Wilhelm II of Germany, and her eldest son and successor, King Edward VII. Queen Victoria also spent her last days with a hated member of her court, the Indian and Muslim Mohammed Abdul Karim, who had served her as Munshi. France as a world power continued to weaken after their defeat in the Franco-German War and the death of Emperor Napoleon III in January of 1873. The French Third Republic was currently led by President Émile François Loubet, who was involved in the Dreyfus Affair political scandal where Captain Alfred Dreyfus—a young Alsatian French artillery officer of Jewish descent—was sentenced to life imprisonment for sharing French military secrets to the German Embassy in Paris. The head of counterespionage, Georges Picquart, identified a French Army major named Ferdinand Walsin Esterhazy as the real culprit. However, the military court unanimously acquitted Esterhazy and the French Army then accused Dreyfus with added charges based on falsified documents. In Spain, the young King Alfonso XIII—who had spent most of his life under the Regency of his mother Maria Christina of Austria and was baptized with water from the River Jordan in Palestine—was plagued by internal turmoil, including increasing Catalan nationalism and foreign wars threatening the Spanish Empire.

Under the Platt Amendment, the U.S. leased the Guantánamo Bay naval base from Cuba and guaranteed the U.S. the right to intervene and placed restrictions on Cuban foreign relations. The first leader of the Republic of Cuba was President Tomás Estrada Palma, who worked with José Martí to gather political support for a revolution. After Martí's death, Estrada Palma became the new leader of the Cuban Revolutionary Party, where he fulfilled the role of chief representative. With this authorization, he was able to form diplomatic relations with other countries—including the United States—and Estrada Palma was also assisted by William Randolph Hearst's newspapers to spread the cause of the Cuban Revolutionary Party by posting articles sympathetic to the revolutionaries.

After a few years of General Leonard Wood's rule in Cuba, elections were to be held on December thirty-first, 1901. There were two Cuban political parties: The Republicans, who were conservative and wanted national autonomy (headed by José Miguel Gómez), and the National Liberals, who were a popular party that wanted Cuba to go toward local autonomy (headed by Alfredo Zayas); both supported Estrada Palma. His opponent, General Bartolomé Masó, withdrew his candidacy, leading to the Presidency of Estrada Palma. He believed in creating a non-racial Cuban Republic, and before his presidency, Estrada Palma promised he would bring 100 public service jobs to Afro-Cubans and repeal American regulations that supported segregation. The United States desired to set up bases close to the Cuban capital of Havana at Bahia Honda, Guantánamo Bay, Cienfuegos, and Nipe Bay. After the Cuban American Treaty of Relations on May twenty-second, 1903, the United States acquired in perpetuity the land surrounding Guantánamo Bay, for use as a naval base and coaling station. President Tomás Estrada Palma won a second term, but with violent opposition from the liberals, who claimed electoral fraud. In response, President Theodore Roosevelt began planning the second occupation of Cuba.

Puerto Rico was now under occupation by the United States and was renamed Porto Rico; the currency was changed from the Puerto Rican peso to the United States dollar. The government lottery was abolished, cockfighting was forbidden, and a centralized public health service was established while the flag of Puerto Rico was traded for the forty-five-star flag of the United States. Various parties formed in Puerto Rico like the Partido Republicano (or Republican Party) led by José Celso Barbosa and the American Federal Party led by Luis Muñoz Rivera; both supported annexation by the United States. Puerto Rico was devastated by two hurricanes in 1899 including the San Ciriaco hurricane which added to Puerto Rico's turmoil.

The Foraker Act of 1900 disbanded the military government in Puerto Rico and established a civil government and free commerce between the island and the United States. The structure of the insular government included a governor appointed by the President of the United States, an executive council the equivalent of a senate for Puerto Rico, and a legislature with thirty-five members—though the executive veto required a two-thirds vote to override. The first appointed civil governor of Puerto Rico was Charles Herbert Allen, and now the current leader was Governor William Henry Hunt. In 1904, the former American Federal Party became the Union of Puerto Rico, which was the most dominant political party.

The United States currently controlled Guam and the Philippines. Guam was used to set up a submarine communications cable on the seabed from Guam to the Philippines. The United States also built cables from the United States' mainland to the conquered islands of Hawaii. Captain James Cook of England previously explored the Pacific Islands, making landfall in January 1778 at Waimea harbor, Kauai. Captain James Cook was the first European to build formal relations with the natives and named the archipelago the "Sandwich Islands" after the fourth Earl of Sandwich—the acting First Lord of the Admiralty. Cook was later killed on February fourteenth, 1779, when he attempted to kidnap Chief Kalaniʻōpuʻu of Hawaii in order to reclaim a cutter stolen from one of his ships.

Kamehameha was raised in the royal court of his uncle Kalaniʻōpuʻu, and he achieved prominence in 1782, upon Kalaniʻōpuʻu's death. The son of Kalaniʻōpuʻu, Kīwalaʻō was soon defeated in the first key conflict—the Battle of Mokuʻōhai—and Kamehameha and his chiefs took power in regions of Hawaii. Kamehameha gained allies from American and British traders who sold him guns and ammunition, including Captain Brown, who guaranteed unlimited supplies from China needed for the formula of gunpowder (which was also given to Kamehameha) as well as sulfur, saltpeter-potassium nitrate, and charcoal, which could also be found in Hawaii. Kamehameha would soon become King Kamehameha I or Kamehameha the Great, and he conquered the chiefs of the Hawaiian Islands, unifying them under his rule in 1795. King Kamehameha I unified the legal system and used the products collected in taxes to promote trade with Europe and the United States.

The House of Kamehameha lost power and the Republic of Hawaii was established in 1893, after Queen Liliʻuokalani was overthrown by a conspiracy involving the United States Minister to the Kingdom of Hawaii (John L. Stevens) and U.S. citizens. Hawaii was currently annexed and was a territory of the United States. Many immigrant groups including Japanese, Puerto Ri-cans, and Koreans soon migrated to Hawaii.

The Philippine American War erupted soon after the Treaty of Paris between the forces of the United States and the Pro-Spanish Philippine Republic on February fourth, 1899. Freemason and leader of the Republic of the Philippines, President Emilio Aguinaldo, led the fight against the United States, which resulted in his victory. The war ended in 1902 and Emilio Aguinaldo was freed, but he continued to support groups that favored independence for the Philippines. The United States continued to increase its power over its new territories as President Theodore Roosevelt enforced the Monroe Doctrine.

President Theodore Roosevelt wrote to the previous Governor of New York, Henry L. Sprague January twenty-sixth 1900, after forcing New York's Republican committee to pull support away from a corrupt financial adviser: "I have always been fond of the West African proverb: 'Speak softly and carry a big stick; you will go far.'" Teddy Roosevelt, as he was affectionally called, attributed the quote to a West African proverb—which was unfounded. However, his supporters regarded the quote as evidence of Teddy Roosevelt's prolific reading habits. The United States also aided the separation of Panama from Colombia in 1903 and helped complete the Panama Canal.

Anibal spoke to his father during a visit to his home in Santo Domingo. Marco Medina stated, "The United States will seek to become a major world power, and her success in the Spanish-American War were the grand entry of the Yankees to the world stage. Despite their presidents, their foreign policy will not change in any major way—and just like all the empires that have come before the United States, they will also seek to dominate the regional nations.

"The Americas will become part of their empire and they will clash with other major empires in the future. My advice to you, my son, is to continue to protect your wife and family and give them the tools they need to succeed as men and women when you and I are no longer part of this world. There will be other Dominican patriots much younger than you or me who will stand up for our people and shed Dominican blood to maintain our sovereignty. The Dominican Republic is a nation of many firsts; the first African slaves arrived in bondage from West African tribes in 1501, and it was in our land near Santo Domingo where black slaves first gathered the bravery to revolt against European colonizers in 1521. Santo Domingo is the oldest continuous city established by Europeans since 1494. A city which is now the Dominican capital and a city which represents Dominican hard work and the Dominican spirit. This is a great land which gave life to the glorious natives like Cacique Caonabo, Anacaona, El Cigüayo, Tamayo, and Cacique Enriquillo that fought so valiantly against the Spaniards from 1519 to 1533."

Anibal smiled as his father stopped momentarily to gather his thoughts. "The West Africans brought their cultures and the religion of Islam to our land, and we welcomed the Jewish people and they became Dominican as well. The natives along with the Africans, Spaniards, and other European groups blended with other Arab migrants arriving from places to include Syria, Palestine, and Lebanon. The Asians that continue to arrive at the Dominican Republic—including the Chinese with their culture and Buddhism—are all blending together to create the Dominican people. We are a respected member of Latin America and our heroes fought against all who have attempted to rule over us. Never forget the wars we participated in and the strengthening of the Dominican identity that resulted from our victories in these wars. We must also fight our own corrupted leaders and we must always seek to uplift the Dominican standard of living. That is when we may rise as a people, my son. We are Dominicans and will always be proud Quisqueyanos."

Anibal would spend more time with his father Marco as he became ill. In September of 1904, Marco Medina passed away in his sleep. There was a great funeral held for him, and although he had lived a long and happy life, Anibal felt a great sadness. He was now the patriarch of the Medina family, and he continued work in the fields, though most of the work was now taken over by his children. This gave him a lot of leisure time to read and play with technology he had brought back from the United States.

Anibal Medina electrified parts of his home in Santo Domingo, which he gave to his oldest son Raul Saladin Medina and his family, as well as his home in San Cristobal, causing many curious Dominicans to visit and inquire about his voyage to New York. Despite his many faults, the previous leader Ulises Heureaux had begun the industrialization of the Dominican Republic and brought the first electric lights to Santo Domingo. Although Santo Domingo was not as extraordinary as New York City, it had made some technological progress and Anibal often spoke to his wife Romina and his family regarding the future of their land with all these advancements.

Anibal built a small library for his home in San Cristobal and spent most of his time reading. Anibal read many of the works of Edgar Allan Poe and he particularly liked the short story The Fall of the House of Usher and the way Edgar Allan Poe described the House of Usher which became another character in the story. The story was ominous, and the ending was surprising with the death and resurrection of Madeline Usher the sister of Roderick Usher and the subsequent death of both characters. Anibal enjoyed the eerie feeling he sometimes had when he read the various stories of Edgar Allan Poe as the plot manifested through his imagination. Anibal remembered the eerie feeling he also experienced as a child when his parents would tell him scary stories of Dominican folklore.

Anibal also recently completed Treasure Island by Scottish author Robert Louis Stevenson. The story spoke of adventures involving buccaneers and buried gold and the age of piracy. Treasure Island was originally titled The Sea Cook: A Story for Boys and the story spoke of treasure maps marked with an "X", schooners, the Black Spot, tropical islands, and one-legged seamen with parrots on their shoulders and a colorful antagonist named Long John Silver. Anibal encouraged his grandchildren to learn foreign languages, particularly English, so they could enjoy the books he and his wife read. The children would be amazed that their island of Hispaniola was featured in Treasure Island and was believed to take place in the mid-eighteenth century. The protagonist was a young boy about thirteen or fourteen years old named Jim Hawkins. The villain, Long John Silver, was the leader of a band of pirates and was one-legged with a parrot on his shoulder named Captain Flint—the same name as his former leader. Long John Silver was the quartermaster serving Captain Flint and his ship named The Walrus. The story entertained Anibal and his family as they wondered which islands and pirates inspired the locations and characters of Treasure Island. It reminded Anibal of his old friend McDonnell and his interest in piracy and their long conversations regarding the subject. Anibal would later give Treasure Island as a gift to Rory McDonnell.

Anibal also read the bestselling book *Ben-Hur: A Tale of the Christ*. The story's protagonist was a wealthy Jewish man named Judah Ben Hur who was falsely accused by his childhood friend Messala of an attempted assassination on Valerius Gratus—the procurator of Judea—and was subsequently enslaved by the Romans. Ben-Hur's mother Miriam and his younger sister Tirzah were imprisoned and Ben-Hur was sentenced to slavery in the Roman galleys. After a naval battle between the Romans and Greek pirates, Judah Ben-Hur survived and was soon adopted by the Roman Quintus Arrius. Judah Ben-Hur later avenged his family by beating his enemy Messala in a chariot race. Judah Ben-Hur married Esther and they financed the building of underground tombs later known as the Catacomb of San Calixto in Rome, where Christian martyrs are buried and venerated

The story of Judah Ben-Hur was the second bestselling book after the Holy Bible and Anibal enjoyed the fictional characters as well as the portrayals of various people in the Bible like the Three Wise Men, John the Baptist, Pontius Pilate, and Jesus Christ. Anibal was fond of silent movies he watched in New York City and would often tell his family that the story of Ben-Hur would be made into a silent movie someday due to its immense popularity. Anibal's family also loved reading—particularly Anibal's son Alejandro Homero Medina, who had already written many short stories in his leisure time.

The Medina family accumulated wealth as Anibal's sons established a long-lasting partnership with the young Selim Andujar and his brother Farid Andujar, who were now running the Andujar family's business affairs after the death of their father Romulo in 1904. This allowed Anibal to plan his retirement and let his children take over both homes in Santo Domingo and San Cristobal. Anibal reduced his workload and enjoyed more leisure time with his wife Romina. He made sure he spent time with his loving wife and his growing family as well as helped grandchildren in their various pursuits. Anibal also began taking an interest in the religious stories and lessons found within Hinduism and its Holy Books. Krishna and Priya Medina sought to learn more about their Indian ancestry and to teach their future children about it. Anibal delighted in the lessons of Hindu Holy Scriptures like the Mahabharata, Ramayana, Rigveda, Upanishads, Vedas, and the Bhagavad Gita (which translated to the Song of God). Anibal enjoyed the teachings of ancient India and often found himself wondering about the possibility that the Indians—who were once occupied by Alexander the Great and the Greeks, the Portuguese, and now the British Empire—would once again reclaim their independence.

Anibal loved to spend time with his grandson Augustin Caonabo Medina, who had a passion for the sport of baseball. Anibal nicknamed Augustin Hermes, after the messenger God because of Augustin's speed and affinity for racing. His son loved practical jokes and was a trickster, which also contributed to his nickname. He was punished often for his misdeeds but in baseball, he found a positive outlet and a sport which helped him learn hard work, discipline, and teamwork.

Baseball quickly spread throughout the Dominican Republic, and the skill level among Dominican baseball players rapidly increased with various teams created throughout the nation. After a meeting at the house of Vicente María Vallejo on El Conde Street in Santo Domingo's Colonial Zone (on November ninth, 1907), a team was founded. Among its first members were George and Cuncún Pou, Luis and Federico Fiallo, Luis and Pinchán Vallejo, Luis Castillo, Salvador Piñeyro, Alvaro Alvarez, Tutú Martínez, Angel and Chichí Mieses, Arturo Perdomo, Bi Sanchez, Virgilio Abreu, Alberto Peña, Arturo Nolasco and Tulio Piña. The team would represent Santo Domingo and was called the Tigres del Licey—nicknamed "El Glorioso". A Puerto Rican accountant and baseball player named Pedro Miguel Caratini would help establish baseball in the Dominican Republic and become the manager for the Tigres del Licey.

Dominican politics were relatively stable compared the chaotic years that Anibal previously lived through. However, instability threatened to return. After the presidency of Carlos Felipe Morales and the Red Party, the Council of Secretaries of State governed the Dominican Republic. Uts members included Manuel Lamarche García, Emiliano Tejera, Andrés Julio Montolío, Francisco Leonte Vásquez Lajara, Carlos Ginebra, Eladio Victoria, and Federico Velásquez y Hernández. The current leader of the Dominican Republic was President Ramón Cáceres, the head of the Red Party. The administration of President Ramon Caceres polarized the Dominican Republic as supporters of Horacio Vásquez called Horacistas (the Red Party) and supporters of Juan Isidro Jimenes Pereyra called Jimenistas (the Blue Party) would lead to a violent confrontation.

Anibal thought about his father's words and the potential turmoil in the Dominican Republic leading to the intervention of the United States.

President Theodore Roosevelt recently won a Nobel Peace Prize in 1906 for his help in making a deal after the shocking Japanese victory over Russia in the Russo-Japanese War. Ironically, President Theodore Roosevelt unleashed his Great White Fleet in a world tour to showcase American Naval Power. Anibal feared for his family's safety in the face of American imperialism, however as an old man, he could only concern himself with the security and affairs of his closest family members.

Anibal and Romina would travel once more to New York City and later to other Caribbean islands such as Cuba, Puerto Rico, Jamaica, Trinidad. Wherever they went, they continued their advocacy for the rights of Caribbean and Dominican working-class people. Anibal spent a lot of time with his grandchildren and sometimes the adult children of his nephew Carlos Medina: Alvaro and Luna Xin (who he called Chinita). Both Alvaro and Chinita were married with children of their own. Anibal enjoyed being with his grandchildren and talking about Dominican folklore that was told to scare young ones into obedience or simply for entertainment. Anibal spoke about El Bacá, which appears when a person makes a pact with the devil, and the Bacá ensures that the person goes through with their end of the bargain. The Bacá is said to appear like a dog from hell with red burning eyes made of hellfire, while other accounts of the Bacá describe it as a shapeshifter. It takes many forms—including a bull or domesticated animals like cows and chickens—that feed on the souls of any human.

El Duende is similar to elves, gnomes, sprites or goblins. Duendes could be good or bad depending on their mood. They are very mischievous creatures that like to play jokes on people, and many times they are blamed for strange noises in a home. Duendes are usually invisible unless they want to be seen and appear as small children with old faces. El Cuco or the boogeyman of Portuguese and Galician origin, was said to snatch children who were misbehaving.

Another popular story involved La Ciguapa, a wild woman-type creature with long dark hair that lives in the forests of the mountains of the Dominican Republic. Many believe the story originated from native Taino, African, as well as Nahuatl folklore. La Ciguapa was beautiful and would lure unsuspecting men and kill them while others might witness a horrendous form of the Ciguapa. They are always naked with long hair which covers their body, and their feet face backward, making it impossible to track them. Dominican lore states that the only way to capture a *ciguapa* is by tracking them at night, during a full moon, with a black and white *perro cinqueño* or polydactyl dog. Stories of the Bruja or the Witch scared many Dominican children as witches were believed to eat children, Dominican parents often used these stories to scare them when they misbehaved.

On a later trip to the United States, Anibal Medina would purchase various horror stories written by William Hope Hodgson, including, The

House on the Borderland, and The Night Land as well as a story which Romina had spoken to him about during his younger years titled *Frankenstein; or The Modern Prometheus* written by Mary Wollstonecraft Shelley and published in 1818.

In 1906, Carlos' son Krishna Medina was married to a beautiful Dominican woman from Bonao with a rich caramel complexion named Valeria Gonzalez. The couple had their first daughter and named her Aida Indira Medina Gonzalez. Krishna loved to hear the stories of the various plays Anibal spoke of and named Aida after the Ethiopian princess from the play Aida. The play involved the love between Aida, a captured Ethiopian princess, and the Egyptian military commander Radamès and his struggle between his love for her and his loyalty to the Pharaoh. The Pharoah's daughter Amneris was also in love with Radamès, heightening the dramatic elements of the play. Other important roles included Ramfis the High Priest and Amonasro the King of Ethiopia. Later, Krishna would name his second child—a boy—Salvador Ashoka Medina Gonzalez. Krishna Medina's sister Priya would marry a History Professor from Santo Domingo named Pablo Alfaro; together they had a son named Cesar Arjuna Alfaro Medina.

Fatima was a quiet girl who mostly liked reading, and Imran was a smart boy who enjoyed working. Anibal thought that perhaps Imran would grow up to become a great businessman and improve his life and the lives of his family. Anibal found himself spending increasing amounts of time with his grandson Augustin Caonabo and he would often watch him play baseball—a sport which he enjoyed almost as much as boxing. Anibal would often speak about the Boston Red Sox and New York Giants and sometimes he would mention the new team called the New York Highlanders (or the Yankees). Anibal and his grandson Augustin would speak mostly about their favorite team, the Tigres del Licey. He quickly became a fan of the sport and would always watch Augustin's games.

On the morning of Three Kings day in 1908, as Dominicans celebrated the three wise men Melchior, Caspar, and Balthazar and their visit to the home of baby Jesus after traveling across the desert for twelve days, Anibal spoke with his wife about their grandchildren. He bought many gifts for his family, and he had chosen a baseball bat and glove for Augustin, who had turned his attention towards becoming a pitcher. Augustin was saddened as he pitched a great game against a good team but lost when the opposing team's best hitter hit a home run against him late in the game.

Anibal looked at his grandson and stated, "We are Medina men. We do not cry after our losses but instead hold our heads up high. We are also humble during times of victory, which is the sign of a true champion. You were named after the brave Taino leader Cacique Caonabo, who fought the Spaniards despite their technological advances. Like Caonabo, you must be brave and persevere through the trials you will face in life. Learn from your mistakes Augustin, and tomorrow you will be better than you are today. That is what Dominicans have always been; a people who have struggled and risen from the ashes of warfare and strife again and again. With hard work and dedication, we as a people can be reborn. Be like the phoenix, for you are a Medina and you are a Quisqueyano!"

Later in the evening, Anibal enjoyed a meal of Mondongo that Romina prepared for him. He smiled as he told her the story of Augustin's sadness after his loss on the baseball field. Anibal explained how his grandson grinned after he comforted him and how he knew Augustin, like the rest of his grandchildren, would grow to become great men and women. Romina smiled and embraced her husband as they sat together watching the sunset in the beautiful Dominican sky. Anibal thought to himself, *I feel complete as a man, my family is joyous and full of health.*

CHAPTER 29
REPUBLICA DOMINICANA

President Ramón Arturo Cáceres Vasquez was assassinated in his horse-drawn carriage on November nineteenth, 1911. General Luis Tejera led the ambush and during the shootout, he was wounded in the leg while President Cáceres was killed. General Tejera and the conspirators fled in an automobile that crashed into a river, where the general was hidden in a nearby hut so his comrades could run to safety. General Tejera was discovered and quickly executed along with over thirty others. In the subsequent power vacuum, General Alfredo Victoria seized control and placed his uncle Senator Eladio Victoria y Victoria as President of the Dominican Republic. Horacio Vásquez soon returned from Puerto Rico to lead his followers (the Horacistas) in a popular rebellion against the new government, joining forces with the border caudillo General Desiderio Arias as the Dominican Republic erupted in Civil War.

Anibal's younger son, Alejandro Homero Medina, was now a lieutenant colonel in the Dominican Army and was ordered to put an end to the rebellion. The Dominican rebels were led by Horacio Vasquez and Desiderio Arias, who received considerable support in Montecristi as well as from the Haitian government and the United States. The Blue Party had split into two: the *bolos pata blanca* (or the white-legged) represented the civilian and intellectual wing of the party, and the *bolos pata negra* (or the black-legged) represented the military wing and the *caudillos*. Together, they were the feet of the rooster. Like many Dominicans, Alejandro Medina was wary of foreign funding and interventionism during political unrest.

The United States soon abandoned the customs houses on the Haitian border used to control imports and exports. The Haitian government, somewhat more stable than previous years, continued to profit from the Dominican Civil War. President William Taft sent a pacification delegation to Santo Domingo in effort to end the conflict. The commission arrived at the Dominican Republic accompanied by 750 U.S. Marines and began negotiating a removal of Chief of the Army while President Eladio Victoria remained in power. However, both men were unpopular with many Dominicans and uncooperative with the United States. This led to negotiations with the Dominican rebels and the establishment of a provisional government under the leadership of President Adolfo Alejandro Nouel, the Archbishop of Santo Domingo. President Adolfo Alejandro Nouel resigned in April 1913 and left for Barahona, and President José Bordaz Baez assumed office that same year.

The Horacistas allied themselves with the Jimenistas and supporters of the southern leader Luis Felipe Vidal called *Vidalistas* in a combined effort to overthrow Bordas. President Woodrow Wilson threatened to dispatch U.S. Marines from Guantanamo Bay to the Dominican Republic if the rebels did not lay down their arms and agree to the appointment of a provisional president. President Bordas soon resigned and the son of the deceased Buenaventura Baez, Ramon Baez Machado, became President of the Dominican Republic on August twenty-seventh, 1914. President Ramon Baez was a physician and politician, and he took advantage of his position to bring the remains of his father to the Dominican Republic. President Ramon Baez also worked to constitute a new government and organize new elections, which eventually voted in Juan Isidro Jimenes Pereyra, who defeated Horacio Vasquez.

Alejandro Homero Medina, now a colonel in the Dominican Army, resigned after he was dismayed by his participation in the violent battles of La Vega and Santiago. Anibal Medina warned his family about the possible occupation of the Dominican Republic by the United States, and his prediction seemed more realistic in 1915 when the United States occupied Haiti. Anibal would pass away in September of 1915, leaving his oldest son Raul Saladin as the patriarch of the Medina family.

Haiti was in political turmoil during the rule of President Jean Vilbrun Guillaume Sam, who was trying to suppress the revolt of Dr. Rosalvo Bobo. The cousin of President Tirésias Simon Sam violently moved against his political opponents and the better educated Haitian mulatto elites. On July twenty-seventh, 1915, President Jean Vilbrun Guillaume Sam ordered the execution of 167 political prisoners—including former president Zamor—held in a Port-au-Prince jail, which angered the Haitian people. President Jean Vilbrun Guillaume fled to the Haitian Embassy, who granted him asylum. Haitian mulatto families were angered by the deaths of their family members in prison and a mob broke into the French Embassy; it was rumored they found the president hiding in a bathroom. They dragged him out and beat him until he was unconscious and then threw his limp body over the embassy's iron fence to the waiting mob, who ripped the president to pieces and paraded the body parts through Port-au-Prince's neighborhoods. For the next two weeks, Haiti was in chaos, leading to its occupation.

In the Dominican Republic, President Juan Isidro Jimenes Pereyra was encouraged by the U.S. State Department to approve the appointment of a U.S. comptroller. President Jimenes promised he would legalize the status of the comptroller once he was sworn in, however Dominican deputies and secretaries rejected the recognition of the U.S. official, leading to open conflict. The United States soon sent the Marines to the Dominican Republic to suppress the Horacistas and Desiderio Arias. The United States placed President Francisco Henríquez y Carvajal as leader, who was born in Santo Domingo to a family descended from Sephardic Jews who immigrated in the nineteenth century from Curaçao from the Netherlands. Henríquez previously moved to Paris for four years, earning a doctorate in Medicine from the University of Paris and later practicing Medicine in the Dominican Republic.

President Francisco Henríquez y Carvajal was replaced by the Vice Admiral of the United States Navy Harry Knapp, who now ruled the Dominican Republic as the first Military Governor. The Government of the United States claimed Desiderio Arias and various Jimenistas were pro-German and a threat to the United States as they entered World War One in 1917. Romina Medina passed away in 1918, at the end of World War One and during the United States occupation of the Dominican Republic. In April 1917, the Dominican National Guard was created to control the revolutionary movements in the Dominican Republic once the marines left. In May 1917, the guard's leaders and commanders were chosen from among the U.S. marine officers to train the native Dominicans according to the rules of the U.S. Marine Corps. Many former members of the Dominican Navy and Republican Guard joined this new National Guard as well as many unemployed youths. One of the new recruits was a former telegraph operator and one-time camp guard for a sugar company in the east named Rafael Trujillo.

Dominican rebels quickly began to fight against the occupation. One of the larger rebel groups was led by Ramon Natera (who also went by General Ramon Natera), and he staged a continuous rebellion against the forces of the United States mostly in the eastern Dominican Republic. Some members of the Medina family aided the rebellion against the United States, but more and more, they stayed out of the political sphere. The Dominican rebels were known as *gavilleros*, and they received support from Dominicans of all classes. Various Dominican rebels galvanized people against U.S. occupation, including Ramon Leocadio Baez (nicknamed Cayo), who told the story of his kidnapping by American forces at the age of sixteen. Ramon Leocadio Baez was captured and tortured for not revealing the hiding place of other Dominicans who fought against the occupation.

Ercilia Pepín was also against the U.S. occupation, and she fought for the rights of women and all Dominicans. She was the director of the Escuela de Niñas del barrio Marilópez (or the School for Girls) of the town of Marilopez. Born to a poor Dominican family from San Miguel, Petronila Angelica Gomez was a writer and activist who spoke out against the U.S. occupation. She would organize the first National Woman's Congress in the Dominican Republic, and in 1917 founded the first feminist Dominican woman's magazine called Fémina, along with Evangelina Rodriguez and Altagracia Dominguez. Dr. Evangelina Rodriguez also spoke against the Yankee occupation and was the first woman to receive a degree in Medicine in the Dominican Republic in 1911.

Ana Teresa Paradas would become the first woman to become a lawyer in the Dominican Republic after a law was passed which allowed this in 1918. Dr. Rodriguez promoted family planning, healthcare for prostitutes and poor women, founded a health center for Dominicans suffering from leprosy and tuberculosis, a health center for maternity and children; she opened a night school to educate poverty-stricken Dominicans who didn't know how to read and did charity work for the poor.

The United States occupation of the Dominican Republic ended in 1924 and the Third Republic of the Dominican Republic was established. All the while, United States occupation continued in Haiti despite stiff resistance from rebel groups—including the Cacos led by Charlemagne Masséna Péralte. He was subsequently betrayed by his officer, Jean-Baptiste Conzé, who led disguised U.S. Marine Sergeant Herman H. Hanneken and Corporal William Button into his rebel camp near Grand-Rivière Du Nord. Charlemagne Masséna Péralte was executed by a shot to the heart at close range in 1919. His body was tied to a door and photographed, then his picture was distributed throughout Haiti to discourage further uprisings. Charlemagne Masséna Péralte was viewed favorably by both Haitian and Dominican nationalists. The Dominican Republic and Haiti continued to fight U.S. occupation after the allied victory ended World War One in 1918. This brought an end to Ottoman Empire and Czarist Russia, leading to the rise of the Soviet Union.

Rafael Trujillo was born in San Cristobal in 1891 to José Pepito Trujillo Valdez (nicknamed Pepito) and a mulatta Franco-Haitian mother named Altagracia Julia Molina Chevalier, whose mother was of Franco-Haitian and mulatto Haitian origin. In 1897, at age six, Trujillo was registered in the school of Juan Hilario Meriño. One year later, he transferred to the school of Broughton, where he became a pupil of Eugenio María de Hostos and remained there for the rest of his primary schooling. After working for about three years as a telegraph operator, Rafael Trujillo would turn to crime: cattle stealing, counterfeiting, and postal robbery. After prison, he formed a violent gang of robbers called the 42.

Rafael Trujillo performed well in the Dominican National Guard, which was now called the Dominican National Police. After the departure of the United States, the Dominican Republic regained its sovereignty in 1924. President Horacio Vásquez would serve his term until 1930, when he was once again reelected, however he was ousted from power. Various Dominican political parties rose in the Dominican Republic with the common issue of re-establishment of Dominican Independence and sovereignty—including the *Union Nacional Dominicana* (or the Dominican National Union) chaired by Emiliano Tejera, the Partido Nacional (or the National Party) composed of the followers of Horacio Vásquez, and the

Partido Progresista (or the Progressive Party) supported by the followers of Federico Velázquez.

Juan Rafael Estrella Ureña previously helped create the Partido Liberal Reformista (or the Liberal Reformist Party), which shared some of its ideology with Eugenio María de Hostos. Juan Rafael Estrella Ureña had gained significant power throughout the years, and now he marched his rebels to Santo Domingo and made a secret agreement with the Chief of the Armed Forces to allow Juan Rafael Estrella Ureña to take power and let Rafael Trujillo run in future elections. When the elderly President Horacio Vasquez ordered Rafael Trujillo to suppress the rebellion, Trujillo commanded the army to remain in their barracks. On March third, 1930, Estrella was proclaimed acting president with Rafael Trujillo confirmed as head of the police and army. As per their agreement, Rafael Trujillo became the presidential nominee of the newly formed Patriotic Coalition of Citizens Party.

Rafael Trujillo would become President of the Dominican Republic on August sixteenth, 1930, with Rafael Estrella Ureña as his Vice President until he resigned in 1932. After its destruction during powerful Hurricane San Zenon, President Rafael Trujillo rebuilt the capital of Santo Domingo in 1930. President Rafael Trujillo dissolved the Blue Party and Red Party and created one called the Dominican Party. In 1934, he promoted himself to the rank of Generalissimo and solidified his power and ruled the Dominican Republic as a dictator. In 1936, at the suggestion of Mario Fermín Cabral, Congress voted overwhelmingly to change the name of the capital from Santo Domingo to Ciudad Trujillo. The province of San Cristobal was changed to Trujillo, and the nation's highest peak, Pico Duarte (named after Juan Pablo Duarte), was renamed Pico Trujillo (or Peak Trujillo). Many other cities were named after Rafael Trujillo's family members.

In 1937, Generalissimo Rafael Trujillo was concerned with the Haitian encroachments on Dominican territory. Haiti was occupied by the United States until 1934 as Generalissimo Rafael Trujillo continued to create a defined border. During the beginning of the twentieth century, the Dominican Republic and Haiti attempted to reach an agreement regarding the frontier line and the issue was resolved in 1929, during the administration of President Horacio Vasquez. Several tens of thousands of Haitians were still living as peasants near the border in the southwest and northwest of the Dominican Republic, working in the sugar industry in the southeast and domestic servants, farmers, or small businessmen in the interior of the Dominican Republic. Haiti claimed several border territories and eventually, Generalissimo Rafael Trujillo and President Vincent agreed on a border and the Dominican government ceded various territories to Haiti. Throughout the history of Hispaniola, Dominican lands were given to Haiti: Hincha (now Hinche), Juana Méndez (now Ouanaminthe), San Rafael de La Angostura (now Saint-Raphaël), San Miguel de la Atalaya (now Saint-Michel-de-l'Attalaye), and Las Caobas (now Lascahobas). These territories were isolated with little communication with the Dominican capital while there was a growing Haitian influence and the gourde circulating as a major currency; in addition to the Spanish language, Haitian Creole was also spoken.

Despite the seemingly friendly relationship between Haiti and the Dominican Republic, a massacre of Haitian people occurred within Dominican territory in October 1937—perpetrated mostly with rifles, machetes, shovels, knives, and bayonets. Black Dominicans were differentiated from Haitians when they were asked to pronounce the word *perejil* (or parsley)—a word that was hard to pronounce due to the Haitians' inability to pronounce the trill "r" in the if they were not fluent. The killings were later referred to the Parsley Massacre. Initial reports listed several hundred to a little over 1,000 deaths, with the number later rising to above 10,000 and then more than 20,000 as public opinion against Trujillo's dictatorship increased. The number of deaths would become a subject of speculation and debate in generations afterwards. In 1938, Generalissimo Trujillo began a new campaign called el *desalojo* (or the eviction) in the southwestern region of the Dominican Republic, resulting in thousands of Haitians fleeing towards Haiti. Generalissimo Trujillo continued to silence his enemies—including Dr. Evangelina Rodriguez, who was tortured and later died in late 1947.

In 1929, the Dominican Republic followed a restricted Jus soli citizenship policy, which excluded from this privilege illegal residents and anyone not having legal permanent residency status. Rafael Trujillo moved to restrict Haitian entrance into the Dominican Republic and develop the border towns. These areas were developed with the addition of modern hospitals, schools, political headquarters, military barracks, and housing projects; highways were constructed to connect the borderlands to major cities. President Franklin Delano Roosevelt and President Sténio Vincent sought reparations of $750,000, of which the Dominican government paid $525,000. However, it was estimated the families of the victims only received two cents per lives lost due to the corruption of the Haitian government. Many spoke out against Generalissimo Trujillo, including Dominican anti-Trujillistas (opponents of Trujillo), who were labeled unworthy Dominicans and traitors to the Homeland for their comments. Among them were Rafael Brache, José Manuel Jimenes, Juan Isidro Jimenes Grullón, and Buenaventura Sánchez.

Generalissimo Rafael Trujillo continued to develop the infrastructure and economy of the Dominican Republic while maintaining political stability in the nation. As Nazi Germany increased its power under Führer und Reichskanzler (Leader and Chancellor) Adolph Hitler, more and more Jewish refugees fled Nazi Germany. President Franklin Delano Roosevelt had a quota that severely limited the number of Jewish refugees entering the United States, and he attempted to deflect criticism. The Évian Conference was convened on July sixth to July fifteenth, 1938, in Évian-les-Bains, France to discuss the refugee problem. It was held at the initiative of United States President Franklin D. Roosevelt, who perhaps hoped to obtain commitments from some of the invited nations to accept more refugees. The conference was attended by representatives from thirty-two countries, and twenty-four voluntary organizations went as observers, presenting plans either orally or in writing. Golda Meir, the attendee from British Mandate Palestine, was not permitted to speak or participate in the proceedings except as an observer. The Dominican Republic was the only nation that came to an agreement to accept Jewish refugees, and the conference became a useful propaganda tool for the Nazis.

The Dominican Republic offered to accept up to 100,000 Ashkenazi Jewish refugees on generous terms, and later Costa Rica joined them. In 1940, an agreement was signed, and Rafael Trujillo donated 26,000 acres of his properties near the town of Sosúa for settlements but only about 800 settlers came. Each Ashkenazi Jewish family was to receive thirty-three hectares (or eighty-two acres) of land, ten cows plus two additional cows per child, a mule and a horse, and a US $10,000 loan (about $166,000) at one percent interest.

After the end of World War II in 1945 and the defeat of the Axis Powers, the United States rose to become a world power alongside the U.S.S.R. King George VI of the United Kingdom. The Dominions of the British Commonwealth would become the last Emperor of India after Indian independence in 1947. Pakistan and its majority Islamic population became independent that year, and after the Bangladesh Liberation War, People's Republic of Bangladesh declared independence in 1972. Queen Elizabeth II, other Commonwealth realms, as well as her heir apparent, Charles, Prince of Wales would rule Britain, which was removed from its previous status as a powerful empire.

Under the leadership of Generalissimo Trujillo, the Dominican Republic signed a treaty with Japan in 1956 to accept migrants for agricultural labor. This would be one of the earliest in a series of treaties signed by Japan's newly established emigration bureau. Generalissimo Trujillo increased his power and numerous titles were bestowed upon him, including *Restaurador de la independencia financiera de la Republica* (or the Restorer of the Republic's financial independence), *El Jefe* (The Chief), *El Benefactor De La Patria* (the Benefactor of the Homeland), and an electric sign was displayed in the capital of Santo Domingo and renamed *Cuidad Trujillo* (Trujillo City). It read *Dios y Trujillo* (or God). Many signs of the dictators were placed inside

Dominican homes. Privately, opponents of Rafael Trujillo nicknamed him *Chapitas* (Bottlecaps) because of his indiscriminate wearing of medals and *El Chivo* (The Goat).

Many Asian nations held animosity towards the former Japanese Empire, and the United States' Gentlemen's Agreement of 1907 and Immigration Act of 1924 as well as Australia's White Australia Policy ended the possibility of Japanese settlement due to anti-Asian sentiments. The Dominican Republic and Latin America became a great area for Japanese settlers. More than 200 Japanese families totaling over 1,318 people braved the month-long ocean voyage and arrived in the Dominican Republic from 1956 to 1959. More than forty-seven families settled in Constanza, however many Japanese left towards other Latin American nations following the assassination of Generalissimo Trujillo in 1961.

After the overthrow of Fulgencio Batista by Fidel Alejandro Castro Ruz and Ernesto Che Guevara, Batista fled to the Dominican Republic and later to Portugal, which was ruled by Dictator Oliveira Salazar. The rise of Fidel Castro in Cuba, who soon became a rival to Rafael Trujillo, brought additional Chinese people from Cuba to the Dominican Republic. Fidel Castro previously planned the overthrow of the governments of the Dominican Republic and Colombia, and as leader of Cuba, he would orchestrate an invasion of the Dominican Republic on June fourteenth, 1959. Cuban-trained guerillas under the leadership of Captain Enrique Jimenez Moya attempted to infiltrate the north coast near Samaná Bay. The rebels departed from Nipe Bay in Oriente Province, Cuba, and three Cuban Navy frigates escorted Moya's two fast motor launches to a point off the coast. However, Dominican Military forces detected the mission and air and naval forces sank both launches. Moya and all of his followers who made it to shore were killed.

At the same time, fifty-six guerrillas boarded a Cuban Air Force plane in Oriente Province, Cuba. Falsely painted with Dominican markings, the plane departed an airfield near Manzanillo. Commander Delio Gomez Ochoa, who commanded the rebel army's Fourth Front during the war against Cuban dictator Fulgencio Batista, led the expedition. The guerrillas landed at Costanza airport and quickly overpowered the stunned Dominican guards, however the guerrilla force was overloaded with ammunition and lacked ground transportation. As a result, it failed in its goal of reaching the mountains and all the members of Gomez Ochoa's column were quickly killed or captured. In total, roughly 200 Dominican exiles and ten Cubans were killed or captured. It was reported that Generalissimo Rafael Trujillo ordered his son Ramfis to lead the hunt for the invaders, boarding two yachts escorted by Cuban gunboats to Great Inagua in the Bahamas. After their capture, the leaders of the invasion were taken aboard a Dominican Air Force plane and then pushed out midair, falling to their deaths.

Generalissimo Rafael Trujillo increased the military strength of the Dominican Air Force, which had been greatly expanded. The extensive development of the Dominican Military during World War II continued unabated after the war with the assistance of arms-dealing countries like Brazil and Sweden, and the large purchases of P-51 Mustang fighters and B-26 Marauder bombers made Generalissimo Trujillo the most powerful leader in the Caribbean. Generalissimo Trujillo and the Dominican Air Force threatened various nations in the Caribbean and Latin America, including Haiti, Cuba, Mexico, and Venezuela.

The popularity of Generalissimo Trujillo quickly declined after the executions of the Mirabal sisters named Patria, Minerva, Maria Teresa on November twenty-fifth, 1960. Generalissimo Rafael Trujillo's failed assassination of the leader Venezuela Rómulo Ernesto Betancourt Bello by his foreign agents in 1960 turned world opinion against him and led the Organization of Ameri-can States (OAS) to sever relations with Rafael Trujillo. An incendiary bomb was planted in President Betancourt's car and exploded, leaving President Betancourt with deep burns. The United States turned on Trujillo and plotted with Dominican conspirators, which included General Juan Tomás Díaz, Pedro Livio Cedeño, Antonio de la Maza, Amado García Guerrero, and General Antonio Imbert Barrera. On Tuesday, the thirtieth of May 1961, Trujillo was shot and killed when his blue 1957 Chevrolet Bel Air was ambushed on a road outside the Dominican capital. Rafael Trujillo's son returned to the Dominican Republic from Paris, France and the *Servicio de Inteligencia Militar* (SIM) (the Military Intelligence Service) under the leadership of Johnny Abbes and began murdering those suspected of conspiring against Rafael Trujillo with their extensive use of *calies* (spies). After the assassination of Generalissimo Rafael Trujillo, a monument was erected in *Autopista 30 de Mayo* (highway 30th of May), named after the date of the Trujillo's killing. The monument celebrates the heroes who ended the Era of Trujillo. Many statues of the dictator and his family members were taken down and cities and towns including the Dominican geography like Pico Trujillo were reverted to their original names.

Generalissimo Rafael Trujillo's long rule further industrialized the Dominican Republic by connecting the nation through roads and bridges. Generalissimo Rafael Trujillo would pay the Dominican *Deuda Externa* (external debt) in 1940 through the Trujillo-Hull Treaty. After World War II new factories opened in the Dominican Republic for cement, chocolate, alcohol, beverages, liquors, paper, cardboard, processed milk, flour, nails, bottles and glass, coffee, rice, marble, medicines, paint, sacks, cord and knitted goods, textiles, clothing, and sugar. From 1938 to 1960, the Dominicans experienced economic growth and the number of manufacturing establishments almost doubled. Capital investments multiplied more than nine times, the number of workers increased more than two and a half times, salaries paid by the industrial sector increased ten times, national raw materials grew fourteen times, fuel and lubricants expenditures increased twenty-two times, and industrial sales grew more than twelve times within a twenty-two-year time frame. The Trujillo regime strengthened the Dominican Republic economically and greatly advanced the nation's infrastructure while expanding the capital of Santo Domingo into an advanced city.

The Trujillo regime brought significant economic advances and stability to the Dominican Republic. However, Trujillo's abuses and the imprisonment and killings of thousands of Haitians and Dominicans polarized people within and without the Dominican Republic. The United States subsequently removed Ramfis Trujillo. Trujillo's funeral was that of a statesman with the long procession ending in his hometown of San Cristobal, where he was first buried. President Joaquín Balaguer gave the eulogy. Ramfis tried to flee with his father's body upon his boat Angelita but was turned back. Balaguer allowed Ramfis to leave the country and relocate his father's body to Paris. There the remains were interred in the Cimetière du Père Lachaise on August fourteenth, 1964, and six years later, they were moved to the El Pardo cemetery near Madrid, Spain. During his life, Rafael Trujillo desired to be buried in the National Pantheon in Santo Domingo. Jesuits held mass there until 1767, when it was used as a tobacco warehouse. In 1860, it was as the first Dominican theater for purely artistic purposes by the society *Amantes de las Letras* (The Lovers of Letters) until 1878, when it became theater La Republicana—which operated until 1917. Afterward, it housed governmental offices until 1956, when Rafael Trujillo ordered Spanish architect Javier Barroso to renovate the structure to serve its new purpose as a national mausoleum. Today it is the place where the most famous persons are honored in the Dominican Republic. Ironically, Trujillo's assassins are also interred here. The Dominican Republic now made significant changes and soon Juan Emilio Bosch Gaviño would be considered the first democratically elected leader of the. Many progressive ideas would be reintroduced in the Dominican Republic and there would be a proliferation of ideas on how to move the Dominican Republic forward.

EPILOGUE

THE FLIGHT OF THE PHOENIX:

THE FUTURE OF THE DOMINICAN REPUBLIC

Born to a Catalan father and a Puerto Rican mother of Galician descent, the leftist intellectual Juan Emilio Bosch Gaviño would become president in 1963 and is regarded by many to be the first democratically elected leader of the Dominican Republic. Previously, he had been the head of the Dominican opposition in exile to the dictatorial regime of Rafael Trujillo for over twenty-five years. He had also founded two of the Dominican Republic's major political parties: the Dominican Revolutionary Party (PRD) founded in 1939 and the Dominican Liberation Party (PLD) founded in 1973. President Juan Bosch would be overthrown in 1963 by Colonel Elías Wessin and replaced by a three-man military junta. The Dominican Republic erupted into civil war between April twenty-fourth and September third, 1965 in Santo Domingo as civilian and military supporters of former President Juan Bosch overthrew the Scottish-Dominican and acting President Donald Reid Cabral. The coup prompted General Elías Wessin y Wessin to organize elements of the military loyal to President Reid (known as loyalists), initiating an armed campaign against the so-called constitutionalist rebels. Allegations of foreign support for the rebels led to a United States intervention in the conflict, which evolved into an occupation by the Organization of American States.

During the subsequent unstable political environment of the Dominican Republic, a massacre occurred when the Dominican government napalmed a community led by Romilio and León Ventura Rodriguez. Twin brothers and liborista priests, they established a new commune north of Palma Sola, near Las Matas de Farfán. The brothers were followers of Olivorio Mateo, (known as Papá Liborio), who previously created a self-reliant commune in the mountains of San Juan de la Maguana. He claimed that he was transported to heaven and was sent back to earth by God; he was received as an incarnate of Jesus Christ and was worshipped. The Dominican government napalmed the commune, killing more than 600 Dominicans as political instability increased.

After the establishment of the Fourth Republic of the Dominican Republic, elections were held in 1966, and President Joaquín Balaguer—the former vice president under the puppet presidency of Rafael Trujillo's brother President Hector—now led the nation. Juan Bosch and Joaquín Balaguer would frequently run against each other after the United States occupation ended (1966). Juan Bosch ran unsuccessfully for president as the PLD candidate in 1978, 1982, 1986, 1990, and 1994; he came closest to winning in 1990, but lost to Joaquín Balaguer— however, there were serious charges of fraud against Balaguer.

Various other dictators would rule in other Latin American nations and Europe, including President François Duvalier of Haiti from 1957 to 1971. The Haitian government was previously able to pay their independence debt to France in 1947, but the rise of President François Duvalier would soon plunge Haiti's weak economy once again into debt. President François Duvalier was a physician, which earned him the title Papa Doc. He would run a populist and black Nationalist campaign. His presidency quickly became authoritarian and his undercover death squad, the Tonton Macoute, killed anyone suspected of being against Papa Doc's regime. In 1964, Papa Doc declared himself President for Life after another faulty election. When bombs were detonated near the Haitian Presidential Palace in 1967, Duvalier had nineteen officers of the Presidential Guard executed in Fort Dimanche. Papa Doc also sought to replace the mulatto Haitian elite in Haiti as he gained the support of the Haitian black majority and the working class. President François Duvalier supported Pan-Africanism and became involved in the négritude movement of Haitian author Jean Price-Mars, which led to his advocacy of Haitian Voodoo. In 1966, President Duvalier hosted the emperor of Ethiopia, Haile Selassie I, in what would be Haiti's only visit by a head of state under Duvalier. During the visit, President Duvalier awarded Haile Selassie the Necklace of the Order of Jean-Jacques Dessalines the Great. In turn, the emperor bestowed upon Duvalier the Great Necklace of the Order of the Queen of Sheba.

President François Duvalier would move against communists and suspected communists to protect his regime and gain favorable attention from the United States. President François Duvalier disliked the Dominican Republic as the leftist President Juan Bosch provided asylum and support to Haitians who plotted against him. This led to the leader ordering his Haitian Presidential Guard to occupy the Dominican Embassy in Pétion-Ville to gather intelligence on a Haitian Army officer believed to have been involved in a plot to capture Duvalier's children by the former leader of the Tonton Macoute, Clément Barbot. President Bosch contemplated sending an invading Dominican force into Haiti, however many Dominican generals and his advisors sought to avoid warfare. President Duvalier also entered in conflict with Fidel Castro, who aided anti-Duvalier Haitians. Duvalier angered Fidel Castro by voting against Cuba in an Organization of American States (OAS) meeting and subsequently at the United Nations, where a trade embargo was imposed on Cuba. Fidel Castro answered by breaking off diplomatic relations and Duvalier subsequently instituted a campaign to rid Haiti of communists.

President François Duvalier would economically devastate Haiti as his dictatorship continued. Some estimates state President François Duvalier killed up to 60,000 Haitians and his leadership led to massive migrations from Haiti's professional class. The Haitian government confiscated peasant landholdings and allotted them to members of the militia who were corrupt and made their living through crime and extortion. Meanwhile, the Haitian government committed rake-offs of industries, bribery, extortion of domestic businesses, and stolen government funds to enrich the lives of President Duvalier and his closest supporters. The Haitian black majority continued to live in poverty and the Haitian mulatto elite, the Arab minority who sometimes married the Haitian elite, along with the white Haitian minority would continue their hold on power in Haiti after the death of President François Duvalier.

President Jean-Claude Duvalier would rule after the death of his father Papa Doc in 1971. Called Baby Doc, he would maintain a lavish lifestyle as corruption increased in Haiti. Jean-Claude Duvalier would plunge Haiti further into poverty as he continued his father's anti-communist policies, which killed thousands of Haitians and led to thousands more fleeing Haiti. On May twenty-seventh, 1980, Duvalier married Michèle Bennett Pasquet in a wedding that cost two million dollars. The Haitian business community and elite angrily responded to the rising corruption among the Duvaliers and the Bennett family's dealings, which included selling Haitian cadavers to foreign medical schools and trafficking narcotics. A report about the increase of HIV/AIDS in Haiti crippled Haiti's tourism industry in the 1980s further destabilizing President Jean-Claude Duvalier's regime and further deepening Haiti into their ongoing economic crisis. Discontent in Haiti spread again in March 1983, when Pope John Paul II visited and spoke against the economic inequality and advocated for an equitable distribution of income, a more egalitarian social structure, and increased popular participation in public life. Pope John Paul helped motivate Haitian popular movements against President Jean-Claude Duvalier and rebuked the corruption in the Haitian government, stating, "All those who have power, riches, and culture so that they can understand the serious and urgent responsibility to help their brothers and sisters."

In January 1986, the Reagan administration began to pressure Duvalier to renounce his rule and leave Haiti. Representatives appointed by Jamaican Prime Minister Edward Seaga served as intermediaries who carried out the negotiations. President Jean-Claude Duvalier would leave for France in February 1988. Environmental crisis in Haiti also impacted its economy like deforestation, which began with the colonial period and increased when coffee was introduced to Haiti in 1730. Upland forests were cleared as roughly a quarter of the land was deforested for coffee. After the Haitian Revolution in 1804, the Haitian government continued the export of timber throughout the 1800s to pay the 90-million-franc indemnity to France. After Hurricane Hazel in 1954, deforestation rose as their logging operations increased in response to Port-au-Prince's intensified demand for charcoal. Deforestation continued into the twenty-first century, causing soil erosion and damaging infrastructures such as dams, irrigation systems, roads, and coastal marine ecosystems. Haitians have crossed the border with the aid of Dominican officials to exploit Dominican forests. Much of the charcoal is sent towards Puerto Rico, the United States, and Haiti as many Dominicans are protesting their government to protect the forests.

In the 1990s, Haiti would decline further through continued government corruption as the Dominican Republic advanced economically, marking an increasing economic difference between the neighboring countries. The government corruption in Haiti would continue throughout the establishment of The United Nations Stabilization Mission in Haiti (MINUSTAH) by Security Council resolution from the first of June 2004 until its departure on the fifteenth of October 2017. Many activists, however, continue to fight for progress in Haiti—including promoting government accountability and progressive efforts like reducing corruption and inequality and supporting environmental programs. Increasing efforts against interventionism—particularly from the U.S. and Canada—and towards Haitian and Dominican cooperation as well as cooperation within the Caribbean community may help improve the government.

In contrast, the Dominican Republic developed laws to protect their environment. Despite how polarizing Rafael Trujillo was, he expanded the Vedado del Yaque, a nature reserve around the Yaque del Sur River. In 1934, he banned the slash-and-burn method of clearing land for agriculture. Throughout the Trujillo Era, the forest warden agency was created to protect the park system, and the Dominican government prohibited the logging of pine trees without Trujillo's permission. During the 1950s, the Trujillo government commissioned a study on the hydroelectric potential of damming the Dominican Republic's waterways. However, the commission concluded that only forested waterways could support hydroelectric dams, leading Rafael Trujillo to ban logging in potential river watersheds. After Trujillo's assassination, logging was renewed, but under President Balaguer, illegal logging was once against targeted and the perpetrators were sometimes violently punished. Recently, Dominicans have protested foreign companies who pol-lute Dominican waters and mining operations which contribute to pollution. Currently, plastics and other garbage have caused problems in rivers and along the coastlines. At the same time, it has contributed to the global problem of plastic in the oceans, leading many environmentalists to advocate for the banning of plastic as well as proper plastic disposal methods.

In Jamaica, a man named Marcus Garvey would gain a large following in the United States. Marcus Garvey was a leader of Pan-Africanism and he founded the Universal Negro Improvement Association and African Communities League (UNIA-ACL). Marcus Garvey attracted many black veterans from World War I, black Americans, and many West Indian immigrants. These were people who were attracted to his message and had suffered injustice and mob violence in New York and throughout the United States—including the infamous Tulsa race riot, which resulted in the burning of the affluent black district of Greenwood Oklahoma (also known as Black Wall Street) in 1921. Marcus Garvey also founded the Black Star Line, a shipping and passenger line which promoted the return of the African diaspora to their ancestral lands. However, many black American leaders condemned his methods and his support for racial segregation. Garveyism would inspire other leaders, ranging from the Nation of Islam to the Rastafari movement, to proclaim Garvey as a prophet. At times, Marcus Garvey conflicted with other black leaders such as W.E.B. Du Bois, who sometimes ridiculed Garvey for his appearance and background as a Jamaican. W.E.B Du Bois helped create the National Association for the Advancement of Colored People (NAACP) in 1909. These early leaders would motivate black leaders during the Civil Rights Era in the United States—including Medgar Evers, Martin Luther King Jr., Malcolm X, and activists like Muhammad Ali. Many laws were passed that terminated segregation in the United States by ending the legal doctrine of separate but equal.

Born in 1924 in New York City, James Baldwin would write and speak about race, sex, and class distinctions in the United States, creating works like Notes of a Native Son, The Fire Next Time, The Devil Finds Work, and a memoir titled Remember This House about his personal thoughts on Malcolm X, Medgar Evers, and Martin Luther King Jr.—which was adapted into an Academy Award-nominated documentary named I Am Not Your Negro. James Baldwin also wrote Giovanni's Room, which brought complex views to homosexuality and bisexuality and initiated public discourse on those themes. James Baldwin commented on popular culture and criticized previous works such as Uncle Tom's Cabin; he was against the emasculation of Uncle Tom and stated that he was, "Robbed of his humanity and divested of his sex," and criticized the African American characters as being two dimensional. Other black leaders during the Harlem Renaissance also criticized Uncle Tom's Cabin, including James Weldon Johnson. Initially written to oppose black stereotypes and minstrel shows and praised by abolitionists like Frederick Douglass, Uncle Tom's Cabin would become a derogatory epithet for a subservient person and a traitor to his own race. However, Uncle Tom's Cabin would be reexamined by critics from various racial and socio-economic backgrounds.

The New Negro Movement which came to be known as the Harlem Renaissance was a powerful social, political, intellectual, and artistic movement which took place in Harlem, New York during the 1920s. It took shape during the African American Great Migration, which included the urban areas of the Northeast and Midwest. Young women preferred short skirts and silk stockings to drop-waisted dresses and cloche hats and men wore loose suits that led to the later style known as the "zoot", which consisted of wide-legged, high-waisted, peg-top trousers, and a long coat with padded shoulders and wide lapels. Men also wore wide-brimmed hats, colored socks, white gloves, and velvet-collared Chesterfield coats, while some men respected their African heritage through a fad for leopard-skin coats, indicating the power of the African animal.

The Harlem Renaissance influenced American culture and brought forth many artists: jazz performers like Eubie Blake, Noble Sissle, Jelly Roll Morton, Luckey Roberts, James P. Johnson, Willie "The Lion" Smith, Fats Waller and Duke Ellington. Other artists included the singers Bessie Smith, Louis Armstrong, Paul Robeson, Bill "Bojangles" Robinson, Josephine Baker, Ella Fitzgerald, Adelaide Hall, Lottie Gee, Cab Calloway, Ethel Waters, Avon Long, Aida Ward, Edith Wilson, Ma Rainey, Fats Waller, Billie Holiday, and Lena Horne. Eleanora Fagan, better known as Billie Holiday, began singing in Harlem and was discovered by producer John Hammond. She would become legendary and influential to artists who came after her.

Various writers would arise during the Harlem Renaissance, including Zora Neale Hurston and Langston Hughes, who was one of the earliest writers in the genre of Jazz poetry. Langston Hughes had a complex ancestry: both paternal great-grandmothers were enslaved African Americans and both of his paternal great-grandfathers were white slave owners in Kentucky. Langston Hughes stated that one of these men was a Scottish American whiskey distiller of Henry County named Sam Clay—said to be the relative of statesman Henry Clay—and the other was Silas Cushenberry, a Jewish American slave trader of Clark County. Langston Hughes' maternal grandmother Mary Patterson was of African American, French, English, and Native American descent who married a mixed-race man named Lewis Sheridan Leary who died after he joined the abolitionist John Brown and his raid on Harpers Ferry. Langston Hughes would also speak about White Supremacy and the One Drop Rule of the United States in his memoirs in 1940, stating, "You see, unfortunately, I am not black. There are lots of different kinds of blood in our family. But here in the United States, the word 'Negro' is used to mean anyone who has any Negro blood at all in his veins. In Africa, the word is purer. It means all Negro, therefore black. I am brown."

Politics in the United States was dynamic and would shift as the two powerful parties—the Democrats and Republicans—realigned. The population of the United States increasingly concentrated into urban areas and went from being mostly Republican in the 1920s to mostly Democrat in the 1930s. The States' Rights Democratic Party, commonly referred to as the Dixie-crats, was a short-lived segregationist political party in the United States. It originated in 1948 as a breakaway faction of the Democratic Party determined to protect state rights to legislate racial segregation from what its members regarded as an oppressive federal government. During the Great Depression, President Franklin D. Roosevelt formed a coalition that would mostly last until 1964 called the "New Deal coalition". Many black Americans who previously voted Republican and moved in greater numbers to northern cities increasingly voted for the Democratic Party, which became champions for the poor and people of color and became a statist party instead of a libertarian one. Many black Americans voted for President John F. Kennedy, and his relationship with Martin Luther King Jr. helped boost his popularity. President Lyndon B. Johnson and the Civil Rights Movement of the 1960s helped fuel many African Americans and immigrants to join the Democratic Party and many southern Democrats to switch to the Republicans and join the Dixiecrats—many of whom also joined the Republicans.

Imperial China had long ended, and Communist China was born under the leadership of Mao Zedong and his successors. The U.S.S.R. would fall in 1991, and many European nations became independent from the Soviet Union. Despite Red Scare in the United States and their false labels on anything Left-Wing sharing the same ideals as corrupt authoritarian regimes, Nordic Nations would rise and provide a shining example of Social Democracy.

Progressive candidates in the United States like the independent senator from Vermont, Bernie Sanders, would challenge the political spectrum of the United States and speak against the increasing Neo-Liberal policies of the Democratic Party. Policies like Universal Healthcare which exists in every first world nation does not exist in the United States. Senator Bernie Sanders ran with the Democrats in the 2016 President Campaign and surprisingly gained a large share of the millennial vote as people of various political affiliations, independents, and progressives made it an impressive run. Many people of color including Latinos supported Bernie Sanders as they questioned the two-party system of the United States and speculated about new political realignments or possibly a new third party. Many voters would also join minor political parties that more closely matched their political and social views.

The rise of Right-Wing Populism also spread throughout the United States, which was supported by the elites as well as a large section of poor whites. Right-Wing Populist ideas spread rapidly throughout various regions of the world, energized by issues such as the rise of illegal immigration and unemployment levels. The respective authoritarian and Right-Wing leaders of these nations harness the fear, anger, and nationalism for their own advantage as they gain power. In the United States, Right-Wing Populism overtook the Republican Party, however many of the poor nationalists who supported Right-Wing Populists also suffered due to the increasing redistribution of wealth to the top one percent. As income inequality continues to increase under both the Republicans and Neo-Liberals who dominate the current Democratic Party, most people in the United States continue to suffer. The two-party system helped continue the increasing income inequality and the restriction of smaller parties and their supporters. Perhaps in the future, more Americans will observe the political systems throughout the world and apply the policies, which will lead to a wider political spectrum and a deeper understanding of issues and reduce income inequality, corruption, poverty, and ensure environmental protections, social mobility, standard of living, education, and quality of life.

Black Americans, Latinos, and other people of color would contribute to the advancement of Civil Rights in the United States. Many Mexicans who lived in the western United States that had previously been Mexico also contributed to Civil Rights. The Mexicans influenced culture in the United States with the vaquero traditions developed from methodology brought to Mesoamerica from Spain and became the foundation for the North American cowboy. The vaqueros of the Americas were the horsemen and cattle herders of Spanish Mexico, who first came to California with the Jesuit priest Eusebio Kino in 1687, and later with expeditions in 1769 and the Juan Bautista de Anza expedition in 1774. They were the first cowboys in the region and the word vaqueros was soon corrupted in English to become the word "buckaroo" and other Spanish words in American English like "rodeo" were taken directly from Spanish rodeo, which roughly translates into English as "roundup".

In Mexico, the dictatorship of Porfirio Díaz ended after he won a fraudulent election in 1910 and his opponent, Francisco I. Madero, issued a call for armed rebellion. This led to the Mexican Revolution and the exile of Porfirio Díaz in France and his death in 1915. Francisco I. Madero was Democratically elected later in the year, but he was overthrown and assassinated in February 1913 by reactionary forces with General Victoriano, who seized power. Anti-Huerta forces in the north of Mexico unified under the northern politician and landowner Venustiano Carranza, the leader of the Constitutionalist faction. In Morelos, peasants under Emiliano Zapata independently also opposed Huerta while in northern Mexico, the conflict took place with organized armies of movement under Constitutionalist generals such as Pancho Villa and Alvaro Obregón and in the center of Mexico. Particularly in the state of Morelos, peasants participated in guerrilla warfare and sought to gain land. During World War II, Mexico became a strong ally to the United States and after the war, Mexico expanded Neo-Liberal policies. After decades of corruption, in 2018, the Mexican people elected the Left-Wing populist Andrés Manuel

López Obrador to the presidency in a landslide victory as they sought a more accountable and fair government.

The Mexicans in the United States would fight for their Civil Rights and the case of Mendez v. Westminster held that the forced segregation of Mexican American students into separate "Mexican schools" was unconstitutional and unlawful. Mendez v. Westminster was ruled in 1947 before Brown v. Board of Education of Topeka in 1954, which declared state laws establishing separate public schools for black and white students to be unlawful. This overturned the Plessy v. Ferguson decision of 1896, which allowed state-sponsored segregation, insofar as it applied to public education. The landmark case Hernandez v. Texas would be the first and only Mexican American civil rights case heard and decided by the United States Supreme Court during the post-World War II period. Unanimously, the court ruled that Mexican Americans and all other nationality groups in the United States had equal protection under the 14th Amendment of the U.S. Constitution. The 14th Amendment covered any national or ethnic groups of the United States for which discrimination could be proved. The ruling was an extension of protection in the Civil Rights Movement to minority groups within the United States and an acknowledgment that, in certain times and places, groups other than African Americans who could prove discrimination would be protected.

The Dominican people began arriving to the United States in the 1940s, however there was a sudden increase of Dominican immigrants in the 1970s. Dominicans would learn about the history of the United States. The Dominican people joined other Latin American groups from Puerto Rico and Cuba in New York City as well as a larger community of Latin Americans throughout the United States—including the large Mexican population concentrated in the western United States. The Cubans and Puerto Ricans who previously settled in the United States were able to form political groups, which enacted change.

The Young Lords under the leadership of José Cha Jimenez was founded in Chicago on September twenty-third, 1968 and were later reorganized on the principles that led to the Grito de Lares. Cha-Cha was born in Caguas, Puerto Rico, to Jíbaro parents: Eugenia Rodríguez Flores of San Lorenzo and Antonio Jiménez Rodríguez of the barrio of San Salvador in Caguas. The Young Lords would be changed into a national civil and human rights movement which subsequently networked to nearly thirty other cities, including three branches in New York City. The Young Lords were soon recruited by Chairman Fred Hampton into the original Rainbow Coalition with the Young Patriots and the Black Panther Party.

Many Puerto Ricans were inspired by leaders like Pedro Albizu Campos, who graduated from Harvard Law School with the highest-grade point average in his law class—an achievement that earned him the right to give the valedictorian speech at his graduation ceremony. However, negative reactions towards his mixed racial heritage would lead to his professors delaying two of his final exams in order to keep Pedro Albizu Campos from graduating on time. He was imprisoned twenty-six years for attempting to overthrow the United States government in Puerto Rico.

Other Latin American groups like Los Boinas Cafes (The Brown Berets), a pro-Chicano organization, emerged during the Chicano Movement in the late 1960s. Founded by David Sanchez, The Brown Berets supported the United Farm Workers, educational reform, and anti-war activism; they also organized against police brutality and some groups remained active after the passage of California Proposition 187. Cesar Chavez along with Dolores Huerta, cofounded the National Farm Workers Association which later became the aforementioned United Farm Workers union (UFW) in 1962. By the late 1970s, Cesar Chavez's tactics had forced growers to recognize the UFW as the bargaining agent for 50,000 field workers in California and Florida, and he popularized the slogan sí, se puede (or yes it can be done), which was later adopted as the 2008 campaign slogan of Barack Obama; he was elected the first black President of the United States.

After the death of Dictator Francisco Franco and the reestablishment of the Spanish Monarchy, the empire of Spain would officially dissolve in 1975. Former colonies of Spain which fell under the control of the United States were now independent, including Cuba and the Republic of the Philippines—which was recognized by the United States in 1946 through the Treaty of Manila. Various colonies would remain under United States control like Guam and Puerto Rico, although movements continue in these territories advocating for independence. The funeral of Francisco Franco was attended by Prince Rainier III of Monaco and Chilean leader General Augusto Pinochet, who modeled his leadership style after the Spanish leader as well as Former U.S. President Richard Nixon called Franco, "A loyal friend and ally of the United States". Upon the abdication of his father, King Juan Carlos I, King Felipe VI of Spain ascended the throne on June nineteenth, 2014.

Many of the Caribbean islands would gain independence in the mid to late 1900s (known as the Commonwealth Caribbean) as well as many of the African colonies under colonial power. The Dominican Republic would become the number one tourist destination in the Caribbean and its economy would continue to increase in the twenty-first century. After the 2010 earthquake in Haiti, massive immigration from that nation increased towards the Dominican Republic and other Caribbean nations like Turks and Caicos and the Bahamas. Protests against the Dominican government erupted, but the issue polarized many Dominicans. Members of Caribbean Community (CARICOM) spoke against the Dominican government while

CARICOM member island nations—including the Bahamas and Turks and Caicos—continued to deport Haitians and children born to Haitian parents within their territories. Other nations in Latin American nations such as Chile, Brazil, Mexico, the United States, and Canada would deport Haitians while the United States and Canada continue their interventionist policies in Haiti and the rest of Latin America. The complex issue brought up old wounds of race and class and the issues of immigration and deportations of the people of various Latin American and Caribbean nations.

The Dominican people have been interconnected with the United States throughout the history of both nations. Juan Rodriguez is believed to be the first documented non-Native American to live on Manhattan Island in what would eventually become New York City, predating the Dutch settlers. He was born in Santo Domingo in the nation of what is now the Dominican Re-public to a Portuguese sailor and an African woman. He is considered the first immigrant, person of African and European heritage, merchant, Latino, and Dominican to settle in Manhattan. Esteban Hotesse, a Dominican native who immigrated to the United States as a child, enlisted during World War II, and served in the lauded Tuskegee Airmen brigade. Gregorio Luperón would have an airport named after him in Puerto Plata, Dominican Republic—the Gregorio Luperón International Airport—and a high school in Manhattan, New York was called the Gregorio Luperón High School for Math & Science. Founding father Juan Pablo Duarte would have a statue in the Avenue of the Americas and Canal Street in Manhattan, New York.

The Dominican Republic would erect monuments representing various heroes and events. Among these were the statue of the Sebastián Lemba, the slave rebel leader who led a prolonged maroon rebellion in the colony of Santo Domingo, a statue of the native Taino rebel leader Cacique Enriquillo, and various others commemorating the battles against England, France, Haiti, Spain, and the United States. The Spanish-Anglo War for Santo Domingo where the Spaniards defeated England and Oliver Cromwell resulted in the celebration of Governor Don Bernardino de Meneses y Bracamonte, Count of Peñalva, and the naming of Puerta del Conde (the Count's Gate). Rafael Trujillo's Monument to Peace (which also commemorated the independence from Haiti in 1844) was rededicated to the heroes of the Restoration War: Gregorio Luperón and Francisco Del Rosario Sanchez.

El Altar de la Patria (The Altar of the Homeland) is a white marble mausoleum within Parque Independencia (Independence Park) in Santo Domingo that houses the remains of the founding fathers of the Dominican Republic: Juan Pablo Duarte, Francisco del Rosario Sánchez, and Ramón Matías Mella—collectively known as Los Trinitarios. The Altar of the Homeland was constructed in 1976 and within the mausoleum, there are statues of the founding fathers carved by Italian sculptor Nicholas Arrighini. There is also an "eternal flame" that is kept lit in memory of the Patriots in Parque Independencia.

The Dominican Republic would spread their music throughout Latin America, the United States, and the world—the most popular being Merengue and Bachata. Another style of Merengue was created northern Cibao region of the Dominican Republic called merengue tipico (or merengue cibaeño), and what was colloquially known as *perico ripiao* (ripped parrot) developed earlier than the merengue and used instruments like the European accordion, bass guitar, güira (metal scraper) influenced by the native Taino, the conga, and the African tambora (drum). Introduced by German traders, the accordion was popularized in the Dominican Republic in the 1880s and quickly became the primary instrument in merengue tipico.

The Dominicans migrated to New York City, making the neighborhood of Washington Heights, Manhattan into the largest Dominican community outside of the Dominican Republic. The Dominicans joined the rich history of New York City and contribute to its diverse culture. New York City received Latino immigrants from various countries like Cuba and Puerto Rico, which helped create the musical form of Salsa. Salsa is primarily Cuban, with a fusion of Spanish cancion, guitar, and Afro-Cuban percussion, which merged with North American music styles of Jazz, Rock, R&B, and Funk.

One of the founding musicians of Salsa was a Dominican named Johnny Pacheco. Composer and bandleader Johnny Pacheco and Italian American lawyer Jerry Masucci founded Fania Records in New York in 1964. The Fania All Stars would showcase many artists, including Willie Colon, Larry Harlow, Ray Barretto, Ralfi Pagan, Luis "Perico" Ortiz, Bobby Valentín, Rubén Blades, Héctor Lavoe, Cheo Feliciano, Adalberto Santiago, Ismael Miranda, and Celia Cruz, who was proclaimed the Queen of Salsa, La Guarachera de Cuba (the Guarachera of Cuba, which spoke of Celia's roots in the Cuban music of Guaracha), as well as The Queen of Latin Music. In 1971, the Fania All Stars sold out Yankee Stadium, and Salsa music moved to Manhattan and the club Cheetah, where promoter Ralph Mercado introduced many future Puerto Rican Salsa stars to Latino audiences and others.

Tite Catalino Curet Alonso was a prolific Puerto Rican writer who composed over 2,000 Salsa songs as well as various Sambas which focused on themes like the plight of Afro-Puerto Ricans and black Caribbeans. His composition Las Caras Lindas (De Mi Gente Negra) or The Beautiful Faces (Of My Black People) which was recorded by Ismael Rivera, is considered by many in Puerto Rico as a classic. Some of the artists who interpreted Tite Curet Alonso's songs include Joe Quijano, Iris Chacón, Wilkins, Cheo Feliciano, Celia Cruz, La Lupe, Willie Colón, Tito Rodríguez, Olga Guillot,

Mon Rivera, Héctor Lavoe, Ray Barretto, Tony Croatto, Rubén Blades, Tito Puente, Ismael Miranda, Roberto Roena, Bobby Valentín, Marvin Santiago, Willie Rosario, Chucho Avellanet, Andy Montañez, Rafael Cortijo, Tommy Olivencia, and Frankie Ruiz. About fifty of Tite Catalino Curet Alonso's compositions became major salsa hits and arguably over 200 became top songs.

The Dominican people would also join the political process of the United States and run for local offices and later higher political offices. The Dominicans became involved in different political parties and support their communities within the United States. The Dominican people would also enter higher education and build small businesses within their communities as well as increasingly enter professional occupations. Dominicans would also contribute artistically to the Dominican Republic and the United States in art, literature, music, and dance. Dominican writers from the past including Carmita Landestoy, Pedro Julio Mir Valentín, and Arístides Sócrates Henríquez Nolasco as well as current writers would write about a wide variety of subjects. New writers would continue to write in the twenty first century. Dominican writers included Fernando Cabrera, Julia Alvarez and her works How the García Girls Lost Their Accents, In the Time of the Butterflies, Elizabeth Acevedo and her works The Poet X, and With the Fire on High, and Angie Cruz and her works Soledad, and Domincana. Dominican writers are currently increasingly writing in various genres including Maya Motayne and her fantasy novel *Nocturna*, while some authors wrote in the genre of science fiction like Josefina de la Cruz and her work Una casa en el espacio or A House in Space.

Dominicans would get involved in all aspects of film and the Dominican Film Festival in New York City would become a great success, attracting Dominican and multicultural audiences and gaining both Spanish and English-speaking audiences. Dominican film is increasing its exposure worldwide to people who speak many languages throughout the world. The Dominican Republic Film Commission would travel to the Cannes Film Festival in France and José Maria Cabral and his film Carpinteros (Woodpeckers) would become the first Dominican film to compete at the Sundance Film Festival as the country's official submission to the 90th Academy Awards' foreign language film category. José Maria Cabral's film Checkmate represented the country at the Oscars in 2012, and the international sales rights of his film The Projectionist would be purchased by the German world sales company Media Luna. José Maria Cabral continues to build his company, Tabula Rasa Films, as many other young Dominicans are involving themselves in all aspects of the business and art of cinema.

The South Bronx, New York would become the birthplace of Hip-Hop music in 1973, which was influenced by Reggae. Robert Nesta Marley, famously known as Bob Marley, was born on the farm of his maternal grandfather in Nine Mile, Saint Ann Parish, Jamaica to a white Jamaican originally from Sussex, England named Norval Sinclair Marley and a black Jamaican singer and songwriter named Cedella Booker. Bob Marley left his Catholic beliefs and converted to Rastafarianism in the 1960s as he began to grow dreadlocks. Bob Marley and the Wailers would help popularize Reggae and Rastafarianism around the world. He was diagnosed with acral lentiginous melanoma in 1977, and later died on May eleventh, 1981 in Miami at age thirty-six. By 1973, Jamaican sound system enthusiast Clive Campbell (or DJ Kool Herc) moved to the Bronx and brought with him Jamaica's sound system culture and teamed up with another Jamaican, Coke La Rock, at the mic. Grandmaster Flowers of Brooklyn and Grandwizard Theodore of the Bronx also contributed to the birth of Hip Hop in New York. These early raps incorporated the dozens—a product of African American culture. Kool Herc & the Herculoids were the first Hip Hop group to be recognized. Many artists would rise to global fame like Grandmaster Flash & The Furious 5, Black Moon, Salt N Pepa, Public Enemy, Fugees, The Lox, Brand Nubian, House of Pain, Run-DMC, N.W.A., De La Soul, Beastie Boys, The Roots, and the Wu-Tang Clan. Many Rappers also gained regional and global fame, including Immortal Technique, Big L, Jay-Z, DMX, KRS-ONE, MC Lyte, Rakim, Big Daddy, Kane, Kool G Rap, Queen Latifah, a rapper from Brooklyn, New York of Jamaican ancestry named Christopher Wallace (known as The Notorious B.I.G.), and Nasir Jones (famously known as Nas) from the Queensbridge projects of Long Island City, New York.

Hip Hop subculture involved MCing/rapping, DJing/scratching with turntables, breakdancing, and graffiti writing. The album Control by Janet Jackson helped create the style of New Jack Swing. New Jack Swing and Hip Hop influenced each other, and Bobby Brown became known as the King of New Jack Swing. The time period of the mid 1980s and 1990s became known as the Golden Age of Hip Hop. In the 1990s, Hip Hop diversified and spread to other regions of the United States, including the west coast and the south. Many Latinos including Puerto Ricans and later Dominicans contributed to Hip Hop culture, creating Spanish Rap—which quickly spread to the Dominican Republic and Latin America. Hip Hop would also influence other genres, including Metal and Reggae. Various rappers would win prestigious awards; Tupac Shakur and Snoop Dogg were elected into the Rock n Roll Hall of Fame while Kendrick Lamar won the Pulitzer Prize for Music in 2018 for his album Damn. Latinos would be influenced by Hip Hop and Reggae and in various nations—including Panama and the island of Puerto Rico—Reggaetón was created, which quickly spread to the Dominican Republic and Latin America. Dem Bow was influenced by Reggae, particularly the music of Dancehall artist Shabba

Ranks and his song Dem Bow, and would spread from Panama to New York City, Puerto Rico, and the rest of Latin America. Dominicans would adopt this music and create Dominican Dem Bow, which was added to the collection of various Dominican musical genres including Ata-bales, Bachata, La Mangulina, Merengue, Palos, Pambiche, Salves, Son Dominicano, and Típico.

In 2019, the Bronx, NY born Dominican Romeo Santos of the band Aventura, would become the first Latino to headline New Jersey's MetLife Stadium while performing for over 80,000 people. Romeo Santos would break the record formerly held by U2 at that stadium. Romeo is given the title of the "King of Bachata" for helping to bring international attention to Bachata music however, Romeo has publicly recognized the Bachata artists of the past who influenced him including Frank Reyes, Raulin Rodriguez, Joe Veras, Zacarias Ferreira, Joe Veras, and Luis Vargas who are featured in album titled Utopia released in 2019. With the increasing Latino population in the United States, Latin Music in general would reach larger audiences. Latino music surpassed Country Music and EDM in the United States in 2019 and may pass other genres in the future.

As the Latino population increases, the community has altered their collective identities. The term Latinx would originate in the United States in the early twenty-first century, which for the supporters of Latinx, made the gendered Spanish language more inclusive. This gender-neutral neologism has sparked debate for and against Latinx from many Latinos including conservatives, liberals, and progressives. Language, like people, change and with that change comes energized debates.

Dominicans would also demonstrate a great love for the sport of baseball. In 1937, Generalissimo Trujillo had merged the Tigres del Licey and the Leones del Escogido into a single team called Los Dragones de Ciudad Trujillo (the Trujillo City Dragons), which was a super team that recruited foreign talent as well as players from the Negro Leagues. The invited players included Josh Gibson, who hit a .453 batting average, Cool Papa Bell, and Satchel Paige; the club also starred the father of Hall of Famer and Puerto Rican great Orlando Cepeda, Petrucho Cepeda. The other players on the team were Antonio "Tony" Castaño, Cy Perkins, Enrique Lantigua, Francisco "Cuco" Correa, Harry Williams, Herman Andrews, Huesito Vargas, Lázaro Salazar, Leroy Matlock, Miguel Solís, Rafael Quintana, Robert Griffin, Rodolfo Fernández, Sam Bank-head, and Silvio García. The Dominican Republic and the Caribbean were great places for players of all races, and many Major and Negro League baseball players competed since there was no segregation in the Caribbean like there was within the United States.

Osvaldo José Virgil Pichardo was born in Monte Cristi, the Dominican Republic in 1932 and moved with his parents to the Bronx, New York, where he graduated from DeWitt Clinton Highschool and enlisted in the United States Marine Corps from 1950 to 1952. Osvaldo José Virgil became the first Dominican player to play in the Major Leagues on September twenty-third, 1956, when he played for the New York Giants starting at third base against the Philadelphia Phillies—a year before the Giants moved to San Francisco, California. On June sixth, 1958, Osvaldo José Virgil became the first player of African descent to take the field for the Tigers, again starting at third base—this time against the Washington Senators. Osvaldo Virgil National Airport serves the Monte Cristi Province in the northern Dominican Republic. The number of Dominicans in Major League Baseball would later surpass the Cubans and Puerto Ricans as Dominicans became the largest foreign-born players in the Major Leagues. Several Dominicans would reach Major League Baseball's highest honor of the Hall of Fame: the legendary pitchers Juan Marichal and Pedro Martinez. On July twenty-ninth, 2018, Vladimir Guerrero would become the first Dominican position player to be inducted in the Hall of Fame. Adding to the rich history of Dominican baseball, various other Dominicans are on their way, including the phenomenal player Albert Pujols. The 2019 World Series champion, Washington Nationals would feature various Dominican players including the young star Juan Soto nicknamed the "Childish Bambino."

In the Caribbean series, the Dominican Republic would become the nation with the most championships represented mostly by the Tigres del Licey. They were followed by two prominent Dominican teams: the *Águilas Cibaeñas* (the Cibao Eagles) and the *Leones del Escogido* (the Lions of Chosen One). Cuba had suffered from the embargo of the United States, but rejoined the Caribbean Series. In 2005, the World Baseball Classic (WBC) was founded and modeled after the FIFA World Cup; it was organized mostly as a response to the International Olympic Committee's decision to remove baseball as an Olympic sport. The Dominicans became a major force in baseball and won a Baseball World Cup in undefeated fashion in 2013, beating out Puerto Rico in the championship while showing strong performances in their other appearances in the World Baseball Classic.

Various sports, including volleyball and basketball, are popular in the Dominican Republic. There is now a Dominican professional basketball league and the Dominican Republic has improved internationally during their participation in the International Basketball Federation (more commonly known as FIBA). Dominicans in the Dominican Republic are increasingly playing basketball, and some are currently playing in the National Basketball Association (NBA) in the United States: Francisco Garcia, Al Horford, and Karl-Anthony Towns. In 2019, the Dominican national basketball team would defeat the German national basketball team in the World Cup. Futbol or soccer is also played in the Dominican

Republic at the professional level, and other sports including Judo are practiced. Luis Castillo also played as a defensive end for the San Diego Chargers in the National Football Lague (NFL) in the United States. In 2014, Victor Estrella became the nation's first top 100 tennis player. Rugby is considered a minor sport in the Dominican Republic and wrestling is watched, starring Dominican wrestlers such as Arcadio Brito, Jack Veneno, and Ramon Alvarez (known as El Bronco No. 1).

The game of Dominoes is immensely popular in the Dominican Republic as well as throughout the Caribbean and Latin America. Card games, Dominoes, and Billiards are great games that bring the Dominican community together and allows social bonding. Dominicans usually talk about politics, sports like basketball, boxing, their favorite teams and players, and social issues concerning Dominican society. The politics of the United States and issues relating to the Dominican diaspora around the world are also discussed. Dominicans of various political and ideological perspectives often debate over the best solutions for the betterment of Dominican society and people. Usually, these board games are played when watching sports or at social gatherings where Dominicans enjoy dancing and having a good time.

The Dominican people celebrate their rich heritage and culture which is portrayed in all aspects of society. The *Himno Nacional de República Dominicana* (the National Anthem of the Dominican Republic) was originally authored by lawyer, writer, and educator Emilio Prud'Homme and composed by José Rufino Reyes Siancas. The first performance of the National Anthem took place on August seventeenth, 1883. The anthem was an instant success, however there were objections to the lyrics for having historical inaccuracies. In 1897, Prud'Homme submitted revised lyrics which stand to this day. On June seventh of the same year, the Congress of the Dominican Republic passed an act adopting the National Anthem with the original music and revised lyrics. However, then-President Ulises Heureaux vetoed the act because the lyric's author, Prud'Homme, was against his administration. The National Anthem was later adopted on the thirtieth of May 1934 and signed into law. The indigenous word Quisqueya representing the Dominican Republic and Quisqueyanos in place of Dominican people (used by Dominicans when referring to one another) appear in the song.

The Dominican Republic is a nation of firsts in the Americas: the land of the first West African slaves, the first Jewish and Muslim settlers, some of the first Europeans, the oldest continuous European established city of Santo Domingo, the first university in the Americas, the first maroons, the first major slave rebellion, and a nation of majority mixed people. A Dominican people with roots in Africa, Europe, and various indigenous groups including the native Tainos; Asians, Middle Easterners, and now new arrivals from other areas of the world including India. As of 2018, the economy of the Dominican Republic has risen to the largest in the Caribbean and Latin America—and may continue to rise. With great leadership, the economy could improve further and help raise the standard of living for most Dominicans in the nation with a better distribution of wealth and a stronger democracy. The future is bright for the Dominican Republic, but only if the Dominican people choose to fight all foreign and internal enemies and show compassion to those most in need. Only one thing is certain: the Dominican story will continue. Dios, Patria, Libertad.

Ulises Heureaux

Máximo Gómez

Rafael Trujillo

President Juan Bosch

Dr. José Francisco Peña Gómez

President Leonel Fernández

President Danilo Medina

ACKNOWLEDGEMENTS

I want to thank the people
that sparked my interests
regarding
Dominican history. I want to
also thank my family and
friends who believed in me
and support my writing.

ABOUT THE AUTHOR

Rafael Morillo was born in the
Bronx, New York. Rafael
studies history and he is an avid
reader of history and historical
fiction. Rafael enjoys sports and
studying about different cultures
and their history. Rafael enjoys
reading historical fiction,
alternate history, science fiction,
and writing historical fiction
from different points of view
that are not traditionally
explored.

Made in the USA
Monee, IL
03 March 2022